THE BEST AMERICAN

NONREQUIRED
READING
2003

THE BEST AMERICAN

NONREQUIRED
READING

2003

■

EDITED BY

DAVE EGGERS

INTRODUCTION BY
ZADIE SMITH

HOUGHTON MIFFLIN COMPANY
BOSTON ■ NEW YORK
2003

issn 1539-316x
isbn 0-618-24695-9
isbn 0-618-24696-7 (pbk.)

Printed in the United States of America

Book design by Robert Overholtzer

MP 10 9 8 7 6 5 4 3 2 1

"What Sacagawea Means to Me" by Sherman Alexie. First published in *Time*, June 30, 2002. Copyright © 2002 by Time, Inc. Reprinted by permission.

"Common Scents" by Lynda Barry. First published in *One! Hundred! Demons!* Copyright © 2002 by Lynda Barry. Reprinted by permission of Darhansoff Verrill Feldman Literary Agents.

"The Littlest Hitler" by Ryan Boudinot. First published in the *Mississippi Review*, Fall 2002. Copyright © 2002 by Ryan Boudinot. Reprinted by permission of the author.

"Tales of the Tyrant" by Mark Bowden. First published in the *Atlantic Monthly*, May 2002. Copyright © 2002 by Mark Bowden. Reprinted by permission of Dunham Literary Agency, Inc., as agents for the author.

"The Meticulous Grove of Black and Green" by Michael Buckley. First published in the *Alaska Quarterly Review*, Fall/Winter 2002. Copyright © 2002 by Michael Buckley. Reprinted by permission of the author.

"Visiting Hours" by Judy Budnitz. First published in *Harper's Magazine*, April 2002. Copyright © 2002 by Judy Budnitz. Reprinted by permission of Darhansoff Verrill Feldman Literary Agents.

"Things We Knew When the House Caught Fire" by David Drury. First published in *Little Engines*, Issue 3. Copyright © 2002 by David Drury. Reprinted by permission of the author.

"A Primer for the Punctuation of Heart Disease" by Jonathan Safran Foer. First published in *The New Yorker*, June 10, 2002. Copyright © 2002 by Jonathan Safran Foer. Reprinted by permission of the author and Aragi, Inc.

CONTENTS

FOREWORD

THIS IS the second year we've put this book together, and we're beginning to have some idea of what we're doing. But do we know exactly what this book is? We do not. The original purpose of the collection was to introduce younger readers — high school and college-age people, more or less — to good writing from contemporary writers. But then the book came out and we discovered that the readership was not what we'd expected. Sure, there were some high school and college readers, but there were also older readers, and younger readers, and readers from every walk of life — police officers, firefighters, animal control experts, air-conditioning repair technicians, and prisoners. It runs the gamut.

Now, your questions answered:

What is the purpose of this book? — Dominique, Santa Monica, CA
Thank you for your question, Dominique. (Such a lovely name!) The purpose of this book is to collect good work of any kind — fiction, humor, essays, comics, journalism — in one place, for the English-reading consumer. The other books in the Best American series are limited by their categories, most particularly the popular but constraining Best American Catholic Badger Mystery Writing. This collection is not so limited, which is why, we think, it dominates all similar collections, making them whimper and cower in a way that is shameful.

Is this book a benefit of some kind? — Dan Carter, Orinda, CA

It's funny you should ask, Dan. The editor's portion of the proceeds of this book goes directly to 826 Valencia, a San Francisco nonprofit that provides students with free tutoring, college scholarships, workshops, SAT prep, and mentoring, and is housed behind a shop that sells supplies to the working buccaneer. To learn more, visit us at www.826Valencia.com, or stop by anytime; we're between 19th and 20th Streets in San Francisco's Mission District.

Who decides what gets into this book? Whoever it is, they're some kind of crazy supra-people! — Helen and Frannie, Nantucket, MA

For the most part, a student committee, operating under my firm, unrelenting, but always warm (though never at the expense of its sternness) guidance. The student committee comprises these people: Kevin Feeney, Alison Cagle, Jeremy Ashkenaz, Adam Tapia-Grassi, Juliet Linderman, Adrienne Mahar, Antal Polony, and Francesca Root-Dodson. They're all high school students from the San Francisco Bay Area.

I would like to know more about these Members. Can you tell me more? — Gerry and Ellen, Marion, IL

This committee is notoriously shy, and sometimes reacts violently to attention of any kind. Without their permission, we can tell you this much:

Adam Tapia-Grassi is a nineteen-year-old freshman at UC Berkeley. (He started on the committee last year, while still in high school.) He has lived in both San Francisco and Marin and is actively involved with Youth Speaks, a literary arts center in the Mission District. He enjoys writing poetry and performing his work at spoken-word venues. He took off his shorts during one performance, and the audience was aghast.

Antal Polony is a sixteen-year-old junior at Berkeley High. He lives in Oakland (he had to transfer into Berkeley High) and has been writing short short stories since he was in fourth grade, and playing the piano for just as long. He has not been published, but he has played the piano at one memorial service and was proud to make a hundred dollars.

Juliet Linderman is a sixteen-year-old junior at Lowell High School. She lives in San Francisco. She loves music and writing songs and poetry. She has three dogs and three cats and likes them all equally.

Adrienne Mahar is a seventeen-year-old at School of the Arts High School. She is a music major and plays the oboe. She has played with the City Music Center Orchestra, the Peninsula Youth Orchestra, the School of the Arts Orchestra, the Carlos Santana Band, and the All-City Orchestra. She loves John Irving, flying on airplanes, and Thai iced tea.

Francesca Root-Dodson is sixteen years old. She attends Marin Academy High School in San Rafael. She attended the Best American Nonrequired meetings with her very good friend . . .

Jeremy Ashkenaz, who also attends Marin Academy. Jeremy and Francesca were the committee's most passionate defenders of the obscure and less emotionally direct. They read a great deal, and they know what they're talking about.

Kevin Feeney is seventeen years old. He attends Saint Ignatius College Prep in San Francisco, and is also the editor of *Thought Magazine*, a literary journal, and *Jack Bandit*, a humor magazine. He reads George Saunders and Ron Carlson and Tobias Wolff, and writes many of his own stories.

Alison Cagle, fourteen years old, started out editing her mother's newspaper columns. She's been an avid reader for years — Nabokov is her favorite — constant to the point of not knowing her way home from any road trip because she opens a book as soon as the car door closes. She's passionate about her studies and current world events, loves jazz and electronica, attends museum lectures, and has been known to meditate on the school bus. With her daughter's reputation on the line, her mother discovered 826 Valencia, where Alison has flourished and has already irrevocably changed the face of the young intellectual.

We also received help and insight from *Alexei Wajchman* and *Max Kuhn*, both high school students and both very handsome men. And *Matt Werner*, now in college, was an enormous help.

How are these decisions made? That is, how are the pieces selected? I assume that witchcraft is involved. — Fernando, Salt Lake City, UT

There was some witchcraft. There is also a good deal of high-intensity water massage. Before either of those elements comes into play, we do this: Basically, over the course of six months, the com-

mittee and I met once a week, during which time we would discuss what we'd read, look through new work, and talk about the
mix of the book. On their own, the members of the committee (the
"Members") would seek out back issues of periodicals, make copies of things they liked, and bring them in for everyone to read.
This was a fairly organized process, with a few copies of each piece
circulating, and all Members required to write their comments on
the back. Those pieces that garnered positive comments from
a majority of readers would make it into the final round, if we had
a final round, which we didn't, really. By the time April came
around and we had to turn in our selections, we knew what we
liked and how the collection would look as a whole. Then the
witchcraft and hoses.

What sorts of things were eligible? Work from any periodical at all?
— Sarah (soon to be Samuel), Louisville, KY
　　Absolutely. We made a very concerted effort to include work
from lesser-known magazines and quarterlies and Web sites, and
we did find some amazing things in some small-circulation publications. Many other magazines we liked, though, produced work
that was just too short or fragmentary for inclusion. A lot of these
magazines are mentioned in the Notable Nonrequired Reading
section in the back, and we hope you will support these smaller periodicals.

Are all the pieces in this collection about adolescence? — Unsigned,
Putney, VT
　　No. But two are; maybe three.

Why aren't there more pieces about badgers? — Reginald, Myrtle
Beach, SC
　　We had plans to include at least seven pieces about badgers —
their manufacture, appearance, and care — but were prevented
from doing so by Zadie Smith. This was a condition of her inclusion in this volume.

In addition to the pieces included in the collection, and Ms. Smith's in-

troduction — or whatever it is — will there be a piece by the editor about a young man with a crush on a sixty-five-year-old woman whose lawn he cuts? — Peter and Nam Mee, Washington, DC

We might have such a piece. It might be immediately following this sentence.

Mrs. Gunderson. Whahaooaoooa. Mrs. Gunderson. This is about Mrs. Gunderson and it gets dirty.

You know she's got to be in her fifties but whahaooaoooa, what is it about her that's got you thinking? She's got great posture. She dresses like some kind of royal person or something, like that American lady who married the king of Jordan. What was her name? Queen Someone. Mrs. Gunderson's prettier, though, and her earrings are so delicate. Hoops like rings you'd reach for if you were very small and riding around her head on some kind of crazy miniature floating carousel. How old is she, anyway? Fifty? Sixty? Man, you just do not know. You'd love to be one of those guys who can guess ages. Your friend Naveed is pretty good at it; when you met him he knew you were a year older and you hadn't told him dick — he just guessed you were ten and . . . you were ten! And you've been friends since, three years now, even after he threw a rock at your head while aiming for a cop car, and you still have a red mark that looks like the one you get from your booster shots — round red dots just under the surface that hardly hurt at all.

But with Mrs. Gunderson's age you have no idea. She's older than your mom, but not as old as your grandparents, who are dead and never spoke to you while alive but looked glittery in pictures, always happy and with drinks, like guests at the party in *Breakfast at Tiffany's*. So that would make Mrs. Gunderson somewhere between forty-five and seventy. Maybe fifty. How old is fifty? Fifty is a hundred. Fifty is Thomas Edison. Fifty is needlepoint and Norse gods. But she looks good; you can't deny that she's a pretty lady, Mrs. Gunderson is, and she's still blond, and she looks like a woman still, doesn't she? Abababada! She does.

Mrs. Gunderson's got a hold on you, doesn't she? What *is* it about her?

You cut her lawn once a week. You push your family lawn mower, which you rent from your dad for two dollars, each day you use it, up the hill, about a mile, to Mrs. Gunderson's house, painted the weak winter sunset yellow of a cockatoo's under-feathers. Every time you see her house, you think of your science teacher's melancholy cockatoo Stephán, and every time you see the melancholy cockatoo named after the teacher's dead son, lost in the lake in January and found in the spring, you think of Mrs. Gunderson. Her name is Deborah Gunderson. You thought it was D-E-B-R-A and you spelled it that way in your assignment notebook, in the section where you rate the girls you know, 1 through 6, but when she paid you with a check that one time — her slender bare fingers, covered in rings of silver knotted with diamonds, but dull and dirty ones — you realized her name had an OH in it. But you would never use her first name; she told you to call her Mrs. G and you do.

But you've been cutting her lawn for three months and you only make thirteen dollars for the job. Which is okay money, but it's still a gyp, actually, when you think about it, because you lose two dollars on the rental, and maybe a buck in gas, so you're really only making ten, and your brother Dan, who cut it for years, made the same thing, so in all that time there hasn't been one damned adjustment for the cost of living. So it is a gyp, you know it's a gyp, even though your mom says *gyp* is short for *gypsies,* and you shouldn't use that word in a derogatory way, but you've never known a gypsy and she's never known a gypsy and why would it be a verb, or whatever, anyway, so what the hell is she talking about?

You half want to be mad at Mrs. G for the ten-dollar gyp but you can't be mad because part of you wants her to maybe . . . offer you a cool pop after you're done. You don't like pop because it feels too scratchy in your throat, so when she offers you a pop you'll say, No thanks, how about some apple juice? And she'll think you're sensible and healthy and maybe then she'll ask you to sit on the couch with her, and . . . maybe then she'd . . . you don't know, maybe hold your head in her lap. Holy crap, that would be weird. That would be something. It's weird to just think about that, *your* head in *her* lap. What would it smell like? You hope it'd be a nice smell, not an old smell, like tarnished silver and taxidermy. You want her lap to smell like Aquafresh. You want her smell to be full-color but simple and clear like Aquafresh. You're pretty sure that such a clean-looking lady would smell good. But so you're lying there and her lap smells of Aquafresh, and then what? You don't know. Probably nothing.

But maybe she'll touch your crotch. Maybe you'll be drinking the cool apple juice and she'll touch your crotch and make something happen. What would happen? Well, that's a tough one. No one can answer a question like that. But it's Friday night and you're thinking, wondering if you should do anything different the next day when you go up the hill to cut her lawn. Should you wear a fedora? She'd think you were pretty suave in a fedora, and you've still got the one Dan gave you when he was obsessed with Duran Duran and he made the two of you recreate the photo shoots from *Rio* and *Seven and the Ragged Tiger,* with him as John Taylor and you as Andy Taylor (no relation).

You're in your room, listening to the radio, waiting for 106.5 The Heat! to play that Human League song so you can tape it. All you need, really, is the first half of the song, because you've got the second half already, and maybe there's some way to splice them together or something. Dan could maybe figure it out. Maybe you'll ask Dan to help you figure it out. You could ask Dan now. No, you'll wait until you get it taped, then ask him. You're listening to the radio on the floor of your bedroom, on the orange carpet, watching an ant jumble over the surface. You flick the ant, and it flies somewhere, maybe dead already — you didn't see where it went. Maybe it entered the next world the second your fingernail catapulted it toward the nether regions of your room.

The "Eye in the Sky" song comes on. That's a stupid song. It's for old people and the band is all old people. Alan Parsons Project is such a stupid name. Like they're all jazz musicians or something, with berets and capes or those long cigarette holders and monocles. Dorks. They're not in a BAND, they're working on a PROJECT. The only thing worse than dorks your age are adult dorks, and those guys have got to be dorks. If there's really an Alan Parsons he's got to be King Damned Dork. *I am Alan Parsons, come work on my Project! Come, come, we are in studio right now, creating fabulous funky audioscapes!*

The song makes you think of that movie *Class of 1984*, where the punk high school kids with the colored hair kill a teacher. They were tough kids and were cruel to everyone. Three guys and one girl. They dressed in leather and had spikes on their clothes. They wouldn't sit down in class and talked back to the teacher, sneering and with bad posture. One of them was rich but still dressed like a punk rocker or transvestite . . . or whatever they're called. Then they killed a teacher by making him drive crazy in his car, and when the car flipped over and burned, they ran to it and warmed their hands on the heat of the fire. They were dancing and laughing like devils. That was the scariest movie you've ever seen, all the way through at least. On the way home from the theater — it was Brian Hernandez's thirteenth birthday party and it sucked — that "Eye in the Sky" song was playing, and it was such a sad song, and the movie was so sad, too, if that was really what high school kids were like now. Were they? You don't know any high school kids outside of your brother Dan, and he doesn't have stupid hair and spikes on his jacket. But maybe in the cities all the kids were like that. It meant that life would always be sad like that — the feeling you got during that movie was the closest you'd ever come to knowing the meaning of the word *sorrow* — and it meant you'd have to stay away from the cities or just decide not to be a teenager or something. It made you so sorry and sad that you had to breathe in deep to avoid crying, and you had to run in place to avoid collapsing. You would never wear black, you decided. For a week after the movie you wore the brightest things you could find because you were happy to be alive and didn't want to kill your teachers. You rooted for the teacher, the other one in the movie, who ended up killing all the bad teenagers. You wanted them dead and would have killed them just like he did — one of them on the half-circle spinning saw in the wood shop.

You turn off the radio and go downstairs because that's where everyone is. Dan's in the kitchen eating a second dinner at nine o'clock because he's trying to gain weight. He's eating spaghetti, and he's looking in the back window, watching his reflection, watching himself eat like a freak show.

"What are you looking at?" you ask.

"Toss off," he says.

Dan's head is too big and his arms are short, which is why some people call him Tattoo. He's almost 5'6" so it doesn't make any sense, because that's not all that short, he's not an actual dwarf or anything, and Tattoo is a dwarf. There are tons of guys the same size as him, but it's because his head is big and his arms are kind of short. But his fingers aren't short or pudgy and his body looks pretty normal otherwise. His legs are normal length and not stubby or bowed, but still they call him Tattoo. Dan is just short for his age; that's what your mom says and you believe her. But since that Stones album came out, it's become more common, the nick-name, which before only a couple of druggies used. Now some of the guys who used to be his friends are saying it, too. You don't know why they used to be his friends and aren't anymore, but you don't see them come by much anymore. They used to drive to school together but now Dan drives himself with Bronwyn and you're not allowed to say the word *tattoo* in the house. In any con-text. For example, you can't say, "Hey Dan, you heard that Stones album, what's it called . . . help me out here . . ." You tried that once and Dan went nutso, punching walls and screaming, but he didn't hit you, which was strange and good and made you like him more, and feel bad for your older brother with the short arms. But you want to point out again that he's not unusual-looking, really. It's just that once you notice it, his short arms and slightly big head, it's like when you meet a guy with a thumb missing or something — it becomes hard to ignore, hard to go back to that first place where you weren't thinking about it at all, when that person was just whatever came out of his mouth, as opposed to that person, whatever comes out of his mouth and also the length of his arms. Sometimes you really want to go back to that place with your brother. Can't you stretch them somehow? Isn't there the technology? You feel awful about this, and about the time when you laughed, the time once when that kid at the bank called him Tattoo and you laughed and even did the "De plane de plane" thing. But now you want to kill those kids with your nunchaku or the Japanese throwing star you made in shop that you haven't tested yet but are sure would fly like a laser and cut like holy fury.

Your mom and dad are sitting on the couch, watching *The Rockford Files*. Your mom is sitting very close to your dad, and he is grinning. James Rockford is investigating something at a country club. A lady walks up to him in a tennis outfit. She's got huge boobies. They talk for a while and then there's a commercial.

"Hey Dad, who's that lady?" you ask.

"Which lady?"

"The tennis lady."

"I don't know," he says, "but whoever she is, she's a very good actress."

You know what? You want to go biking. You feel like getting on your bike and maybe riding by Mrs. Gunderson's. You've got an urge to get out there in the night air. You go get your shorts on and get your biking gloves and your bad-ass yellow biking cap and you go to the garage.

You leave your community-service-officer-mandated bike light on until you turn from the driveway and then you stop to disconnect it. You're at the mailbox and looking back, making sure no one inside is seeing you. Your house looks strange. Your house is not quite straight. The roof is slanted or something. For some reason it doesn't look as straight as most of the other houses. You have many times sat on your lawn, trying to figure out just what about your house makes it look kind of crooked or sloping but have yet to discern just what it is. There is a gutter on the front of the roof that definitely slants; that much is clear; it goes from left to right and descends easily a foot en route. So maybe that's it. Sometimes you wish your house were more upstanding and rigid-seeming, and other times you like it because at night it seems haunted, and though you hate haunted houses because they're stupid and retarded you wouldn't mind living in one if you knew what was what about that haunted house. Your house was white but now looks sort of beige, or the color of paper when held briefly over a candle. Your house is in a corner of your town, on a cul-de-sac with heavy pines, where you can't see the neighbors readily, a shady and overgrown enclave where the UPS man parks when he wants to nap or organize his packages.

But now your light is detached and it is time. It is time to ride! (Say this last word, *ride*, to yourself, as if receiving a wedgie mid-word. This is the proper way to pronounce this verb.) You will ride, and you will ride in the dark. You are part of the dark. When you ride at night you are a black ghost-rider, a nocturnal thing, an element of the night, like a wolf or a tree or an automatic sprinkler or something.

You get on your bike and your bike feels fast with the tires so full and you're up the hill faster than ever before. Your Toshiba walkman is clipped to your shorts in back, and you've got your Smiths mix on. You've fast-forwarded to "Well I Wonder" and you swerve a little to prove to the song that you love it. Why does this song speak to you? You are not sure. Maybe it's that, like Mr. Morrissey, you aren't sure yet whether this is the world you were intended for. You walk lightly on this earth, you don't get too attached, because at any moment you might be taken away, by someone from another planet or by a French academy of some kind, one for the truly singular, where they train you to be a philosopher or an opera singer or whatever. And so when they come to claim you, you don't want to miss anyone too much. You turn the song up and close your eyes — you ride a whole block, blind, meandering, tempting doom, demonstrating your devotion.

The night is warm and the road is empty and the lights of the houses are few.

Your T-shirt is hiding your walkman so its silver casing doesn't reflect when cars go by. You can't have cars seeing you. Your T-shirt is black and your shorts are blue and you are not wearing shoes. You are the barefoot bike boy. You are the barefoot bike boy who can ride faster than cars or wolves or wind. Cars are pussies and wolves are pussies and the wind, compared to you and your speed, is also a pussy. And you're barefoot and this makes you only you, wholly apart from every stupid rancid boring loud whining crying person in the goddamn world. If aliens came to Earth they would recognize you as the most highly evolved of all humans, would discern your individuality and your skill on your bike and your originality for not wearing shoes and would take you with them. You would be selected above all, above the president and above Gil Gerard and Erin Gray and maybe even Mark Hamill. You would go with the aliens and teach them everything and see everything — planets of purple, covered in water the color and viscosity of blood, and then you'd come back with incredible powers and you would be able to kill the bad teenagers in *Class of 1984* in a way never before seen by mankind.

The teeth of the pedals are biting your instep, but you can handle the pain. Yes, you can. People keep telling you you have a high threshold for pain, and then you tell other people or anyone who will listen about your extraordinarily high threshold for pain. Dr. Sonya, the dentist who gave you your last filling, told you that, that you have a high threshold for pain, and you walked home banging your head on tree trunks to corroborate her thesis. You went home and cut your palm a little with a steak knife, and stuck a needle through a flap of flesh on your calf, and it bled more than you thought it would but it hardly hurt at all. Your threshold for pain is totally amazing and you wonder how the hell to make sure everyone knows about this without bragging too much. You should go on *That's Incredible!* Maybe you could meet the host, Cathy Lee Crosby, and she'd be so intrigued by your high threshold for pain that she'd touch your crotch. Everyone's going to find it damned fascinating and you're going to have to hire a manager for all the girls wanting to touch your crotch. People will throw you money and you'll have to move into a castle with a moat, so people won't always be wanting to test your threshold for pain. Evel Knievel will come out of nowhere and want to test you, too, and you will crush him without mercy! Man, the aliens, when they find out about your complete and utter indifference to pain that would cripple or kill any mortal man let alone someone of your tender age they'll want you to be their damned king or something.

You put your bike down in the hedge in front of Mrs. Gunderson's house. There is a light on, in the living room, lit as if with butter, if butter gave off light, which it very well might — they make fuel from peanuts! She could be home. You'll wait a minute or two more while you rewind "Well I Wonder." The song becomes at all meaningful, of course, only after seven consecutive plays; but even then it's not close to enough. Between seven and twenty plays one begins to grasp its power, but not until you've reached thirty do you pay it the respect it's due; only then do you know its nuances, have you earned the right to listen while swaying, to listen while lying on the lawn of Mrs. G's house; only then have you walked a mile in the shoes of Mr. Morrissey, who you wish would stop wearing the hearing aid and would button up his shirt so he doesn't look so . . . loose. You are in her yard, behind a tree they cut down about ten feet up — it's like a very tall stump, like they made a mistake or forgot where to cut the tree . . . and you stare into her living room window. No one is there. She's out. She's dead. She's on a date with your typing teacher. Damn! You should have told her about your threshold for pain before now, because if you had she'd already be talking about you and touching you because you're so tough it's scary.

Wait. Is that the end of the story? — Susan B. & Anthony, Concord, MA

Well, technically, no. But it's all we have finished right now. There existed a certain ending for this story, but it was much too scatalogical, and there were complaints from the author's cousins and, again, from Zadie Smith, who you would think would be more open-minded. Nevertheless, we hope you enjoy this collection. We tried hard.

DAVE EGGERS

INTRODUCTION

Dead Men Talking

FOR YOUNG readers and young writers, here are half a dozen commonplaces concerning the act of reading, required or otherwise:

1. **Dr. Johnson:** *"A man ought to read just as inclination leads him; for what he reads as a task will do him little good."*

In principle I agree with this — but I'm not quite this sort of reader. Not *confident* enough to be this reader. "Inclination" is all very well if you are born into taste or are in full possession of your own, but for those of us born into families who were not quite sure what was required and what was not — well, we fear our inclinations. For myself, I grew up believing in the Western literary canon in a depressing, absolutist way. I placed all my faith in its hierarchies, its innate quality and requiredness. The lower-middle-class, aspirational reader is a very strong part of me, and the only books I wanted to read as a teenager were those sanctified by my elders and betters. I was certainly curious about the nonrequired reading of the day (back then, in London, these were young, edgy men like Mr. Self and Mr. Kureishi and Mr. Amis), but I didn't dare read them until my required reading was done. I didn't realize then that required reading is never done.

My adult reading has continued along this fiercely traditional and cautiously autodidactic path. To this day, if I am in a bookshop, browsing the new fiction, and Robert Musil's *A Man Without Qualities* happens to catch my eye from across the room, I am shamed out of the store and must go home to try to read that monster again before I can allow myself to read new books by young people. Of course, the required nature of *The Faerie Queene,* books 3 through 10 of *Paradise Lost,* or the *Phaedrus* exists mostly in my head, a rigid idea planted by a very English education. An education of that kind has many advantages for the aspiring writer, but in my case it also played straight and true to the creeping conservatism in my soul. Requiredness lingers over me. When deciding which book of a significant author to read, I pick the one that appears on reading lists across the country. When flicking through a poetry anthology, I begin with the verse that got repeated in the film that took the Oscar. I met an Englishwoman recently, also lower middle class, who believed she was required to read a book by every single Nobel laureate, and when I asked her how that was working out for her, she told me it was the most bloody miserable reading experience she'd ever had in her life. Then she smiled and explained that she had no intention of stopping. I am not that bad, but I'm pretty bad. It is only recently, and in America, that the hold required reading has had on me has loosened a little.

Tradition is a formative and immense part of a writer's world, of the creation of the individual talent — but experiment is essential. I have been very slow to realize this. Reading this collection made me feel the literary equivalent of "Zadie, honey, you need to get *out* more"; I began to see that interesting things are going on, more and more things, and that I can't keep up with them, and that many of them cause revolt in the required-reading part of my brain (I get very concerned by the disappearance of some of the more expressive punctuations: the semicolon, the difference between long and short dashes, the potential comic artfulness of the parentheses), and yet, I so enjoyed myself that even if what I have read in this book is the clarion call of my own obsolescence, it seems essential to defend experiment and nonrequiredness from those who would attack it.

Thing is, the very young and very talented are not beholden. Nor are the readers who would approach them. The great joy of non-requiredness seems to me that as a young reader, you have this opportunity to hold opinions that are not weighed down by the opinions that came before. It is up to *you* to measure the worth of the writers in your hand, for you are young and they are young and actually I am still young and we are all in this thing together. And I feel pride when I see that, collectively, we are not only writing and reading weird stories, but also writing and reading serious journalistic nonfiction and comics and satire and histories, and we are doing all these things with the sort of rigor and attention that no one expected of us, *and* we are managing this rigor and attention in a style entirely different from our predecessors'. We are so good, in fact, that we cannot hope to stay nonrequired very long. We, too, will soon become required, which comes with its own set of problems.

2. **Logan Pearsall Smith:** *"People say that life is the thing, but I prefer reading."*

How important is the "touch of the real"? Should the young man hankering after a literary life read through his massive dictionaries or stand upon a pile of them to reach the high shelf where the whiskey is kept? When I was in my teens, making a few stabs at writing, I had a very low opinion of experience. It did not seem to me that trekking to the cobwebbed corners of the world for six months and returning with a pair of ethnic trousers made anybody a more interesting fellow than when they left. Weary, stale, flat, and unprofitable were all the uses of the world to me — which meant, of course, that I was not much good at anything and had no friends. No matter what anybody says, it is a mixture of perversity and stomach-sadness that makes a young person fashion a cocoon of other people's words. If the sun was out, I stayed in; if there was a barbecue, I was in the library; while the rest of my generation embraced the sociality of Ecstasy, I was encased in marijuana, the drug of the solitary. It was suggested to me by a teacher that I might "write about what you know, where you live, people you see," and in response I wrote straight pastiche: Agatha

Christie stories, Wodehouse vignettes, Plath poems — all signed by their putative authors and kept in a drawer. I spent my last free summer before college reading, among other things, *Journal of the Plague Year, Middlemarch,* and the Old Testament. By the time I arrived at college I had been in no countries, had no jobs, participated in no political groups, had no lovers, and put myself in no physical danger apart from an entirely accidental incident whereupon I fell fifty feet from my bedroom window while trying to reach for a cigarette I'd dropped in the guttering. In short, I was perfectly equipped to go on to write the kind of fiction I did write: saturated by other books; touched by the world, but only very vicariously. Welcome to the house that books built: my large rooms wallpapered with other people's words, through which one moves like a tourist through an English country manor — somewhat impressed, but uncertain whether anyone really lives there.

These days, given the choice between a week in the Caribbean and a week reading *A High Wind in Jamaica,* I would probably still choose the book and the sofa. But this is no longer a proud rejection, only a stiffened habit. To read many of the pieces in this collection is to discover the uses of the world, of experience, is to be shown how life can indeed be the thing, if only you let it. I am impressed by this strong, noble, journalistic trend in American writing, to be found in this very book, dispassionately exercising itself over Saddam's daily existence, or what it is like to live in South Central L.A. I had never met with this kind of journalism until I came to America. It has since been explained to me that most Americans read *In Cold Blood* when they are fifteen, but I read it only two years ago, and not since *Journal of the Plague Year* had I felt writing like that, and I mean *felt* it; writing that gets up inside you, physically, giving you back the meaning of the word *unnerve*. When you read too many novels, and then when you happen to write them as well, you develop a sort of hypersensitivity to the self-consciously "literary" as it manifests itself in fictional prose — it's a totally irrational, violent, and self-defeating sensitivity, and you *know* that, but still, every time you see it, including in your own stuff, it makes you want to scream. So to read what purports to be the truth — no matter how decorated — feels to me like the palate-cleansing green tea that follows a busy meal of monosodium glutamate.

The point is, my mind has changed about experience. I thought I didn't like memoirs, I thought I didn't like travelogues, I thought I didn't like autobiographical books written by people under forty, but the past three years of American writing have proved me wrong on all these counts. It is never too late to change your mind about what you require. I see now that I am required, and more than this, that *I* require, I *need,* to do something else with my life than solely to read fiction and write it. I've got to get out there, abroad and up close; I've got to smell things, eat them, throw them across a park, sail them, dig them up, and see how long I can survive without them, or with them.

As I write this, I am at a college with a novelist younger than me, and at a recent lunch he put before me a hypothetical choice. Should a young man stay the university distance for those four long years? Or should he drop out and seek the experiences that are owed him? Which decision makes the better writer? I argued the case for college, listing the writers on my side of the Atlantic who stayed the course even while indulging in such various activities as storing a bear in their room (Byron), ditching class to walk up hills (Wordsworth), spending most of the time having suits made (Wilde), stopping soccer balls at the goal's mouth (Nabokov), or scribbling obscenities in library books (Larkin). He naturally countered with all the Americans who quit while they were ahead, or earlier (Mark Twain, William Faulkner, Herman Melville, Walt Whitman, Jack London). He won the argument because I had no experience with which to argue against it. By definition Emersonian experience cannot be rejected without any experience of it; it must be passed through and felt and only then compared to the Miltonic experience: the dark room, a book, the smell of the lamp. I'm not qualified to make the judgment, no, not yet — although I intend to be. I want to travel properly next year. See some stuff. In the meantime, maybe we should heed the advice of the Web site www.education-reform.net/dropouts.htm and

Shaun Kerry, M.D. (diplomate, American Board of Psychiatry and Neurology), who comes down firmly on the side of life:

> Ultimately, what distinguishes the aforementioned individuals from the rest of us is their passion for learning that transcends the structured environment of the classroom. Instead of limiting their education to formal schooling, they were curious about the world around them. With their fearless spirit of exploration and their desire to experiment, these individuals discovered their true passions and strengths, which they built upon to achieve success later in life.
>
> Imagine what a loss for the world it would have been if Walt Disney had confined his learning to the requirements of his school's curriculum, and followed only the guidance of his teachers, rather than his own internal motivation. His extraordinary animated features may have never been created.

Imagine.

3. **Laurence Sterne:** *"Digressions, incontestably, are the sunshine; they are the life, the soul of reading."*
Yet, somehow, digressions have gone and got themselves a bad name. The name might be indulgence. Digressions, supposedly, are for writers who cannot control themselves, or else writers who seek to waste the hard-earned time of the no-bullshit reader who has little patience for frippery. The attitude: Writer, do not take me down this strange alley when I mean to get from A to B, and don't think that, just because I am from the Midwest or Surrey, I'll allow some New York or London wiseass to take me on an unnecessary, circuitous journey and charge me too much while they're at it. And less of the chat — I don't need a tour guide — Christ, I know this city like the back of my hand. *And* please note that I'm man enough to use honest language like "back of my hand," which is more than you can say for these namby-pamby *writers*.

And then on the other side of the street, you've got your folks who care *only* for digression. They don't feel they've got their money's worth unless, while trying to get from Williamsburg to the Upper East Side, the writer takes them by way of Nairobi, a grandparent's first romance, the Guadeloupean independence struggle of the 1970s, through the stink of the Moscow sewer system and up through the bud-mouth of an unborn child. But these folks are few.

Among the majority, digression has fallen from favor, along with many of the great digressors, of which Sterne was the mighty progenitor. Maybe "digression" has been confused and twinned with "complexity," but if that's so, then someone should explain that a path off a main road needn't be busy or populated — it can be plain, flat, straight, almost silent. But for all digressions to be of this kind would seem to me a shame. To be so strict about it, I mean. I do like a sunny, busy lane. And I like a memory-saturated, melancholic one as well. I think of W. G. Sebald's *The Emigrants*, that ode to digression, structured like a labyrinth of lanes leading away from a historical monument that is itself too painful to be looked at directly. This might be a model. Things are so painful again just now.

Maybe I worry too much about these things, but like a silent minority of transvestite schoolboys and wannabe drag kings, I imagine a whole generation of not-yet-here writers who feel great shame when contemplating their closet full of adjectival phrases, cone-shaped flashbacks, multiple voices, scraps of many media, syzygy, footnotes, pantoums. I worry that they will never wear them out for fear of looking the fool.

Look: Wear your black some days, and wear your purple others. There is no other rule besides pulling it off. If you can pull off, for example, blocks of red and yellow in horizontal stripes, feathers, tassels, lace, toweling, or all-over suede, then for God's sake, girl, *wear* it.

Here is a beautiful digression from a master digressor. He is meant to be discussing his sixteen-year-old cousin, Yuri:

> He was boiling with anger over Tolstoy's dismissal of the art of war, and burning with admiration for Prince Andrey Bolkonski — for he had just discovered *War and Peace* which I had read for the first time when I was eleven (in Berlin, on a Turkish sofa, in our somberly ro-

coco Privatstrasse flat giving on a dark, damp back garden with larches and gnomes that have remained in that book, like an old postcard, forever).

4. **James Joyce:** *"That ideal reader suffering from an ideal insomnia"*
The ideal reader cannot sleep when holding the writer he was meant to be with.

Sometimes you meet someone who is the ideal reader for a writer they have not yet heard of. I met a boy from Tennessee at a college dinner who wore badly chipped black nail polish and a lip ring, had perfect manners, and ended any disagreement or confusion with the sentence "Well, I'm from Tennes*see*." He was the ideal reader for J. T. Leroy and did not know it, having never heard of him. This was a very frustrating experience. Multiple recommendations did not seem sufficient — I wanted to take him at that moment, in the middle of the dinner, to the bookstore so he might meet the two novels he was going to spend the rest of his life with.

A cult book, of course, is one that induces the feeling of "being chosen as ideal" in every one of its readers. This is a rare, mysterious quality. The difference between, for example, a fine book like Philip Roth's *The Human Stain* and a cult book like J. D. Salinger's *Raise High the Roof Beam, Carpenters* is that no one is in any doubt that Roth's book was written for the general reader, whereas a Salinger reader must fight the irrational sensation that the book was written for her alone. It happens more often in music: Prince fans thought Prince their own private mirage; all the boys who liked Morrissey thought he sang for each of them; I had the same feeling with the initial album of Marshall Mathers, and also the first time I heard Mozart's Requiem. It is all of it delusional, probably, like simultaneous orgasm, but to think of oneself as the perfect receptacle for an artwork is one of the few wholly benign human vanities.

Ideal reading is aspirational, like dating. It happens that I am E. M. Forster's ideal reader, but I would much prefer to be Gustave

Flaubert's or William Gaddis's or Franz Kafka's or Borges's. But early on Forster and I saw how we suited, how we fit, how we felt comfortable (too much so?) in each other's company. I am Forster's ideal reader because, I think, nothing that he left on the page escapes me. Rightly or wrongly, I feel I get all his jokes and appreciate his nuances, that I am as hurt by his flaws as I am by my own, and as pleased when he is great as I would be if I did something great. I *know* Morgan. I know what he is going to say before he says it, as if we had been married thirty years. But at the same time, I am never bored by him. You might know three or four writers like this in your life, and likely as not, you will meet them when you are very young. Understand: They are not the writers you most respect, most envy, or even most enjoy. They are the ones you *know*. So my advice is, choose them carefully so that people don't roll their eyes at you at parties (this happens to me a lot).

The definition of a genius might be the reader who is ideal for multiple writers, each of them as dazzling and distant from each other as religions.

Maybe you are the ideal reader for a writer in this collection.

5. **Sir Francis Bacon:** *"Reading maketh a full man; conference a ready man; and writing an exact man."*

I've tried to deal a little with how full reading can make you, and how empty also. "Conference" we can file alongside "experience" — it is the main portion of experience. Otherwise known as the necessary habit of rubbing up against people in the world, other people and their variousness. The central significance of such rubbing, or frotting, being that it plays a key part in forming the kind of human being who might one day write a book that isn't utterly phony and doesn't make you feel sick when you read it.

"If fiction isn't people it is nothing, and so any fiction writer is obligated to be to some degree a lover of his fellowmen, though he may, like the Mormon preacher, love some of them a damn sight better than others." Wallace Stegner said that, and though Wallace Stegner is not the reason I wake up in the morning, if you don't believe that sentence in some small part then you have no business writing fiction at all. You don't know what it is. And you're probably right, the me-

dium *is* beneath you, it *is* dying, it *is* intellectually defunct — so why don't you just leave it alone, go on, move along now. It's a silly business — leave it to fools.

But if you are going to continue with it, then meet some people, won't you? Care for them, conference with them. It will make you ready. Nobody contains within themselves multitudes, no, not Shakespeare, not Dickens, not Tom Wolfe, not nobody. You need to get some conference. *Ready* — this is absolutely the right word. I am not ready. Are you?

On Sir Francis's last point: It is a commonplace to say that writing is a kind of exactitude, and it feels natural enough (to the writer) to speak of writing as the act of striving for precision, of making the artwork on the page a replica of the ideal artwork in one's mind. Particularly if the writer is on a festival panel and cornered suddenly by a question regarding "process," then she will most likely answer along these broadly Platonic lines, while retaining a guilty sense that the truth is more ambivalent, and too liquid to grasp in your hand and throw to the questioner with the microphone at the back of the hall.

When I write, the kind of exactitude that most concerns me is a bit tricky to explain. I'll try, quickly. So you know the rhythm and speed of reading? Okay, keep that in mind. Now remember the rhythm and speed of writing — the jaggedy, retentive, tortured, unnatural lack of flow. Okay. Now to me, the mystery of exactitude lies in finding the perfect fit between *what you know it is to write* and *what you know it is to read*. If you are writing, and have forgotten the rhythm and speed and, actually, the texture, of what it is to read, you're in trouble. But *at the same time*, to keep the idea of reading in mind too strongly while you're writing is to grow fearful at the keyboard, dreading all that you might write that would be complex, awkward, resistant (to the ear, to the brain), intimate, and seemingly unshareable.

Mr. Stegner called writing the "dramatization of belief." I find it useful to think of that phrase as pertinent not simply to what appears on the page in terms of narrative content but to the relation between two opposite, but umbilically connected, acts: reading and writing. To me, each writer's prose style dramatizes their belief regarding what reading may demand of writing and vice versa. Hemingway, for example, believed in the primacy of reading; he thought that there should be no artificial interruption in its natural smoothness and speed. He subjugated the vanities of writing to the realities of reading. Nabokov, on the other hand, thought Hemingway was a Philistine. Nabokov thought reading should equal the performative act of writing, that it should be a reenaction of the act of writing (although no reader, except possibly his wife, proved equal, in Nabokov's mind, to the task).

Somewhere between the writing that has forgotten entirely what reading is and the writing that is a slave to what reading is — that's where I try to be.

(*N.B.* I guess you know how Sir Francis Bacon died.)

6. **Vladimir Nabokov:** *"A work of art has no importance whatever to society. It is only important to the individual, and only the individual reader is important to me."*

Role models — individuals endowed with wide-ranging socio-symbolic significance — have no place in fiction. Role models are bullshit. People who move through the world playing roles, attending to roles, aspiring to roles, looking for models to help them find new roles — these people are not partaking fully in this whole existence-thing, which is about doing it for real. We would rather not read that way (leaning over a pond, waiting for the water to settle, and all so our own mirrored faces might rise toward us like Plath's "terrible fish"), no, nor write that way either. To this some folks will object. *Oh, I see. So you're not political.* No! Don't believe it! You are political! You are the most political fucking person in the world because when you read, when you write, you won't let a single human being be obscured behind the dread symbolic bulk of somebody or something else. Every time you open a novel or put pen to paper you dramatize your belief in the miraculous, incommensurable existence of a society of six billion individuals. One of whom died three hundred and seventy-seven years ago while attempting to freeze a chicken.

ZADIE SMITH

THE BEST AMERICAN

NONREQUIRED
READING

2003

SHERMAN ALEXIE

■

What Sacagawea Means to Me

FROM *Time*

IN THE FUTURE, every U.S. citizen will get to be Sacagawea for fifteen minutes. For the low price of admission, every American, regardless of race, religion, gender, and age, will climb through the portal into Sacagawea's Shoshone Indian brain. In the multicultural theme park called Sacagawea Land, you will be kidnapped as a child by the Hidatsa tribe and sold to Toussaint Charbonneau, the French-Canadian trader who will take you as one of his wives and father two of your children. Your first child, Jean-Baptiste, will be only a few months old as you carry him during your long journey with Lewis and Clark. The two captains will lead the adventure, fighting rivers, animals, weather, and diseases for thousands of miles, and you will march right beside them. But you, the aboriginal multitasker, will also breastfeed. And at the end of your Sacagawea journey, you will be shown the exit and given a souvenir T-shirt that reads, IF THE U.S. IS EDEN, THEN SACAGAWEA IS EVE.

Sacagawea is our mother. She is the first gene pair of the American DNA. In the beginning, she was the word, and the word was possibility. I revel in the wondrous possibilities of Sacagawea. It is good to be joyous in the presence of her spirit, because I hope she had moments of joy in what must have been a grueling life. This much is true: Sacagawea died of some mysterious illness when she was only in her twenties. Most illnesses were mysterious in the nineteenth century, but I suspect that Sacagawea's indigenous immune system was defenseless against an immigrant virus. Perhaps Lewis and Clark infected Sacagawea. If that is true, then certain postcolonial historians would argue that she was murdered not by germs but by colonists who carried those germs. I don't know much about the science of disease and immunities, but I know enough poetry to recognize that individual human beings are invaded and colonized by foreign bodies, just as individual civilizations are invaded and colonized by foreign bodies. In that sense, colonization might be a natural process, tragic and violent to be sure, but predictable and ordinary as well, and possibly necessary for the advance, however constructive and destructive, of all civilizations.

After all, Lewis and Clark's story has never been just the triumphant tale of two white men, no matter what the white historians might need to believe. Sacagawea was not the primary hero of this story either, no matter what the Native American historians and I might want to believe. The story of Lewis and Clark is also the story of the approximately forty-five nameless and faceless first- and second-generation European Americans who joined the journey, then left or completed it, often without monetary or historical compensation. Considering the time and place, I imagine those forty-five were illiterate, low-skilled laborers subject to managerial whims and nineteenth-century downsizing. And it is most certainly the story of the black slave York, who also cast votes during this allegedly democratic adventure. It's even the story of Seaman, the domesticated Newfoundland dog who must have been a welcome and friendly presence and who survived the risk of becoming supper during one lean time or another. The Lewis and Clark Expedition was exactly the kind of multicultural, trigenerational, bigendered, animal-friendly, government-supported, partly French-Canadian project that should rightly be celebrated by liberals and castigated by conservatives.

In the end, I wonder if colonization might somehow be magical. After all, Miles Davis is the direct descendant of slaves and slave owners. Hank Williams is the direct descendant of poor whites and poorer Indians. In 1876 Emily Dickinson was writing her poems in an Amherst attic while Crazy Horse was killing Custer on the banks of the Little Big Horn. I remain stunned by these contradictions, by the successive generations of social, political, and artistic mutations that can be so beautiful and painful. How did we get from there to here? This country somehow gave life to Maria Tallchief and Ted Bundy, to Geronimo and Joe McCarthy, to Nathan Bedford Forrest and Toni Morrison, to the Declaration of Independence and Executive Order No. 1066, to Cesar Chavez and Richard Nixon, to theme parks and national parks, to smallpox and the vaccine for smallpox.

As a Native American, I want to hate this country and its contradictions. I want to believe that Sacagawea hated this country and its contradictions. But this country exists, in whole and in part, because Sacagawea helped Lewis and Clark. In the land that came to be called Idaho, she acted as diplomat between her long-lost brother and the Lewis and Clark party. Why wouldn't she ask her brother and her tribe to take revenge against the men who had enslaved her? Sacagawea is a contradiction. Here in Seattle, I exist, in whole and in part, because a half-white man named James Cox fell in love with a Spokane Indian woman named Etta Adams and gave birth to my mother. I am a contradiction; I am Sacagawea.

LYNDA BARRY

■

Common Scents

FROM *One! Hundred! Demons!*

BUT THERE WERE BAD MYSTERIES TOO, LIKE THE MYSTERY OF THE BLEACH PEOPLE, WHOSE HOUSE GAVE OFF FUMES YOU COULD SMELL FROM THE STREET. WE KEPT WAITING FOR THAT HOUSE TO EXPLODE. THE BUGS DIDN'T EVEN GO IN THEIR YARD.

THE GIRL WHO SHOCKED ME WITH THE NEWS ABOUT THE SMELL OF MY HOUSE WAS THE ONE WHOSE HOUSE SMELLED LIKE THE FRESH BUS BATHROOM. HER MOTHER WAS THE MOST DISINFECTING, AIR FRESHENER SPRAYING PERSON THAT EVER LIVED.

SHE HAD THOSE CAR FRESHENER CHRISTMAS TREE THINGS HANGING EVERYWHERE. EVEN THE MARSHMALLOW TREATS SHE MADE HAD A FRESH PINE-SPRAY FLAVOR. SHE WAS FREE WITH HER OBSERVATIONS ABOUT THE SMELL OF OTHERS.

YOUR ORIENTALS HAVE AN ARRAY, WITH YOUR CHINESE SMELLING STRONGER THAN YOUR JAPANESE AND YOUR KOREANS FALLING SOMEWHERES IN THE MIDDLE AND DON'T GET ME STARTED ON YOUR FILIPINOS.

SHE DETAILED THE SMELLS OF BLACKS, MEXICANS, ITAL-IANS, SOME PEOPLE I NEVER HEARD OF CALLED "BO-HUNKS" AND THE DIFFERENCE IT MADE IF THEY WERE WET OR DRY, FAT OR SKINNY. NATURALLY I BROUGHT THIS INFORMATION HOME.
AIE N'AKO! WHITE LADIES SMELL BAD TOO, NAMAN! SHE NEVER WASH HER POOKIE! HER KILI-KILI ALWAYS SWEAT-SWEATING! THE OLD ONES SMELL LIKE E-HEE! THAT LADY IS TUNG-AH!

RYAN BOUDINOT

■

The Littlest Hitler

FROM *Mississippi Review*

THEN THERE'S THE TIME I went as Hitler for Halloween. I had
gotten the idea after watching World War II week on PBS. My dad
helped me make the costume. I wore tan polyester pants and one
of his khaki shirts, with sleeves so long they dragged on the floor
unless I rolled them up. With some paints left over from when we
made the pinewood derby car for YMCA Indian Guides, he
painted a black swastika in a white circle on a red bandanna and
tied it around my left arm. Using the Dippity-Do he put in his hair
every morning, he gave my own hair that plastered, parted style
that had made Hitler look as if he was always sweating. We clipped
the sides off a fifty-cent mustache and adhered it to my upper lip
with liquid latex. I tucked my pants into the black rubber boots I
had to wear whenever I played outside and stood in front of the
mirror. My dad laughed and said, "I guarantee it, Davy. You're going to be the scariest kid in fourth grade."

My school had discouraged trick-or-treating since the razor
blade and thumbtack incidents of 1982. Instead, they held the
Harvest Carnival, not officially called "Halloween" so as not to upset the churchy types. Everyone at school knew the carnival was for
wimps. All week before Halloween the kids had been separating
themselves into two camps, those who got to go trick-or-treating
and those who didn't. My dad was going to take me to the carnival,
since I, like everybody else, secretly wanted to go. Then we'd go
trick-or-treating afterward.

There were problems with my costume as soon as I got on the bus that morning. "Heil Hitlah!" the big kids in the back chanted until Mrs. Reese pulled over to reprimand them. We knew it was serious when she pulled over. The last pulling-over incident occurred when Carl Worthington cut off one of Ginger Lopez's pigtails with a pair of scissors stolen from the library.

"That isn't polite language appropriate for riding the bus!" Mrs. Reese said. "Do you talk like that around the dinner table? I want you both in the front seats, and as soon as we get to school I'm marching you to Mr. Warneke's office."

"But I didn't do anything!"

I felt guilty for causing this ruckus. Everybody was looking at me with these grim expressions. It's important, I suppose, to note that there wasn't a single Jewish person on the bus. Or in our school, for that matter. In fact, there was only one Jewish family in our town, the Friedlanders, and their kids didn't go to West Century Elementary because they were home-schooled freaks.

When I got to school Mrs. Thompson considered me for a moment in the doorway and seemed torn, both amused and disturbed at the implications of a fourth-grade Hitler. When she called roll I stood up sharply from my desk, did the salute I'd been practicing in front of the TV, and shouted, "Here!" Some people laughed.

After roll was taken we took out our spelling books, but Mrs. Thompson had other ideas. "Some of you might have noticed we have a historical figure in our class today. While the rest of you dressed up as goblins and fairies and witches, it looks like Davy is the only one who chose to come as a real-life person."

"I'm a real-life person, too, Mrs. Thompson."

"And who would you be, Lisette?"

"I'm Anne Frank."

Mrs. Thompson put a hand to her lips. Clearly she didn't know how to handle this. I'd never paid much attention to Lisette before. She'd always been one of the smart, pretty girls everyone likes. When I saw her rise from her desk with a lopsided Star of David made of yellow construction paper pinned to her Austrian-looking frock or whatever you call it, I felt the heat of her nine-year-old loathing pounding me in the face.

"This is quite interesting," Mrs. Thompson said. "You both came as figures from World War II. Maybe you can educate us about what you did. Davy, if you could tell us what you know about Hitler."

I cleared my throat. "He was a really, really mean guy."

"What made him so mean?"

"Well, he made a war and killed a bunch of people and made everybody think like him. He only ate vegetables, and his wife was his niece. He kept his blood in jars. Somebody tried to kill him with a suitcase, and then he took some poison and died."

"What people did he kill?"

"Everybody. He didn't like Jesse Owens because he was Afro-American."

"Yes, but mostly what kind of people did he have problems with?"

"He killed all the Jews."

"Not all Jews, fortunately, but millions of them. Including Anne Frank."

The classroom was riveted. I didn't know whether I was in trouble or what. Lisette smirked at me when Mrs. Thompson said her character's name, then walked to the front of the class to tell us about her.

"Anne Frank lived in Holland during World War II. And when the Nazis invaded she lived in someone's attic with her family and some other people. She wrote in her diary every day and liked movie stars. She wanted to grow up to write stories for a newspaper, but the Nazis got her and her family and made them go to a concentration camp and killed them. A concentration camp is a place where they burn people in ovens. Then somebody found her diary and everybody liked it."

When Lisette was done everybody clapped. George Ford, who sat in front of me and was dressed as Mr. T, turned around, lowered his eyes, and shook his fist at me. "I pity the foo' who kills all the Jews."

*

Recess was a nightmare.

I was followed around the playground by Lisette's friends, who were playing horse with a jump rope, berating me for Anne Frank's death.

"How would you like it if you had to live in an attic and pee in a bucket and couldn't walk around or talk all day and didn't have much food to eat?"

It didn't take long for them to make me cry. The rule about recess was you couldn't go back into the building until the bell, so I had to wait before I could get out of my costume. I got knots in my stomach thinking about the parade at the end of the day. Everybody else seemed so happy in their costumes. And then Lisette started passing around a piece of notebook paper that said "We're on Anne Frank's Side," and all these people signed it. When my friend Charlie got the paper he tore it up and said to the girls, "Leave Davy alone! He just wanted to be a scary bad guy for Halloween and he didn't really kill anybody!"

"I should just go as someone else," I said, sitting beneath the slide while some kids pelted it with pea gravel. This was Charlie's and my fort for when we played GI Joe.

"They can kiss my grits," Charlie said. He was dressed as a deadly galactic robot with silver spray-painted cardboard tubes for arms and a pair of New Wave sunglasses. "This is a free country, ain't it? Hey! Stop throwing those son-of-a-bitching rocks!"

"Charlie!"

"Oops. Playground monitor. Time for warp speed." Charlie pulled on his thumb, made a clicking sound, and disappeared under the tire tunnel.

Despite Charlie's moral support, I peeled my mustache off and untied my armband as soon as I made it to the boys' room. There were three fifth-graders crammed into a stall, going, "Oh, man! There's corn in it!" None of them seemed to notice me whimpering by the sink.

Mrs. Thompson gave me her gray-haired wig to wear for the parade.

"Here, Davy. You can be an old man. An old man who likes to wear khaki."

I knew Mrs. Thompson was trying to humor me and I resented her for it. Lisette, for whatever reason, maybe because her popularity in our classroom bordered on celebrity worship, got to lead the parade. I was stuck between Becky Lewis and her pathetic cat outfit and Doug Becker, dressed as a garden. His mom and dad were artists. Each carrot, radish, and potato had been crafted in meticulous papier-mâché, painted, lacquered, and halfway embedded in a wooden platform he wore around his waist. The platform represented a cross section, with brown corduroys painted with rocks and earthworms symbolizing dirt, and his fake-leaf-covered shirt playing the part of a trellis. For the third year in a row Doug ended up winning the costume contest.

By the time our parade made it to the middle school I was thoroughly demoralized. I had grown so weary of being asked, "What are you?" that I had taken to wearing the wig over my face and angrily answering, "I'm lint! I'm lint!"

My dad made wood stoves for a living. When my mom left he converted our living room into a shop, which was embarrassing when my friends came over, because the inside of our house was always at least ninety degrees. My dad was genuinely disappointed when he learned of my classmates' reactions.

"But everyone knows you're not prejudiced. It's Halloween, for crying out loud." He folded the bandanna, looking sad and guilty. "I'm sorry, Davy. We didn't mean for it to turn out like this, did we? Tell you what. Let's go to Sprouse-Reitz and buy you the best goddamn costume they got."

We drove into town in the blue pickup we called Fleetwood Mack. Smooth like a Cadillac, built like a Mack truck. The Halloween aisle at 6:30 p.m. on October 31 is pretty slim pickings. There was a little girl with her mom fussing over a ballerina outfit — last-minute shoppers like us. I basically had a choice between a pig mask, some cruddy do-it-yourself face paint deals, and a discounted Frankenstein mask with a torn jaw.

"Hey! Lookit! Frankenstein!" my dad said, trying to invest some enthusiasm in the ordeal. "Don't worry about the jaw, we'll just duct tape it from the inside. Nobody'll even notice."

"I want a mask with real hair. Not fake plastic lumpy hair," I said.

"You don't really have a choice here, Davy. Unless you want the pig mask."

"Fine. I'll go as stupid Frankenstein."

My dad grabbed me by the elbow and spun me around. "Do you want a Halloween this year or not? You can't go trick-or-treating without a costume, and this is about your only option. Otherwise it's just you and me sitting on our asses in front of the television tonight."

That night the grade school gym floor was covered with the same smelly red tarp they used every year for the PTA ham dinner. Teachers and high school students worked in booths like the Ring Toss, Goin' Fishin', and the Haunted Maze, a complex of cardboard duct-taped together. All the parents were nervously eyeing Cyndy Dartmouth, who'd come as a hooker. She was the same seventh-grader who'd shocked everybody by actually dyeing her hair blond for her famous-person report on Marilyn Monroe. Her parents ran the baseball card shop in town, and every middle school guy in West Century wanted to get in her pants. She seemed womanly and incredibly sophisticated to me as we stood in line together for the maze. I liked her because she stuck up for me on the bus and one time told me what a tampon was.

They let you into the maze two at a time, and Cyndy and I ended up going in together.

"You go first," I said as we entered the gaping cardboard dragon's mouth. She got on her hands and knees in front of me, and for an incredible moment I saw her panties under her black leather skirt.

The maze took a sharp right turn, and the light disappeared. Cyndy reached back and grabbed my arm. I screamed. She laughed, and I tried to pretend I wasn't scared. The eighth-graders had done a really good job building this place. There were glow-in-the-dark eyes on both walls and a speaker up ahead playing a spooky sound effects album. I held on to her fishnet ankle and begged her to let us go back. We passed a sign reading "Watch Out for Bears!!!" and entered a tunnel covered in fake fur. I started crying. Cyndy held me, whispering that it was all just made up, none of it was real, it was just cardboard stuck together with tape, holding my face in that magical place between her breasts that smelled like perfume from the mall.

Suddenly light streamed in on us. One of the high school volunteers had heard me crying and opened a panel in the ceiling.

"Ross! Mike! Check it out! They're totally doing it in here!" the guy laughed. I looked up to see four heads crowding around the opening.

"Leave us alone, you fuckers!" Cyndy said, and it seemed a miraculous act of generosity that she didn't tell them the real reason for our embrace.

We quickly crawled through the rest of the maze. When we emerged a group of kids was waiting for us.

"Hey Cyndy, why don't you crawl through the tunnel with a guy who's actually got pubes?"

I panicked, hoping my dad wouldn't hear. I didn't want Cyndy to get picked on, but I kind of liked the idea that the other kids thought I'd done something raunchy with her in the maze. When Ross Roberts asked me if I'd gotten any, I sort of shrugged, as if to suggest that I had, although I didn't completely understand what it was I could have gotten.

Cyndy bit her bottom lip and disappeared into the girls' room with three other girls who would end up sending me hate notes on her behalf the next day at school. The rest of the carnival was awful after that. I carried my Frankenstein mask upside down because I'd forgotten to bring a candy bag. Most of the candy at the carnival was that sugarless diabetic crap, handed out simply because one kid in sixth grade had diabetes and we all had to be fair to him. My dad walked around the perimeter of the gym, pretending to be interested in each grade's autumn crafts project, not really mingling with any of the other adults, even though he'd sold wood stoves to a few of them. I could tell he didn't want to be here and when I told him I wanted to leave he nodded and said it was time to do some serious trick-or-treating.

I liked my dad because he didn't seem to follow a lot of the rules other grownups seemed obligated to follow. He let me watch R-rated movies, showed me how to roll joints, and told me how to sneak into movie theaters. We bought our Fourth of July fireworks from the Indian reservation and used them to blow up slugs. The only times I felt that he was a real grownup were when he was figuring out the bills or being sad about my mom. But tonight we were co-conspirators. In Fleetwood Mack we sang along to the Steve Miller *Greatest Hits* tape and picked the richest-looking neighborhoods to trick-or-treat on. With a greasy Burger King bag salvaged from the floor of the truck, we went door-to-door, my dad hanging out behind me, waving politely. Somebody even tossed him a can of beer.

I didn't know we were at the Friedlanders' house until Mrs. Friedlander opened the door. Word had it they were among the parents who didn't let their kids go trick-or-treating since the razor blade and thumbtack scare of 1982. Hannah Friedlander sat on the steps up to the second story of their split-level house, leaning over in her sorceress costume to see who it was. Mike, her brother, came up the stairs from the rec room and joined her, breathing dramatically in his Darth Vader mask. I wanted to do something nice for them, wanted to just hand them my whole bag, but I couldn't bring myself to do it. I'd be too embarrassed, I'd make my father angry, I'd call too much attention to the fact that they couldn't go trick-or-treating. So I chose to do nothing but accept Mrs. Friedlander's individually wrapped Swiss chocolate balls and thanked her, then walked back to Fleetwood Mack with my dad and went home, looking at all the Halloween displays through the nostrils of Frankenstein's nose.

"So, did you have an okay Halloween after all?" my dad said, carrying me upstairs to my bedroom. I nodded and got into my PJs. He pulled the covers over my face and bit my nose through the blanket as he did every night. Later, when I could hear him snoring through the wall, I took the bag of candy from my dresser and tiptoed downstairs to what used to be our living room. There was a stove hooked up to each of our three chimneys, one which was cold, one with some embers inside, the third filled with flames. I opened the door to the flaming stove and thought about throwing my whole bag in there, but then remembered the rule: wood and paper only. Besides, I had an entire Snickers bar in there; I wasn't insane. I sat for a long time eating chocolates, one by one, in front of the fire. Then I reached into the stove to see how far I could go before it really started to hurt.

MARK BOWDEN

■

Tales of the Tyrant

FROM *Atlantic Monthly*

Shakhsuh (His Person)

> Today is a day in the Grand Battle, the immortal Mother of All Battles. It is a
> glorious and a splendid day on the part of the self-respecting people of Iraq
> and their history, and it is the beginning of the great shame for those who
> ignited its fire on the other part. It is the first day on which the vast military
> phase of that battle started. Or rather, it is the first day of that battle, since
> Allah decreed that the Mother of All Battles continue till this day.
>
> — Saddam Hussein, in a televised address to the Iraqi people,
> January 17, 2002

The tyrant must steal sleep. He must vary the locations and times.
He never sleeps in his palaces. He moves from secret bed to secret
bed. Sleep and a fixed routine are among the few luxuries denied
him. It is too dangerous to be predictable, and whenever he shuts
his eyes, the nation drifts. His iron grip slackens. Plots congeal in
the shadows. For those hours he must trust someone, and nothing
is more dangerous to the tyrant than trust.

Saddam Hussein, the Anointed One, Glorious Leader, Direct
Descendant of the Prophet, President of Iraq, Chairman of its
Revolutionary Command Council, field marshal of its armies,
doctor of its laws, and Great Uncle to all its peoples, rises at about
three in the morning. He sleeps only four or five hours a night.
When he rises, he swims. All his palaces and homes have pools.

Water is a symbol of wealth and power in a desert country like Iraq, and Saddam splashes it everywhere — fountains and pools, indoor streams and waterfalls. It is a theme in all his buildings. His pools are tended scrupulously and tested hourly, more to keep the temperature and the chlorine and pH levels comfortable than to detect some poison that might attack him through his pores, eyes, mouth, nose, ears, penis, or anus — although that worry is always there too.

He has a bad back, a slipped disk, and swimming helps. It also keeps him trim and fit. This satisfies his vanity, which is epic, but fitness is critical for other reasons. He is now sixty-five, an old man, but because his power is grounded in fear, not affection, he cannot be seen to age. The tyrant cannot afford to become stooped, frail, and gray. Weakness invites challenge, coup d'état. One can imagine Saddam urging himself through a fixed number of laps each morning, pushing to exceed the number he swam the previous year, as if time could be undone by effort and will. Death is an enemy he cannot defeat — only, perhaps, delay. So he works. He also dissembles. He dyes his gray hair black and avoids using his reading glasses in public. When he is to give a speech, his aides print it out in huge letters, just a few lines per page. Because his back problem forces him to walk with a slight limp, he avoids being seen or filmed walking more than a few steps.

He is long-limbed, with big, strong hands. In Iraq the size of a man still matters, and Saddam is impressive. At six feet two he towers over his shorter, plumper aides. He lacks natural grace but has acquired a certain elegance of manner, the way a country boy learns to match the right tie with the right suit. His weight fluctuates between about 210 and 220 pounds, but in his custom-tailored suits the girth isn't always easy to see. His paunch shows when he takes off his suit coat. Those who watch him carefully know he has a tendency to lose weight in times of crisis and to gain it rapidly when things are going well.

Fresh food is flown in for him twice a week — lobster, shrimp, and fish, lots of lean meat, plenty of dairy products. The shipments are sent first to his nuclear scientists, who x-ray them and test them for radiation and poison. The food is then prepared for him by European-trained chefs, who work under the supervision of al Himaya, Saddam's personal bodyguards. Each of his more than twenty palaces is fully staffed, and three meals a day are cooked for him at every one; security demands that palaces from which he is absent perform an elaborate pantomime each day, as if he were in residence. Saddam tries to regulate his diet, allotting servings and portions the way he counts out the laps in his pools. For a big man he usually eats little, picking at his meals, often leaving half the food on his plate. Sometimes he eats dinner at restaurants in Baghdad, and when he does, his security staff invades the kitchen, demanding that the pots and pans, dishware, and utensils be well scrubbed, but otherwise interfering little. Saddam appreciates the culinary arts. He prefers fish to meat, and eats a lot of fresh fruits and vegetables. He likes wine with his meals, though he is hardly an oenophile; his wine of choice is Mateus rosé. But even though he indulges only in moderation, he is careful not to let anyone outside his most trusted circle of family and aides see him drinking. Alcohol is forbidden by Islam, and in public Saddam is a dutiful son of the faith.

He has a tattoo on his right hand, three dark blue dots in a line near the wrist. These are given to village children when they are only five or six years old, a sign of their rural, tribal roots. Girls are often marked on their chins, forehead, or cheeks (as was Saddam's mother). For those who, like Saddam, move to the cities and come up in life, the tattoos are a sign of humble origin, and some later have them removed, or fade them with bleach until they almost disappear. Saddam's have faded, but apparently just from age; although he claims descent from the prophet Muhammad, he has never disguised his humble birth.

The president-for-life spends long hours every day in his office — whichever office he and his security minders select. He meets with his ministers and generals, solicits their opinions, and keeps his own counsel. He steals short naps during the day. He will abruptly leave a meeting, shut himself off in a side room, and return refreshed a half-hour later. Those who meet with the president have no such luxury. They must stay awake and alert at all times. In 1986, during the Iran-Iraq war, Saddam caught Lieutenant General Aladin al-Janabi dozing during a meeting. He stripped the general of his rank and threw him out of the army. It was years before al-Janabi was able to win back his position and favor.

Saddam's desk is always immaculate. Reports from his various department heads are stacked neatly, each a detailed accounting of recent accomplishments and spending topped by an executive summary. Usually he reads only the summaries, but he selects some reports for closer examination. No one knows which will be chosen for scrutiny. If the details of the full report tell a story different from the summary, or if Saddam is confused, he will summon the department head. At these meetings Saddam is always polite and calm. He rarely raises his voice. He enjoys showing off a mastery of every aspect of his realm, from crop rotation to nuclear fission. But these meetings can be terrifying when he uses them to cajole, upbraid, or interrogate his subordinates. Often he arranges a surprise visit to some lower-level office or laboratory or factory — although, given the security preparations necessary, word of his visits outraces his arrival. Much of what he sees from his offices and on his "surprise" inspections is doctored and full of lies. Saddam has been fed unrealistic information for so long that his expectations are now also uniformly unrealistic. His bureaucrats scheme mightily to maintain the illusions. So Saddam usually sees only what those around him want him to see, which is, by definition, what he wants to see. A stupid man in this position would believe he had created a perfect world. But Saddam is not stupid. He knows he is being deceived, and he complains about it.

He reads voraciously — on subjects from physics to romance — and has broad interests. He has a particular passion for Arabic history and military history. He likes books about great men, and he admires Winston Churchill, whose famous political career is matched by his prodigious literary output. Saddam has literary aspirations himself. He employs ghostwriters to keep up a ceaseless flow of speeches, articles, and books of history and philosophy;

his oeuvre includes fiction as well. In recent years he appears to have written and published two romantic fables, *Zabibah and the King* and *The Fortified Castle;* a third, as-yet-untitled work of fiction is due out soon. Before publishing the books Saddam distributes them quietly to professional writers in Iraq for comments and suggestions. No one dares to be candid — the writing is said to be woefully amateurish, marred by a stern pedantic strain — but everyone tries to be helpful, sending him gentle suggestions for minor improvements. The first two novels were published under a rough Arabic equivalent of "Anonymous" that translates as "Written by He Who Wrote It," but the new book may bear Saddam's name.

Saddam likes to watch TV, monitoring the Iraqi stations he controls and also CNN, Sky, al Jazeera, and the BBC. He enjoys movies, particularly those involving intrigue, assassination, and conspiracy — *The Day of the Jackal, The Conversation, Enemy of the State.* Because he has not traveled extensively, such movies inform his ideas about the world and feed his inclination to believe broad conspiracy theories. To him the world is a puzzle that only fools accept at face value. He also appreciates movies with more literary themes. Two of his favorites are the *Godfather* series and *The Old Man and the Sea.*

Saddam can be charming, and has a sense of humor about himself. "He told a hilarious story on television," says Khidhir Hamza, a scientist who worked on Iraq's nuclear weapons project before escaping to the West. "He is an excellent storyteller, the kind who acts out the story with gestures and facial expressions. He described how he had once found himself behind enemy lines in the war with Iran. He had been traveling along the front lines, paying surprise visits, when the Iranian line launched an offensive and effectively cut off his position. The Iranians, of course, had no idea that Saddam was there. The way he told the story, it wasn't boastful or self-congratulatory. He didn't claim to have fought his way out. He said he was scared. Of the troops at his position, he said, 'They just left me!' He repeated 'Just left me!' in a way that was humorous. Then he described how he hid with his pistol, watching the action until his own forces retook the position and he was again on safe ground. 'What can a pistol do in the middle of battle?' he asked. It was charming, extremely charming."

General Wafic Samarai, who served as Saddam's chief of intelligence during the eight-year Iran-Iraq war (and who, after falling out of favor in the wake of the Persian Gulf War, walked for thirty hours through the rugged north of Iraq to escape the country), concurs: "It is pleasant to sit and talk to him. He is serious, and meetings with him can get tense, but you don't get intimidated unless he wants to intimidate you. When he asks for your opinion, he listens very carefully and doesn't interrupt. Likewise, he gets irritated if you interrupt him. 'Let me finish!' he will say sharply."

Saddam has been advised by his doctors to walk at least two hours a day. He rarely manages that much time, but he breaks up his days with strolls. He used to take these walks in public, swooping down with his entourage on neighborhoods in Baghdad, his bodyguards clearing sidewalks and streets as the tyrant passed. Anyone who approached him unsolicited was beaten nearly to death. But now it is too dangerous to walk in public — and the limp must not be seen. So Saddam makes no more unscripted public appearances. He limps freely behind the high walls and patrolled fences of his vast estates. Often he walks with a gun, hunting deer or rabbit in his private preserves. He is an excellent shot.

Saddam has been married for nearly forty years. His wife, Sajida, is his first cousin on his mother's side and the daughter of Khairallah Tulfah, Saddam's uncle and first political mentor. Sajida has borne him two sons and three daughters, and remains loyal to him, but he has long had relationships with other women. Stories circulate about his nightly selecting young virgins for his bed, like the Sultan Shahryar in *The Thousand and One Nights*, about his having fathered a child with a longtime mistress, and even about his having killed one young woman after a kinky tryst. It is hard to sort the truth from the lies. So many people, in and out of Iraq, hate Saddam that any disgraceful or embarrassing rumor is likely to be embraced, believed, repeated, and written down in the Western press as truth. Those who know him best scoff at the wildest of these tales.

"Saddam has personal relationships with women, but these stories of rape and murder are lies," Samarai says. "He is not that kind of person. He is very careful about himself in everything he does. He is fastidious and very proper, and never wants to give the wrong impression. But he is occasionally attracted to other women, and he has formed relationships with them. They are not the kind of women who would ever talk about him."

Saddam is a loner by nature, and power increases isolation. A young man without power or money is completely free. He has nothing, but he also has everything. He can travel, he can drift. He can make new acquaintances every day, and try to soak up the infinite variety of life. He can seduce and be seduced, start an enterprise and abandon it, join an army or flee a nation, fight to preserve an existing system or plot a revolution. He can reinvent himself daily, according to the discoveries he makes about the world and himself. But if he prospers through the choices he makes, if he acquires a wife, children, wealth, land, and power, his options gradually and inevitably diminish. Responsibility and commitment limit his moves. One might think that the most powerful man has the most choices, but in reality he has the fewest. Too much depends on his every move. The tyrant's choices are the narrowest of all. His life — the nation! — hangs in the balance. He can no longer drift or explore, join or flee. He cannot reinvent himself, because so many others depend on him — and he, in turn, must depend on so many others. He stops learning, because he is walled in by fortresses and palaces, by generals and ministers who rarely dare to tell him what he doesn't wish to hear. Power gradually shuts the tyrant off from the world. Everything comes to him second- or third-hand. He is deceived daily. He becomes ignorant of his land, his people, even his own family. He exists, finally, only to preserve his wealth and power, to build his legacy. Survival becomes his one overriding passion. So he regulates his diet, tests his food for poison, exercises behind well-patrolled walls, trusts no one, and tries to control everything.

Major Sabah Khalifa Khodada, a career officer in the Iraqi army, was summoned from his duties as assistant to the commander of a terrorist training camp on January 1, 1996, for an important meeting. It was nighttime. He drove to his command center at Alswayra, southwest of Baghdad, where he and some other military officers were told to strip to their underwear. They removed their clothing, watches, and rings, and handed over their wallets. The clothing was then laundered, sterilized, and x-rayed. Each of the officers, in his underwear, was searched and passed through a metal detector. Each was instructed to wash his hands in a disinfecting permanganate solution.

They then dressed, and were transported in buses with blackened windows, so that they could not see where they were going. They were driven for a half-hour or more, and then were searched again as they filed off. They had arrived at an official-looking building, Khodada did not know where. After a time they were taken into a meeting room and seated at a large round table. Then they were told that they were to be given a great honor: the president himself would be meeting with them. They were instructed not to talk, just to listen. When Saddam entered, they were to rise and show him respect. They were not to approach or touch him. For all but his closest aides, the protocol for meeting with the dictator is simple. He dictates.

"Don't interrupt," they were told. "Don't ask questions or make any requests."

Each man was given a pad of paper and a pencil, and instructed to take notes. Tea in a small glass cup was placed before each man and at the empty seat at the head of the table.

When Saddam appeared, they all rose. He stood before his chair and smiled at them. Wearing his military uniform, decorated with medals and gold epaulets, he looked fit, impressive, and self-assured. When he sat, everyone sat. Saddam did not reach for his tea, so the others in the room didn't touch theirs. He told Khodada and the others that they were the best men in the nation, the most trusted and able. That was why they had been selected to meet with him, and to work at the terrorist camps where warriors were being trained to strike back at America. The United States, he said, because of its reckless treatment of Arab nations and the Arab people, was a necessary target for revenge and destruction.

American aggression must be stopped in order for Iraq to rebuild and to resume leadership of the Arab world. Saddam talked for almost two hours. Khodada could sense the great hatred in him, the anger over what America had done to his ambitions and to Iraq. Saddam blamed the United States for all the poverty, backwardness, and suffering in his country.

Khodada took notes. He glanced around the room. Few of the others, he concluded, were buying what Saddam told them. These were battle-hardened men of experience from all over the nation. Most had fought in the war with Iran and the Persian Gulf War. They had few illusions about Saddam, his regime, or the troubles of their country. They coped daily with real problems in cities and military camps all over Iraq. They could have told Saddam a lot. But nothing would pass from them to the tyrant. Not one word, not one microorganism.

The meeting had been designed to allow communication in only one direction, and even in this it failed. Saddam's speech was meaningless to his listeners. Khodada despised him, and suspected that others in the room did too. The major knew he was no coward, but, like many of the other military men there, he was filled with fear. He was afraid to make a wrong move, afraid he might accidentally draw attention to himself, do something unscripted. He was grateful that he felt no urge to sneeze, sniffle, or cough.

When the meeting was over, Saddam simply left the room. The teacups had not been touched. The men were then returned to the buses and driven back to Alswayra, from which they drove back to their camps or homes. The meeting with Saddam had meant nothing. The notes they had been ordered to take were worthless. It was as if they had briefly visited a fantasy zone with no connection to their own world.

They had stepped into the world of the tyrant.

Tumooh (Ambition)

The Iraqis knew that they had the potential, but they did not know how to muster up that potential. Their rulers did not take the responsibility on the basis of that potential. The leader and the guide who was able to put that potential on its right course had not yet emerged from amongst them. Even when some had discovered that potential, they did not know how to deal with it. Nor did they direct it where it should be directed so as to enable it to evolve into an effective act that could make life pulsate and fill hearts with happiness.

— Saddam Hussein, in a speech to the Iraqi people, July 17, 2000

In Saddam's village, al-Awja, just east of Tikrit, in north-central Iraq, his clan lived in houses made of mud bricks and flat, mud-covered wooden roofs. The land is dry, and families eke out a living growing wheat and vegetables. Saddam's clan was called al-Khatab, and they were known to be violent and clever. Some viewed them as con men and thieves, recalls Salah Omar al-Ali, who grew up in Tikrit and came to know Saddam well in later life. Those who still support Saddam may see him as Saladinesque, as a great pan-Arab leader; his enemies may see him as Stalin-esque, a cruel dictator; but to al-Ali, Saddam will always be just an al-Khatab, acting out a family pattern on a much, much larger stage.

Al-Ali fixed tea for me in his home in suburban London last January. He is elegant, frail, gray, and pale, a man of quiet dignity and impeccable manners who gestures delicately with long-fingered hands as he speaks. He was the information minister of Iraq when, in 1969, Saddam (the real power in the ruling party), in part to demonstrate his displeasure over Arab defeats in the Six-Day War, announced that a Zionist plot had been discovered, and publicly hanged fourteen alleged plotters, among them nine Iraqi Jews; their bodies were left hanging in Baghdad's Liberation Square for more than a day. Al-Ali defended this atrocity in his own country and to the rest of the world. Today he is just one of many exiled or expatriated former Iraqi government officials, an old socialist who served the revolutionary pan-Arab Baath Party and Saddam until running afoul of the Great Uncle. Al-Ali would have one believe that his conscience drove him into exile, but one suspects he has fretted little in his life about human rights. He showed me the faded dot tattoos on his hand which might have been put there by the same Tikriti who gave Saddam his.

Although al-Ali was familiar with the al-Khatab family, he did not meet Saddam himself until the mid-sixties, when they were both socialist revolutionaries plotting to overthrow the tottering government of General Abd al-Rahman Arif. Saddam was a tall, thin young man with a thick mop of curly black hair. He had recently escaped from prison, after being caught in a failed attempt to assassinate Arif's predecessor. The attempt, the arrest, the imprisonment, had all added to Saddam's revolutionary luster. He was an impressive combination: not just a tough capable of commanding respect from the thugs who did the Baath Party's dirty work, but also well read, articulate, and seemingly open-minded; a man of action who also understood policy, a natural leader who could steer Iraq into a new era. Al-Ali met the young fugitive at a café near Baghdad University. Saddam arrived in a Volkswagen Beetle and stepped out in a well-cut gray suit. These were exciting times for both men. The intoxicating aroma of change was in the air, and prospects for their party were good. Saddam was pleased to meet a fellow Tikriti. "He listened to me for a long time," al-Ali recalled. "We discussed the party's plans, how to organize nationally. The issues were complicated, but it was clear that he understood them very well. He was serious, and took a number of my suggestions. I was impressed with him."

The party seized control in 1968, and Saddam immediately became the real power behind his cousin Ahmad Hassan al-Bakr, the president and chairman of the new Revolutionary Command Council. Al-Ali was a member of that council. He was responsible for the north-central part of Iraq, including his home village. It was in Tikrit that he started to see Saddam's larger plan unfold. Saddam's relatives in al-Awja were throwing their newly ascendant kinsman's name around, seizing farms, ordering people off their land. That was how things worked in the villages. If a family was lucky, it produced a strongman, a patriarch, who by guile, strength, or violence accumulated riches for his clan. Saddam was now a strongman, and his family was moving to claim the spoils. This was all ancient stuff. The Baath philosophy was far more egalitarian. It emphasized working with Arabs in other countries to rebuild the entire region, sharing property and wealth, seeking a better life for all. In this political climate Saddam's family was a throwback. The local party chiefs complained bitterly, and al-Ali took their complaints to his powerful young friend. "It's a small problem," Saddam said. "These are simple people. They don't understand our larger aims. I'll take care of it." Two, three, four times al-Ali went to Saddam, because the problem didn't go away. Every time it was the same: "I'll take care of it."

It finally occurred to al-Ali that the al-Khatab family was doing exactly what Saddam wanted them to do. This seemingly modern, educated young villager was not primarily interested in helping the party achieve its idealistic aims; rather, he was using the party to help him achieve his. Suddenly al-Ali saw that the polish, the fine suits, the urbane tastes, civilized manner, and the socialist rhetoric were a pose. The real story of Saddam was right there in the tattoo on his right hand. He was a true son of Tikrit, a clever al-Khatab, and he was now much more than the patriarch of his clan.

Saddam's rise through the ranks may have been slow and deceitful, but when he moved to seize power, he did so very openly. He had been serving as vice chairman of the Revolutionary Command Council, and as vice president of Iraq, and he planned to step formally into the top positions. Some of the party leadership, including men who had been close to Saddam for years, had other ideas. Rather than just hand him the reins, they had begun advocating a party election. So Saddam took action. He staged his ascendancy like theater.

On July 18, 1979, he invited all the members of the Revolutionary Command Council and hundreds of other party leaders to a conference hall in Baghdad. He had a video camera running in the back of the hall to record the event for posterity. Wearing his military uniform, he walked slowly to the lectern and stood behind two microphones, gesturing with a big cigar. His body and broad face seemed weighted down with sadness. There had been a betrayal, he said. A Syrian plot. There were traitors among them. Then Saddam took a seat, and Muhyi Abd al-Hussein Mashhadi, the secretary-general of the Command Council, appeared from behind a curtain to confess his own involvement in the putsch. He had been secretly arrested and tortured days before; now he spilled out dates, times, and places where the plotters had met. Then he started naming names. As he fingered members of the audience one by one, armed guards grabbed the accused and escorted them from the hall. When one man shouted that he was innocent, Saddam shouted back, *"Itla! Itla!"* — "Get out! Get out!" (Weeks later, after secret trials, Saddam had the mouths of the accused taped shut so that they could utter no troublesome last words before their firing squads.) When all of the sixty "traitors" had been removed, Saddam again took the podium and wiped tears from his eyes as he repeated the names of those who had betrayed him. Some in the audience, too, were crying — perhaps out of fear. This chilling performance had the desired effect. Everyone in the hall now understood exactly how things would work in Iraq from that day forward. The audience rose and began clapping, first in small groups and finally as one. The session ended with cheers and laughter. The remaining "leaders" — about three hundred in all — left the hall shaken, grateful to have avoided the fate of their colleagues, and certain that one man now controlled the destiny of their entire nation. Videotapes of the purge were circulated throughout the country.

It was what the world would come to see as classic Saddam. He tends to commit his crimes in public, cloaking them in patriotism and in effect turning his witnesses into accomplices. The purge that day reportedly resulted in the executions of a third of the Command Council. (Mashhadi's performance didn't spare him; he, too, was executed.) During the next few weeks scores of other "traitors" were shot, including government officials, military officers, and people turned in by ordinary citizens who responded to a hotline phone number broadcast on Iraqi TV. Some Council members say that Saddam ordered members of the party's inner circle to participate in this bloodbath.

While he served as vice chairman, from 1968 to 1979, the party's goals had seemed to be Saddam's own. That was a relatively good period for Iraq, thanks to Saddam's blunt effectiveness as an administrator. He orchestrated a draconian nationwide literacy project. Reading programs were set up in every city and village, and failure to attend was punishable by three years in jail. Men, women, and children attended these compulsory classes, and hundreds of thousands of illiterate Iraqis learned to read. UNESCO gave Saddam an award. There were also ambitious drives to build schools, roads, public housing, and hospitals. Iraq created one of the best public-health systems in the Middle East. There was admiration in the West during those years, for Saddam's accomplishments if not for his methods. After the Islamic fundamentalist revolution in Iran, and the seizure of the U.S. embassy in Tehran in 1979, Saddam seemed to be the best hope for secular modernization in the region.

Today all these programs are a distant memory. Within two years of his seizing full power, Saddam's ambitions turned to conquest, and his defeats have ruined the nation. His old party allies in exile now see his support for the social-welfare programs as an elaborate deception. The broad ambitions for the Iraqi people were the party's, they say. As long as he needed the party, Saddam made its programs his own. But his single, overriding goal throughout was to establish his own rule.

"In the beginning the Baath Party was made up of the intellectual elite of our generation," says Hamed al-Jubouri, a former Command Council member who now lives in London. "There were many professors, physicians, economists, and historians — really the nation's elite. Saddam was charming and impressive. He appeared to be totally different from what we learned he was afterward. He took all of us in. We supported him because he seemed uniquely capable of controlling a difficult country like Iraq, a difficult people like our people. We wondered about him. How could such a young man, born in the countryside north of Baghdad, become such a capable leader? He seemed both intellectual and practical. But he was hiding his real self. For years he did this, building his power quietly, charming everyone, hiding his true instincts. He has a great ability to hide his intentions; it may be his greatest skill. I remember his son Uday said one time, 'My father's right shirt pocket doesn't know what is in his left shirt pocket.'"

What does Saddam want? By all accounts, he is not interested in money. This is not the case with other members of his family. His wife, Sajida, is known to have gone on million-dollar shopping sprees in New York and London, back in the days of Saddam's good relations with the West. Uday drives expensive cars and wears custom-tailored suits of his own design. Saddam himself isn't a hedonist; he lives a well-regulated, somewhat abstemious existence. He seems far more interested in fame than in money, desiring above all to be admired, remembered, and revered. A nineteen-volume official biography is mandatory reading for Iraqi government officials, and Saddam has also commissioned a six-hour film about his life, called *The Long Days,* which was edited by Terence Young, best known for directing three James Bond films. Saddam told his official biographer that he isn't interested in what people think of him today, only in what they will think of him in five hundred years. The root of Saddam's bloody, single-minded pursuit of power appears to be simple vanity.

But what extremes of vanity compel a man to jail or execute all who criticize or oppose him? To erect giant statues of himself to adorn the public spaces of his country? To commission romantic portraits, some of them twenty feet high, portraying the nation's Great Uncle as a desert horseman, a wheat-cutting peasant, or a construction worker carrying bags of cement? To have the nation's television, radio, film, and print devoted to celebrating his every word and deed? Can ego alone explain such displays? Might it be the opposite? What colossal insecurity and self-loathing would demand such compensation?

The sheer scale of the tyrant's deeds mocks psychoanalysis. What begins with ego and ambition becomes a political movement. Saddam embodies first the party and then the nation. Others conspire in this process in order to further their own ambitions, selfless as well as selfish. Then the tyrant turns on them. His cult of self becomes more than a political strategy. Repetition of his image in heroic or paternal poses, repetition of his name, his slogans, his virtues, and his accomplishments, seeks to make his power seem inevitable, unchallengeable. Finally he is praised not out of affection or admiration but out of obligation. One *must* praise him.

Saad al-Bazzaz was summoned to meet with Saddam in 1989. He was then the editor of Baghdad's largest daily newspaper and the head of the ministry that oversees all of Iraq's TV and radio programming. Al-Bazzaz took the phone call in his office. "The president wants to ask you something," Saddam's secretary said.

Al-Bazzaz thought nothing of it. He is a short, round, garrulous man with thinning hair and big glasses. He had known Saddam for years, and had always been in good odor. The first time Saddam had asked to meet him had been more than fifteen years earlier, when Saddam was vice chairman of the Revolutionary Command Council. The Baath Party was generating a lot of excitement, and Saddam was its rising star. At the time, al-Bazzaz was a twenty-five-year-old writer who had just published his first collection of short stories and had also written articles for Baghdad newspapers. That first summons from Saddam had been a surprise. Why would the vice chairman want to meet with him? Al-Bazzaz had a low opinion of political officials, but as soon as they met, this one struck him as different. Saddam told al-Bazzaz that he had read some of his articles and was impressed by them. He said he knew of his book of short stories, and had heard they were very good. The young writer was flattered. Saddam asked him what writers he admired, and after listening to al-Bazzaz, told him, "When I was in prison, I read all of Ernest Hemingway's novels. I particularly like *The Old Man and the Sea*." Al-Bazzaz thought, This is something new for Iraq — a politician who reads real literature. Saddam peppered him with questions at that meeting, and listened with rapt attention. This, too, al-Bazzaz thought was extraordinary.

By 1989 much had changed. Saddam's regime had long since abandoned the party's early, idealistic aims, and al-Bazzaz no longer saw the dictator as an open-minded man of learning and refine-ment. But he had prospered personally under Saddam's reign. His growing government responsibilities left him no time to write, but he had become an important man in Iraq. He saw himself as someone who advanced the cause of artists and journalists, as a force for liberalization in the country. Since the end of the war with Iran, the previous year, there had been talk of loosening con-trols on the media and the arts in Iraq, and al-Bazzaz had lobbied quietly in favor of this. But he wasn't one to press too hard, so he had no worries as he drove the several miles from his office to the Tashreeya area of Baghdad, near the old Cabinet building, where an emissary from the president met him and instructed him to leave his car. The emissary drove al-Bazzaz in silence to a large villa nearby. Inside, guards searched him and showed him to a sofa, where he waited for half an hour as people came and went from the president's office. When it was his turn, he was handed a pad and a pencil, reminded to speak only if Saddam asked a direct question, and then ushered in. It was noon. Saddam was wearing a military uniform. Staying seated behind his desk, Saddam did not approach al-Bazzaz or even offer to shake his hand.

"How are you?" the president asked.

"Fine," al-Bazzaz replied. "I am here to listen to your instruc-tions."

Saddam complained about an Egyptian comedy show that had been airing on one of the TV channels: "It is silly, and we shouldn't show it to our people." Al-Bazzaz made a note. Then Saddam brought up something else. It was the practice for poems and songs written in praise of him to be aired daily on TV. In recent weeks al-Bazzaz had urged his producers to be more selective. Most of the work was amateurish — ridiculous doggerel written by unskilled poets. His staff was happy to oblige. Paeans to the president were still aired every day, but not as many since al-Bazzaz had changed the policy.

"I understand," Saddam said, "that you are not allowing some of the songs that carry my name to be broadcast."

Al-Bazzaz was stunned, and suddenly frightened. "Mr. President," he said, "we still broadcast the songs, but I have stopped some of them because they are so poorly written. They are rubbish."

"Look," Saddam said, abruptly stern, "you are not a judge, Saad."

"Yes. I am not a judge."

"How can you prevent people from expressing their feelings toward me?"

Al-Bazzaz feared that he was going to be taken away and shot. He felt the blood drain from his face, and his heart pounded heavily. The editor said nothing. The pencil shook in his hand. Saddam had not even raised his voice.

"No, no, no. You are not the judge of these things," Saddam reiterated.

Al-Bazzaz kept repeating, "Yes, sir," and frantically wrote down every word the president said.

Saddam then talked about the movement for more freedoms in the press and the arts. "There will be no loosening of controls," he said.

"Yes, sir."

"Okay, fine. Now it is all clear to you?"

"Yes, sir."

With that Saddam dismissed al-Bazzaz. The editor had sweated through his shirt and sport coat. He was driven back to the Cabinet building, and then drove himself back to the office, where he immediately rescinded his earlier policy. That evening a full broadcast of the poems and songs dedicated to Saddam resumed.

Hadafuh (His Goal)

You are the fountain of willpower and the wellspring of life, the essence of earth, the sabers of demise, the pupil of the eye, and the twitch of the eyelid. A people like you cannot but be, with God's help. So be as you are, and as we are determined to be. Let all cowards, piggish people, traitors, and betrayers be debased.

— Saddam Hussein, addressing the Iraqi people, July 17, 2001

Iraq is a land of antiquity. It is called the Land of Two Rivers (the Tigris and the Euphrates); the land of Sumerian kings, Mesopotamia, and Babylon; one of the cradles of civilization. Walking the streets of Baghdad gives one a sense of continuity with things long past, of unity with the great sweep of history. Renovating and maintaining the old palaces is an ongoing project in the city. By decree, one of every ten bricks laid in the renovation of an ancient palace is now stamped either with the name Saddam Hussein or with an eight-pointed star (a point for each letter of his name spelled in Arabic).

In 1987 Entifadh Qanbar was assigned to work on the restoration of the Baghdad Palace, which had once been called al-Zuhoor, or the Flowers Palace. Built in the 1930s for King Ghazi, it is relatively small and very pretty; English in style, it once featured an elaborate evergreen maze. Qanbar is an engineer by training, a short, fit, dark-haired man with olive skin. After earning his degree he served a compulsory term in the army, which turned out to be a five-year stint, and survived the mandatory one-month tour on the front lines in the war with Iran.

Work on the palace had stalled some years earlier, when the British consultant for the project refused to come to Baghdad because of the war. One of Qanbar's first jobs was to supervise construction of a high and ornate brick wall around the palace grounds. Qanbar is a perfectionist, and because the wall was to be decorative as well as functional, he took care with the placement of each brick. An elaborate gate had already been built facing the main road, but Qanbar had not yet built the portions of the wall on either side of it, because the renovation of the palace itself was unfinished, and that way large construction equipment could roll on and off the property without danger of damaging the gate.

One afternoon at about five, as he was preparing to close down work for the day, Qanbar saw a black Mercedes with curtained windows and custom-built running boards pull up to the site. He knew immediately who was in it. Ordinary Iraqis were not allowed to drive such fancy cars. Cars like this one were driven exclusively by al Himaya, Saddam's bodyguards.

The doors opened and several guards stepped out. All of them wore dark green uniforms, black berets, and zippered boots of reddish brown leather. They had big mustaches like Saddam's, and carried Kalashnikovs. To the frightened Qanbar, they seemed robotic, without human feelings.

The bodyguards often visited the work site to watch and make trouble. Once, after new concrete had been poured and smoothed, some of them jumped into it, stomping through the patch in their red boots to make sure that no bomb or listening device was hidden there. Another time a workman opened a pack of cigarettes and a bit of foil wrapping fluttered down into the newly poured concrete. One of the guards caught a glimpse of something metallic and reacted as if someone had thrown a hand grenade. Several of them leaped into the concrete and retrieved the scrap. Angered to discover what it was, and to have been made to look foolish, they dragged the offending worker aside and beat him with their weapons. "I have worked all my life!" he cried. They took him away, and he did not return. So the sudden arrival of a black Mercedes was a frightening thing.

"Who is the engineer here?" the chief guard asked. He spoke with the gruff Tikriti accent of his boss. Qanbar stepped up and identified himself. One of the guards wrote down his name. It is a terrible thing to have al Himaya write down your name. In a country ruled by fear, the best way to survive is to draw as little attention to yourself as possible. To be invisible. Even success can be dangerous, because it makes you stand out. It makes other people jealous and suspicious. It makes you enemies who might, if the opportunity presents itself, bring your name to the attention of the police. For the state to have your name for any reason other than the most conventional ones — school, driver's license, military service — is always dangerous. The actions of the state are entirely unpredictable, and they can take away your career, your freedom, your life. Qanbar's heart sank and his mouth went dry.

"Our Great Uncle just passed by," the chief guard began. "And he said, 'Why is this gate installed when the two walls around it are not built?'"

Qanbar nervously explained that the walls were special, ornamental, and that his crew was saving them for last because of the heavy equipment coming and going. "We want to keep it a clean construction," he said.

"Our Great Uncle is going to pass by again tonight," said the guard. "When he does, it must be finished."

Qanbar was dumbfounded. "How can I do it?" he protested.

"I don't know," said the guard. "But if you don't do it, you will be in trouble." Then he said something that revealed exactly how serious the danger was: "And if you don't do it, we will be in trouble. How can we help?"

There was nothing to do but try. Qanbar dispatched Saddam's men to help round up every member of his crew as fast as they could — those who were not scheduled to work as well as those who had already gone home. Two hundred workers were quickly assembled. They set up floodlights. Some of the guards came back with trucks that had machine guns mounted on top. They parked alongside the work site and set up chairs, watching and urging more speed as the workers mixed mortar and threw down line after line of bricks.

The crew finished at nine-thirty. They had completed in four hours a job that would ordinarily have taken a week. Terror had driven them to work faster and harder than they believed possible. Qanbar and his men were exhausted. An hour later they were still cleaning up the site when the black Mercedes drove up again. The chief guard stepped out. "Our Uncle just passed by, and he thanks you," he said.

Walls define the tyrant's world. They keep his enemies out, but they also block him off from the people he rules. In time he can no longer see out. He loses touch with what is real and what is unreal, what is possible and what is not — or, as in the case of Qanbar and the wall, what is just barely possible. His ideas of what his power can accomplish, and of his own importance, bleed into fantasy.

Each time Saddam has escaped death — when he survived, with a minor wound to his leg, a failed attempt in 1959 to assassinate

Iraqi President Abd al-Karim Qasim; when he avoided the ultimate punishment in 1964 for his part in a failed Baath Party uprising; when he survived being trapped behind Iranian lines in the
Iran-Iraq war; when he survived attempted coups d'état; when he
survived America's smart-bombing campaign against Baghdad, in
1991; when he survived the nationwide revolt after the Gulf War
— it has strengthened his conviction that his path is divinely inspired and that greatness is his destiny. Because his worldview is
essentially tribal and patriarchal, destiny means blood. So he has
ordered genealogists to construct a plausible family tree linking
him to Fatima, the daughter of the prophet Muhammad. Saddam
sees the prophet less as the bearer of divine revelation than as a
political precursor — a great leader who unified the Arab peoples
and inspired a flowering of Arab power and culture. The con-
cocted link of bloodlines to Muhammad is symbolized by a six-
hundred-page hand-lettered copy of the Koran that was written
with Saddam's own blood, which he donated a pint at a time over
three years. It is now on display in a Baghdad museum.

If Saddam has a religion, it is a belief in the superiority of Arab
history and culture, a tradition that he is convinced will rise up
again and rattle the world. His imperial view of the grandeur that
was Arabia is romantic, replete with fanciful visions of great palaces and wise and powerful sultans and caliphs. His notion of history has nothing to do with progress, with the advance of knowledge, with the evolution of individual rights and liberties, with any
of the things that matter most to Western civilization. It has to do
simply with power. To Saddam, the present global domination by
the West, particularly the United States, is just a phase. America is
infidel and inferior. It lacks the rich ancient heritage of Iraq and
other Arab states. Its place at the summit of the world powers is
just a historical quirk, an aberration, a consequence of its having
acquired technological advantages. It cannot endure.

In a speech this past January 17, the eleventh anniversary of
the start of the Gulf War, Saddam explained, "The Americans have
not yet established a civilization, in the deep and comprehensive
sense we give to civilization. What they have established is a me-

tropolis of force . . . Some people, perhaps including Arabs and plenty of Muslims and more than these in the wide world . . . considered the ascent of the U.S. to the summit as the last scene in the world picture, after which there will be no more summits and no one will try to ascend and sit comfortably there. They considered it the end of the world as they hoped for, or as their scared souls suggested it to them."

Arabia, which Saddam sees as the wellspring of civilization, will one day own that summit again. When that day comes, whether in his lifetime or a century or even five centuries hence, his name will rank with those of the great men in history. Saddam sees himself as an established member of the pantheon of great men — conquerors, prophets, kings and presidents, scholars, poets, scientists. It doesn't matter if he understands their contributions and ideas. It matters only that they are the ones history has remembered and honored for their accomplishments.

In a book titled *Saddam's Bombmaker* (2000), Khidhir Hamza, the nuclear scientist, remembers his first encounter with Saddam, when the future dictator was still nominally the vice chairman. A large new computer had just been installed in Hamza's lab, and Saddam came sweeping through for a look. He showed little interest in the computer; his attention was drawn instead to a lineup of pictures that Hamza had tacked to the wall, each of a famous scientist, from Copernicus to Einstein. The pictures had been torn from magazines.

"What are those?" Saddam asked.

"Sir, those are the greatest scientists in history," Hamza told him.

Then, as Hamza remembers it, Saddam became angry. "What an insult this is! All these great men, these great scientists! You don't have enough respect for these great men to frame their pictures? You can't honor them better than this?"

To Hamza, the outburst was irrational; the anger was out of all proportion. Hamza interpreted it as Saddam's way of testing him, of putting him in his place. But Saddam seemed somehow *personally* offended. To understand his tantrum one must understand

the kinship he feels with the great men of history, with history itself. Lack of reverence for an image of Copernicus might suggest a
lack of reverence for Saddam.

In what sense does Saddam see himself as a great man? Saad al-
Bazzaz, who defected in 1992, has thought a lot about this question, during his time as a newspaper editor and TV producer in
Baghdad, and in the years since, as the publisher of an Arabic
newspaper in London.

"I need a piece of paper and a pen," he told me recently in the
lobby of Claridge's Hotel. He flattened the paper out on a coffee table and tested the pen. Then he drew a line down the center. "You
must understand, the daily behavior is just the result of the mentality," he explained. "Most people would say that the main conflict
in Iraqi society is sectarian, between the Sunni and the Shia Muslims. But the big gap has nothing to do with religion. It is between
the mentality of the villages and the mentality of the cities.

"Okay. Here is a village." On the right half of the page al-Bazzaz
wrote a *V* and beneath it he drew a collection of separate small
squares. "These are houses or tents," he said. "Notice there are
spaces between them. This is because in the villages each family
has its own house, and each house is sometimes several miles
from the next one. They are self-contained. They grow their own
food and make their own clothes. Those who grow up in the villages are frightened of everything. There is no real law enforce-
ment or civil society. Each family is frightened of each other, and
all of them are frightened of outsiders. This is the tribal mind. The
only loyalty they know is to their own family, or to their own village. Each of the families is ruled by a patriarch, and the village is
ruled by the strongest of them. This loyalty to tribe comes before
everything. There are no values beyond power. You can lie, cheat,
steal, even kill, and it is okay so long as you are a loyal son of the
village or the tribe. Politics for these people is a bloody game, and
it is all about getting or holding power."

Al-Bazzaz wrote the word "city" atop the left half of the page. Beneath it he drew a line of adjacent squares. Below that he drew

another line, and another. "In the city the old tribal ties are left behind. Everyone lives close together. The state is a big part of everyone's life. They work at jobs and buy their food and clothing at markets and in stores. There are laws, police, courts, and schools. People in the city lose their fear of outsiders, and take an interest in foreign things. Life in the city depends on cooperation, on sophisticated social networks. Mutual self-interest defines public policy. You can't get anything done without cooperating with others, so politics in the city becomes the art of compromise and partnership. The highest goal of politics becomes cooperation, community, and keeping the peace. By definition, politics in the city becomes nonviolent. The backbone of urban politics isn't blood, it's law."

In al-Bazzaz's view, Saddam embodies the tribal mentality. "He is the ultimate Iraqi patriarch, the village leader who has seized a nation," he explained. "Because he has come so far, he feels anointed by destiny. Everything he does is, by definition, the right thing to do. He has been chosen by Heaven to lead. Often in his life he has been saved by God, and each escape makes him more certain of his destiny. In recent years, in his speeches, he has begun using passages and phrases from the Koran, speaking the words as if they are his own. In the Koran, Allah says, 'If you thank me, I will give you more.' In the early nineties Saddam was on TV, presenting awards to military officers, and he said, 'If you thank me, I will give you more.' He no longer believes he is a normal person. Dialogue with him is impossible because of this. He can't understand why journalists should be allowed to criticize him. How can they criticize the father of the tribe? This is something unacceptable in his mind. To him, strength is everything. To allow criticism or differences of opinion, to negotiate or compromise, to accede to the rule of law or to due process — these are signs of weakness."

Saddam is, of course, not alone in admiring the *Godfather* series. They are obvious movies for him to like (they were also a favorite of the Colombian cocaine tycoon Pablo Escobar). On the surface it is a classic patriarchal tale. Don Vito Corleone builds his criminal empire from nothing, motivated in the main by love for his family. He sees that the world around him is vicious and corrupt, so he outdoes the world at its own cruelty and preys upon its vices, creating an apparent refuge of wealth and safety for himself and his own. We are drawn to his single-mindedness, subtle intelligence, and steadfast loyalty to an ancient code of honor in a changing world — no matter how unforgiving that code seems by modern standards. The Godfather suffers greatly but dies playing happily in the garden with his grandson, arguably a successful man. The deeper meaning of the films, however, apparently evades Saddam. The *Godfather* saga is more the story of Michael Corleone than of his father, and the film's message is not a happy one. Michael's obsessive loyalty to his father and to his family, to the ancient code of honor, leads him to destroy the very things it is designed to protect. In the end Michael's family is torn by tragedy and hatred. He orders his own brother killed, choosing loyalty to code over loyalty to family. Michael becomes a tragic figure, isolated and unloved, ensnared by his own power. He is a lot like Saddam.

In Saddam's other favorite movie, *The Old Man and the Sea*, the old man, played by Spencer Tracy, hooks a great fish and fights alone in his skiff to haul it in. It is easy to see why Saddam would be stirred by the image of a lone fisherman, surrounded by a great ocean, struggling to land this impossible fish. "I will show him what a man can do and what a man endures," the old man says. In the end he succeeds, but the fish is too large for the dinghy, and is devoured by sharks before the trophy can be displayed. The old man returns to his hut with cut and bleeding hands, exhausted but happy in the knowledge that he has prevailed. It would be easy for Saddam to see himself in that old man.

Or is he the fish? In the movie it leaps like a fantasy from the water — a splendid, wild, dangerous thing, magnificent in its size and strength. It is hooked, but it refuses to accept its fate. "Never have I had such a strong fish, or one that acted so strangely," the old man proclaims. Later he says, "There is no panic in his fight." Saddam believes that he is a great natural leader, the likes of which his world has not seen in thirteen centuries. Perhaps he will fail in the struggle during his lifetime, but he is convinced that his courage and vision will fire a legend that will burn brightly in a future Arab-centered world.

Even as Saddam rhapsodizes over the rich history of Arabia, he concedes the Western world's clear superiority in two things. The first is weapons technology — hence his tireless efforts to import advanced military hardware and to develop weapons of mass destruction. The second is the art of acquiring and holding power. He has become a student of one of the most tyrannical leaders in history: Joseph Stalin.

Saïd Aburish's biography, *Saddam Hussein: The Politics of Revenge* (2000), tells of a meeting in 1979 between Saddam and the Kurdish politician Mahmoud Othman. It was an early-morning meeting, and Saddam received Othman in a small office in one of his palaces. It looked to Othman as if Saddam had slept in the office the night before. There was a small cot in the corner, and the president received him wearing a bathrobe.

Next to the bed, Othman recalled, were "over twelve pairs of expensive shoes. And the rest of the office was nothing but a small library of books about one man, Stalin. One could say he went to bed with the Russian dictator."

In the villages of Iraq the patriarch has only one goal: to expand and defend his family's power. It is the only thing of value in the wide, treacherous world. When Saddam assumed full power, there were still Iraqi intellectuals who had hopes for him. They initially accepted his tyranny as inevitable, perhaps even as a necessary bridge to a more inclusive government, and believed, as did many in the West, that his outlook was essentially modern. In this they were gradually disappointed.

In September of 1979 Saddam attended a conference of unaligned nations in Cuba, where he formed a friendship with Fidel Castro, who still keeps him supplied with cigars. Saddam came to the gathering with Salah Omar al-Ali, who was then the Iraqi ambassador to the United Nations, a post he had accepted after a long period of living abroad as an ambassador. Together Saddam and al-Ali had a meeting with the new foreign minister of Iran. Four years earlier Saddam had made a surprise concession to the soon-to-be-deposed shah, reaching an agreement on navigation in the Shatt-al-Arab, a sixty-mile strait formed by the confluence of the Tigris and Euphrates Rivers as they flow into the Persian Gulf. Both countries had long claimed the strait. In 1979, with the shah roaming the world in search of cancer treatment, and power in the hands of the Ayatollah Khomeini (whom Saddam had unceremoniously booted out of Iraq the year before), relations between the two countries were again strained, and the waters of the Shatt-al-Arab were a potential flash point. Both countries still claimed ownership of two small islands in the strait, which were then controlled by Iran.

But al-Ali was surprised by the tone of the discussions in Cuba. The Iranian representatives were especially agreeable, and Saddam seemed to be in an excellent mood. After the meeting al-Ali strolled with Saddam in a garden outside the meeting hall. They sat on a bench as Saddam lit a big cigar.

"Well, Salah, I see you are thinking of something," Saddam said. "What are you thinking about?"

"I am thinking about the meeting we just had, Mr. President. I am very happy. I'm very happy that these small problems will be solved. I'm so happy that they took advantage of this chance to meet with you and not one of your ministers, because with you being here we can avoid another problem with them. We are neighbors. We are poor people. We don't need another war. We need to rebuild our countries, not tear them down."

Saddam was silent for a moment, drawing thoughtfully on his cigar. "Salah, how long have you been a diplomat now?" he asked.

"About ten years."

"Do you realize, Salah, how much you have changed?"

"How, Mr. President?"

"How should we solve our problems with Iran? Iran took our lands. They are controlling the Shatt-al-Arab, our big river. How can meetings and discussions solve a problem like this? Do you know why they decided to meet with us here, Salah? They are weak is why they are talking with us. If they were strong there would be no need to talk. So this gives us an opportunity, an opportunity that only comes along once in a century. We have an opportunity here to recapture our territories and regain control of our river."

That was when al-Ali realized that Saddam had just been playing with the Iranians, and that Iraq was going to go to war. Saddam had no interest in diplomacy. To him, statecraft was just a game whose object was to outmaneuver one's enemies. Someone like al-Ali was there to maintain a pretense, to help size up the situation, to look for openings, and to lull foes into a false sense of security. Within a year the Iran-Iraq war began.

It ended horrifically, eight years later, with hundreds of thousands of Iranians and Iraqis dead. To a visitor in Baghdad the year after the war ended, it seemed that every other man on the street was missing a limb. The country had been devastated. The war had cost Iraq billions. Saddam claimed to have regained control of the Shatt-al-Arab. Despite the huge losses, he was giddy with victory. By 1987 his army, swelled by compulsory service and modern Western armaments, was the fourth largest in the world. He had an arsenal of Scud missiles, a sophisticated nuclear weapons program under way, and deadly chemical and biological weapons in development. He immediately began planning more conquest.

Saddam's invasion of Kuwait, in August of 1990, was one of the great military miscalculations of modern history. It was a product of grandiosity. Emboldened by his "victory" over Iran, Saddam had begun to plan other improbable undertakings. He announced that he was going to build a world-class subway system for Baghdad, a multi-billion-dollar project, and then proclaimed that he would construct a state-of-the-art nationwide rail system along with it. Ground was never broken for either venture. Saddam didn't have the money. One thing he did have, however, was an army of more than a million idle soldiers — easily enough men to overrun the neighboring state of Kuwait, with its rich oil deposits. He gambled that the world would not care, and he was wrong. Three days after

Saddam's takeover of the tiny kingdom President George Bush announced, "This will not stand," and immediately began assem-
bling one of the largest military forces ever in the region.

Through the end of 1990 and into 1991 Ismail Hussain waited
in the Kuwaiti desert for the American counterattack. He is a
short, stocky man, a singer, musician, and songwriter. The whole
time he was forced to wear a uniform, he knew that he did not
belong in one. Although some of the men in his unit were good
soldiers, none of them thought they belonged in Kuwait. They
hoped that they would not have to fight. Everyone knew that the
United States had more soldiers, more supplies, and better weapons. Surely Saddam would reach an agreement to save face, and
his troops would be able to withdraw peacefully. They waited and
waited for this to happen, and when word came that they were actually going to fight, Hussain decided that he was already dead.
There was no hope: He foresaw death everywhere. If you went toward the American lines, they would shoot you. If you stayed in
the open, they would blow you up. If you dug a hole and buried
yourself, American bunker-buster bombs would stir your remains
with the sand. If you ran, your own commanders would kill you —
because they would be killed if their men fled. If a man was killed
running away, his coffin would be marked with the word *jaban*, or
"coward." His memory would be disgraced, his family shunned.
There would be no pension for them from the state, no secondary
school for his children. *Jaban* was a mark that would stain the
family for generations. There was no escaping it. Some things are
worse than staying with your friends and waiting to die. Hussain's
unit manned an antiaircraft gun. He never even saw the American
fighter jet that took off his leg.

It was apparent to everyone in the Iraqi military, from con-
scripts like Hussain to Saddam's top generals, that they could not
stand up against such force. Saddam, however, didn't see it that
way. Al-Bazzaz remembers being shocked by this. "We had the
most horrible meeting on January 14, 1991, just two days before
the allied offensive," he told me. "Saddam had just met with the
UN Secretary General, who had come at the final hour to try to ne-

gotiate a peaceful resolution. They had been in a meeting for more than two and a half hours, so hopes were running high that some resolution had been reached. Instead Saddam stepped out to address us, and it was clear he was going to miss this last opportunity. He told us, 'Don't be afraid. I see the gates of Jerusalem open before me.' I thought, What is this shit? Baghdad was about to be hit with this terrible firestorm, and he's talking to us about visions of liberating Palestine?"

Wafic Samarai was in a particularly difficult position. How does one function as chief of intelligence for a tyrant who does not wish to hear the truth? On the one hand, if you tell him the truth and it contradicts his sense of infallibility, you are in trouble. On the other, if you tell him only what he wants to hear, time will inevitably expose your lies and you will be in trouble.

Samarai was a lifelong military officer. He had advised Saddam throughout the long war with Iran, and he had seen him develop a fairly sophisticated understanding of military terminology, weaponry, strategy, and tactics. But Saddam's vision was clouded by a strong propensity for wishful thinking — the downfall of many an amateur general. If Saddam wanted something to happen, he believed he could will it to happen. Samarai kept up a steady stream of intelligence reports as the United States and its allies assembled an army of nearly a million soldiers in Kuwait, with air power far beyond anything the Iraqis could muster, with artillery, missiles, tanks, and other armored vehicles decades more advanced than Iraq's arsenal. The Americans didn't hide these weapons. They wanted Saddam to understand exactly what he was up against.

Yet Saddam refused to be intimidated. He had a plan, which he outlined to Samarai and his other generals in a meeting in Basra weeks before the American offensive started. He proposed capturing U.S. soldiers and tying them up around Iraqi tanks, using them as human shields. "The Americans will never fire on their own soldiers," he said triumphantly, as if such squeamishness was a fatal flaw. It was understood that he would have no such compunction. In the fighting, he vowed, thousands of enemy prisoners would be taken for this purpose. Then his troops would roll unopposed into eastern Saudi Arabia, forcing the allies to back down. This was his plan, anyway.

Samarai knew that this was nothing more than a hallucination. How were the Iraqis supposed to capture thousands of American soldiers? No one could approach the American positions, especially in force, without being discovered and killed. Even if it could be done, the very idea of using soldiers as human shields was repulsive, against all laws and international agreements. Who knew how the Americans would respond to such an act? Might they bomb Baghdad with a nuclear weapon? Saddam's plan was preposterous. But none of the generals, including Samarai, said a word. They all nodded dutifully and took notes. To question the Great Uncle's grand strategy would have meant to admit doubt, timidity, and cowardice. It might also have meant demotion or death.

Still, as chief of intelligence, Samarai felt compelled to tell Saddam the truth. Late in the afternoon of January 14 the general reported for a meeting in Saddam's office in the Republican Palace. Dressed in a well-cut black suit, the president was behind his desk. Samarai swallowed hard and delivered his grim assessment. It would be very difficult to stand fast against the assault that was coming. No enemy soldiers had been captured, and it was unlikely that any would be. There was no defense against the number and variety of weapons arrayed against Iraq's troops. Saddam had refused all previous military advice to withdraw the bulk of his forces from Kuwait and move them back across the Iraqi border, where they might be more effective. Now they were so thinly strung out across the desert that there was little to stop the Americans from advancing straight to Baghdad itself. Samarai had detailed evidence to back up his views — photographs, news reports, numbers. The Iraqis could expect nothing more than swift defeat, and the threat that Iran would take advantage of their weakness by invading from the north.

Saddam listened patiently to this litany of pending disaster. "Are these your personal opinions or are they facts?" he asked. Samarai had presented many facts in his report, but he conceded that some of what he was offering was educated conjecture.

"I will now tell you my opinion," Saddam said calmly, confidently. "Iran will never interfere. Our forces will put up more of a fight than you think. They can dig bunkers and withstand America's aerial attacks. They will fight for a long time, and there will be many casualties on both sides. Only we are willing to accept casualties; the Americans are not. The American people are weak. They would not accept the losses of large numbers of their soldiers."

Samarai was flabbergasted. But he felt he had done his duty. Saddam would not be able to complain later that his chief intelligence officer had misled him. The two men sat in silence for a few moments. Samarai could feel the looming American threat like a great weight pressing on his shoulders. There was nothing to be done. To Samarai's surprise, Saddam did not seem angry with him for delivering this bad news. In fact, he acted appreciative that Samarai had given it to him straight. "I trust you, and that's your opinion," he said. "You are a trustworthy person, an honorable person."

Heavy aerial attacks began three days later. Five weeks after that, on February 24, the ground offensive began, and Saddam's troops promptly surrendered or fled. Thousands were pinned at a place called Mutla Ridge as they tried to cross back into Iraq; most were incinerated in their vehicles. Iran did not invade, but otherwise the war unfolded precisely as Samarai had predicted.

In the days after this rout Samarai was again summoned to meet with Saddam. The president was working out of a secret office. He had been moving from house to house in the Baghdad suburbs, commandeering homes at random in order to avoid sleeping where American smart bombs might hit. Still, Samarai found him looking not just unfazed but oddly buoyed by all the excitement.

"What is your evaluation, general?" Saddam asked.

"I think this is the biggest defeat in military history," Samarai said.

"How can you say that?"

"This is bigger than the defeat at Khorramshahr [one of the worst Iraqi losses in the war with Iran, with Iraqi casualties in the tens of thousands]."

Saddam didn't say anything at first. Samarai knew the president wasn't stupid. He surely had seen what everyone else had seen — his troops surrendering en masse, the slaughter at Mutla Ridge, the grinding devastation of the U.S. bombing campaign. But even if Saddam agreed with the general's assessment, he could not bring himself to say so. In the past, as at Khorramshahr, the generals could always be blamed for defeat. Military people would be accused of sabotage, betrayal, incompetence, or cowardice. There would be arrests and executions, after which Saddam could comfortably harbor the illusion that he had rooted out the cause of failure. But this time the reasons for defeat rested squarely with him, and this, of course, was something he could never admit. "That's your opinion," he said curtly, and left it at that.

Defeated militarily, Saddam has in the years since responded with even wilder schemes and dreams, articulated in his typically confused, jargon-laden, quasi-messianic rhetoric. "On this basis, and along the same central concepts and their genuine constants, together with the required revolutionary compatibility and continuous renewal in styles, means, concepts, potentials, and methods of treatment and behavior, the proud and loyal people of Iraq and their valiant armed forces will win victory in the final results of the immortal Mother of All Battles," he declared in a televised address to the Iraqi people in August of last year. "With them and through them, good Arabs will win victory. Their victory will be splendid, immortal, immaculate, with brilliance that no interference can overshadow. In our hearts and souls as in the hearts and souls of the high-minded, glorious Iraqi women and high-spirited Iraqi men, victory is absolute conviction, Allah willing. The picking of its final fruit, in accordance with its description which all the world will point to, is a matter of time whose manner and last and final hour will be determined by the Merciful Allah. And Allah is the greatest!"

To help Allah along, Saddam had already started secret programs to develop nuclear, chemical, and biological weapons.

Qaswah (Cruelty)

The flood has reached its climax and after the destruction, terror, murder, and sacrilege practiced by the aggressive, terrorist, and criminal Zionist entity, together with its tyrannical ally, the U.S., have come to a head against our brothers and our faithful struggling people in plundered Palestine. If evil achieves its objectives there, Allah forbid, its gluttony for more will increase and it will afflict our people and other parts of our wide homeland too.

— Saddam Hussein, in a televised address to the Iraqi people, December 15, 2001

In the early 1980s a mid-level Iraqi bureaucrat who worked in the Housing Ministry in Baghdad saw several of his colleagues accused by Saddam's regime of accepting bribes. The accusations, he believes, were probably true. "There was petty corruption in our department," he says. The accused were all sentenced to die.

"All of us in the office were ordered to attend the hanging," says the former bureaucrat, who now lives in London. "I decided I wasn't going to go, but when my friends found out my plans, they called me and urged me to reconsider, warning that my refusal could turn suspicion on me." So he went. He and the others from his office were led into a prison courtyard, where they watched as their colleagues and friends, with whom they had worked for years, with whose children their children played, with whom they had attended parties and picnics, were marched out with sacks tied over their heads. They watched and listened as the accused begged, wept, and protested their innocence from beneath the sacks. One by one they were hanged. The bureaucrat decided then and there to leave Iraq.

"I could not live in a country where such a thing takes place," he says. "It is wrong to accept bribes, and those who do it should be punished by being sent to jail. But to hang them? And to order their friends and colleagues to come watch? No one who has witnessed such cruelty would willingly stay and continue to work under such conditions."

Cruelty is the tyrant's art. He studies and embraces it. His rule is based on fear, but fear is not enough to stop everyone. Some men and women have great courage. They are willing to brave death to oppose him. But the tyrant has ways of countering even this. Among those who do not fear death, some fear torture, disgrace, or humiliation. And even those who do not fear these things for themselves may fear them for their fathers, mothers, brothers, sisters, wives, and children. The tyrant uses all these tools. He commands not just acts of cruelty but cruel spectacle. So we have Saddam hanging the fourteen alleged Zionist plotters in 1969 in a public square, and leaving their dangling bodies on display. So we have Saddam videotaping the purge in the Baghdad conference hall, and sending the tape to members of his organization throughout the nation. So we have top party leaders forced to witness and even to participate in the executions of their colleagues. When Saddam cracks down on Shia clerics, he executes not just the mullahs but also their families. Pain and humiliation and death become public theater. Ultimately, guilt or innocence doesn't matter, because there is no law or value beyond the tyrant's will; if he wants someone arrested, tortured, tried, and executed, that is sufficient. The exercise not only serves as warning, punishment, or purge but also advertises to his subjects, his enemies, and his potential rivals that he is strong. Compassion, fairness, concern for due process or the law, are all signs of indecision. Indecision means weakness. Cruelty asserts strength.

Among the Zulu, tyrants are said to be "full of blood." According to one estimate, in the third and fourth years of Saddam's formal rule (1981 and 1982) more than three thousand Iraqis were executed. Saddam's horrors over the more than thirty years of his informal and formal rule will someday warrant a museum and archives. But lost among the most outrageous atrocities are smaller acts that shed light on his personality. Tahir Yahya was the prime minister of Iraq when the Baath Party took power, in 1968. It is said that in 1964, when Saddam was in prison, Yahya had ar-

ranged for a personal meeting and tried to coerce him into turning against the Baathists and cooperating with the regime. Yahya
had served Iraq as a military officer his whole adult life, and had at
one time even been a prominent member of the Baath Party, one
of Saddam's superiors. But he had earned Saddam's enduring
scorn. After seizing power, Saddam had Yahya, a well-educated
man whose sophistication he resented, confined to prison. On
his orders Yahya was assigned to push a wheelbarrow from cell
to cell, collecting the prisoners' slop buckets. He would call out
"Rubbish! Rubbish!" The former prime minister's humiliation
was a source of delight to Saddam until the day Yahya died, in
prison. He still likes to tell the story, chuckling over the words
"Rubbish! Rubbish!"

In another case Lieutenant General Omar al-Hazzaa was over-
heard speaking ill of the Great Uncle in 1990. He was not just sentenced to death. Saddam ordered that prior to his execution his
tongue be cut out; for good measure, he also executed al-Hazzaa's
son, Farouq. Al-Hazzaa's homes were bulldozed, and his wife and
other children left on the street.

Saddam is realistic about the brutal reprisals that would be un-
leashed should he ever lose his grip on power. In their book *Out of
the Ashes* (1999), Andrew and Patrick Cockburn tell of a family
that complained to Saddam that one of their members had been
unjustly executed. He was unapologetic, and told them, "Do not
think you will get revenge. If you ever have the chance, by the time
you get to us there will not be a sliver of flesh left on our bodies."
In other words, if he ever becomes vulnerable, his enemies will
quickly devour him.

Even if Saddam is right that greatness is his destiny, his legend
will be colored by cruelty. It is something he sees as regrettable,
perhaps, but necessary — a trait that defines his stature. A lesser
man would lack the stomach for it. His son Uday once boasted to a
childhood playmate that he and his brother Qusay had been taken
to prisons by their father to witness torture and executions — to
toughen them up for "the difficult tasks ahead," he said.

Yet no man is without contradictions. Even Saddam has been

known to grieve over his excesses. Some who saw him cry at
the lectern during the 1979 purge dismiss it as a performance,
but Saddam has a history of bursting into tears. In the wave of executions following his formal assumption of power, according to
Saïd Aburish's biography, he locked himself in his bedroom for
two days and emerged with eyes red and swollen from weeping.
Aburish reports that Saddam then paid a brazen though apparently sincere condolence call on the family of Adnan Hamdani,
the executed official who had been closest to him during the previous decade. He expressed not remorse — the execution was *necessary* — but sadness. He told Hamdani's widow apologetically that
"national considerations" must outweigh personal ones. So on occasion, at least, Saddam the person laments what Saddam the tyrant must do. During the Civil War, Abraham Lincoln drew a
sharp distinction between what he personally would do — abolish
slavery — and what his office required him to do: uphold the Con-
stitution and the Union. Saddam ought to feel no such conflict; by
definition, the interests of the state are his own. But he does.

The conflict between his personal priorities and his presiden-
tial ones has been particularly painful in his own family. Two of
his sons-in-law, the brothers Saddam and Hussein Kamel, fled to
Jordan and spilled state secrets — about biological, chemical, and
nuclear weapons programs — before inexplicably returning to Iraq
and their deaths. Uday Hussein, Saddam's eldest son, is by all reports a sadistic criminal, if not completely mad. He is a tall, dark-
skinned, well-built man of thirty-seven, who in his narcissism and
willfulness is almost a caricature of his father. Uday has all his father's brutal instincts and, apparently, none of his discipline. He is
a flamboyant drunk, and famous for designing his own wild ap-
parel. Photographs show him wearing enormous bow ties and
suits in colors to match his luxury cars, including a bright red one
with white stripes, and one that is half red, half white. Some of his
suit jackets have a lapel on one side but not the other.

Ismail Hussain, the hapless Iraqi soldier who lost his leg in the
Kuwaiti desert, attracted Uday's attention as a singer after the war.
He became the first son's favorite performer, and was invited to

sing at the huge parties Uday threw every Monday and Thursday night. The parties were often held at a palace, which Saddam built, on an island in the Tigris near Baghdad. The opulence was eye-popping. All the door handles and fixtures in the palace were made of gold.

"At the parties," says Ismail, who now lives in Toronto, "I would be performing, and Uday would climb up on the stage with a machine gun and start shooting it at the ceiling. Everyone would drop down, terrified. I was used to being around weapons, bigger weapons than Uday's Kalashnikov, so I would just keep on singing. Sometimes at these parties there would be dozens of women and only five or six men. Uday insists that everyone get drunk with him. He would interrupt my performance, get up on stage with a big glass of cognac for himself and one for me. He would insist that I drink all of it with him. When he gets really drunk, out come the guns. His friends are all terrified of him, because he can have them imprisoned or killed. I saw him once get angry with one of his friends. He kicked the man in the ass so hard that his boot flew off. The man ran over and retrieved the boot and then tried to put it back on Uday's foot, with Uday cursing him all the while."

Uday's blessing paves the way for a singer like Ismail to perform regularly on Iraqi television. For this service Uday demands a kickback, and he can unmake a star as quickly as he can make one. The same is true in sports. Raed Ahmed was an Olympic weightlifter who carried the Iraqi flag during the opening ceremonies of the Atlanta games, in 1996. "Uday was head of the Olympic Committee, and all sports in Iraq," Ahmed told me early this year, in his home in a suburb of Detroit. "During training camp he would closely monitor all the athletes, keeping in touch with the trainers and pushing them to push the athletes harder. If he's unhappy with the results, he will throw the trainers and even the athletes into a prison he keeps inside the Olympic Committee building. If you make a promise of a certain result, and fail to achieve it in competition, then the punishment is a special prison where they torture people. Some of the athletes started to quit when Uday took over, including many who were the best in their sports. They just decided it was not worth it. Others, like me, loved their sports, and success can be a steppingstone in Iraq to better things, like a nice car, a nice home, a career. I always managed to avoid being punished. I was careful never to promise anything that I couldn't deliver. I would always say that there was a strong possibility that I would be beaten. Then, when I won, Uday was so happy."

Ahmed sat like a giant in his small living room, his shoulders nearly as wide as the back of the couch. The world of Saddam and Uday now strikes him as a bizarre wonderland, an entire nation hostage to the whims of a tyrant and his crazy son. "When I defected, Uday was very angry," he said. "He visited my family and questioned them. 'Why would Ahmed do such a thing?' he asked. 'He was always rewarded by me.' But Uday is despised."

Saddam tolerated Uday's excesses — his drunken parties, his private jail in the Olympic Committee headquarters — until Uday murdered one of the Great Uncle's top aides at a party in 1988. Uday immediately tried to commit suicide with sleeping pills. According to the Cockburns, "As his stomach was being pumped out, Saddam arrived in the emergency room, pushed the doctors aside, and hit Uday in the face, shouting: 'Your blood will flow like my friend's!'" His father softened, and the murder was ruled an accident. Uday spent four months in custody and then four months with an uncle in Geneva before he was picked up by the Swiss police for carrying a concealed weapon and asked to leave the country. Back in Baghdad, in 1996, he became the target of an assassination attempt. He was hit by eight bullets, and is now paralyzed from the waist down. His behavior has presumably disqualified him from succeeding his father. Saddam has made a show in recent years of grooming Qusay, a quieter, more disciplined and dutiful heir.

But the shooting of Uday was a warning to Saddam. Reportedly, a small group of well-educated Iraqi dissidents — none of whom has ever been apprehended, despite thousands of arrests and interrogations — carried it out. The would-be assassins are rumored to be associated with the family of General Omar al-Hazzaa, the

officer whose tongue was cut out before he and his son were executed. This may be true; but there is no shortage of aggrieved parties in Iraq.

As Saddam approaches his sixty-sixth birthday, his enemies are
numerous, strong, and determined. He celebrated the 1992 elec-
toral defeat of George Bush by firing a gun from a palace balcony.
Ten years later a new President Bush is in the White House, with a
new national mission to remove Saddam. So the walls that protect
the tyrant grow higher and higher. His dreams of pan-Arabia and
his historical role in it grow ever more fanciful. In his clearer moments Saddam must know that even if he manages to hang on to
power for the remainder of his life, the chances of his fathering
a dynasty are slim. As he retreats to his secret bed each night, sitting up to watch a favorite movie on TV or to read one of his
history books, he must know it will end badly for him. Any man
who reads as much as he does, and who studies the dictators of
modern history, knows that in the end they are all toppled and dis-
dained.

"His aim is to be leader of Iraq forever, for as long as he lives,"
Samarai says. "This is a difficult task, even without the United
States targeting you. The Iraqis are a divided and ruthless people.
It is one of the most difficult nations in the world to govern. To ac-
complish his own rule, Saddam has shed so much blood. If his
aim is for his power to be transferred to his family after his death,
I think this is far into the realm of wishful thinking. But I think he
lost touch with reality in that sense long ago."

This, ultimately, is why Saddam will fail. His cruelty has created
great waves of hatred and fear, and it has also isolated him. He is
out of step. His speeches today play like a broken record. They no
longer resonate even in the Arab world, where he is despised by
secular liberals and Muslim conservatives alike. In Iraq itself he is
universally hated. He blames the crippling of the state on UN
sanctions and U.S. hostility, but Iraqis understand that he is the
cause of it. "Whenever he would start in blaming the Americans
for this and that, for everything, we would look at each other and

roll our eyes," says Sabah Khalifa Khodada, the former Iraqi major who was stripped and decontaminated for a meeting with the Great Uncle. The forces that protect him know this too — they do not live full-time behind the walls. Their loyalty is governed by fear and self-interest, and will tilt decisively if and when an alternative appears. The key to ending Saddam's tyranny is to present such an alternative. It will not be easy. Saddam will never give up. Overthrowing him will almost certainly mean killing him. He guards his hold on the state as he guards his own life. There is no panic in his fight.

But for all the surrounding threats, Saddam sees himself as an immortal figure. Nothing could be more illustrative of this than the plot of his first novel, *Zabibah and the King.* Set in a mythical Arabian past, it is a simple fable about a lonely king, trapped behind the high walls of his palace. He feels cut off from his subjects, so he sets out on occasion to mingle. On one such outing, to a rural village, the king is struck by the beauty of the young Zabibah. She is married to a brutish husband, but the king summons her to his palace, where her rustic ways are at first scorned by the sophisticated courtiers. In time Zabibah's sweet simplicity and virtue charm the court and win the king's heart — although their relationship remains chaste. Questioning his own stern methods, the king is reassured by Zabibah, who tells him, "The people need strict measures so that they can feel protected by this strictness." But dark forces invade the kingdom. Infidel outsiders pillage and destroy the village, aided by Zabibah's jealous and humiliated husband, who rapes her. (The outrage occurs on January 17, the day in 1991 when the United States and allied powers began aerial attacks on Iraq.) Zabibah is later killed; the king defeats his enemy and slays Zabibah's husband. He then experiments with giving his people more freedoms, but they fall to fighting among themselves. Their squabbles are interrupted by the good king's death and their realization of his greatness and importance. The martyred Zabibah's sage advice reminds them: The people need strict measures.

And so Saddam champions the simple virtues of a glorious

Arab past, and dreams that his kingdom, though universally scorned and defiled, will rise again and triumph. Like the good king, he is vital in a way that will not be fully understood until he is gone. Only then will we all study the words and deeds of this magnificent, defiant soul. He awaits his moment of triumph in a distant, glorious future that mirrors a distant, glorious past.

MICHAEL BUCKLEY

■

The Meticulous Grove of
Black and Green

FROM *Alaska Quarterly Review*

Film Study: *Dogmouth*, Written and Directed by Marcus Bigg

It opens on a normal alley. The buildings that border it are an old, sea-stained concrete mess run through with hurricane fencing and long glass windows. There is no sound. Then the explosion comes and glass bursts from both sides of the alley like champagne bubbles at the ecstatic moment of the cork's removal; loose bricks are thrown like skipping stones through the air; jagged chunks of rock collide then fall to the bed of the alley. Still there is no sound. Then a squat, rusting tank turns into the alleyway, pulling itself over curbs and crushing the broken stones under it. For a long half-minute the tank defines the reality of the destruction with its obscene weight. With its blind force. Then soldiers spill around it, hunched with their rifles in their arms. They move quickly. They are terrified and strong.

Character Study: Self

I am lanky and tall and all shirts are either too big for me or too small and all pants sit too high on my legs, leaving my socks exposed in the light. When I was young I felt I needed to choose my socks very carefully because of this. Now I always wear white athletic socks, no matter what anyone says about it. Unlike Bigg I've been with the same woman for fifteen years. Her name is Carrie. When we were young, after we made love, she would lie in a way that made her look as if she were posing for a painting. Her right arm would be behind her head and her left arm would be at her side so her fingers rested on the inside of her thigh like long thin boats on a moonlit brown ocean. The light that surrounded her was always perfect. It lay subdued on her powerful breasts like the flashpoint before the flash, like fingers before snapping, like teeth before biting; full of potential sensation and memories of the future. Now she wears loose flannel boxer shorts around her (as it turns out) barren, strip-mined hips. She wears my loose T-shirts to bed and seems to move away from the light, to its muddled, unfocused underbelly. We adopted a child a year ago. His name is Anthony and he's retarded, although she doesn't like it when I call it that. She calls his impairment nothing and treats it like an ever-present, whispering ghost. I feel it is an injustice to him to ignore his retardation, considering that it came to him from his own father kicking him, again and again, in the head. I think his suffering should be remembered and respected, but as she has told me before and probably will again, my sensibility is for art, not life. He has fine brown hair spread over his overly large head. It is as soft as an infant's prebirth growth.

Thoughts on What Led to the Accident

It was ten years ago, of course, and that should count for something, but it doesn't. When you fall into the trap of viewing your life as a kind of long, boring movie you associate great significance with times and places in which you forgot your lines, or were just plain scripted to fail. You think of these times and places as turning points in which, for one instant, a lifelong dream stuck its big toe out of the surreality of your water glass and you could've grabbed it, you could've, you wish you had, but you didn't. And so you remember the beauty of that toe and daydream about the whole different life and the whole different you that was attached to it like a leg leading to hips to a chest and arms and to a head, all hiding, all could've been but wasn't. My turning point was in New York ten years ago. Bigg was there filming a movie and I was there, fresh and confused from a weeklong bus ride, and from sleeping on a friend's floor, and from eating in cheap fast food places where the screaming pace of the city sat around me like a methodical riot. The friend I was staying with was there too. (His name is Steve, and a study will follow.) We had heard that Bigg was seeking a writer to collaborate with. Five of us were chosen from the crowd by an assistant of Bigg's and we were driven to a restaurant constructed completely of glass and old solid wood and the overwhelming smell of pleasure. We were seated at a table and after we'd waited for an hour Bigg himself came in, and he was larger and more violent than any picture could've captured. He existed outside of the moment that day like an idea that had been written down. He sat at a table near to us, with his back to us, and when one of the writers spoke to his vast, still shoulders he ignored her. We stared at his back for a long time and after a while I began to believe he was some kind of statue, a representation of a demigod, as if he were made of my expectation, as if he stunk of it. Finally his assistant came back and after staring at all of us for a second he put his hand on my shoulder. You, he told me. You first. They seated me across from Bigg and brought us both ice water with very thin slices of lemon floating at the top of the glass. I was nervous, and Bigg was impassive and quiet even after I greeted him. I tasted the water and accidentally sucked ice cubes into my mouth and thought then, as I do now, that water tastes tainted when it has lemon in it. Have you ever been in a barfight? Bigg finally said to me, and I crushed the ice cubes between my teeth and thought, staring first at the boiling, bearded, grimacing mess of his face, then at his monstrous paws laid out on the table in front of him. Between his thumbs and forefingers it looked like golf balls sat under the skin, written over in thick, meandering veins, covered in tiny, beautiful, fading cuts. No, I said. He stared at me for another few seconds and I felt the tension drain out from between us like a warm tide ebbing out to the sunsetting ocean. Next, he said loudly. Steve was next, of course, and it was ten years ago and no doubt it's distorted by memory's long tunnel that is slippery with dreams, that is narrow with other memories of later disappointments superimposed over that one that day in that restaurant which I'd barely felt until Bigg asked Steve, Have you ever been in a barfight? and Steve smiled the biggest actor's grin in the world and said, I once beat every tooth out of a lumberjack's head and took each and every one of 'em home in my shirt pocket. Bigg ordered them each a Jack Daniel's and a beer then, and their collaboration began. Bigg's assistant ushered the rest of us out. The sound of the restaurant's immense wooden doors quietly closing behind our backs and leaving us among buildings that sweated gold and people who walked dogs that had thin, shaved, prancing legs, that sound; I heard it yesterday afternoon as I woke up from an aching reverie just before I rear-ended a big blue pickup truck. I was on my way to pick up Anthony from school because they'd called and said he had green mucus.

Film Study: *Angel*, Written and Directed by Marcus Bigg

It opens on a soldier slowly removing his uniform. He starts with his shoes and ends with his military issue, olive drab briefs. When he is completely naked he begins to cry. As the film progresses we watch the soldier in the hellish, wet, stinking trenches of World War I, with apocalyptic flares bursting over him like stars being broken by boys with BB guns, and with corpses talking to themselves in the mud next to him about their ancient, immovable grudges.

"One Man": A Film Concept, Turned Down by Fourteen Studios As of Last Week. Writer: Me

It is the story of a Japanese soldier after World War II. He is deep in the otherworld sweat of the jungle on an island in the Pacific.

He believes the war is still being fought. The film chronicles his thirty years on the island. A definitive scene in the script is when, half an hour into the film, weeping, he tries to bury himself in mud. It doesn't work.

Thoughts

Although *Angel* is widely considered to be Bigg's best film, I feel it chronicles the spiritual dismemberment of the soldier with a mallet, rather than with a scalpel. I believe "One Man" could be better, if anyone would buy it.

We study our betters because we hope to learn something, and in doing so, to own it.

Character Study: Self

The morning routine is always, always, always the same and always, always, always in the monotony of Carrie scrubbing herself in the shower as I stand in the closet trying to choose clothes to wear I feel old, old, old. When I've chosen what I'm going to wear I walk into Anthony's room. He always wakes up as I open his door, which Carrie has shut during the night after he falls asleep.

Guh muh-ning, he says.

Good morning, I say.

Guh foooo, he says, shaking one of his tiny fists in the air.

Good food, I say. It's time for breakfast.

I take him downstairs into the kitchen of the modern tract home we live in. The kitchen lights up like a church on Christmas noon when I clap my hands. Anthony claps his hands too, but we've adjusted the Clapper so it won't respond to the quiet noise of his little-boy's hands. Before we'd adjusted it, when we'd first brought Anthony home, we'd had long Clapper battles with him — me clapping, then him, turning the lights back off, then Carrie clapping so they'd come back on, then me clapping belatedly and turning them back off, then Anthony clapping, turning them on, then off again, then on. We finally adjusted them because he'd sit awake all night clapping his room into light then back to darkness. He likes being the god of light and dark, I thought one day, and almost told Carrie, but didn't.

I cook him eggs and potatoes and bacon usually, because despite his body which is like a tiny, tiny old man's, he is voracious. As I cook he sits at the breakfast table and stares at the light above his head.

Shih, he says when he smells the food. He means shit. I sometimes picture a myna bird sitting in Anthony's soft, squarish head pulling words out of his frozen past and putting them onto the tip of his huge tongue, among his jumbled teeth. It's hard to teach him new words. It takes months and months of repetition. In the year that we've had him we've only been able to teach him two phrases: good morning, and good food.

Watch your mouth, I tell him.

Mommy guh fooooo, he says.

I'm not your mommy and good food is on the way, I tell him.

When I'm finished cooking he eats and I drink coffee and watch him. When he chews the food sometimes it falls out of his mouth and past his large, round bottom lip. He picks the chewed food up with his greasy, small fingers and puts it back in his mouth. The grease on his hands lights them up in an unnatural way.

Carrie comes downstairs. Usually she says, You let him sit in the kitchen in his underwear? I can't remember what she says when she doesn't say that.

He gets food all over his clothes, I say.

She goes back upstairs to get him a shirt.

Shih, he says.

When she comes back down she makes him get up and pulls the shirt over his head.

Fuckah bitch, he yells.

She tells him to watch his language, young man.

I think she's ashamed of the scars on his belly. There is one small circular one from a gastric tube he'd had in place when he was younger and had just had the sense freshly kicked out of him, and had forgotten how to chew. The other scar stretches from his navel up to the bottom of his ribcage and no one we've talked to seems to know what it's from. Surgery, probably, Carrie said, when we first got him. I asked him once what happened, and I touched him with a finger on the long scar. Shih, he said, owie.

Don't let him sit in the kitchen in his underwear, she tells me, almost every day.

I forgot, I tell her, and think, Who cooked his damn breakfast? Then I wonder what Bigg would do, faced with Anthony and Carrie. He would probably calmly spread his philosophy of independence and strength over the breakfast table in place of the food.

Character Study: Bigg (excerpted from a 1982 interview in *Playboy*)

P: *You seem to mention that in all of your interviews.*

B: It's something that's very important to me. It is me. My movies are me. I don't make movies because I want to. I have to. They're me, on film, in different people's bodies.

P: *You mean characters?*

B: I mean other bodies. I don't believe in characters. I believe in versions of myself. A man can't tell a story right if he's not talking about himself. I'll never make a movie about a woman or a gay man or an attorney. Those things don't have any of me in them.

P: *But many of your movies have women in them. And attorneys; I think in "Angel" one of the soldiers was a lawyer from Houston.*

B: But the story was told from one point of view, and that was mine. What you're seeing is me in war, me in death, me in love. Me on film. I'm passionate about capturing the transcendent state that men can achieve through conflict. Men often rise above petty or worldly shit when heated in the midst of aggression. They become their actions, they lose themselves. To me that's the only proof of being; actions, the results of actions.

P: *Do you mean men as an all-inclusive grouping, as in humanity? Or just men?*

B: Men. Men only.

P: *Isn't that sexist?*

B: Is it? I only know about me. My approach to life is that it must be held by the balls at all hours of the day and night. Life is like a war. People who don't realize that never charge up the hill, and end up dying in obscurity in the ranks of the pack animals. Can women do that? I don't know. I don't care. I only know me. I only want to know me. Let's change the subject.

P: *It says here you played rugby while you attended film school at Berkeley.*

B: Yes.

P: *Why did you quit?*

B: I was knocked out once very badly. I lost two days of my life. My mother was alive then, she told me no more rugby.

P: *Your mother?*

B: Every man has to listen to his mother.

Green Mucus

I cleaned up after rear-ending the blue truck and ended up at Anthony's school twenty minutes after they called me. It is always a race when the school calls; if you take more than half an hour to get there the teachers and aides talk about what a bad parent you are, they talk about endangerment, and they go cold and frozen the second you walk into class.

When I opened the door to the room and I came in, most of the class was sitting around a small table covered in cut-up construction paper. There was an inhuman wailing that swept around me as the door closed, which fell from a deep crying to a breathless warbling then rose again. The sound made me want to close my eyes.

"Hi," the teacher said over the wailing, off to the right, and I saw her sitting on a chair holding a twisted, sweating, screaming child in her lap; his face and head were small but they were formed almost wholly of a huge round mouth surrounded by thin lips that dripped spittle into his gaping throat. She was rocking him back and forth.

"Should I call a doctor?" I asked.

"What?" she said, and one of the aides at the table with the children started laughing, I could barely hear it over the crying, which fell then rose again in volume. The child started trembling and thrusting his legs. His pants were too high on his legs like mine were and I could see braces made of plastic and fabric extending from his shoes up past the tight cuffs.

"No," the teacher yelled over the child. "He's just fussing. Anthony honey, Daddy's here."

Anthony walked over to me. He had a long green drop hanging out of his nose onto his upper lip.

"Guh fooooo," he said.

"See? He has green mucus," the teacher said.

"Yeah, I'll take him home."

"He needs to see a doctor," one of the aides said from the table.

"I will," I said.

"What happened?" the teacher yelled to me. She was staring at my face, which I could feel swelling under its skin and spreading blue and red under my broken nose.

"Nothing," I said. "Kind of a car accident."

"Oooh . . ." she said.

"I meant *Anthony* needs to see a doctor," the aide yelled.

"I will, take him to one," I yelled back and dragged him out of the room, even though I'd forgotten his jacket and backpack, and I walked him down the hall and could hear that insane crying all the way out to the parking lot. I wondered why I hadn't heard it when I came in. I took Anthony to my car. Its crushed hood broke the sunshine up within it.

"Fuckah bitch," Anthony said.

"Does he always cry like that?" I asked him.

"Guh foooo," he said.

"We'll go to McDonald's."

"Guh foooo," he said again.

Character Study: Steve

I met Steve in a restaurant we both worked at in Los Angeles. It was a fast-moving, tight dining room that opened through silver doors to a kitchen of frantic cooking and chopping and screaming orderorderorder pickup move your ass, and Steve and I avoided the kitchen as much as we could. Being waiters, we stayed in the ordered traffic and bath of conversation in the dining room. Steve had trained me when I started working there. He would tell me, through a fake smile, a waiter always needs to look happy, but don't look too happy, it's not a party we're at, for fuck's sake. Always be attentive. Look around all the time. Watch people eat but don't let them see you doing it. Once Steve yelled at me for dropping a plate of food in the kitchen. Jesus Christ, he said, there's fifteen minutes, you moron. Fuck you, I told him, fuck you and leave me alone. After that he did leave me alone, until he told me at his going-away party, which took place in the kitchen of the restaurant after it was closed, to come and see him in New York if I wanted to. We were both drunk and when he told me that I imagined a bursting dream of success in that city that beats like a heart all night long and lives in its boiling juices all day.

Thoughts

Of course Steve had heard me talking to Bigg that day he interviewed us in the restaurant. He heard the barfight question and changed his answer when my own (lie) failed. I think now about how much better it would've been if I'd said, even the stupid truth, yes, I'd been sucker-punched once in a bar by one of Carrie's old boyfriends. Steve has never been in a barfight and of course he never knocked all of the teeth out of a lumberjack's head, although I have to give him credit for the idea, which was good. I've heard from Steve, off and on, over the years. After he and Bigg finished their shots and beers they walked out of those same massive restaurant doors that kept me away from that bursting dream life and they collaborated on *Dogmouth* and *Angel* and all of Bigg's other movies. Recently Steve came out with a movie, a study of which will follow.

Character Study: Self

My forming idea is this:

It opens on a set of working abdominal muscles, etched in perfect tan, sweating, rhythmic. The shot will pan back and eventually show us the actor (who wears small red shorts and has, hopefully, a very real intensity on his face) and the workout machine itself, the Angleflex. I hope the Angleflex people will like this because they've rejected my last four ideas and I think soon they will find a new director. They are tired of telling me I'm too artistic. One of them even told me I'm too esoteric, and I asked him what that meant but he didn't answer because he didn't have to.

Earlier this week I was coming out of the shower and Carrie was lying on the bed in her boxer shorts and her big shirt and she was reading a book. I sat over her long brown legs and ran my fingers over the tips of her toes.

"Remember how your toes used to stick out of the hole in those purple socks you used to wear?" I asked her.

"You better find a way to write me in soon," she said. "I may not be here if I'm not going to be a character in this thing."

"I was just talking about your toes," I said. "*Your* toes."

"You were talking about how we used to be. You always talk about how we used to be."

"As opposed to?" I asked her, and even as I said it I could picture myself, the image of understanding and reason, trying to make her feel as if her words didn't make any sense. I can't help it. But her words don't, really, make any sense.

Anthony began screaming in his bedroom.

"Did you close his door before he was asleep?" she asked, getting off the bed. "How could you do that?"

"He was asleep," I said, and as she left the bedroom I could hear him clapping frantically between his hoarse screams.

It's her fault, I thought, the fault of her crazy jailed ex-boyfriends and all the abortions she had. The silent reason sitting in

her gently scarred inner hips why we have Anthony and not someone with the gracefully arched feet she used to have and the
knobby, dented knees I still have, someone with the soft brown
eyes she used to want me to paint, someone with my visible ribs
and thin hair. I've always been thirsty for her to take up the weight
of our present life onto her shoulders, for her to say yes, my fault,
my fault there's no child and my fault Anthony has so many scars
set in such soft skin and my fault you're tired all the time and can't
come up with good ideas for the Angleflex people. But I can't mention the abortions, because she wouldn't let that be taken back. Because that would live forever in the space between us and the tract
house around us.

Write me in soon, she said, as if I were writing this thing we live
in. I feel often like I'm shooting the movie of our whole lives but
for God's sake, I'm definitely not writing it.

Film Study: *Bugger*, Written and Directed by Marcus Bigg

It opens on the factory that dominates the characters' lives, that
lives around them like a throbbing, iron father. It is a wide shot
taken from the cavernous ceiling and it encompasses all of the
sweating, struggling laborers as they rush and lunge and shout to
each other amid a wash of noise. The mild panic of frantic work
fills their faces. The sound is immense, it is the sound of a thousand machines running high at once, the sound of a whole society
fit onto the tip of a pin, and this sound dominates the entire film.

Notes on the Collaboration

Although they collaborated on every film Bigg made after they
met, he rarely mentions Steve in his interviews. He most often
discusses his personal philosophy of life as war, although sometimes he talks about sports or models he's been seen around town
with. He never talks about the films he makes. Between them and
their maker is a vast grove of mystery that Bigg maintains meticulously. Steve once told me that as they collaborated, he and Bigg,
Steve would present an idea, and Bigg would have three seconds

to veto the idea. At first, Steve said, this was difficult. He'd throw his best ideas at Bigg and Bigg would knock them away like rotten apples, in his simple monotone, saying no, no, no. After about forty-five minutes, usually, Bigg would finally say, hearing one of Steve's harangued, picked-apart ideas, all right, let's do it. Steve realized after a while that Bigg always accepted the sixty-third idea. He'd tested this, one day as they sat down to write, by inserting a transparent and shitty idea about a factory run on desperation and oppression into the sixty-third spot. He told me over the phone that Bigg had taken it, but probably nothing would come of it. When I went to see *Bugger* (alone, as I always am in the temple of Bigg's movies) I burst out laughing into the industrial roar of the film's opening because here was the shitty idea made into poetry for the timeless eyes, here was the lie that Steve spoke into that vacuum of manly trust between him and Bigg, here was proof that the prophet was listening to a voice other than God's.

But still, he'd made poetry. He'd made a wonderfully long movie filled with machine grease and the calloused, stony palms that slathered it into the guts of the functions.

We study our betters in hopes of emulating them, because when one is enough like Christ, one will be able to stroll across water.

Boxing Lessons

Bigg, of course, dabbles in boxing. He once said in an interview that the motions and spirit of boxing defined the boundaries and sensibilities of his filming style. This was three years ago when a short film of mine was being refused by film festival after film festival, all the way down to the lowest, most mediocre festival that Bigg could've shaken to pieces with a sneeze. One day I called one of this mediocre festival's directors (I don't remember which one because I don't have to) and asked him why, for Christ's sake, didn't they take my film? Because it's limp, he said after I pressed him, it's too esoteric, it's like, I don't know, white bread sitting in the rain. I hung up, of course. And I didn't ask him if he knew what esoteric meant because I'm sure he did.

So after that I searched for and found a boxing gym as far away from the tract housing as I could manage and I showed up one day with a pair of gloves I'd bought at a sporting goods store. The place was clean and square and simple inside and the walls were covered in pictures of very, very serious warriors in gloves. I lifted weights for a while but became embarrassed when they clanged together, because every unsmiling, muscular man in the room would cast me a sidelong kind of glare when they did, so I went to punching the heavy bag which was actually very heavy and after a while a man tapped me on the shoulder and asked me if I wanted to get in the ring. He was a short, thin man in lots of sweat clothes with the very short tips of jet black hair shaved just over the gentle moon of his skull and his eyes were very intense and didn't waver, didn't look away, like Bigg's probably (surely) don't, like two cameras grown in a face, and so I said fuck yes, let's do it, I could use it. We got into the ring and I went to a corner and the other man just stared, there from the center of the ring, so I went out to meet him. Fuck him, I thought, as I came toward him with my hands up, fuck him and everybody, let's leave the ranks of the pack animals and charge this motherfucker and fuck all the wrongs done to you by life and fuck the silent murder they deposit in your chest to fester and rot and here and now I will burst this murder all over this other man like the lancing of an abscess and so then, I threw what felt to me like a flurry of punches that landed all over him, that left him no room for escape, that smothered his humanity in flying hands and a dodging head, and then, before I could react, I saw first one explosion, then another, I heard the sound of metal falling into metal, then I landed on my back and found I couldn't open my eyes or close my mouth. Shit, sorry man, my opponent said, after a few minutes, pulling me to my feet. I thought you saw those coming. You came on so strong I thought you really wanted to do it. I just wanted to spar.

So I left. And later Carrie asked me why I was holding an unopened beer can to my forehead, and I felt like saying because I feel too sick to drink it but I really said, I boxed, honey. You did? she asked. Why? I don't know, I told her, and she was quiet for a long time. The back of my throat hurts, I said, and then I looked up and she wasn't in the room anymore. So I drank the beer and poured myself a glass of Jack Daniel's, figuring I'd at least salvage the machismo of Bigg's drinking habit, but I fell asleep in the chair I was in, and woke up to find the Jack Daniel's untouched on the coffee table in the flower-petal light of the thieving dawn.

Film Study: *Treetip*, by Steven Spires

It opens in darkness. The camera pulls back from what we see is dirt on the floor of a forest, then back more, showing a flat covering of wet foliage, then back and back, straight up, through the dense canopy of trees. Finally we see, from above, a vast sea of water-engorged rain forest swaying back and forth in a — we are left to assume — warm breeze.

Thoughts

Steve's movie fails for many reasons. I feel the most important reason is his insistence on making the stretch of rain forest the film's main character. We are forced to suffer through the opening of the film, which takes place at the beginning of time, then through a twenty-minute sequence of fecund nature footage that catalogues the functions and organs of the forest like a surgeon fingering through a body. Finally the indigenous peoples of the area show up and deal with each other in subtitles. They build a society that we watch destroyed, in choppy, bloody, clinical scenes. The implication of fire in the conquistadors' guns (which, in the film, Steve cares so much about) culminates in the burning of the village, which is orgiastic and prolonged. At one point a conquistador wears the head of a dead villager like a mask. I personally don't believe anyone would do that, if they realized how much blood would get on them. Later we watch the stretch of forest as recent history marches past it and I have to say that I, for one, was happy when the yellow earthmovers finally came to tear down all of the trees. That is how the film ends, after a ten-minute-long snake's-eye view of the bare, churned dirt and the muddy (Steve would say bloody) tires of the bulldozers.

Although his movie was widely released, it has had almost no commercial success. Sometimes I think that's because Bigg cursed the film somehow, as only a force like him could. Steve obviously kept the idea for his film away from Bigg's director's appetite; he was probably afraid it would get swallowed into a better movie than he could possibly make, one which would sail under the flags of Bigg's fame.

Character Study: Bigg, cont.

Bigg was married for ten years before he became famous, at which point he was married no more. When asked in an interview why he had gotten divorced, Bigg said simply, a man has to go his way. After that, in subsequent interviews, he wouldn't discuss it. To Bigg, I think, all of the interviews are like one long one. He'll carry on this interview until the day he dies, whether or not anyone is listening, and of course they probably will be.

Last week, as I was watching the goddamned TV after a long, stupid day of trying to talk the Angleflex people into a more artistic (esoteric, they said) approach, I saw Bigg on the news. He was taking refuge in the American embassy in Saigon, where he'd been filming his new movie. It was said that earlier that day he'd broken the jaw of an old Vietnamese villager after the man had refused to pull his water buffalo from his farm over to Bigg's set. Both Bigg and the suit-wearing Americans on TV vehemently denied the story, but crew members and Vietnamese villagers told, on the same news show, about the violence with which Bigg had held the man's face in the ankle-deep mud surrounding his set. That man is lucky he isn't dead, said one unnamed actor, who probably hadn't tried to help anyway. Bigg's reputation will blow all of this out into the thick silence of the forests around Saigon, where no one will care, where only the villagers will whisper about it. Here in America, in the bone-white sunbleach of Los Angeles, it will make him more famous. More *known*.

Directors, especially American directors, especially Bigg, think the whole world is a movie set and all the people of the world are confused extras. Boys like Anthony are scarred and movies are made about them. These movies show us how to see the world but leave Anthony and his belly scars alone, staring into the kitchen light. Surely one day someone will make a movie about the Godman that is Bigg.

Thoughts

Even though we may be unlike our betters we can find salvation in their faults. Even their worst part is better than our best part if it made them what we'd like to be.

Character Study: Self

I try as hard as I can to cheat on Carrie but I can't find anyone to do it with. For weeks now I've tried with a production assistant on the set of the Angleflex commercial (which has become more *direct,* more *intense,* more about muscle, less about brains). Bigg once said something about all of the hope found in the sound of a woman's high heels walking on concrete, and one day when I heard the production assistant coming toward me, I hoped. But when I talk to her I say stupid things and talk too much, and she says stupid things too out of her perfect, floral mouth.

I resolved a long time ago, after missing my opportunity at collaboration with Bigg, to get into every fight I had a chance to. The problem is, in all of these years, there's been *no* chance to. The people in my tract housing are nice and quiet and ignore me like I pretend to ignore them.

Thoughts

How are you supposed to charge a hill when it keeps moving? Or when there isn't a hill in front of you? Or when you wouldn't recognize a hill if you saw one?

Character Study: Bigg

Bigg details his philosophy of productive aggression in his new book, *Man Unbound.* He rails against society and its constraints at once, then against the pathetic nature of suburban men's back-to-nature movements, where they bang on drums and dance and cry together to regain their manhood and their sense of purpose. He laughs at gyms and neo-fat-boot camps that take civilians and train them as if they were in the military. He claims that someone without physical power, that is, as he says, without the ability to effect real change on a listless world, isn't really a person at all. The critics, of course, tear his book apart and call him a fascist. But the people who really know, the nameless millions who congregate in the cities like campers around a fire, the people who give a movie success or failure, the people whose every action directors and executives try to predict, buy the book in droves. They drag it out of bookstores and hold their little piece of Bigg on their shelves, between their fake paintings and their family pictures, over their fireplaces. They laugh at the critics who should know but somehow don't, the critics made of all brain and no flesh. I buy the book too, and find myself, after Anthony and Carrie are asleep, staring at the black-and-white picture of Bigg on the dust jacket. The picture seems more real than the silent, divided world of the bedroom I am in.

Thoughts on the Accident Itself

I rear-end the blue pickup truck and see the hood of my car, first normal, then pushed up and crushed toward the front so its paint is ripped at the seams of the crush and the silver underneath looks white in the sunlight. I put the car in first gear and turn it off and get out. There is a line of cars in front of me that stretches for blocks and ends with a red light that shimmers and sits disembodied over the heat bleeding off of the cars in the street. A bus is broken down halfway through the congestion; its engine compartment is open and gaping and I can see the bus driver standing on its roof, shielding his eyes, looking off toward the red light as if he were looking for a coming flood. Then the man from the pickup truck gets out and slams his door behind him and looks for a second at his rear bumper. You fuckin idiot, you stupid ass goddamn moron, he says to me. You stopped too quickly, I say to him. Fuck you, he says, and I feel suddenly the need to hit him and break the power he's robbed from me all over his sweating face. I want to see him lying on his back, gripping at blood spilling out of his mouth. So I swing my fist and he's too close to me so my forearm hits his ear, and he explodes into motion and before I can react my head is being slammed into the side of his truck and I'm seeing those same explosions again, like loud ringing bells, like the crunch of steel of the two colliding cars. Then I'm on my back and the man is in his truck. He U-turns and drives the opposite way and I feel sick in the wash of heat and exhaust that sweeps over me. I get back into my car and in the car next to mine a middle-aged woman is staring at me and I yell to her so she can hear, Don't worry it's not bad, but she doesn't say anything, just stares, and then I realize my shirt's covered in blood, in long bright strips of it, in the vibrant shapes of the shadows of fauna, so much more alive than it ever looks in the movies. I hold some loose papers I'd written on up to my bleeding nose as the traffic creeps up, and only after I'm past the red light and the world is moving around me again do I think of calling the police. I think of telling them how someone hit me for rear-ending them and I feel so stupid I don't stop until I get to Anthony's school. I put the bloody papers into the trunk and I put an old jacket on to cover the bloodstains on my shirt.

Thoughts

How can we live in a world we can't change? That is, how can we live in a world we're too weak for?

A New Movie Idea of Mine

A loose line of sunburned farm workers are walking across a bright tan field of wheat. Their farm tools dangle from their dirty hands and they yell jokes to each other, and they laugh alone. Off ahead of them is a grove of eucalyptus trees, meticulously kept, black and green against the white sky. They notice trails of gray smoke first, then they notice flames coming from the bases of the trees they can't see, have never seen, but which surely must be immense and too thick to reach arms around. There is no smoke. The living orange of the fire gulps the thin, strong trees in long, sweeping dresses against the sky, and one of the laborers thinks, Lord help us, the trees are burning. I don't know, yet, why he thinks this, why he cares about the distant grove.

The Now of Yesterday Afternoon, After the Accident

As Anthony and I leave his school and get into the car, Carrie's car pulls up. They must've called her too, seeing as (I was once told) green mucus is contagious. She gets out and walks around to Anthony's side of the car. I roll down the window for her.

"My God, what happened?" she says.

"Car accident," I tell her.

"You're hurt."

"I think my nose is broken."

"Guh fooo," Anthony says.

"We're going to McDonald's, don't worry," I say, wondering at the same time why she would worry but God my broken nose hurts so much I have to breathe through my mouth.

"I'll go," she says.

"What?"

"I'll go. Why don't you take Anthony to the park down the street? I'll come with the food."

"Shih," Anthony says.

"Okay," I tell her.

"Drive carefully," she says and I get mad for a second and start to say Jesus Christ you think it's my fault this happened but I look up at her and she's smiling, and I'm confused, and don't know what to do.

She walks back to her car and I pull out of the school's parking lot, which I notice, for the first time, is surrounded by rusted hurricane fencing with barbed wire along its top.

"Punk bitch," Anthony says.

"Relax. You'll eat soon."

We drive down the street and park in the neighborhood by the park and as we walk toward the park Anthony holds my hand and keeps his head low so the sun doesn't get in his eyes, the sun that opens up the whole neighborhood of trees and soft, small houses into a gentle kind of noon in which I can vaguely smell the jasmine of the waiting nighttime.

The park is made of sloping, sea-salted green hills that have hard, short trees growing between them. In the middle of the park is a playground constructed of plastic piping looped and coiled in on itself in an ecstasy of red and yellow and green and Anthony runs to this when he sees it, laughing, not listening to me telling him to wait. I shout to him over the windy grass between us but to my ears it almost sounds like I'm telling him to run faster, faster in the time before the food gets here and the dusk comes.

I sit at a plastic blue picnic table and watch Anthony play. He crawls into the tunnels built into the structure of the playground and disappears for a while, then comes out again and screams curses loud into the sky, with a smile on his face. After a while he runs back to me, and sits next to me, panting through his big lips and his mess of teeth.

"Guh muh-ning," he says.

"It's afternoon, not morning," I say.

Carrie comes and I can see her from far away walking over hills of grass, holding bags of food in her hands. She's watching her feet and places them very carefully on the grass. The jacket she's wearing is blown open by the wind and it plasters her clothes to her body as if they were wet. She's so much fatter than she used to be, I think.

"Mommy, owie," Anthony says, touching his nose.

"Yes," I say, "and it fucking hurts."

"Fuckah bitch," he says.

I place my hand on his soft, warm head, looking at the light blue webwork of veins under his skin. I wish he was mine. I wish his heart had the same blood that I'm carrying now for the millions of people who came before me in time. I wish he was mine biologically, but then, here I am with him. Here we are in the park, like father and son. And here Carrie comes with food, smiling over the blowing sweet grass, holding the bags up high as if they had gold in them.

JUDY BUDNITZ

■

Visiting Hours

FROM *Harper's Magazine*

HE PRETENDED TO be asleep nearly every time I came to visit. He'd have the sheet drawn precisely up to his neck, his head neatly centered on the pillow and his hands laid palms up on either side, surrendering, an angelic smile on his face. He liked tricks, fooling around, liked faking accents and doing imitations. He was bad at it but everyone told him he was hilarious. He'd try to scare me sometimes — I'd come in and lean close, trying to decide if he was still breathing, and then he'd suddenly bug open his eyes or snatch my face or yell.

Maybe he did it in the hope that I would leave him alone and let him sleep. But I don't think so.

My brother, when he's really asleep, curls up on his side, hands pressed between his thighs, mouth wide open. He likes a pillow over his head, likes the closeness, his own warm breath in his face. He has hot feet, can't sleep unless they're sticking out, no matter what the temperature.

After he feigned waking, he liked to show off with the mechanical bed, pressing the buttons to raise his feet or his head, folding himself up in a V shape.

The bed next to his was always empty. The lights in the room were always on. The bulb above his head shone a sickly violet light on him, like those lamps people use to grow orchids. The fluorescent tubes on the ceiling gave off an incessant angry buzz. The table beside the bed was covered by a white towel, and on the towel were always an empty kidney-shaped pan, a glass with a rust-colored residue in the bottom, an empty pill cup, a pad of paper but no writing implement, a tiny pair of forceps. What were these things for? I didn't want to know. They were always there, carefully lined up like a place setting at a fancy restaurant.

The floor was a dull checkerboard: gray and beige squares of linoleum.

I used to bring him things to brighten the room — grocery-store bouquets, balloons, greeting cards with kittens and fuzzy rabbits on them. Sometimes I grabbed the wrong thing by mistake: a HAPPY ANNIVERSARY or NEW BABY!!! but they were still pretty. They were always gone the next time I came to visit. When I asked him about it, he said the nurses had brought the stuff to the poor little sick kiddies just down the hall; they needed cheering up more than he did.

I can't possibly get any more cheerful than I am now, he'd said and grinned so wide I could see his dead molar, the one that had gone gray. Most of the time his lips were loose and fluttery, too big for his face, but when he smiled they got pulled tight and firm, and his eyes crinkled up in the corners.

As I was leaving the hospital that evening I walked up and down the halls and saw nothing but the intensive-care unit, tubing and blipping machines and shrunken elderly people with their mouths open. No children, and no balloons either.

Perhaps he was mixed up. But it was more likely the nurses had been lying to him and had kept his things for themselves. Filling their cheap apartments with silver balloons and teddy bears, sticking the carnations and Gerber daisies in their stiff frizzy hair. The bitches.

I decided I would not tell him. It would only upset him. I'd let him believe he was helping some unhappy kids. After all, it's the thought that counts.

I came puffing into the room one day and waited for his eyes to open.

"You're so late," he said. "What did you do, actually go to school for once and stay the whole day?"

The room was so warm it was hard to breathe. The snow on my

coat had turned to water drops, and I felt sweat sliding down the sides of my nose and popping out on my upper lip. I would have little pink colonies of pimples there by tomorrow.

"I missed the bus, so I had to run it."

"Sit down," he said. "Take a load off."

There were no chairs in the room. There was a window with a nice wide ledge, but it was a few inches too high for sitting and anyway it was too far from the bed. I took off my damp coat. Sweat was trickling down my chest; my clothes were clammy. I told myself it was cleansing, like taking a shower from the inside out. I started to put my coat on the floor, but then I thought of all the other things that had probably touched that floor and decided not to.

So I hugged the coat and sort of crouched by the bed, which was uncomfortable but it's supposed to be good strengthening exercise for the back-of-the-leg muscles, just like those exercises described in women's magazines for the girl-on-the-go with no time for a conventional workout.

"You didn't have to run," he said. "I'm not going anywhere. I might even be here tomorrow."

"I know," I said. "You're looking better," I said, and thought: You look terrible.

"Thanks," he said, which meant: I know and I don't care. He liked looking tough; when he was younger he used to draw fake scars on his arms with a pen. His eyes were bloodshot, lashes damp and matted together.

"Have you been smoking pot in here?"

"I wish," he said. And then, "Could you get me some?"

"No."

"You goody-goody," he said. They had had to shave off big map-like sections of his hair, and the patches that were left stuck up in sticky clumps. It made him look punk. The bare bits of scalp were paler than his face. I could see the big black stitches. I did not like looking at them; I wished the doctor had left the bandages on. The air was supposed to make them heal faster, but why did I have to look at them?

"You're getting quite a beard," I said, even though he wasn't.

He rubbed the side of his face and looked proud. "It's nothing. They won't give me a razor yet. Afraid I'll tear something."

He used only his right hand to gesture. The left one didn't move much. I was afraid to ask about it. Whether he couldn't move it or chose not to. And the parts of his body beneath the sheet, I never saw those. There were tubes that snaked in under the covers, and tubes that came out. Sometimes when he shifted I heard the crackle and squeak of plastic sheeting. And I could see his feet, white and bony, sticking out. That was all.

There was yellow crust rimming his nostrils. I wanted to scrape it away for him.

"Goddamn," he said. "You're just dying to be Florence Nightingale, aren't you? I bet you're dying to wipe the sweat from my poor brow and say, 'There, there.'"

That would have been nice, I would have liked to do that, except he wasn't really sweating, and his face was so raw-looking that I would be afraid to touch it, afraid of unraveling the little black stitches or jarring loose a scab that held in a flood.

He said, "If you saw the things these nurses do, you wouldn't find it so damn romantic."

After a moment I said, "Mother and Dad were talking about you last night. They said next time they come —"

"I don't want to talk about them."

"But they said to tell you —"

"I don't want to hear about it."

"But —"

"It's boring," he said.

We both looked up at the dark television screen. I could hear someone squealing in laughter or pain very far away, echoing; or it could have been one squeaky wheel on a stretcher rolling down a distant corridor. The distant squeal went on and on. I imagined someone having a baby, or falling out a window, or being operated on without anesthesia. That squealing. Why didn't someone make it stop? Ezra closed his eyes. It was probably just a stretcher. The simplest explanation is usually the right one. We learned that in school. Occam's ratchet, or something like that.

"Should I turn it on?" I asked.

"It's broken. Somebody kicked it."

We both looked at the silent TV that hung from the ceiling on a little metal seat like a trapeze.

Ezra gazed over at the vacant bed. "I'm so bored. I wish there was someone in that bed over there. A good-looking girl with all her parts intact."

"But you can't even get out of bed."

"I'd find a way," he said, and showed me the gray tooth.

I took his hand and held it. The left hand. I don't think he minded, because he didn't pull it away.

"Tell me a story," he said.

"All right," I said. "Last night, Mother and Dad and I were sitting around the dinner table and Dad said —"

"No. I said a story. The made-up kind. You know, the kind you used to tell. The vampires and wooden stakes, the man with a hook for a hand waiting in the woods, and all that shit."

"But that was years ago. I can't remember."

"So make up a new one. The gorier the better."

"I don't like to even think about those things anymore. They're not real, they can't happen in the real world. Oh, don't go to sleep. All right, all right. Once there were these three bears. They lived in a little house in the forest. There was —"

"Bor-ing."

"What? Are you too old for that story?"

"I don't think I was ever young enough for that story."

"All right. Once upon a time there were four bears. Poppa-bear, Momma-bear, and, um, Son-bear and Baby-bear. They lived in a house in the forest and ate their porridge and went to bed. And one day —"

"I hope this gets more interesting," Ezra said. "I hope there's a farmer's daughter involved or something."

"Hush. One day when all the bears were out in the forest, a little girl named Goldilocks came to the house. She tasted the porridge and she tried the chairs and then went to sleep in the little bed that was just right. Then all the bears came home and

Goldilocks woke up and came down the stairs. Who is that? Momma-bear said, and Poppa-bear laughed and said, Oh, nobody, just a friend, and slapped Goldilocks on her rear and Goldilocks smiled. Momma-bear began to scream, and Goldilocks ran out of the house and Poppa-bear chased after her, but he couldn't see very well and kept running into trees and running red lights, and one time he drove right up on the curb and nearly hit a fire hydrant —"

"In the forest?"

"He came home alone, much later, and found Momma-bear in the kitchen still stirring the porridge, and he said, Is it hot enough for you yet? And he took the pot and poured the porridge down her front, and she said nothing, just looked down while all the porridge ran down and stuck in her pretty fur that she had spent all day combing and curling. Baby-bear tried to help her, but she screamed at him to go away — she did not like to be seen with her fur all matted down and ugly."

Ezra's eyes were shut. "This story sucks," he said. "Where was Son-bear during all this?"

"I don't know," I said.

"It's your story. Make something up."

"But I don't know."

My father started eating even before my mother had finished lighting the candles. "Darling," he said, "this is fantastic. You've outdone yourself."

My mother unfolded her napkin in her lap. "Thank your daughter," she said. "It was her idea. She found the recipe. Without her around I'd be cooking the same thing night after night."

My father put down his fork. "My thanks to the both of you then," he said, and raised his glass. He liked to make dramatic gestures. Then he seized my mother's hand and kissed it. She laughed, and blushed, and soon they were kissing over the table. I looked away. They were always acting like that, kissing and giggling like characters in a sappy old movie.

"Lydia," my father said, "pour your daughter some wine."

"Honey, no. I don't care how smart she is, or how mature she acts — she's still only fourteen. And it's a school night."

"Just a sip," my father said. "We have something to celebrate."

"What?" I said.

"Oh, just something a little bird told me," he said. "I hear there's a new actress in the house. How does the part go?" He made his voice high and fluttery. "There's rosemary, that's for remembrance . . ."

"Oh Daddy, stop." Now I was blushing.

"I'm not the barbarian you think I am. I've studied a little Mr. Will in my time."

"How did you know? Mother! You weren't supposed to tell! I wanted it to be a surprise!"

"I couldn't help it," my mother said. "I was so excited for you. Beating out all the older girls to get Ophelia. I had to tell your father."

"I'm so proud of you, I can't begin to tell you," he said. He looked at my mother. "You two are unbelievable. Honestly, I feel like the luckiest man in the world."

"I can't wait until Ezra comes home," I said.

My mother said, "Then we'll be a real family again."

The next time I visited I found a nurse with him. She was not like the sexy nurses on soap operas; she was thick all around, with a big unlined slab of a face and those white nurse shoes with puckered seams. Her hair was much longer than mine, though, a fat braid all the way to her waist. I saw her hand him a little cup.

"What are you giving him?" I said.

"Blue ones are for pain, white ones are antibiotics," she said. She hugged a tray full of little pill cups up against her big chest like a mother coming to the door on Halloween. "I'm going to make sure you take them this time," she told my brother. He grinned at her.

"What do you mean?" I said. "Has he not been taking his medication?"

She ignored me, watched him gulp water.

"Ezra?"

He waited until the nurse had left, then reached into his cheek and pulled out the two white pills. He stashed them away somewhere behind his bed.

"What are you doing? I'm going to tell —"

"You tell on me and I'll tell someone that you've been skipping school and hiding out in here," he said. He pushed the buttons and raised the end of the bed until his feet were right in my face. He wiggled his toes and smiled. His face looked greasy. He was not allowed to wash it yet, for fear of disturbing the stitches. He was not allowed to brush yet, either, and his breath was swampy.

I said, "Look at your beard." Not much more than peach fuzz on his cheeks, but it always pleased him to have it noticed. There were five or six long wispy hairs growing out of his upper lip. I thought of catfish.

When we were little he used to build me sandcastles, tree houses, bed-sheet tents — secret, closed-in places full of his voice and his smell. He'd let me make up the names for the hideouts and we'd spend hours inside.

"When are Mom and Dad coming to visit?"

"They came yesterday," I said.

He was tracing lines on the sheet with his finger. I wanted to touch him but was not sure where he was beneath the covers. What if there was nothing there? I didn't want to know. I reached out and held his feet. They were like river stones, smooth and cool. He had a new sore at the corner of his lips, as if he had stretched his mouth open past its limits. It looked as if maybe someone had bitten him there. As if someone had started kissing him and not known how to stop.

"Yesterday," he said.

"The doctors said this would happen. They said your short-term memory would be gone. Because of the concussion. They said it will get better over time."

"Oh. Right."

"Mom and Dad have been coming every day. Well, every other day."

"Really?"

"Yes. They said . . . Mother said . . ."

"Never mind, I don't want to know what they said. I mean, I'll see them tomorrow, right?"

"Of course."

He looked away. "Why don't you tell me a story then?" he said. Something clenched in his face; suddenly a thick lumbering clot oozed out of his nostril. His hand leapt up to hide it. "Got a tissue?"

There were none in the room. I had to give him a crumpled one from my pocket. "Shouldn't I get a nurse?"

"Nah. Don't want to bother them. Don't want to wear out my welcome, heh."

"You never used to be so considerate."

"It's the new me. The concussion gave me a brand-new personality, hey? Tell the story. Anything." He lay back. I saw his throat working, swallowing the blood.

"You don't look too good," I said. "Can't I go tell someone?"

"You're no beauty queen yourself," he said. "Aw . . . Stop that. Just tell the story."

"Should I finish the old one or start a new one?"

"The stupid bears? Whatever. As long as it's scary, no wussy girl shit about flowers and princes and ponies."

"I'm not trying to be scary, it just turns out . . . Well, the four bears . . . actually before there were four bears there were five. There was a fifth, a bear smaller than Baby-bear, a little bear cub too young to have a name. One day Poppa-bear was at home with the baby cub, and Poppa-bear was very worried because he kept thinking there were hunters waiting outside the house with their guns. Soon he was certain the hunters were knocking at the door, so he picked up the baby bear cub and hid him in the broom closet to save him."

"So the hunters shot him, right? Blammo?"

"Well, he opened the front door and there weren't any hunters after all. But Poppa-bear was afraid, and he went out and hid in the forest for a while. Much, much later all the bears came home and they opened the closet and there was the cub, lying there curled in a tiny ball next to the bottles of detergent, not exactly breathing anymore. And Poppa-bear said he hadn't known, said they had been playing hide-and-seek and the kid had been trying to hide from him, he had been looking everywhere and couldn't find him, he loved that baby, how could he know the kid was hiding in the broom closet drinking drain cleaner? It wasn't his fault."

"And then what?"

"Momma-bear asked him to leave. So he did, but he came back in the middle of the night and stood out in the street and shouted at her, and threw bottles at her window until it broke, and Baby-bear came rushing in and found the window shattered, and broken glass shining all over the quilt, and her mother screaming. And after that Poppa-bear moved back in, and nobody talked about it, and Baby-bear stayed hidden in her room worrying because she knew, somehow, what her father had done, but she was too much of a coward to do anything about it —"

"I thought he was a he."

"What?"

"The one named Baby-bear. Last time you said he was a he. Now you're saying she."

"Oh. What does it matter? He, she. They're just fucking bears."

"Don't get mad. Hey. Where was Son-bear this time?"

"I don't know. He was never around. He could usually take care of himself, I guess."

Ezra's face hardly looked like his; everything was swollen out of shape, splotched with bruises, his hair sprouting unevenly. He reminded me of something he used to do to scare me when we were younger. He'd hold me down on the floor and crouch over my head so that he could bring his upside-down face close to mine. Upside down his eyebrows looked like a sort of mustache, his forehead became a broad jaw, his hair was like a spiky beard. It was horrifying — the eyes were the same, looking right at me and winking, but everything else was deformed and huge and alien. It used to make me cry, because it made me forget what he really looked like.

"What's wrong? You don't seem yourself tonight," my father said. He looked at me worriedly.

"Nothing."

"How's your brother doing?" my mother asked. "I can't tell you how proud your father and I are of you, the way you've been keeping him company. It really means a lot to him, giving up your free time to cheer him up. It makes such a difference. Your father and I wish we could get out there more."

"I want to do it," I said. "It's not a chore."

She said, "You don't have to say it. I know you've been sacrificing your friends to be with him, even the school dance. Good deeds don't go unnoticed."

"Well, actually . . ." I said.

"What?" my father said, studying me closely.

"Someone has been noticing. I mean, Principal Borden. I mean, I should tell you I've been leaving school early. To get to the hospital sooner. And sometimes I don't go to school at all. I take the bus and just wait in the lobby or the gift shop or the parking garage until visiting hours." They had both put down their forks and were staring at me.

"And now Mr. Borden says I'm going to get suspended, or worse, if I keep skipping school, and skipping detention. He says he's going to call you to discuss it. If he hasn't already."

My parents looked at each other. My father angrily pushed himself away from the table. He slammed the chair back with his fist and walked to the wide bay windows at the far end of the dining room. He stood looking out, at the tarpaulin covering the pool, the snow-covered flower beds, the birdbath, the night sky, with his hands pressing the small of his back, clearing his throat again and again.

I was gripping my fork, digging the tines into my thumb. My mother took it from me and covered my hand with her cool one. "Honey," she said, "you do what you need to do."

I looked at her hand, at the big wedding ring and the perfectly manicured nails. It was a beautiful hand.

"Your brother is more important than school right now," she said. "You just keep doing what you're doing." She glanced at my father's back. "We'll worry about Mr. Borden."

"But what if I get suspended?"

"Some people just don't understand what's important," she said. "I guess some people don't care about their family the way we do."

I heard footsteps. My father's shadow fell across my plate and then I felt his hands on my shoulders. He breathed more slowly as he tried to control himself.

"Don't get angry at Mr. Borden, dear," my mother said brightly. "He just doesn't understand. He probably has a miserable home life. He has no idea what it's like." She kept her hand on mine and put her other over my father's. We remained linked like that, looking at Ezra's empty chair, my father's breath warming my hair, until my mother said, "Now who wants ice cream?"

That nurse with the flat face was with him again when I came in. She was sitting on the bed close to him, feeling his forehead; his face was flushed beneath her white hand. The skin all along his stitches looked red and juicy.

"Looks like there's an infection setting in," she said. "If there is, we'll have to keep you here an extra week, give you a course of antibiotics intravenously." Sitting made her thighs look even bigger; they were straining her slacks, spreading all over the bed, probably crushing him.

He grimaced painfully as she poked at him, but she must have thought he was smiling because she got angry. "You think it's a joke? You won't be able to go home for another week. You think that's funny?" She swept out of the room with her tray of pills rattling.

"So how are Mom and Dad?" Ezra said. His eyes looked dingy. Not bloodshot, but dark and smudged like dirty cue balls. The sore on his mouth was still there. He was wearing the same black T-shirt he'd worn for days. Maybe he was attached to it. I do that sometimes, I just don't feel like changing. Or maybe he had several identical ones.

"Dad was just here this morning," I said.

"Was he." Not quite a question.

"He came in because he has to go on a business trip for a few days and wanted to see you before he left. Don't you remember?

He left these for you." I pointed to the pile of books on the bedside table next to the glass. Stephen King paperbacks, last week's *Rolling Stone*.

"You brought me those," he said. "I saw you. Yesterday. You put them there as you were leaving. Yesterday evening. You thought I was asleep."

"That's right," I said. "I forgot. Dad asked me to bring them. He was afraid he'd forget them this morning, what with his trip and all."

"Jesus, who do you think you're kidding?"

"At least the nurses didn't steal them," I said. "I was afraid they would."

"Give it up," he said tiredly.

"Look," I said. "I'll be perfectly honest with you. The doctor said you might have lapses. He said you might forget things, or you might recall things that never actually happened. He said if that happened we were supposed to humor you, you know, go along with it rather than make a big deal out of it. He said it would upset you to be reminded that you can't remember everything."

"I think you're the crazy one here."

"I know it's hard for you to sit in this room all day. But don't take it out on me. You should just concentrate on getting better so you can come home."

"Concentrate on getting better," he mimicked.

"Having an accident doesn't give you the right to be a jerk."

"Yes it does."

"Listen, since you don't remember seeing Dad, do you want me to tell you what they were saying about you last night? Mother still sets a place for you at the table every night. Ever since I told her your TV doesn't work she's been taping all your shows for when you come home. She says now she'll even let you get your ear pierced, if you still want to. Then Dad said one more hole in your head won't make any difference. You know Dad. They laughed, but then they got sort of quiet and sad. Mom still cries a lot, goes in your room and cries. Dad doesn't say much. But once he said — he didn't know I was listening — he told Mother he was thinking of getting a car for you, so you'd stop tearing up his. Don't tell him I told you, I think it's supposed to be a surprise."

"Jesus. I don't want to hear this. Story, please."

"All right. Bears?"

"No more bears."

"Here's a story I thought of for English. We were supposed to write a fable. So one day there were these two praying mantises, sitting there eating leaves or whatever, when they saw a lemming run by. Then another lemming and another, and soon there were hundreds of lemmings stampeding by, all running down to a cliff by the sea, where they flung themselves into the water and splashed till they drowned. The praying mantises watched as more and more lemmings streamed past, and then one said: Don't they realize what they're doing? Why don't they just stop, instead of running to their deaths? Are they crazy? And the other praying mantis said: Yes, they're mad, they're completely mad, and then she bit off her husband's head and mated with the rest of his body, because that's how mantises do it."

At last I'd gotten him to smile.

"And the moral, see, is that it's easier to recognize madness in other people than to see it in yourself."

"I think the moral should be, don't piss off the wife, or you'll get chewed out and fucked over."

"That's not what it means."

"No, no, that was good. Tell me another."

"How are the play rehearsals going?" asked my father.

"They're all right."

"Want me to go over your lines with you? I could be your Hamlet."

"That's okay, Daddy, really."

"I guess you think your old dad is more of a doddering old Polonius anyway."

"No, not at all."

"I could drive you to the mall for a couple of hours. You could use some new clothes. Kids wear such strange things these days,

but they'd look so cute on you. You're growing up, can't go around
looking like Daddy's little girl forever."

"No thanks."

"You know that fishing trip that your brother and I were going
to take? How would you like to go instead? Just the two of us, some
father-daughter bonding?"

"Maybe. I don't know."

"All right. I understand." He turned and knelt by the fireplace,
feeding more wood to the flames. The room was warm, we didn't
need the fire, but it looked so nice. I went to my mother, who was
curled up on the sofa with her feet tucked beneath her, working on
her needlepoint. I didn't know how she could see what she was doing in the dim light. I lay down and put my head in her lap.

She ran her cool fingers through my hair. "Oh honey," she said.
"I still remember when you were born. When I went in the hospital there was snow all over the ground, everything was gray and
cold and horrible, just like the weather's been lately. I went into
the hospital and it was so easy, you were the easiest baby in the
world, you hardly even cried when you were born. Your father was
the one who cried, because he was so happy. And then he fainted
and the nurses had to spend more time on him than they did on
you. Or did he faint first and then cry? Oh, it doesn't matter. What
matters is that when we left the hospital, the sun was shining, and
everywhere all the daffodils and crocuses had come up, they had
come up just in the short time I'd been inside, and now they were
blooming everywhere."

"Where was Ezra?"

"Oh, he was too little to come. He was waiting at home for you."

"Go on."

"Well, Poppa-bear stayed home much more than he did before, because every time he went into the woods he thought he
heard the hunters coming for him. He'd begun having night-
mares, thrashing around in his sleep. The Momma-bear stopped
taking care of herself, didn't paint her nails or shave under her
arms. She said all she wanted was to go somewhere quiet and hi-

bernate and never wake up. Poppa-bear mostly ignored Baby-bear, but once she was sitting in his chair and he lifted her out of it by her hair and said he wished she'd never been born. Baby-bear did not know what to do. She asked her brother, and Son-bear said, I'll blow his damn head off, that's what I'll do. So she did not ask him again."

Ezra lay back with his eyes closed. A bag of liquid hung on a stand beside the bed and dripped down through a tube and through a needle stuck into the inside of his elbow. I'd seen him fooling around with the tubing when I came in earlier, but he'd stopped when he saw me. Now he lay so limply, as if a giant invisible hand were pressing him down into the bed.

"That Son-bear," he said, and laughed. "He's a son of a gun."

"How is your brother doing?" my mother asked.

"His doctor told me he'll be coming home real soon," my father said. "They say he's made an unbelievable recovery. Wait till he sees what's waiting for him in the garage."

"I think you deserve some of the credit," my mother told me. "You've been amazing."

"I don't want to talk about it," I said.

We watched the snow falling outside the windows. My mother toyed with her amethyst necklace. My father played with his silverware. He had big meaty hands, with thick brown hair above the knuckles. He had taken off his suit the minute he came home from work and was now wearing his favorite red flannel shirt. He handled the fork and knife as if he did not quite know what to do with them.

"Want to practice some lines from that school play?"

"No."

Silence again.

"Darling," my father said, "this is fantastic. You've outdone yourself."

My mother reached out to light the candles, but they were already lit. "Thank your daughter," she said. "It was her idea, this recipe. If it wasn't for her I'd be cooking the same old thing night after night."

My father raised his glass to me. "My thanks to both of you then." He drank, then looked around the table and said, "I'm so unbelievably lucky to have the two of you. I feel like the luckiest man in the world." He reached for my mother's hand, but she was busy unfolding her napkin.

The snow was piling up on the windowsills.

"May I be excused?" I said.

I went up the stairs to my bedroom and closed the door. I could have read one of my books, because I had hundreds of books, or I could have watched my TV, or called one of my friends, because I had lots of friends, but I didn't. And I didn't listen to music. I just sat in the middle of the bed with the lights off, a canopy bed with a down comforter, I sat and I waited and I listened for my father's footsteps on the stairs.

I knew something was different the moment I walked in the door. There was a smell in the room that had not been there before. The floor was sticky.

Ezra had his hands clasped behind his neck, in an attempt to look casual. There was a cast encasing his leg from hip to ankle. His head was wrapped in a turban of bandages again, the way it had been in the beginning. The purple circles had darkened beneath his eyes.

"What happened to you?" he said.

"Me?" I said. "What happened to you?"

"Your hand. What's wrong with your hand?"

"Nothing," I said. I pulled down the sleeve of my sweater to cover it. "Somebody grabbed me. Some stupid girl. When we were playing basketball. In gym class."

"You haven't been to school in ages. I can tell. You don't even bother to fake it anymore. You've stopped dragging your backpack and notebooks around."

"I have been to school —"

"The nurses say they see you hanging around in the snow, waiting to come in here. They've seen that sleeping bag in the parking lot. They think you're nuts."

"What happened to you? What happened to your leg?"

The nurse plowed in right then, as if she'd been hiding outside the door just waiting for a good moment to make her entrance. I smelled baby powder and chicken soup as she brushed past.

She sat in her usual spot beside him, too close, and said, "I don't know how he even made it out of bed, but early this morning we found him way at the other end of the hospital, three floors down. Looked like he had slipped on some wet floors. We had to reset the leg. Banged himself up pretty good." She narrowed her eyes at him. "One custodian swears he saw someone sliding around like an ice skater, having a grand old time."

Then she glared at me. Her eyes were light brown, almost yellow, nasty. She puttered around, pretending to check Ezra's tubes and stitches and bandages. She wiped his nose for him. "What were you thinking?" she said. "Running around in the middle of the night, in the shape you're in? Undoing all the good work the doctors did?"

I did not like the way she looked at him. She was old enough to be his mother. He grinned at her, and she slapped his cheek in a way that would have been playful if he hadn't had dozens of stitches in his head. He never let me sit on the bed.

Finally she stood up, and the mattress sprang back to its original shape. "I don't understand it," she said. "If I didn't know better I'd think you wanted to stay here."

I watched her leave, her hips heaving. I could see her panty line.

"I've got six pins in my leg," Ezra announced. "I'm the bionic man."

"You've got to come home," I said. "You've just got to."

"You think I like this dump?" he said.

I looked at the bedside table. Some of the items had been moved around. The forceps were missing. I put the kidney-shaped pan and the dirty glass back in their proper places. I tugged the string to pull down the shade because I did not like looking at the dirty pigeons pecking in the snow on the roof opposite. White pigeon droppings on white snow — how could you ever tell the dirty from the clean? Then I knelt at his bedside so that our eyes were on the same level. Or they would have been, if he had only turned his head.

"Once upon a time —"

"Why don't you tell me about the accident," he said.

"You said you didn't like true stories."

"I changed my mind," he said, picking at the bandages on his head. "I don't remember it too well. Tell me how I got this."

"Well," I said. The radiator hissed and clanked. The fluorescent lights buzzed, a high-pitched whine like a dog whistle, just barely audible. It was enough to drive you crazy. "Well. Maybe you remember, you were riding your skateboard, in the street, even though Dad's told you a thousand times not to, and, well, there was a car. There was a car coming very fast because, well, we found out later it was because the driver's wife was going into labor — she was having a baby right in the back seat! And he was rushing to bring her to the hospital. And also the sun was in his eyes. And also you were wearing your Walkman, it got totally smashed up. So that's what happened —"

"No it's not."

"It is. I keep telling you, the doctor said it's because of your concussion —"

"I was riding my skateboard in the snow?"

"Yes."

"I sold my board to Ian months ago —"

"You must have borrowed one —"

"You can do better than that."

"What do you mean?"

"All right," he said. "Now it's my turn."

"Stop," I said. "Don't. Just . . ." I had a sudden vision of the upside-down-face trick again, Ezra's eyes gazing right at me but the rest of the features reversed and twisted, eyebrows waggling beneath the eyes and a mouth grinning in the middle of the new forehead.

Ezra's mouth said, "I've got a story for you, a good one. It's a story about Dad."

DAVID DRURY

■

Things We Knew When the House Caught Fire

FROM *Little Engines*

WHEN THE NEIGHBOR'S HOUSE burned down, the massive motorized doors on the firehouse would not open. Why the doors jammed, why the fire trucks never rolled out, we of Magnolia Park Drive did not know. But we saw it all. The firehouse was less than a block away.

They were the Bainers, and while their house blazed and smoked, the rest of us gathered on the safe side of the street. It was morning, early and cold. First light in the sky, frost quivering on the grass in anticipation of the sun. And as the adults took their positions, tightening bathrobes and blowing steam off coffee mugs, the newspaper delivery man came rattling around the corner in his station wagon, right on schedule, steering with one hand, launching papers from his window with the other. Fabulous terror registered on his face. I was just one kid, but speaking on behalf of all the neighborhood kids, we couldn't have been more ecstatic.

Calamity, tragedy, houses afire. You see, these are the daydreams that children dream. High-flying motorcycles, ninjas wielding samurai swords, the playground bully falling backward from a kick to the neck. Godzilla versus monster trucks. Bank robbers with two guns apiece. High-speed car chases that end with police vehicles lifting off the ground and spiraling through the air, lights and sirens a-blazing. Explosions that end with money raining down out of the sky. Wolves fighting bears. And houses burning to the ground. Even if those houses belonged to Bainers. Especially if those houses belonged to the Bainers.

They were the bad neighbors. That was the thinking. But let me back up.

Here is a list of things:

- BMW (him)
- Sport utility vehicle (her)
- Franchise coffee (whole bean, bought by the pound, kept in the freezer)
- A Martha Stewart garden you pay someone to garden
- A clean house, brightly lit
- A divorce
- A family who downhill skis (with helmets on) and participates in organized community sports
- A sixty-hour work week
- A daycare where you pay overtime
- A babysitter who sleeps over
- A dog with a new leash who eats biscotti

The perfect suburb is a delicate thing. It takes a careful balance of ingredients — all the perks of being near to the big city without all the ugly side effects that would turn it into a strip mall or ghetto: crime, traffic, malt liquor billboards, diapers, and dog food cans blowing around in the street like urban tumbleweeds.

Larkspur, California, was a cozy "high-income" community one bridge-length north of San Francisco, tucked in the shadow of Mount Tamalpais. The schools all won national awards, the streets were kept clean and safe. Then came the Bainers, tracking mud inside our paradise.

The family inherited the house from an aunt and rather than sell it through real estate agents they picked up and moved to California from one of the states in the middle. Brought their yellow-ing RV and parked it right out front. Because of an addendum in the "General Unsightliness" parking ordinance, they were forced to move it within three days, but not before the tow truck actually showed up.

Mr. Bainer brought daughter Allaray and son Kendall from his first marriage. Mrs. Bainer brought sons Kennel and baby Glen from hers. At eleven years, Allaray was the oldest and shrewdest. Kendall and Kennel, made brothers by the union of parents, not only shared nearly identical names, which would have been strange enough, but they had been born on the same day nine years ear-lier. We thought of them as twins. Baby Glen, old enough to walk but young enough to slobber, was born of giants. He was huge. A freak of nature. We clung to the belief that he outweighed his siblings.

The Bainers did not fit. You needed only catch sight of them to know it. Dirty bare feet. Tattered corduroys. Little-House-on-the-Prairie dresses worn over jeans. T-shirts with stretched-out neck holes and peeling iron-ons: The Incredible Hulk, ET, Heroes of Motocross. And there was never a time they didn't have Kool-Aid-stained faces and purple-popsicle tongues. By comparison we must have looked like model citizens or department store manne-quins, decked out in our squeaky white Reeboks, Bugle Boys, de-signer backpacks, and twenty-five-dollar haircuts. We even acces-sorized.

They didn't look the part, and it was our duty to make them aware of it. What did I know? I was just a kid among kids. None of us tall enough yet to see that the world was bigger than Magnolia Park Drive. Each and every one of us with that secret desperate longing to fit. The transition from childhood to adulthood is one long freeze-frame moment when the needle has been pulled off the record and there aren't enough musical chairs for everybody. Though all are equal participants in scrambling for a seat, every-one suspects that it will be only a little while before he or she is squeezed out, exposed, rejected, the die cast, the number up, and the parents stand around ever-smiling in party hats, unaware of the magnitude of this.

There's no time for conjecture. You don't stop and ask why the need is so strong or how you will meet it. It's the law of the jungle. Survival instinct doesn't pause for introspection. It moves too fast to be held to the scientific method. It is spirit-material. It floats in the air. But fitting is everything. In high school, it would express itself in want of popularity or scholastics, or jackets with square letters and sports accomplishments sewn on so no one will forget. But for now, while we ourselves were searching to fit, we felt a sense of place in at least knowing that the Bainers did not.

They didn't look right, they didn't play right. They were mischief makers, always up to something. Digging holes in the neighbor's yard, walloping the sidewalks with golf clubs. Clearly they exerted their will over the Bainer parents. From our vantage point they were never spanked, never put on restriction, never punished. They seemed happy, but had they earned it? Not on our Swatches. We wasted no time in finding opportunity to let them know it.

When we approached, all four Bainer kids were sitting on the curb, smashing worms with a rock. "You better not do that," we scowled. "Why are you doing that?"

Allaray shrugged as if it didn't matter why.

"Because it's fun," one of the boys said without looking up.

"Where did you come from? Why'd you move here? Can't you talk? Are you retarded? I guess you must be retarded then. Ha ha, you're retarded." Our volley of inquiries came so quickly nobody could actually answer them. We laughed and pointed until we were oxygen deprived and had to catch our breath.

"We just moved in," said Allaray, biting at a hangnail.

"Didn't you hear us? We already knew that. Are you going to our school? We have a tree house but you can't come. We have Atari, but you can't play. How much is your allowance? Where'd you get those clothes?" No response. Now they were absorbed in flattening a Hot Wheels convertible with the rock, after placing a worm in the front seat. When they were finished pounding, they smiled up at us as if we would be pleased to share in their accomplishment. Baby Glen licked the worm-smashing rock clean and giggled.

It was no use. We failed to coax out of them the tears we were looking for. No crying. No running home to Mommy. No swearing. No giving the finger. It was only as we walked away, when we threw rocks at their feet and told them to dance, that we got a response. Little Allaray picked up the rocks and, with a naive joy in her face, threw them back at us with deadly aim.

Allaray might have been a skin-and-bones little girl, but she also had the best rock-throwing arm we'd ever seen. A Major League Baseball arm. A catapult. She could have taken out a first-grader at forty yards. A kindergartner at fifty. And as she fired on us, she was smiling. Giggling. Hopping up and down holding her sides, stringy blond hair bouncing in her face, her brothers clapping behind her. She didn't throw like she was vengeful or afraid. She had no fear. She threw rocks for the fun of seeing us run scared. Like our insults had been the anticipated opening volley in some time-honored game, some ritual of glee, and now it was her turn to play. She was the happiest rock thrower we knew.

Of course we ran away laughing victoriously, but beneath the shelter of our little arms covering our little heads as the rocks rained down upon us we secretly felt cheated. Like the sword got knocked out of our hands.

A day later, the three oldest children were riding their Schwinns in the street. We pedaled past them on our lightweight shiny racing bikes. After a few passes we popped wheelies. A few more passes and we were whistling inches from them. We circled like vultures, teasing them, throwing insults to the air, calling attention to their duct-taped banana seats, goosey handlebars, and mismatched reflectors.

We reconvened, conceived a new plan, and dispersed again. One of us called out that he had found a wounded bird in the gutter. We all dropped our bikes and went running. The Bainers followed suit, curious to see for themselves what we had found. That was the cue. Three of us, myself included, made a dash for *their* bikes, hopping on and pedaling away furiously. Not for our own, not to steal or destroy, but just long enough to gloat and play an innocent game of keep-away.

They stood there contemplating whether they would take the

bait and run after us. We passed back and forth, faces hot with insults and wind. The Bainers just watched. They didn't take chase.
We made closer passes, swerving as if we might hit them, making
more direct our insults. They turned and ran into their garage. To
get their parents. Ha. They folded, I thought. They would come
back, sucking their fingers to stop the tears, forcing their parents
to intervene, opening new avenues of insult and humiliation for
weeks to come.

But when they returned, it was not parents they dragged with
them, but something else, down the driveway and into the middle
of the street. A wooden structure pounded full of nails. A plywood
ramp nailed to a stack of two-by-fours. And the Bainers looked
back at us to see what we would do. They didn't have to say anything. We were suckers. We went straight for it. Pedaling like mad
for liftoff. It was only when my front tire hit the ramp that I wondered, What if this is a ploy? The collapsing ramp trick, the perfect
revenge, and they would have the last laugh as I went sprawling
in the street? But then I was airborne, my buddies right behind
me, and on my wobbly landing, it was the Bainers, clapping and
jumping and whooping like *we* were the Heroes of Motocross
ironed onto their T-shirts. Our own cheering section. "More! More!
More!" they squealed. "Higher! Faster! Farther!" I bit my smiling
lip into a straight face. And hit the jump again.

The Bainer family stood on their lawn, fixed like pegs in a sun-
dial, and watched their home go up. Only their shadows moved,
flickering and lengthening as the house burned toward the
ground. Their dog, Furler, stood beside them and whimpered.
And we all sensed a final justification. Retribution. Revenge. We
could barely contain ourselves. What goes around, man, it comes
around.

"Move out of the way, kids!" Mr. Stuckey barked out the window
as he frantically backed his Cadillac Seville from the street onto
the driveway and into his garage, afraid, in his paranoia, that the
fire might spread to his luxury sedan. "God dammit!" he tacked on
at the end. Until Mr. Stuckey, I had believed that all old people
went to church and never sinned.

Ash and cinders swirled around the Bainers, settling in their hair and on their sleeping clothes and obscuring them nearly from view at times. They were frozen there, like plastic figures in a giant horrible snow globe, the kind you shake up to see the white flakes swirl around a pleasant little cityscape and settle to the bottom. But the snow was black, and their expressions lacked that Christmas spirit that is always captured so well in plastic. They were the anti-carolers in a snow globe of shame — and it was God who did the shaking. For the eleven months leading up to this day, when the house was not on fire, the neighborhood adults had, muttered similar sentiments with the same folding of arms and tsk-tsks in their appraisals that they were muttering now. That they didn't appreciate having a squalid unkempt wreck of a home framed in their picture windows. Unsightliness is next to ungodliness.

As the newspaper delivery man came upon the unsettling scene, his sense of duty must have been throttled by the pandemonium. He leaned on the gas pedal as he passed. We know because we heard the engine gunning. And in his confusion, his arm already crooked out the window with a thousand rubber-band bracelets waving in the wind, he let fly a paper with force and trajectory such that it sailed up on to the Bainers' roof. The paper promptly burst into flames and fell into the living room through the collapsing ceiling. We children were so enthralled at all the chaos we cheered and did jumping jacks in our pajamas and bed hair.

We wanted to see the Bainer kids suffer. Just a little. No more than any other person. Just general panic and loss type suffering. Learning life's lessons. We had been under their curse forever. We wanted fairness. Balance. But we weren't alone. Our parents were in on it too. They had their reasons.

Apparently the Bainer parents, who were rarely ever seen by us, were also rarely seen, if at all, at community meetings, council sessions, and parent-teacher events. They attended no church, they gave to none of the local charities, they didn't frequent the local businesses. They seemed fine with letting their children wreak unsupervised havoc in public view. But improprieties in lawn care were the greatest of their sins.

If measured in terms of devotion and attention, the Bainers ranked among squatters, recluses, and heroin junkies when it came to lawn maintenance. They let the grass grow. They let the weeds take over. The front sidewalk was consumed, the path to their door impeded. The tallest weeds tickled their windows. The "It-Gets-the-Corners" sprinkler that was on the lawn when they moved in, hose snaking back to the house, had never moved and was soon swallowed in the undergrowth. A cloud of pollen and dander hung in the air. Allergy season hit our street hard. Something finally appeared on the town council agenda, and no wonder, considering that the moniker "Our Town Is a Clean Town" took larger billing than "Welcome to Larkspur" on the beaten copper signpost erected at the edge of town. At first the council issued an official request that the Bainers cut their lawn, but nothing changed. Dragonflies came to nest.

In a show of smug solidarity, we local kids, with the trickle-down politics of our parents, came wielding scissors (household, fabric, safety, toenail). We handed them out among ourselves and stooped down and snipped at the grass, taunting with gestures that we intended to carry out the council ruling. At first, Allaray, with that silly smile, charged at each one of us through the weeds, a child torso coming at us like a cartoon ghost, driving us back and knocking us off our balance. She blasted a third-grade boy so hard he rolled backwards, right off the sidewalk and into the street.

When we started closing in, Allaray improvised her reign of terror. She ducked down, out of our line of sight, then reemerged with the long-buried hose and sprinkler. She gripped the hose halfway back to the spigot. She lifted it up over her head and began swinging it around, the bulky sprinkler out in front, churning like a helicopter blade. Faster. Rustling the tops of the waist-high weeds. Her brothers, who were behind her, dropped to the ground. The rest of us moved back with a ripple, knowing that stitches and ugly scars would be branded on anyone who came in contact with the hunk of metal at the end of the hose. She swung it around. Faster, higher, letting out slack. You could hear the hose beating the air with a heavy hum and the sprinkler warbling and whistling its warning. There we were, gathered on the outermost edges of the lawn, the corners, out of the death radius, but still on the lawn when one of us realized the truth and yelled out, "It gets the corners!" immediately scattering us in a panic. Except me. I held my ground. I was not willing to let this undernourished girl rule us with fear.

I postured. I sneered. I tried to look undaunted, even though my muscles were prepared to bolt at the last possible second. I lurched forward a step as if I might take the offensive. That's when my foot came down wrong, on some toy or ball hidden in the thick grass, and I fell hard, flattening the weeds below me. The breath went out of me. On my back, looking up — that was the moment when I knew. The momentum, the trajectory, the angle of her arm and the arc of the sprinkler coming around like brass knuckles on a right hook. There was no stopping it. I would get what I deserved. In that half-second I made eye contact with Allaray. And though I knew she could hardly change the laws of momentum now, much less want to, I'd like to think I saw a brief softness in her eyes, the slightest tweak in her wrist, a kink in the affectation of her rotor, the delayed release that saved my life. Instead of lodging in my temple, the sprinkler turned a few degrees north, whistling through the air, smashing through the Bainers' front window and landing on their dining room table. My buddies ran home, their siren cries of "Ooooh . . . You're gonna get in TROU-BLE" fading down the street behind them. Allaray Bainer stood staring at me. Our second of shared silence lasted long enough to make me wonder if she really *had* missed me on purpose. And Kendall and Kennel shuttled through the weeds giggling, racing to see who could turn the spigot on first.

The council eventually exercised a more reasonable and effective tactic when it came to cleaning up the overgrown lawn. Volunteer firemen were handed weed whackers and clippers on a Saturday afternoon in August; paid from an emergency fund to give the house a once-over. The neighborhood came out, even set up lawn chairs to watch.

The firemen could have walked the few hundred feet from the firehouse at the end of the block, but they loaded up the big red fire truck with lawn mowers, trimmers, and the rest and pulled up out front. They went right to work on the yard. The tactic would have been an embarrassment to any other family in town, but the Bainers acted as though they had won a prize. At least the children did. They joined in the work. Kendall brought out very sharp adult scissors and stabbed and cut at the grass, until he swung too wildly and nearly stabbed a fireman in the knee. The other Bainer kids were running in circles through the grass, pulling up fistfuls of it and throwing it above them in a ritual dance. The Bainer mother came out with a tray of lemonade, gushing as though the volunteer landscapers were truly there of their own good will.

One of the firemen gathered the kids together. We could see him talking to them and shooing them toward the fire truck, and that was the moment our hearts dropped. The most undeserving kids on the whole block, and they get an invite to play on a million-dollar playground. The daydreams that children dream, when they are not dreaming of houses burning to the ground, are of living in the toy store and playing on fire trucks without adult supervision. To scramble unfettered and free over the smooth red surfaces, leave your breath on the shiny chrome gadgets, make fingerprints on the mirrors, tug on the handles, climb over the step-ups, slide behind the wheel, burrow and nestle in the hiding places. It was the Promised Land on wheels. We couldn't have been more jealous.

Meanwhile it was hot, and the firemen, now freed from ambling children, were ready to work. They pulled off their heavy coats and hats and set them on the sidewalk. They didn't seem to notice or care when the kids came off the truck to try on the heavy garments. Allaray struggled to button one of the coats while it was freestanding on the sidewalk like a big yellow teepee. Kendall's thin greasy head popped out one arm of the coat. Kennel's out the other. Finally Allaray slid underneath and her head came out the top. They looked frightening, like a melting girl giant with two heads for hands. Allaray reached out between buttons in the coat to grab a red helmet and put it on her head. Furler, freed for the day from his backyard collar, barked and growled at them while they stumbled up one side of the driveway, down the other, and into the street, where they eventually fell apart. Baby Glen saw all of this and tried to mimic them, but his head got stuck in the sleeve and he began screaming. While the two older brothers pulled him free, Allaray abruptly crossed the street and came over to all of us who had been watching. She was holding something in her hands and offering it to us. She had found a stash of candies in one of the pockets of the fireman's jacket, and went up and down the row of neighbor kids, placing them in our begrudging, out-stretched little hands until they were gone. She crossed back and joined her brothers as they all donned fire helmets and head-butted each other.

When the firemen finished their exercise, the neighborhood folded up its lawn chairs and went inside to escape the heat. Disdain by way of yard irreverence was abated for a time. But yard irreverence would rear its head again and reach blasphemous new levels against a backdrop of cardinal neighborhood virtues that blossomed during Christmas season.

Our town was one of *those* communities, where extravagant displays of light and sound and decoration were a matter of home-owner pride. A matter of communal pride, where a dizzying display of lights and Santas and angels and reindeer and holiday exclamations meant that the Christmas spirit lived here, and more so than elsewhere. We expected, I think, the Bainers to bow out of this to-do, owing to the notion that they probably didn't believe in Christmas, much less participate in neighborhoodliness. And for the first half of the month their property looked like a black tooth in our street's Christmas smile. But the Bainer kids finally caught on. Their first plan, since they didn't have their own stockpile of holiday regalia, consisted of stealing one item of decoration from each house and placing it on their own lawn. That worked until 8 A.M. the next morning when all the neighbors came by and loudly snatched up their absconded items. The next plan was to utilize that which they did have. They spread their toys out over the yard, inside a corral made of Legos, army men, Hot Wheels, stuffed animals, and a Barbie with burned hair.

"Those are the shepherds," Allaray told us, first pointing to the army men, "and those are the wise men, and the animals, and that is Mary," pointing to the Barbie doll. Then she ran in the house and returned with the baby Jesus, a Cabbage Patch doll with crayon all over its face. She laid it in the center of the yard, gently resting its head on the sprinkler. Creator of Heaven and Earth, Savior of Lost Souls, Teacher of Army Men, Son of Barbie. The boys were busy tying flashlights to the shrubs to shine like spotlights on the nativity scene. At night, the Bainer crèche looked eerie, especially in the glow of all the rest of the lights on the street. But the biggest blow was yet to come.

Coordinators for Larkspur's annual Christmas Craft Fair were raffling off a delicate blown-glass Baby Jesus this year, hand-painted and detailed, wrapped in silk swaddling clothes. Blemishless Jesus. With jewels for eyes, and a hole in his back for lighting purposes. Everyone who came to the event got one ticket, and you could buy more for five dollars each. The elementary school was raising money for a new playground with scientifically engineered tanbark — the kind of tanbark that won't give you slivers and that makes you something-percentage safer from breaking your spine or neck, or someone else's spine or neck. The glass Jesus was the creation of a world-renowned glass-blowing artist, one of our most famous local residents, a man who never came around really, but spent a lot of time in Europe and drinking wine on his yacht. Baby Jesus raised the eyebrows of more than a few. The latest trend in holiday yard-spirit was to prove you knew more of the "real meaning" of Christmas and employ a manger scene with hay and life-size or mechanical moving animals and figures. A throwback. The glass-blown baby Jesus was going to make a nice prize pony for anyone who wished to not just one-up other yard display participants, but blow the competition out of the water. It was appraised at a value of between $5,000 and $9,000, and came with a motion sensor alarm, so that thieves or Bainers would be discouraged from selfish urges.

When the ticket was drawn and the number announced, bounding down front were none other than the Bainer children with the winning ticket in hand. The artist made the presentation and handed Jesus to them, pleased to the core of his philanthropic ego to see the jubilation of the recipients. Had he known the Bainers, he would have hesitated. Kendall grabbed Baby Jesus by one foot and hoisted him up over his head like a carnival prize. He ran around the room with the other kids chasing. We all sat stunned. They were going to break Jesus into a million shards or value him at less than he had been appraised. They had no consideration for the quality craftsmanship, value, and beauty of the piece of art with which they ran whooping with joy, shoelaces untied and flapping behind them.

The Bainers didn't sell Jesus. Maybe they didn't realize they could. It would have been for the best. The parents let the kids have him and the kids went bouncing up a ladder and tied him to the chimney with lengths of yellow rope (stolen, we believed, from both tetherball poles at school). The ascending Jesus, with a flashlight in his baby backside.

Now, by holy and cleansing fire, God was bringing the hammer of justice down, and He was saying, "No more!" Parents shook their heads at the prospect of having a burnt-out black shell on their block for weeks and months to come. They whispered back and forth that they had seen this coming, what with the way the parents kept the house, and the way they probably let their children play with matches.

"It's too bad. It's a shame, and at Christmastime," they sighed. But they wouldn't have had it any other way. This was the great purging, a judgment handed down from on high, things being made right again.

Only none of us was convinced that even now — with their house on fire — the Bainers were getting it. Leave it to the Bainer kids to rejoice in tragedy. To wear it like the "S" on Superman's cape. Little Kendall lay down and made snow angels in the two inches of black gunk that covered the lawn. He had feared the delights of winter were a thing of the past, gone forever when his family moved to California. After watching the cast of *Sesame Street* doing snow angels in Central Park, Kendall had mourned out loud, yelling that *he* wanted to do snow angels. He hadn't stopped yelling it for fourteen weeks. Now he saw his chance to do snow angels, be it in snow or wet black residue from his burning home. His parents didn't stop him. Kennel jumped up and down with glee and sucked on all ten fingers. Baby Glen clutched his mother's leg with one hand, and with the other reached for the dewy ash, putting it into his mouth one baby fistful at a time. Once he discovered that it turned his baby-white skin black he rubbed it all over himself, on his face and diaper and up and down his mother's leg. Mr. Stuckey was swearing out loud again, fumbling with a ladder and tugging on the garden hose in his yard. He propped his ladder against the roof, careful not to set the legs in the garden plot beneath his window, and began climbing with the hose looped over his arm and tucked into his belt. He was shaking as he made his way up, trying to keep his balance as best an old seething man can, and his ladder rattled against the rain gutters. With his head cocked to one side he yelled for someone to turn on the hose, and he began spraying his roof.

We squirmed with delicious excitement, and while our house-socks and pajama bottoms soaked up morning dew like thirsty trees in the grass, we listened for sirens. We never heard them. The firehouse doors did not budge. The shiny red fire engines did not come.

Mr. Stuckey noticed it too, convinced his roof would catch fire before the firemen ever arrived. He pulled hard to get a kink out of his hose. He yanked once and then again. The water barely trickled. He cut the air to one side and then the other as if he was doing karate with his old arms, a series of epileptic seizures aimed at unkinking the hose. Finally, with one mighty yank, reeling in an imaginary two-hundred-pound fighting sturgeon, he tore the hose right at the spigot and water gushed out, instantly drowning his precious garden. The floodwaters spilled over, carrying potting soil and flower petals into the garage through the eight inches of cat space in the garage door.

We looked back at the fire station. Where were they? We could hardly contain ourselves. Our thoughts were malicious. That the firemen were playing a well-thought-out prank on the Bainers. For having to come cut their lawn. The Bainers were facing the music. Reaping what they had sowed. The world made sense again.

The firemen must have sat in their trucks for a full two minutes, waiting for the doors to go up, certain that they would at any second. When it was clear that there was a problem they got out of the truck and tried to manually lift the doors from the inside. We heard something, even over the roar of the fire and the snapping of timbers. We heard banging, men yelling. Then we saw them. Firemen pouring out through side doors like bees from a thumped hive. Swarming around the doors. Scrambling and tugging at them from the outside. Trying to free their rolling firefighting machines. It was the trucks that gave them strength, that made them firemen. It was the trucks that held the tools and hoses and power to form water into the kind of H_2O cannon that could put out a burning house. They were useless without them. But the doors were too heavy.

When the firemen finally gave up, they barely knew what to do. They turned and came sprinting down the street, pulling on heavy fire coats as they ran, gripping things tightly — small fire extinguishers, loose hoses dangling, large shiny axes. They were dedicated civil servants to the end, but they were in a state of emotional distress. It was written all over their faces. Panic. They'd lost their cool. They'd broken the first rule.

A fireman on the verge of breaking down and weeping in the road is a confusing and sad sight to see. Something from the pages of *Life* magazine or on a heart-wrenching television documentary, but not on your own street. However, here they were. Large men who had trained and lifted weights and dreamed the daydreams that young men dream — being a life-saving hero in the face of danger. These who had practiced CPR on rubber corpses, ridden in parades, who led school assemblies on how to not panic in a fire. They were running past our lawn chairs and pa-jamas and Hula-Hoops and cups of coffee, and they were sobbing loudly, dragging equipment behind them, the most frightened faces I have ever seen. One lost a boot while running. Others nearly tripped over themselves. They were out of their element. Emotion blistered on the thick skin and moistened their old-world mustaches. The tears rolled back from their eyes, dripping off their ears.

Groaning, crying, screaming. Gnashing of teeth. Visible regret. Profound sorrow. We wanted all these things, but we wanted them from the Bainers, not the firemen.

And, though no one ever knew for sure why, in that moment of confusion, little Allaray Bainer charged back at her burning home. She disappeared into the thick smoke. The Bainers' dog, Furler, cited in police logs for noise and meanness, broke charac-ter. Sensing this new desperation maybe, he stood in and crooned his own sad siren laments while the house crackled like a record player.

We couldn't know if any of Allaray's family would have run in af-ter her. The firemen were arriving now, moving the family back and dashing in after Allaray. The firemen kept running in and out, asking Mr. Bainer if anyone else was inside. He plainly told them each time that no, everybody was here. The firemen, still unorga-nized, ran wildly, fumbling with their equipment and bumping into each other. They circled the house, kicking in doors and yell-ing. One of them injured a shoulder knocking down a door. An-other stepped through a floorboard and fell headlong into a smol-dering section of wall, breaking his leg.

When the smoke cleared for a moment in front of the house, we saw Allaray. Our mouths fell open. She was standing beneath the chimney, gripping the bright green yard hose, spraying it up onto the roof as best she could manage in the blinding smoke. She was focused. We stared, frozen, making no sound, too shocked to gasp or pull her back ourselves before a wall fell on her.

If Mr. Stuckey was watching her from his rooftop, he was cer-tainly regretting his eighty-six years of life on this earth, for he must have been forced to admit he couldn't handle a Sears garden hose the way Allaray did — thumb pressed over the ring spout for maximum velocity, sweeping back and forth. She stood her ground until a fireman ducked into the smoke and retrieved her under his arm.

The fire, which had burned so intensely, began dying down now. There wasn't much left to burn, and the firemen finally were getting hoses on the flareups and smoldering ruins. The Salvation Army arrived and put blankets on the Bainers' shoulders. Some of the firemen sat on the curb hanging their heads and passing around a cigarette, and while the medics gave Allaray oxygen on a stretcher, the Bainer boys threw off their blankets and tromped through the ashes, round and round the chimney. Allaray, by her efforts it appeared, had saved the chimney (nonflammable), the front window (badly melted), and a jagged halo of roof around the chimney. Was Allaray a hero? Saving what needed no saving? But there it stood, nonetheless.

At the top of the chimney was the true, confirmed miracle — Baby Jesus, swallowed in smoke but still hanging on, his ropes blackened and frayed, but not burned through. No way it could have been from Allaray keeping them wet. The ropes should have snapped, the delicate glass object smashed against the ground. And in any case, Jesus should have melted in the heat, like the windows.

It was one of the neighbor children who told me that Allaray spent a night or two in the hospital. She was so close to the fire she had breathed in smoke and suffered minor burns on her face. They said that the only part of her face not red from her burns were two thin lines from the corners of her eyes to underneath her chin where a small but steady stream of tears had protected her eleven-year-old skin.

When the Bainers came back one last time a few days later, they came with their large ugly mobile home and parked it right out front. The kids ran around while the parents sifted through the mess looking for anything they could salvage. The kids found the blackened aluminum ladder where the garage had been and hauled it to the chimney, where they leaned it precariously. Up the ladder ambled Allaray, bandages on her face and all.

We kids had seen the emergence of Glass Jesus. Stunned when the smoke cleared, only then did we so fervently wish he had broken, melted, and dripped into the rain gutters. I know I did. Wished his ropes had snapped and his value devalued when he smashed to the ground. In a moment like that, why did I continue to wish suffering upon the Bainers? Why even after their instances of unfounded generosity and the preservation of my life by Allaray? Why, after the example of the firemen whose civic love overlooked grudges? What did the Bainers ever possess that made me so jealous?

As soon as the Bainers and the firemen had left on the day of the fire, we stood around with knowing looks, asking ourselves who would be the first to attempt it. We children, pirates till death, wanted to loot Jesus for his eyes. Those precious gems would wipe clean under faucet water. But who would dare? We all argued about it and did rock paper scissors a hundred times or more, and who won it I don't remember because in the end we knew we were still afraid to do it. For the risk of playing in a danger zone full of splinters, nails, and glass? Maybe. For the punishment we would receive if caught? Possibly. For fears unstated? Most likely. The idea of casting lots for Jesus' very eyes gave us pause. Especially in view of the miracle we had all been witness to. The glass baby survived an all-consuming fire, suspended for everyone to see like a supernatural exclamation point atop the heap of burnt-out home.

But now I gritted my teeth and burned inside and cursed Allaray when I saw her positioning the ladder. Mine! Mine! It should be mine! I wanted to scream. But the decision was no longer mine to make, nor the rest of the neighborhood kids'. She would lay claim to the prize, the image of her final victory over us. We could only hope those jewels were burnt-up black coals after all.

Up Allaray went, and I seethed. She pulled on the ropes. Still strong. Still tight. She spit on her jacket and rubbed Jesus' face. The visage of the baby emerged from the soot, and the two little shining jewel eyes came alive. Cursewords! The eyes had survived the fire intact, brighter than ever. The Bainers would have the last laugh. Allaray reached around Jesus and fumbled for the flashlight that had occupied the hole in his back. "Still here!" she yelled down to the others. Allaray turned the flashlight on. She admired the display while descending the ladder, and then from the ground. And the Bainer kids ran around in the ash until their legs were black from it and they looked like legless floating ghosts against the dark mound of their former home. Beneath the lit face and eyes of Jesus, eerily affixed above them, they floated like transparent spirits. And then they piled in their RV and drove away, leaving the charred, but illuminated face of Jesus behind them.

JONATHAN SAFRAN FOER

■

A Primer for the Punctuation of Heart Disease

FROM *The New Yorker*

THE "SILENCE MARK" SIGNIFIES an absence of language, and there is at least one on every page of the story of my family life. Most often used in the conversations I have with my grandmother about her life in Europe during the war, and in conversations with my father about our family's history of heart disease — we have forty-one heart attacks between us, and counting — the silence mark is a staple of familial punctuation. Note the use of silence in the following brief exchange, when my father called me at college, the morning of his most recent angioplasty:

"Listen," he said, and then surrendered to a long pause, as if the pause were what I was supposed to listen to. "I'm sure everything's gonna be fine, but I just wanted to let you know —"

"I already know," I said.

"□"

"□"

"□"

"□"

"O.K.," he said.

"I'll talk to you tonight," I said, and I could hear, in the receiver, my own heartbeat.

He said, "Yup."

■ The "willed silence mark" signifies an intentional silence, the conversational equivalent of building a wall over which you can't climb, through which you can't see, against which you break the bones of your hands and wrists. I often inflict willed silences upon my mother when she asks about my relationships with girls. Perhaps this is because I never have *relationships* with girls — only *relations*. It depresses me to think that I've never had sex with anyone who really loved me. Sometimes I wonder if having sex with a girl who doesn't love me is like felling a tree, alone, in a forest: No one hears about it; it didn't happen.

⁇ The "insistent question mark" denotes one family member's refusal to yield to a willed silence, as in this conversation with my mother:

"Are you dating at all?"
"□"
"But you're seeing people, I'm sure. Right?"
"□"
"I don't get it. Are you ashamed of the girl? Are you ashamed of me?"
"■"
"⁇"

¡ As it visually suggests, the "unxclamation point" is the opposite of an exclamation point; it indicates a whisper.
The best example of this usage occurred when I was a boy. My grandmother was driving me to a piano lesson, and the Volvo's wipers only moved the rain around. She turned down the volume of the second side of the seventh tape of an audio version of *Shoah,* put her hand on my cheek, and said, "I hope that you never love anyone as much as I love you¡"
Why was she whispering? We were the only ones who could hear.

¡¡ Theoretically, the "extraunxclamation points" would be used to denote twice an unxclamation point, but in practice any whisper that quiet would not be heard. I take comfort in believing that

at least some of the silences in my life were really extraunxcla-
mations.

!! The "extraexclamation points" are simply twice an exclama-
•• tion point. I've never had a heated argument with any member of my family. We've never yelled at each other, or disagreed
with any passion. In fact, I can't even remember a difference
of opinion. There are those who would say that this is unhealthy.
But, since it is the case, there exists only one instance of extraexclamation points in our family history, and they were uttered by
a stranger who was vying with my father for a parking space in
front of the National Zoo.

"Give it up, fucker!!" he hollered at my father, in front of my
mother, my brothers, and me.

"Well, I'm sorry," my father said, pushing the bridge of his
glasses up his nose, "but I think it's rather obvious that we arrived
at this space first. You see, we were approaching from —"

"Give . . . it . . . up . . . fucker!!"

"Well, it's just that I think I'm in the right on this particu —"

"GIVE IT UP, FUCKER!!"

"Give it up, Dad¡" I said, suffering a minor coronary event as my
fingers clenched his seat's headrest.

"Je-sus!" the man yelled, pounding his fist against the outside of
his car door. "Giveitupfucker!!"

Ultimately, my father gave it up, and we found a spot several
blocks away. Before we got out, he pushed in the cigarette lighter,
and we waited, in silence, as it got hot. When it popped out, he
pushed it back in. "It's never, ever worth it," he said, turning back
to us, his hand against his heart.

⁓ Placed at the end of a sentence, the "pedal point" signifies a
    thought that dissolves into a suggestive silence. The pedal
point is distinguished from the ellipsis and the dash in that the
thought it follows is neither incomplete nor interrupted but an
outstretched hand. My younger brother uses these a lot with me,
probably because he, of all the members of my family, is the one
most capable of telling me what he needs to tell me without hav-

ing to say it. Or, rather, he's the one whose words I'm most convinced I don't need to hear. Very often he will say, "Jonathan~" and I will say, "I know."

A few weeks ago, he was having problems with his heart. A visit to his university's health center to check out some chest pains became a trip to the emergency room became a week in the intensive care unit. As it turns out, he's been having one long heart attack for the last six years. "It's nowhere near as bad as it sounds," the doctor told my parents, "but it's definitely something we want to take care of."

I called my brother that night and told him that he shouldn't worry. He said, "I know. But that doesn't mean there's nothing to worry about~"

"I know~" I said.

"I know~" he said.

"I~"

"I~"

"□"

Does my little brother have relationships with girls? I don't know.

↓ Another commonly employed familial punctuation mark, the "low point," is used either in place — or for accentuation at the end — of such phrases as "This is terrible," "This is irremediable," "It couldn't possibly be worse."

> "It's good to have somebody, Jonathan. It's necessary."
>
> "□"
>
> "It pains me to think of you alone."
>
> "■↓"
>
> "??↓"

Interestingly, low points always come in pairs in my family. That is, the acknowledgment of whatever is terrible and irremediable becomes itself something terrible and irremediable — and often worse than the original referent. For example, my sadness makes my mother sadder than the cause of my sadness does. Of course, her sadness then makes me sad. Thus is created a "low-point chain":⏐⏐⏐⏐⏐...∞.

❄ The "snowflake" is used at the end of a unique familial phrase — that is, any sequence of words that has never, in the history of our family life, been assembled as such. For example, "I didn't die in the Holocaust, but all of my siblings did, so where does that leave me?❊" Or, "My heart is no good, and I'm afraid of dying, and I'm also afraid of saying I love you.❊"

☺ The "corroboration mark" is more or less what it looks like. But it would be a mistake to think that it simply stands in place of "I agree," or even "Yes." Witness the subtle usage in this dialogue between my mother and my father:

> "Could you add orange juice to the grocery list, but remember to get the kind with reduced acid. Also some cottage cheese. And that bacon-substitute stuff. And a few Yahrzeit candles."
> "☺"
> "The car needs gas. I need tampons."
> "☺"
> "Is Jonathan dating anyone? I'm not prying, but I'm very interested."
> "☺"

My father has suffered twenty-two heart attacks — more than the rest of us combined. Once, in a moment of frankness after his nineteenth, he told me that his marriage to my mother had been successful because he had become a yes man early on.

"We've only had one fight," he said. "It was in our first week of marriage. I realized that it's never, ever worth it."

My father and I were pulling weeds one afternoon a few weeks ago. He was disobeying his cardiologist's order not to pull weeds. The problem, the doctor says, is not the physical exertion but the emotional stress that weeding inflicts on my father. He has dreams of weeds sprouting from his body, of having to pull them, at the roots, from his chest. He has also been told not to watch Orioles games and not to think about the current administration.

As we weeded, my father made a joke about how my older brother, who, barring a fatal heart attack, was to get married in a few weeks, had already become a yes man. Hearing this felt like having an elephant sit on my chest — my brother, whom I loved more than I loved myself, was surrendering.

"Your grandfather was a yes man," my father added, on his knees, his fingers pushing into the earth, "and your children will be yes men."

I've been thinking about that conversation ever since, and I've come to understand — with a straining heart — that I, too, am becoming a yes man, and that, like my father's and my brother's, my surrender has little to do with the people I say yes to, or with the existence of questions at all. It has to do with a fear of dying, with rehearsal and preparation.

✂🕸 The "severed web" is a Barely Tolerable Substitute, whose meaning approximates "I love you," and which can be used in place of "I love you." Other Barely Tolerable Substitutes include, but are not limited to:

→|←, which approximates "I love you."
🖉□, which approximates "I love you."
🕯, which approximates "I love you."
×✈, which approximates "I love you."

I don't know how many Barely Tolerable Substitutes there are, but often it feels as if they were everywhere, as if everything that is spoken and done — every "Yup," "Okay," and "I already know," every weed pulled from the lawn, every sexual act — were just Barely Tolerable.

• • Unlike the colon, which is used to mark a major division in
• • a sentence, and to indicate that what follows is an elaboration, summation, implication, etc., of what precedes, the "reversible colon" is used when what appears on either side elaborates, summates, implicates, etc., what's on the other side. In other words, the two halves of the sentence explain each other, as in the

cases of "Mother::Me," and "Father::Death." Here are some examples of reversible sentences:

> My eyes water when I speak about my family::I don't like to speak about my family.
> I've never felt loved by anyone outside of my family::my persistent depression.
> 1938 to 1945::□.
> Sex::yes.
> My grandmother's sadness::my mother's sadness::my sadness::the sadness that will come after me.
> To be Jewish::to be Jewish.
> Heart disease::yes.

← Familial communication always has to do with failures to communicate. It is common that in the course of a conversation one of the participants will not hear something that the other has said. It is also quite common that one of the participants will not understand what the other has said. Somewhat less common is one participant's saying something whose words the other understands completely but whose meaning is not understood at all. This can happen with very simple sentences, like "I hope that you never love anyone as much as I love you¡"

But, in our best, least depressing moments, we *try* to understand what we have failed to understand. A "backup" is used: We start again at the beginning, we replay what was missed and make an effort to hear what was meant instead of what was said:

> "It pains me to think of you alone."
> "← It pains me to think of me without any grandchildren to love."

{ } A related set of marks, the "should-have brackets," signify words that were not spoken but should have been, as in this dialogue with my father:

> "Are you hearing static?"
> "{I'm crying into the phone.}"
> "Jonathan?"
> "□"

"Jonathan~"

"■"

"??"

"I::not myself~"

"{A child's sadness is a parent's sadness.}"

"{A parent's sadness is a child's sadness.}"

"←"

"I'm probably just tired¡"

"{I never told you this, because I thought it might hurt you, but in my dreams it was *you*. Not me. *You* were pulling the weeds from my chest.}"

"{I want to love and be loved.}"

"☺"

"☺"

"↓"

"↓"

"♟"

"☺"

"□↔□↔□"

"↓"

"↓"

"⏭○⏮"

"■ + ■ → ■"

"☺"

"♪ □"

"⊠ ⊠¡'"

"◎□✧●◆○○□◆⊙●"

"■"

"{I love you.}"

"{I love you, too. So much.}"

Of course, my sense of the should-have is unlikely to be the same as my brothers', or my mother's, or my father's. Sometimes — when I'm in the car, or having sex, or talking to one of them on the phone — I imagine their should-have versions. I sew them together into a new life, leaving out everything that actually happened and was said.

LISA GABRIELE

■

The Guide to Being a Groupie

FROM Nerve.com

BE A GIRL. Be born sad. Be from a big family, or be an only child. Either way, make sure your parents are distracted and overwhelmed. They should hate your moodiness and scoff at any discussion of fresh and freaky ways to wear your hair. Notice that as your parents' arguments, debt, and beer bottles pile up on the kitchen table at night, the volume on your radio dial rises. Through process of elimination, rock and roll, loud, is the only thing that drowns out the downstairs cacophony. You are twelve. You learn to stay out of the way of what's going to happen.

Don't panic when lyrics to songs by Van Halen, Aerosmith, Led Zeppelin, and Journey fill the space in your brain previously reserved for algebra problems, figure-skating schedules, and your dad's new phone number. Realize that you can memorize a song after hearing it only three times. Trace a Rush album cover onto the title page of your English composition binder. Ask your mom if you can take guitar lessons. She tells you to dry the dishes, and when you're done, to take the garbage out. Drag the flimsy bag over the gravel, check to see if any neighbors are around, then sing into the dark suburban sky: *She's just a small-town girl . . . She took the midnight train going anywhere . . .* Wonder if Steve Perry wrote that song after he peered behind your homemade curtains into the 3-bdr, 2-bath, crpt, frplc, wtw shag, split-level and watched you, alone at the kitchen table, illuminated by the light over the stove, waiting for the avocado phone to ring.

Get a job at a jeans store in the mall. Go to Faces for a free makeover on your lunch break. In between sips of your Dairy Queen shake, watch as a twenty-one-year-old's face is smeared atop your sixteen-year-old features. Notice how that girl in the mirror looks old and young, wary and naive at the very same time. Ask yourself, Where did she come from? Memorize the combination of shading and shine before scrubbing it off in the washroom after shift. Your mom's picking you up in front of the mall. It's important that she recognizes you, for now.

Become best friends with Linda G., the assistant manager of the jeans store, who is four years older and has tits and money in spades. Plus a driver's license. Plus knowledge of radio station concerts and the names of doormen at the Alexander Tavern and the Riviera by the expressway. Diamonds Lounge is okay, she says, but you go there last, because it's the easiest to get into. There, let an older man dance with you. Make casual movie conversation. Ask him what he does for a living. When he tells you he's an accountant, pretend you know what that is. He asks you the same. You say student. *What's your major?* You say English. He asks for your number. Give him the wrong one. Your mom's home all the time now. Plus, he's her age, and that creeps you out. You're not here for the men; you're still here for the boys. But they have a hard time getting into these places without the benefit of scaffolded hair and three-inch feather earrings, which brush your collarbones and complement your Heart jersey perfectly.

Be certain that the first time the lead singer from Hustler makes eye contact with you, he's addressing his song to the sky-high blonde on your left. The CanAm Tavern is dark; it's an easy mistake to make. Feel Linda nudge you in the ribs the second time he finds your eyes. When she says *he's looking right fucking at you,* there's only the tiniest bit of jealousy in her voice. Because no one has searched you out or locked eyes with you so intently in so long, return the gaze with the kind of intensity you're sure will make the bar spontaneously combust. Feel joy and fear, like you've done something beautifully bad. Then recoil your attention, smack the love off your face, and enjoy the drinks he's sent to your round, tippy table. Be unaware this is the last time you act coy by accident.

Nod intently when Dale tells you that Hustler is just a starter band. As soon as he gets his shit together and buys a new amp, he's going to find a better band that will launch him into the stratosphere. Realize that the fact that he has a plan for tomorrow turns you on like nothing else. He puts his tongue in your ear and his hand on your thigh, near your crotch. He tells you he writes his own songs. Maybe one day, he'll write one about your brown eyes, which now reflect blurry love. Suddenly you have a plan too. You will be the girl in his songs. That job will require you simply to show up and satisfy his needs. This is easy, because you've never really discovered any of your own.

When Linda gives you a look that says *your fucking ride's leaving*, say goodbye and promise to see him tomorrow. Be careful to keep the word "curfew" out of your new rock vernacular.

When the new doorman questions the veracity of your fake ID, say, *I'm with the band*. Demand that he get Dale; Dale is expecting you. Dale makes it good with the guy, then parts the sea, guiding you to a table by the stage. The drummer's wife is there. She excuses herself to check with the babysitter, respray her crimped hair, and shove cheap coke up her French-Canadian nose. Swear that she and the drummer are brother and sister. Dale kisses you fiercely, gratefully, expertly, draping his skinny tattooed arm around your bare shoulders like an owner. Feel marvelous to belong to something. For the first time in your life, feel proud of yourself and the things you do and the people you know.

Stack your spare classes on Friday morning to accommodate your new lifestyle. Find it difficult to remember the last time you made it to afternoon gym and drama. Realize that being in a classroom Monday to Thursday is like living between concrete brackets. Exist only for Thursday, Friday and Ladies Nites when Dale's on stage, when you can finally, fully look at him. Imagine how you would fit into his big life, which is sure to get bigger than this tavern. Between sets, when Dale sits with you, he eats up all the oxygen. Find it hard to breathe, which has something to do with the fact that his mouth is constantly smothering yours and the broom closet in the backstage area of the Riv is only big enough to do it standing up. Enjoy the furtive sex, but prefer this open-air affection, when everyone in the room is reminded of who you really are.

Act positive that at some time or another you probably told Dale pretty much exactly how old it is that you were, or maybe that it never really came up. And whose fault is that? Try to remember the last time Dale ever asked you questions about yourself. Fucker doesn't even know your last name. Fucker never bought you a burger or phoned you at home. True, you told him not to, but fucker only ever *really* expected you to show up where he was playing, and to sit your sweet ass down on the vinyl chairs to watch. He didn't know about your strep throat or that your mom's been crying more than usual. Fucker didn't even write that song about your eyes, which are now brimming over with Great Lash Ebony and Alice Coopering down your Maybelline cheeks. You want to be in a song, but not this song. The last thing you ever wanted to be was the girl who bawls drunkenly in public washrooms because no one ever writes about her. Unless they're punk. And that's not your bag yet.

Be fashionably late when Soldier, Stripes, and The Look are playing the RockFest bandshell. Know almost everyone there. The drummer's wife, who is smoking and teetering on her heels in the rain, lets you into the backstage area behind the Port-a-Pottys. Fail to spot Dale, but catch a glimpse of Angelo from Soldier. He sees you too. Feel his big hug as he pulls you into his skinny body and fat bulge. Hear him tell you it's good to see you, that he's heard about you and Dale. He tells you Dale's an asshole and his band's crap and why don't you and Linda make yourselves comfortable on the picnic table and watch their show from there. Feel the click of comfort, of belonging to a place with these people, how things seem normal again. See Dale with that redheaded bitch from the Riv, the one who always hovered near the tippy table acting like she was total friends with everyone. Don't let it bother you. She is older than you by a lot, and Dale's totally fucking welcome to her.

Don't give a shit when Angelo ignores you after their set, because the keyboardist doesn't. It feels like musical sluts the way the two of you wound up side by side on the least-crowded picnic table. Have a deep discussion about horoscopes, dogs, and divorce, which makes you feel gorgeous about yourself. Watch as Jay Jr. circles your nipple with the mouth of his sweaty Black Label.

Ignore your mother when she starts in on you again. Run toward the honking until her yelling disappears in the hum of Jay's I-Roc. At the club, smile as he whisks you past the doorman, past the crowded stage area and into a real greenroom. This is where you keep other bored girls company while boys play. Some girls you know, the rest you don't really want to. Get high. Watch Jay come backstage after a set you didn't bother to watch. Be unimpressed with a few songs he wrote, all of which seem a bit gay. You knew which words were coming, even before you committed the lyrics to memory. When Jay asks you to shove over on the ratty couch, you get up. Someone else's ex-girlfriend drives you home in a dark-blue van.

Notice a guitar leaning up against the console in the upstairs hallway. It's small and used and untuned. Ask your mother whom it belongs to. She says you, if you want it. Reply that you don't know how to play guitar. Try teaching yourself something new for a change, she says. Try making up your own mind about things instead of accommodating these fucking guys who keep pulling up our goddamn driveway but never bother to come to our front fucking door, she says.

Laugh secretly at the guy on the cover of *How to Play Guitar in Ten Easy Steps:* a gaylord with a red, fuzzy Afro who's smiling idiotically. Hide the book in your purple satin bag, the one you made in home ec for which you received your first A-. Learn a song, sitting cross-legged on the bathroom vanity. It's "Leaving on a Jet Plane." Picture what it must feel like to do that. Realize you can't, because you've never been on an airplane. Consider writing a song about that very real dilemma. When your brother pounds on the bathroom door saying hurry up, that he has to use the bathroom, tell him to fuck off and use the one downstairs, because you've got the room right now. Tell him all eyes are on you, and both of them are wide fucking open.

AMANDA HOLZER

■

Love and Other Catastrophes:
A Mix Tape

FROM *Story Quarterly*

ALL BY MYSELF, *Eric Carmen*. Looking for Love, *Lou Reed*. I Wanna Dance with Somebody, *Whitney Houston*. Let's Dance, *David Bowie*. Let's Kiss, *Beat Happening*. Let's Talk About Sex, *Salt 'n' Pepa*. Like a Virgin, *Madonna*. We've Only Just Begun, *The Carpenters*. I Wanna Be Your Boyfriend, *The Ramones*. I'll Tumble 4 Ya, *Culture Club*. Head Over Heels, *The Go-Go's*. Nothing Compares to You, *Sinead O'Connor*. My Girl, *The Temptations*. Could This Be Love? *Bob Marley*. Love and Marriage, *Frank Sinatra*. White Wedding, *Billy Idol*. Stuck in the Middle with You, *Steelers Wheel*. Tempted, *The Squeeze*. There Goes My Baby, *The Drifters*. What's Going On? *Marvin Gaye*. Where Did You Sleep Last Night? *Lead-belly*. Who's Bed Have Your Boots Been Under? *Shania Twain*. Jealous Guy, *John Lennon*. Your Cheatin' Heart, *Tammy Wynette*. Shot Through the Heart, *Bon Jovi*. Don't Go Breaking My Heart, *Elton John and Kiki Dee*. My Achy Breaky Heart, *Billy Ray Cyrus*. Heart-break Hotel, *Elvis Presley*. Stop! In the Name of Love, *The Supremes*. Try a Little Tenderness, *Otis Redding*. Try (Just a Little Bit Harder), *Janis Joplin*. All Apologies, *Nirvana*. Hanging on the Telephone, *Blondie*. I Just Called to Say I Love You, *Stevie Wonder*. Love Will Keep Us Together, *Captain and Tennille*. Let's Stay Together, *Al Green*. It Ain't Over 'til It's Over, *Lenny Kravitz*. What's Love Got to

Do with It? *Tina Turner.* You Don't Bring Me Flowers Anymore, *Barbra Streisand and Neil Diamond.* I Wish You Wouldn't Say That, *Talking Heads.* You're So Vain, *Carly Simon.* Love Is a Battlefield, *Pat Benatar.* Heaven Knows I'm Miserable Now, *The Smiths.* (Can't Get No) Satisfaction, *Rolling Stones.* Must Have Been Love (But It's Over Now), *Roxette.* Breaking Up is Hard to Do, *Neil Sedaka.* I Will Survive, *Gloria Gaynor.* Hit the Road, Jack, *Mary McCaslin and Jim Ringer.* These Boots Were Made for Walking, *Nancy Sinatra.* All Out of Love, *Air Supply.* All By Myself, *Eric Carmen.*

CHUCK KLOSTERMAN

∎

The Pretenders

FROM *New York Times Magazine*

RANDY TRASK'S HAIR is naturally blond. He likes it that color, and it looks just fine. It's what his hair is supposed to look like. But in his line of work, blond hair is a problem, and he knows it.

"I am going to dye my hair red," he assures me. "That is definitely in the works. It's just that the last time I tried, it turned sort of pink. And for some reason, people get scared of you when you have red hair. I don't know why that is, but it's true. They just don't warm up to you the way they do if you're blond."

Trask is telling me this at ten minutes to midnight. We are sitting in his 1997 extended-cab Ford Ranger pickup, which we will soon be driving from Cincinnati to Harrisonburg, Virginia, for his gig tomorrow night. Trask is the lead singer in a band called Paradise City, and like any frontman, he cares about his image. But Trask has a whole set of concerns — like the specific tint of his hair — that most singers don't need to worry about. He doesn't just want to look good; he wants to look exactly like W. Axl Rose, the lead singer of Guns N' Roses, the late-eighties pop-metal band that Paradise City imitates, as precisely as possible, in every show it plays.

It's roughly a ten-hour drive to Harrisonburg, so leaving in the middle of the night should get us to town just in time to check into the Hampton Inn and take an afternoon nap. There is some concern about this trip, because the last time the band stayed in

Harrisonburg, they were banned for life from the Econo Lodge. They need to make sure things go smoothly at the Hampton Inn this weekend; there just aren't that many hotels in Harrisonburg to choose from.

Our pickup is idling outside the home of Paul Dischner, Trask's bandmate, who is inside, still packing for our voyage. Our conversation moves on from Trask's hair issues to larger questions. "I initially had a problem with the idea of doing a Guns N' Roses tribute, because I didn't want anyone to think I was discrediting Axl," Trask says. "That was always my main concern. If Axl was somehow against this, I'd straight-up quit. I would never do this if he disapproved. But I really think we can do his songs justice. People constantly tell me, 'You sound better than Axl,' but I always say, 'Whoa now, slow down.' Because I like the way I sing Axl's songs, but I *love* the way Axl sings them. That's the main thing I'm concerned about with this article: I do not want this to say anything negative about Guns N' Roses. That's all I ask."

I am the first reporter who has ever done a story on Paradise City. This is less a commentary on Paradise City — named after one of Guns N' Roses' biggest hits — and more a commentary on the phenomenon of tribute bands, arguably the most universally maligned sector of rock 'n' roll. These are bands mired in obscurity and engaged in a bizarre zero-sum game: If a tribute band were to succeed completely, its members would essentially cease to exist. Their goal is not to be somebody; their goal is to be somebody else.

Though the Beatles and Elvis Presley were the first artists to spawn impersonators, the modern tribute template was set by groups like Strutter, Hotter Than Hell, and Cold Gin, all of which found success in the early nineties by looking, acting, and singing like the 1978 version of Kiss. It turned out that people would sooner pay ten dollars to see four guys pretending to be Kiss than five dollars to see four guys playing original songs nobody had ever heard before. There are now hundreds — probably thousands — of rock bands who make a living by method acting. There's the Atomic Punks, a Van Halen tribute that celebrates the

David Lee Roth era. Planet Earth are L.A.-based Duran Duran clones. Bjorn Again claims to be Australia's finest ABBA tribute. AC/DShe is an all-female AC/DC cover group from San Francisco. There are tributes to groups who weren't that popular to begin with (Badfinger, Thin Lizzy), and there are tributes to bands who are not altogether difficult to see for real (Dave Matthews Band, Creed). And though rock critics deride Stone Temple Pilots and Oasis for ripping off other artists, people pay good money to watch tribute bands rip off Stone Temple Pilots and Oasis.

Being consciously derivative is not simple; Trask and Dischner can talk for hours about the complexity of feeding their appetite for replication. There are countless qualifications that must be considered when auditioning potential members in a tribute. This was especially obvious when Paradise City had to find a new person to play Slash, GN'R's unforgettable lead guitarist. It is not enough to find a guy who plays guitar well; your Slash needs to play guitar like Slash. He needs to play a Les Paul, and he needs to tune it like Slash. He needs to have long black hair that hangs in his face. Preferably, he should have a dark complexion, an emaciated physique, and a willingness to play shirtless. And if possible, he should drink Jack Daniel's.

The Slash in Paradise City fulfills about half of those requirements.

"Bobby is on thin ice right now, and he knows he's on thin ice," says Trask, referring to lead guitarist Bobby Young. "I mean, he's an okay guy, and he's a good guitar player. But we have ads out right now for a new Slash, and he knows that. I want someone who is *transfixed* with being Slash. We want someone who is as sick about Slash as I am about Axl."

What is odd about Young's shortcomings as Slash is that in a traditional band, his job would likely be the most secure: He is clearly the most skilled musician in Paradise City, with a degree from Cincinnati's conservatory of music. "I was classically trained, so I'm used to everything being built around minor chords," he tells me. "But Slash plays almost everything in a major chord, and his soloing is very different than mine. It's all in chromatic keys. I really thought I could learn all of these Guns N' Roses songs in two days, but it took me almost two weeks."

Unfortunately, Young can't learn how to look like a mulatto former heroin addict, and he holds the only position in America for which that is a job requirement. He only vaguely resembles Slash, and his bandmates tell him he looks like an Oompa-Loompa from *Willy Wonka and the Chocolate Factory*. There's a similar problem with Paradise City's bassist, an affable, laid-back blond named Spike. Spike is built a little too much like a farmer. His shoulders are broad, and he actually looks more like Larry Bird than Duff McKagan, the bassist in Guns N' Roses. Spike is also partly deaf from playing heavy metal for so many years (he can't hear certain frequencies, including high-end feedback), but — amazingly — this doesn't seem to pose a problem.

Visually, the rest of Paradise City succeeds to varying degrees. Rob (the Monster) Pohlman, the drummer, could pass perfectly for Steven Adler — if Pohlman hadn't just shaved his head and dyed the remaining bristles orange. (Dischner is upset about Pohlman's new haircut; a few days earlier, he had explained to me proudly that "what sets us apart from the twenty-two other Guns N' Roses tribute bands in America is that we don't wear wigs.") Trask is eight inches too tall to be Axl Rose, but he has the voice and — more important — the desire. He wills himself into Axlocity.

Dischner is the only Paradise City member who naturally looks like his assigned doppelganger, Izzy Stradlin', Guns N' Roses' original rhythm guitarist. He's also the guy who makes the trains run on time: He handles the cash, coordinates the schedules, and keeps his bandmates from killing one another. Before Paradise City, Dischner played in an Yngwie Malmsteen–influenced heavy metal band called Premonition, a group whose entire existence was based on the premise that Juan Carlos, the king of Spain, is in fact the Antichrist. To this day, Dischner adheres to this theory and insists it can be proved through biblical prophecy. He lives with his wife, Kristi (an aspiring vampire novelist), in a small suburb of

Cincinnati, and he peppers his conversation with a high-pitched, two-note laugh that sounds like "wee *hee!*" Over the next thirty-six hours, he will make that sound approximately four hundred times.

By the time we pull out of Dischner's driveway at 12:30 A.M., it has already been an incredibly long day for Trask. He awoke at 2 A.M. at his home in Ravenna, Ohio, and immediately drove four hours to the outskirts of Cincinnati, where he spent the day cutting down a troublesome tree in Dischner's yard. After a brief nap, the band hooked up for a few hours of rehearsal before supper. Now Trask is about to drive the entire way to Virginia, nonstop. He almost never sleeps. Trask once drove twenty-two straight hours to Hayes, Kansas, and played a show immediately on arrival. If the real Axl Rose had Trask's focus, Guns N' Roses would have released two albums a year.

There was a time when Paradise City had a tour bus, but they lost it last summer. This is not a euphemism; they literally can't find it. It broke down on a trip to Kansas City, and they had to leave it in a Missouri garage to make it to the club on time. Somehow, they lost the business card of the garage and have never been able to find their way back. Dischner tells me this story three times before I realize he's completely serious.

"We drove back through Missouri a bunch of times, we put up a picture on our Web site, and we even called the highway patrol," Dischner says. "But we lost the bus. And I guess there's some law that states you only have thirty days to find your bus."

The band is now traveling in two vehicles. Randy/Axl will use his truck to pull the Haulmark trailer that holds their gear; he'll drive, I'll ride shotgun, and Paul/Izzy will curl up in the extended cab. A friend of the band — some dude named Teddy — will follow in his Ford Mustang, which will also carry Bobby/Slash and Rob/Steven. The pickup box is covered with a topper, so Spike/Duff will lie back there with Punky.

Trask and Dischner do not know who Punky is.

At departure time, only 40 percent of the band is not under the influence of some kind of chemical. Twenty minutes into the trip, that percentage will fall to zero. Even before we get on the road, this Punky character looks drunk enough to die; amazingly, he's just getting started. They're *all* just getting started. It remains to be seen if these guys can sound like Guns N' Roses, but they clearly have the self-destructive thing mastered.

Our vehicles barrel into the darkness of Kentucky. Spike and Punky are freezing in the box of the pickup, and they try to stay warm by drinking Bud Light. Inside the toasty cab, faux Axl, faux Izzy, and I discuss the question most people have about tribute bands, which is "Why on earth do you do this?" It seems antithetical to the whole concept of art; the notion of creativity has been completely removed from the equation. Wouldn't the members of Paradise City be happier if they could write their own songs, dress however they want, and — quite simply — be themselves?

Not really.

"Obviously, being in an original band is the ultimate dream, but it mostly sucks," Dischner says. "You don't get to tour. You don't get no money. You have to beg your own friends to come to the show. But being a mock star is awesome."

Paradise City will earn $1,100 for the Harrisonburg show. After their manager takes his 15 percent and they pay for gas and promotions, they will be left with $655, which — split between five people — ends up being $131 each. Obviously, this is almost nothing. But the operative word is "almost." If the same five guys in Paradise City performed their own material, they would have to pay club owners for the chance to play; relatively speaking, $1,100 is good money.

"The thing about being in a tribute band is that your fans already exist," Trask says. "You show up at the bar, and there's immediately a few hundred people who love Guns N' Roses and therefore love you. We don't think of ourselves as Guns N' Roses. But our fans are Guns N' Roses fans — they're not really fans of Paradise City. We're not deluding ourselves."

This is true; no one in Paradise City seems confused about the social significance of the group. But they're obsessed with convincing themselves that it's still worth it. They love talking about how "life on the road" is a hard yet satisfying experience. They make grand proclamations that sound like outtakes from VH1's *Behind the Music:* It's all about the fans, it's all about the music, it's all about the awe-inspiring majesty of rock; it's all about something, and then it's all about something else entirely. But they're never lying — when you're in a tribute band, all those clichés are true. Paradise City cares more about Guns N' Roses than the actual members of Guns N' Roses care about the song "Paradise City."

In fact, the guys in Paradise City care about *all* music with more enthusiasm than any group of musicians I've ever encountered. The truck stereo never plays an artist they dislike. They have positive things to say about Aerosmith, Nickelback, Celine Dion (!), Black Sabbath, Pink Floyd, and Alabama. When Jewel's "You Were Meant for Me" comes on the radio, Dischner mentions that the song always makes him wish it was raining; ten minutes later, he tells me that Rush is "just about the greatest three-piece band ever," and then gives a similar compliment to the Rush tribute band 2112.

We hit the Virginia border around dawn. Trask begins scanning radio stations in the hope of hearing "the commercial." This is a radio spot promoting Paradise City's concert at the Mainstreet Bar and Grill in Harrisonburg. The band gets excited about hearing "the commercial" in the same way normal bands get excited about hearing their first single on the radio. When we finally hear it, it refers to Paradise City's "triumphant return" to Virginia. Highfives are exchanged all around.

For the next hour, Trask and I discuss the real Guns N' Roses, a topic we are both obsessed with (albeit in very different ways). Just like mine, Trask's first musical love was Mötley Crüe (before Paradise City, he fronted a Mötley tribute called Bastard), but he slowly grew obsessed with the more combustible GN'R. Guns N' Roses made its debut in 1987 as L.A.'s most dangerous band, blowing the doors off pop metal with *Appetite for Destruction*, arguably the strongest debut album ever. They followed with an EP titled *GN'R Lies,* which is best remembered for the ballad "Patience" and the controversial song "One in a Million," a track that managed to be racist, homophobic, and xenophobic all in just over six minutes. In 1991, Guns released two massive albums on the same day, *Use Your Illusion I* and *II,* cementing their place as the biggest band in the world. Yet by 1997, it had all collapsed; one by one, every member — except the mercurial Axl Rose — either quit or was fired. Rose became a virtual recluse, endlessly working on an alleged masterpiece, titled *Chinese Democracy,* that may never be released.

But history is not an issue for Paradise City; for them, the past is no different than the present, and the future will be identical. Every day, Axl Rose grows a little older, but Paradise City never ages beyond the summer of '91.

There are no fashion don'ts inside the Mainstreet Bar and Grill in downtown Harrisonburg. You want to wear a headband? Fine. You want to wear a Fubu sweatshirt and a baseball hat featuring the Confederate flag? No problem. This is the kind of place where you will see a college girl trying to buy a $2.25 glass of Natural Light on tap with her credit card — *and have her card denied.*

The Mainstreet is not trendy. But it's still cool, or at least gritty, and Paradise City has sold it out. Almost five hundred people (mostly kids from nearby James Madison University) have paid twelve dollars each to get inside, which is as big an audience as the Mainstreet will draw for next week's show by Dokken, an eighties metal act trying to make a comeback. One can only wonder how the real guys in Dokken feel about being as popular as five fake guys in Guns N' Roses.

The opening act is a local collegiate jam band called Alpine Recess; they look as if they'd rather be opening for a Phish tribute band, but the crowd is polite. Meanwhile, Paradise City is dressing downstairs in the basement, drinking free beer in the storeroom and leaning against the water heater. They have decided to open with the song "Nighttrain," even though it includes an extended five-minute guitar solo that Young worries might anesthetize the audience.

Unlike the real GN'R, Paradise City hits the stage on time. Trask moves his hips in Axl's signature snakelike sway, and the crowd sings along with everything. Paradise City may not always look like Guns N' Roses, but they certainly sound like them; when I go to the bathroom and hear the music through the door, it's impossible not to think that this is how it would have sounded to urinate on the Sunset Strip in 1986.

"This next song is dedicated to everybody who ever told you how to live," Trask tells us as he prowls the twenty-five-foot stage. "This is for everybody who told you not to smoke weed or not to drink beer every day."

This soliloquy leads into the bubbling bass intro of "It's So Easy," the angriest three minutes on *Appetite for Destruction.* Girls begin crawling onstage to dance on top of the amplifiers, and the band couldn't be happier. Ultimately, this is why they do this: Onstage they're paying tribute to the music of Guns N' Roses, but deep down they're paying tribute to the Guns N' Roses lifestyle. They're totally willing to become other people, just so long as those other people party all the time, live like gypsies, and have pretty girls dancing on their amplifiers. This is why guys create rock bands; Paradise City just created somebody else's.

After the show, a few girls (most of whom seem *very* young) accompany the band back to the Hampton, and the frivolity lasts until dawn. The gig is an undeniable success. There is a casualty, however: The next morning, something is clearly amiss with Punky. It turns out he fell down a flight of stairs before the concert and spent the entire Paradise City set lying on the concrete floor of their basement dressing room. He still managed to party with the band for most of the night, but in the morning — when the clarity of sobriety finally emerged — little Punky realized his wrist was broken, and he had to be rushed to the hospital by ambulance.

Oddly (or perhaps predictably), the band simply drove back to Ohio. We left Punky with no car and no ride, broken and battered, in a town where he knew absolutely no one. Axl would have completely approved.

K. KVASHAY-BOYLE

∎

Saint Chola

FROM *McSweeney's*

SKATER. HESHER. Tagger. Lesbo-Slut. Wannabe. Dweeb. Fag.
Prep. What-up. Bad-ass. Gangster. Dork. Nerd. Trendy. Freaky.
In a few weeks it'll be solid like cement, but right now nobody
knows yet. You might be anything. And here's an example: Meet
Mohammadee Sawy. Hypercolor T-shirt, oversize overalls with
just one hook fastened, the other tossed carefree over the shoulder
like it's no big thing. In walks Mohammadee, short and plump
and brown, done up for the first day with long fluffy hair and a
new mood ring, but guess what, it's not *Mohammadee* anymore.
Nope, because Dad's not signing you up today, you're all by yourself and when you get the form where it says Name, Grade, Homeroom, you look around and take the pen Ms. Yoshida hands you
and you write it in big and permanent: Shala M. Sawy. And from
now on that's who you are. Cool.

It's tough to do right but at least you learn what to want. You
walk the halls and you see what's there. I want her jeans, I want
her triple-pierce hoops, I want her strut, I want those boobs, I
want that crowd, I want shoes like those, I want a wallet chain, I
want a baby-doll dress, I want safety pins on my backpack, I want a
necklace that says my name. Lipstick. I want lipstick. Jelly bracelets. Trainer bras from Target. It could be me. I could be anyone.
KISS FM, POWER 106, Douche-bag, Horn-ball. Fanny packs! Biker
shorts! And suddenly, wow, Shala realizes that she has a surge of

power inside that she never knew was there. Shala realizes that she's walking around and she's thinking Yup, cool, or No way! Lame!

Shala? That sounds good. And that's just the way tiny Mrs. Furukawa says it in homeroom when she calls roll. She says *Shala.* And Shala Mohammadee Sawy? She smiles. (But not so much as to be uncool because she's totally cool.) And she checks out the scene. There's a powerhouse pack of scary Cholas conspiring in the back row, there's aisle after aisle of knobby, scrawny white-boy knees sprouting like weeds from marshmallow sneakers, and there are clumps of unlikely allies haphazardly united for the first time by the pride of patriotism: Serrania Avenue, row three, Walnut Elementary, row five, or MUS, first row. Forty faces. Shala knows some of them. Ido, Farah, Laura Leaper, Eden, Mori Leshum, oh great, and him: Taylor Bryans. Barf. But the rest? They're all new.

In Our World, fourth period, Shala learns current events. It's social studies. The book's heavy. But then there's a war. And then Shala's embarrassed to say Niger River out loud, and she learns to recognize Kuwait and a kid named Josh gets a part in a movie with Tom Hanks, but that's nothing she tells Lucy because she used to roller-skate at Skateland with the kid from *Terminator II.* And he's cuter. Way cuter.

It's L.A. Unified where there's every different kind of thing, but it's just junior high so you're just barely starting to get an idea of what it means to be some different kind of thing. There are piercings. There are cigarettes. Even drug dealers. And with all that, there's the aura of danger all around, and you realize, for the first time, that you could get your ass kicked. You could get pounded after school, you could get jumped in the bathroom, you could get jacked up, beat up, messed up, it's true, and the omnipresent possibility swells every exchange.

Mrs. Furukawa's new husband is in the army. She says so. She wears the highest heels you've ever seen a person wear. Her class reads *The Diary of Anne Frank* but you know you're set, you already read it. Plus *A Wrinkle in Time,* and you read that one too. At home your mom says Get out the flag, we want them to know what side we're on.

On television every night Bush says Sad-dum instead of Suhdom and your dad says it's a slap in the face. Your dad, the Mohammad Sawy from which your Mohammadee came, says it's on purpose, just to drive that bastard nuts. You practice saying the name both ways, the real way and the slap-his-face way.

Gym class is the worst because you have to get naked and that is the worst. Gym is what your friends feared most in fifth grade when you thought about junior high and you tried so hard to imagine what it would be like to be with other people and take your clothes off (Take your clothes off? In front of people? Strangers-people? Oh yeah right. Get real. No way.) and you started trying to think up the lie you'd have to tell your parents because they just wouldn't get it. A big important thing is Modesty. You know that. It's your cultural heritage, and naked is certainly not Modesty. On the first day just to be sure, you raise your hand and ask, If you were a nonstrip every day would you fail? And Ms. DeLuca says, Yes.

Some kids ditch but it's been three months. It's too late now. You're stuck with who you are by now and even though you're finally Shala you're still a goody-good brainy dweeb. And dweebs just don't ditch. Not like you want to anyway. Except in gym. That's when you do want to. You sit on the black asphalt during roll call with your gym shirt stretched over your knees so that it's still all bagged out twenty minutes later when the volleyball crashes bang into your unprotected head for the fifteenth time like it's been launched from some mystery rocket launcher and it's got a homing device aimed straight for you.

At twelve, no one knows anything yet, so what kind of name is Shala? Who can tell? And, plus, who'd even consider the question if parents didn't ask it? Sometimes kids slip up to you in the crush of the lunch line and speak quick Spanish and expect you to answer. Sometimes kids crack jokes in Farsi and then shoot you a sly glance just before the punch line. Sometimes you laugh for them

anyway. Sometimes you'll try and answer *Sí*, and disguise that An-
glo accent the best you can. *Sí, claro.* But the best is when a sleep-
over sucks and you want to go home and you call up your mom
and mumble Urdu into the telephone and no one knows when
you tell your mom I hate these girls and I want to leave.

On Tuesday a kid wears a T-shirt to school and it says NUKE 'EM
and when Mrs. Furukawa sees it she's pissed and she makes him
go to the office and when he comes back he's wearing it inside out.
If you already saw it you can still kind of tell though. ME' EKUN.

After school that day your cousin asks if you want to try Girl
Scouts with her. Then she gets sick and makes you go alone.
When you get there it's totally weird for two reasons. First, your
cousin's older by one year and she already wears a hijab and when
you went over to get her she dressed you up. So now you're wearing a hijab and lipstick and your cousin's shirt, which says CHILL
OUT. Uncool. But what could you say? She's all sick and she kept
cracking up whenever you put something else of hers on and she's
so bossy all the time and then before you knew it the carpool's
honking outside and your aunt shouts that you have to go right
now. So you do. Then, second of all, you don't know anybody here.
They're all seventh-graders. It sucks.

They're baking banana nut bread and the girl who gave you a
ride says that you smell funny. What's worse than smelling funny?
The first thing you do is you go to the bathroom and wash your
hands. Then you rinse out your mouth. You try to keep the lipstick
from smearing all over the place. You sniff your armpits. As far as
you can tell, it seems normal. In the mirror you look so much
older with Aslana's hijab pinned underneath your chin like that.

When you walk out of the bathroom you bump into the Girl
Scout mom and almost immediately she starts to yell at you like
you spilled something on the carpet.

Um, excuse me but this is a feminist household and hello?
Honey, that's degrading, she says.

She must be confused. At first you wonder, is she really talking
to me, and like in a television sitcom, you turn around to check if
there's someone else standing behind you.

Don't you know this is America, sweetheart? I mean have you heard of this thing feminism?

Yeah, I'm one too, you say, because you learned about it in school and it means equality between the sexes and that's a good idea.

That's sweet. She looks at you. But get that thing off your head first, she says. You know you don't have to wear it. Not here. No one's gonna arrest you. I didn't call the police or anything, honey — what's your name?

The Girl Scout mom shakes her Girl Scout head and she's wearing a giant Girl Scout outfit that fits her. She looks weird. Like an enormous kid, super-sized like French fries. You can just be yourself at our house, honey, she assures you. You can. What, your mom wears that? She's forced to? Right? Oh, Jesus Christ. Look at you. Well you don't have to, you hear me? Here, you want to take it off? Here, com'ere, honey.

And when you do she helps you and then after you're ashamed that you let her touch it. Then you mix the banana nut dough and you think it looks like throw-up and that same girl says that you still smell like a restaurant she doesn't like. You really, really want to leave. Maybe if you stand still, you think, no one will notice you. On the wall there's a picture of dogs playing cards. Your cousin's hijab is in your backpack and you hold your whole self still and imagine time flowing away like milk down your throat until it's gone and you can leave.

There are Scud missiles, yeah, but in sixth grade at LAUSD, there are more important things. Like French kisses. There's this girl who claims she did one. You just have to think, What would that be? because no one would ever kiss you. At least until you're married. Lucy Chang says it's slutty anyway. Lucy Chang is your best friend. You tell her about Girl Scouts and she says Girl Scouts is lame.

On the way home from school you get knocked down by a car. With a group of kids. It's not that bad, kind of just a scary bump, from the guy doing a California-stop, which means rolling through the stop sign. At first he says sorry and you say it's okay. But when you suck up all your might and ask to write down his license plate number he says no. Your dad must be a lawyer, he says, is that it? What, look, you're not even hurt, okay? Just go home.

You have some friends with you. You guys were talking about how you could totally be models for a United Benetton ad if someone just took a picture of you guys right now. You're on your way to Tommy's Snack Shack for curly fries and an Orange Julius. Uhh, I think we should probably just go, all right? Noel says. It's not that bad so we should just go.

Yeah, go, the man says. Don't be a brat, he says. Just go.

Okay fine, you say, fine, I'll go, but FIRST I'm gonna write it down.

He's tall and he looks toward the ground to look at you. Just mind your own business, kid, she doesn't want you to. No one wants you to, he says.

Well I'm gonna, you say.

Look, you're not hurt, nobody's hurt, what do you need to for?

Just in case, you say. If it scares him you're happy. You're in junior high. You know what to do. Stand your ground. Make your face impassive. You are made of stone. You repeat it more slowly just to see if it freaks him out. *Just. In. Case,* you say and you're twelve and if you're a brat then wear it like a badge.

At mosque there's a broken window. It's a disgrace, your father says, Shala, I tell you it's a damn disgrace. The hole in the window looks jagged like a fragile star sprouting sharp new points. It lets all the outside noise in when everybody's trying to pray and cars rush past grinding their brakes.

There's a report in Language Skills, due Monday, and you have to have a thesis so on the way home from mosque your mom helps you think of one. Yours is that if you were living in Nazi times you would have saved Anne Frank. Your mom says that's not a thesis. Hers is that empathy and tolerance are essential teachings in every religion. You settle for a compromise: Because of Anne Frank's tolerance she should be a saint.

*

At home while your mom makes dinner she stands over the stove as you peel the mutant-looking ginger root and there are lots of phone calls from lots of relatives. What are we going to do, your mom keeps demanding each time she talks into the phone. What? Tell me. What are we going to do?

Saddam does something. You know it because there are television reports. Everyone's worried for your older brother. He's studying in Pakistan with some friends and if he leaves now then he'll be out one whole semester because his final tests aren't for two more months. He's big news at the mosque. Also people are talking about the price of gas and how much it costs just to drive downtown.

Then Bush does something back, and the phone cord stretches as your mom marches over and snaps the TV off like she's smashed a spider.

The ginger and the asafetida and the mustard seed sauté for a long time until they boil down and then it is the usual moment for adding in the spinach and the potato and the butter but instead the moment comes and goes and the saag aloo burns for the first time that you can remember and the delicate smell of scorched spice swirls up through the room as you watch your mom demand her quite angry Urdu into the receiver and you realize that she doesn't even notice.

You know why she's upset. It's because everyone can tell Ahmad's American and he can't disguise it. He smells American, he smiles American, and his T-shirts say JUST DO IT like a dare. And lots of people hate America. Plus, in that country, in general in that country, it's much more dangerous. Even just every time you visit, you swallow giant pills and still your weak sterile body gets every cold and all the diarrhea and all the fevers that India has to offer. It's because of the antiseptic lifestyle, your mother insists. Too clean.

In Science, fifth period, you learn that everything is made out of stardust from billions of years ago. Instead of it being as romantic as Mr. Kane seems to think it is, you think that pervasive dust feels sinister. You know what happened to Anne Frank, and you can't believe that when she died she turned back into people dust, all mixed up with every other kind of dust. Just piles and piles of dust. And all of it new.

There are plenty of other Muslim kids. Tons of them at school. Everyone's a little freaked out. In the hall, after science, you see an eighth-grader get tripped on purpose and the kid who did it shouts, Send Saddam after me, mofo, I'll kick his ass too!

After school that day at Mori Leshum's house everyone plays a game called Girl Talk, which is like Risk, except it takes place at the mall. It gets old fast. Next: crank calls! 1-800-SURVIVAL is 1, 8, 0, 0, 7, 8, 7, 8, 4, 8, 2, 5. Uh hi, I just got in a car accident and YOU SUCK A DICK! You laugh and laugh, but when it comes time for your turn to squeal breathy oinks into the phone the way you've heard in movies, you chicken out and everyone concludes that oh my god you're such a prude. Well at least I'm not a total perv, you say. Oi, oi, oh! Wooo! Ahh! moans Jackie and when Mori's shriveled grandma comes in the room to get you guys pizza, you all shut up fast for one quick second and then burst into hilarity. The grandma laughs right back at you and she has a dusty tattoo on her arm and it's not until years later that you realize what it is. Oh, that, says Mori. It's just her boyfriend's phone number. She says she put it there so she won't get it lost.

Some things that you see you can't forget. On your dad's desk in his office where you're not supposed to touch anything, you see a book called *Vietnam*, and it's as thick as a dictionary and it has a glossy green cover. At random you open it up and flip. In the middle of a sentence is something about sex so you start to read quick. And then you wish you didn't. You slam it shut. You creep out of the office. You close your eyes and imagine anything else, and for a second the shattered starshape of your mosque window flashes to the rescue and you cling tight and you wish on it and you wish that you hadn't read anything at all. Please, you think, and you try to push the devastation shoved out through the sharp hole the same way you try to push out the sound of horns and shouts when you say prayer. Please, you think, but it doesn't work and nothing swoops in to rescue you.

Sex ed is only one quarter so that for kids like you, whose parents won't sign the release form, you don't miss much. Instead of switching midsemester, you take the biology unit twice and you become a bit of an expert on seed germination. Lucy tells you everything anyway. Boys get wet dreams and girls get cramps, what's that all about? she says. You look at her handouts of enormous outlined fallopian tubes and it just sort of looks like the snout of a cow's face and you don't see what the big deal is. You do ask, though, Is there a way to make your boobs grow? And Lucy says that Jackie already asked and no, there isn't. Too bad. Then Lucy says, I must, I must, I must increase my bust! And then you call her a Horndog and she calls you a Major Skank and then you both bust up laughing.

When it happens it happens in the stall at McDonald's. Paula Abdul is tinny on the loudspeaker. Lucy's mom asks what kind of hamburger you want and you say you don't eat meat, it has to be fish filet, please. With sweet-and-sour sauce, please. Then Lucy says, Grody! and then you and Lucy go off to the bathroom together and while she's talking to you about the kinds of jeans that Bongo makes, and every different color that there is, and how if you got scrunchies to match, wouldn't that be cool? you're in the stall and you realize it like a loose tooth. Lucy, oh my god Lucy, check this out, wow! It happened!

Are you serious? she says. Are you serious? Oh my god, are you sure?

I'm sure, you say, and you breathe in big chalky breaths that stink of bathroom hand soap, powdered pink. When you guys come back to the table and you eat your meal it seems like a whole different thing being in the world. And it is.

That night you ask your mom if you can stay home from school on account of the occasion. She doesn't let you. She does ask you if you want to try her hijab on, though, and you don't tell her about Aslana's. Shala, she says, Shala, I don't know about right now. This

just may not be the time. But it has to be your choice. You don't
have to if you don't want to, but you do have to ask yourself how do
you represent yourself now as a Muslim woman in this country
where they think that Muslims are not like you, Shala, and when
you choose this, Shala, you are showing them that they know you
and that you are nice and that you are no crazy, no religious nut.
You are only you, and that is a very brave thing to show the world.

Now when you guys walk home, you're way more careful about
not trusting any cars to do anything you expect them to. When you
get to the 7-Eleven, you try different ways of scamming a five-
finger discount on the Slurpees. The woman behind the counter
hates kids. Timing is everything. Here's how it goes: One person
buys and you mix every color all together and try to pass from
mouth to mouth and suck it gone before it melts. It's hard because
of brain freeze. You try to refill and pass off, which the woman
says counts as stealing and is not allowed, but that's only when she
catches you. Trick is, you have to look like you're alone when you
buy the cup or she'll be on to you and then she'll turn around and
watch the machine. So everyone else has to stand outside with the
bum named Larry and then go in one by one and sit on the floor
reading trashy magazines about eye shadow while the buyer waits
in line. Today that's you. You wait in line. You've got the collective
seventy-nine cents in your hand. You freeze your face still into a
mask of passivity and innocence.

As the trapped hot dogs roll over, sweating on their metal coils,
you hear the two men in front of you discussing politics and waiting with their own single flavor Slurpees already filled to the brim
and ready to be paid for in full.

Same goddamn ground war we had in 'Nam, and hell knows
nobody wants to see their baby come home in a body bag. Hey.

The way I see it is, you got two choices, right? Nuke the towel-
heads, use your small bombs, ask your questions later, or what you
do is convert.

With you on the first one, buddy.

No, no listen: *convert*. Hell yeah, whole country. To Islam. To
mighty Allah.

Shit, man, you and the rag-heads?

But I got a point, right? Right? 'Cause what'd you think these fuckers want? Right? Oh yeah, hey uh, pack of Lucky Strikes, huh? And how 'bout Superlotto? Yeah, one of those, thanks.

Next: you. You try to gauge how much this straggly woman sees. Can she tell? Muslim? Mexican? Does she know that your clothes are Trendy, that your grades are Dweeby, that your heart is Goody-goodie? Your face: unreadable, innocent, frozen. One Slurpee. Please.

You walk around the counter and toward the magazines and when your friends see you, you try to look triumphant and cool and with it. But you feel like a cheat. Like maybe if it is stealing, you might not be such a good Muslim, you might be letting your kind of people look bad.

Not *stealing*, says Lucy. Sharing. It's just sharing.

So you share. You slurp cherry-cola-blueberry-cherry layers until your forehead aches. Then Jackie opens up her mouth and throws her head back and gets down on her knees and another girl pulls the knob and you all stop to watch the Slurpee slurped straight from the machine. Gross, someone says, but you're all impressed with the inventiveness and Jackie's daredevil status is elevated in everyone's eyes.

Oh, for Christssake! Give me a break! You goddamn good-for-nothing kids, get out of here! Get! Never again! You're banned, you hear me? Banned! Out! Get out!

Scatter giggling and shrieking across the parking lot, and the very next day dare each other to go back like nothing happened and you know you can because you know she can't tell the difference between any of you anyway. You could be anyone for all she knows.

The day you try it out as a test, someone yanks hard from behind and when it gets ripped off your head a lot of hair does too. You think about how when hard-ass what-up girls fight they both stop first and take out all their earrings. It hurts enough to make you cry but you try hard not to. Please don't let me cry, please, please don't let me cry. First period, and Taylor Bryans sees your chubby lower lip tremble and he remembers the time you corrected his wrong answer in front of the whole class (Not pods! *Seeds!* Duh!) and he starts up a tough game of Shala-Snot-Germs and the cooties spread from hand to hand all around the room as your face gets hotter and hotter and your eyeballs sting and your nose drips in sorrow. Your dignity gathers and mounts as you readjust the scarf and re-pin the pin. You can't see anyone pass germs, you can't hear anyone say your name. You are stone. You are cool. You will not cry. Those are not tears. The bell rings.

Then the bell rings six more times at the end of six periods and when you get home that day you have had the hijab yanked on seven occasions, four times in first period, and you've had your feet stomped twice by Taylor Bryans in the lunch line, and after school a group of eighth-graders, all of them past puberty and huge with breasts in bras, surrounded you to gawk and tug in unison. And you've made up your mind about the hijab. It stays. No matter what. The fury coils in your veins like rattlesnake lava, the chin pushes out to be held high, the face is composed and impervious and a new dignity is born outraged where there used to be just Shala's self-doubt. It stays, you think. No matter what.

Still, at home you cry into your mom's sari and you shout at her like she's one of the merciless. I'm just regular, you wail. I'm the same as I ever was!

Oh, baby, come on, shhh, it's going to be okay, she says. And then your mom suggests that maybe right now might not be the right time to start wearing this. She assures you that you are okay either way, that you can just take it off and forget about it. She says all this, sure, but she wears hers knotted firmly underneath her own chin as she strokes your back with reassurance.

That night, before you get into bed, you think about your brother and what it must be like for him. You look in the bathroom mirror and you slip the hijab on over your young hair and you watch like magic as you're transformed into a woman right before your very eyes. You watch like magic as all of the responsibilities and roles shift and focus.

You get it both ways. In your own country you have to worry, you have to get your hair pulled. And in India there you are: the open target, so obvious with your smooth American feet and your mini Nike backpack, the most hated. With anger and envy and danger all around you. The most hated. The most spoiled. An easy mark. A tiny girl. With every thing in the world, and all of it at your disposal.

You think about your brother and you wonder if he's scared.

As you get dressed for bed you check things out with a hand mirror. You poke at the new places you hadn't looked at before. You look at the shape in the hand mirror and you think, Hello, me. It's embarrassing even though it's only you. You feel a whole new feeling. You think about how much you hate Taylor Bryans. Indignation rises up like steam. You stand there in the bathroom with blood on your hands and you know it. I am Muslim, you think, I am Muslim, hear me roar.

In third-period PE the waves of hot Valley sun bake off the black-top asphalt and from a distance you see squiggly lines of air bent into mirage and your head is cooking underneath the scarf and your ears feel like they're burning in the places where they touch the cloth and your hair is plastered to the back of your neck with sticky salty sweat and when you group up for teams, someone yanks hard. You topple right over. You scrape your knees and through the blood they're smudged sooty black. Everyone turns around to look, and a bunch of girls laugh quietly behind hands. The hijab is torn from where the pin broke loose and your dad is right, it's way better that it isn't a knot or you might choke. Your neck is wet with a hair-strand of blood from where the popped-open pin tip slipped along skin. And you figure, That's it. Forget it. I quit. I'm ditching. I hate you.

Someone says, Aw shit, girl, you okay?

You scramble up and walk tall and leave the girls in their bagged-out PE uniforms and you go back into the cool dank locker room where you can get naked all by yourself for once. As you wash the gravel out of your hands you stare at yourself in the mirror. You think Bloody Mary and squeeze your eyes shut tight, but when you open them it's still just your face all alone with rows and rows of lockers. No demon to slice you down.

Now when you walk in late you're not Nobody anymore, you're not Anyone At All. Instead, now, when you walk in you have to brace yourself in advance, and you have to summon up a courage and a dignity that grows strong when your eyes go dull and you stare into unfocused space inches away while Taylor Bryans and Fernando Cruz snicker and snicker until no one's looking and then they run up and shout in your face: Arab! Lard-ass! Damn, you so ugly you ooogly!

Your inner reserves fill to full when Fernando stomps on your feet and your white Reeboks get all smeared up and your face doesn't even move no matter how much it hurts.

The bell rings. Lunch. You push and shove your way into the cluster of the Girls' Room, and there's no privacy and you try to peer into the tagged-up piece of dull-shine metal that's bolted to the wall where everyone wants a mirror, but there are girls applying mascara and girls with lip liner and the only air is a fine wet mist of aerosol Aqua Net and it's too hard to breathe and you can't see if it's still pinned straight, because that last snatch was like an afterthought and it didn't even tug all the way off. But you can't make your way up to the reflection and you can't see for sure. So here it comes, and then you're standing there in the ebb and flow of shoulders and sneakers and all of a sudden here it comes and you're sobbing like you can't stop.

Hey girl, why you crying? You want me to kick some motherfucker's ass for you, girl? 'Cause I'll do it, bitch, I'm crazy like that. You just show me who, right, I'll do it, homegirl.

And through your tears you want to throw your arms around the giant mountainous chola and her big-hearted kindness and you want to kiss her Adidas and you want to say Taylor Bryans's name and you want to point him out and you want his ass kicked hard, but you stop yourself. You picture the outcome, you picture the humiliation he'd feel, a skinny sixth-grader, a scrub, the black eye, the devastation of public boy-tears, the horror of having someone who means it hit you like an avalanche. You look over your back and past all the girl-heads, the stiff blondes and permed browns and braided weaves, the dye jobs, the split ends, all of them elbowing and pushing in to catch a dull distorted glimpse in graffitied monochrome, and you smooth over the folds of your safe solid black hijab and you snuffle up teary dripping snot and you picture what it would be.

You picture her rush him: Hey BITCH, yeah I'm talking to you, *pendejo,* that's right you better run outta my way whiteboy, cuz I'm going to whup your ass, punk-ass motherfucker! You picture her and she's like a truck. Taylor Bryans stops cold and then he startles and turns to flee but she's already overcome him like a landslide, and she pounds him like muddy debris crushing someone's million-dollar home. You picture the defeat, the crowd of jeering kids, Fight! Fight! Fight! The tight circle of locked arms, elbow in elbow so the teachers can't break it up, the squawk of adult walkie-talkies and then the security guards, the assistant principal, and all the teachers on yard duty, all of them as one, all charging over to haul kids out of the fray and into detention, and all the while you can picture him like he's a photograph in your hand: the tears, the scrapes, the bruises, the giant shame in his guilty nasty eyes and you know that it wouldn't solve a thing and you suspect that it probably wouldn't even stop him from pulling your hair out and stomping on your feet and you picture it and you open up your heart and you forgive him.

Then you gather up all that new dignity, and then you look up at her, stick your covered head out of the girls' bathroom, and point.

DYLAN LANDIS

■

Rana Fegrina

FROM *Tin House*

LORELEI YASSKY keeps a switchblade in her sock.

Lorelei Yassky has B.O.

Lorelei Yassky did it in her parents' bed and a week later they had crabs so bad they were in their *armpits*.

The Gospel of Lorelei Yassky is graven into desks with house keys and the blood of Bics; it is written in the glances of girls — low arcs of knowing that span the hallways and ping off the metal lockers.

Lorelei Yassky walks with her books soldered to her chest.

Lorelei Yassky bites her nails until a quarter-moon of roseate nail bed rises at the top of each finger. When she laughs, her eyes narrow; the laugh is bitter and quick in her throat.

Lorelei Yassky once stuck a hot dog up inside herself and couldn't get it out and her parents had to drive her to the hospital.

Lorelei Yassky eats lunch with two older girls: Ivy, who has a forehead broad as a man's, and a girl whose brother Keith went to jail for almost killing a guy. Ivy and the other girl are blond the way Lorelei is blond, with ribbons of brown raveling along their side parts. They are juniors. They could get Keith to fuck you up. No one calls them a slut.

In the beginning is the word and there is no making it go away. Leah's finger polishes the dark scars in her honeyed desk: the jagged s, the glottal LUT. The word is appended to the initials L.Y. In Leah's mind the name LORELEI is a ribbon unfurling. She traces the secretive o and the lascivious curl of that EI at the end, like the tip of someone's tongue.

When she gets tired of reading her desk she tries reading Mr. Jabor's T-shirt backwards, searching for hidden meaning. Forwards it says I'D RATHER BE WRITING MY NOVEL in inky typewriter type.

Mr. Jabor's hair stands straight up, which is why he cuts it to a fuzz. His arms jut from his sleeves like splints and he has earnest knees, perpetually bent. Mr. Jabor is the only teacher Leah knows who comes to work in sneakers. She gets a good look at them because she sits in the second row, and Mr. Jabor reads poetry standing on his desk.

The kids are supposed to call him Rick.

"Walt is not just another dead poet, ladies and gentlemen," Rick says. A cigarette bobs and jabs in the corner of his mouth. The freshman English class stares at him much of the time, waiting for him to light up. Sometimes he does.

"Listen to this," says Rick. "This is so good it'll make you want to pee in your pants."

Leah considers the option. In three and a half periods she will have to carve something far more elemental than a word into the thoracic-abdominal cavity of *Rana Fegrina,* a creature as tender and green as a gingko leaf. Everyone will look at her because she got a bad lab partner, a partner who has been held back and has B.O., and this will somehow appear to be Leah's fault and she will have to mouth-breathe for the entire fifty-five minutes.

The atmosphere is not a perfume, says Rick, his knees shooting off little sparks with each bounce. *It has no taste of the distillation, it is odorless, it is for my mouth forever, I am in love with it.*

Rick's sneakers squeak on his desk and Leah looks away. She hates Rick's sneakers for being so excitable and sympathetic and she hates the name Walt.

Rick has been reading poetry to them all semester, Coleridge who was an opium addict and John Donne whose son died, and the one who peed in his pants over a Grecian urn, Keats. No matter what Rick says, Leah cannot name one thing that poetry heals. For example, poetry does not heal adenocarcinoma of the lung. Leah's father smells like formaldehyde and he's still alive, and that is a mystery not even Walt can explain.

She writes on the inside cover of her notebook: *Rana Levinson. Leah Fegrina. Rana Leah Fegrina.*

I will go to the bank by the wood and become undisguised and naked, says Rick. *I am mad for it to be in contact with me.*

Leah hears tittering. Peripheral movement of hands, a shard of briefly floating white: A note is being passed. Leah does not have the kind of school friendships that involve communication by note, or even, for the most part, by speech. This is due partly to being a girl five-nine with acutely red hair, which causes people to look at her, which causes her to think that large bells are clanging above her head.

Rick grips his book with both hands, like a preacher. "This man is talking about rejoicing in the physical universe," he says. "Are you listening? Because some of you really need to hear this." *My respiration and inspiration, the beating of my heart, the passing of blood and air through my lungs.*

It is thirty seconds to 10:35. Even Rick can see that. The instant his shoulders deflate, backpacks slam onto desks; fingers fly over clasps.

"Wait!" yells Rick. "Gimme one thing you learned from Walt. One thing."

"Get naked in the woods," says Andy Sak.

Leah doesn't turn around because Andy Sakellarios is too lovely to look at directly, just as when Leah's father opens his eyes anymore in his metal bed and looks directly at his daughter, she has to study a crease in the sheet. The crease floats over his chest like the ghost of his scar. Leah knows that Andy Sak's mouth is slightly open, like a cup. She knows that the curvature of his skull is elegant in the way that mathematicians use the word.

"Yeah?" says Rick. "You're close. Relish the natural world, and remember that you are a part of it."

*

Kingdom Animalia. Subkingdom Metazoa. Section Deuterostomia. Phylum Chordata. Subphylum Vertebrata. These are the places where Leah seeks beauty: in the classification of living things, in books arranged by height, in closets with hangers precisely one and one-half inches apart and clothing zoned by color. She seeks purity in the blamelessness of a clean-swept desk. She seeks forgiveness in each new sheet of loose-leaf paper. Class Amphibia. Order Anura. Biological name Rana Fegrina of the long green hands.

They've had three days to memorize the exact position of the frog in the biological universe. Leah was born with the words in her bones; she took ten minutes.

"Remember the finger-prick?" says Mr. Lack. "If you had trouble with the finger-prick, raise your hand."

The arms of girls shoot into the air. Leah's rises halfway. A few boys who had trouble with the finger-prick start shoving, or maybe it's the word that gets them going. Not *finger*. The other one. Lorelei Yassky doesn't raise her hand. She's ransacked the dissection kit without waiting for instructions and is stroking the scalpel down the inside of her arm, dragging it lightly, almost weightlessly, so no weal of red unrolls behind it.

Leah takes a small step back.

"Those of you with hands aloft," says Mr. Lack, clasping his own behind his back and strolling among the lab tables, "may have a little trouble with today's dissection. For this subpopulation I have one piece of advice." He gathers the moment. "Get over it," he says.

Leah watches the point of the scalpel whisper across Lorelei Yassky's wrist.

"Get over it, people," says Mr. Lack. "Be glad the frogs are dead. In my day we pithed our frogs." He holds an invisible needle high in the air and stirs.

Lorelei dips her head. "That's the eighth plague," she says behind a curtain of hair. "Pithing frogs."

Rana Fegrina is larger than Leah expected; he is nearly the size of her hand, with limbs extended in full leap. Did he die this way, or did they flatten him under a book? Most of his green has drained away. Chlorophyll, Leah thinks stupidly, as Mr. Lack turns and strolls down her aisle.

"And any girl who utters the words 'Eew, it's so gross,' regardless of intonation, loses ten points," says Mr. Lack. He wheels around, guided by sonar. "Boys lose twenty-five," he snaps. "And *Miss* Yassky, please desist from the dissection of your own hand."

Lorelei lowers the scalpel until it is the merest inch above the lab table. Then she drops it. It sounds like a tiny piece of glass breaking.

"Miss Yassky joins us for the second year," says Mr. Lack.

The top of Leah's head bursts into flame. She takes another step back. Lorelei spreads her fingers, revealing a small red smear in the vicinity of her lifeline. Then she hides it in her fist.

"Open your kits," says Mr. Lack, "pin the frog, and decide which among you shall make the first cut."

Leah is now standing four feet from her partner. It won't do. She steps closer to Lorelei. All she smells is formaldehyde. Rana Fegrina, on his back on the dissection tray, looks up at her through the blind eye of his belly.

"I'll pin if you cut," whispers Leah, looking at the frog instead of at Lorelei.

"I cut last year," says Lorelei.

Lorelei's voice has exactly the same drape as her hair. Leah can't tell if she's being ironic. Also, she has never stood this close to a slut. She thought a slut would have yellow teeth. She wants to check Lorelei's teeth and sniff her neck and rifle her backpack for notes and pierce the curtain of hair with her finger, as if breaking the sleek vane of a feather.

She wants to say: Is it true?

"I'll do absolutely everything if you just cut," says Leah, frantic. As a sign of good faith she plucks up the first pin and positions it over Rana Fegrina's gray-green palm. She has to duck her head so she won't see it break the skin. Instead she concentrates on Lorelei Yassky's bellbottoms. They are perfect, these bellbottoms. They clump over Lorelei's sneakers in front, and in back they're frayed from being stood on. The jeans taper and flare as if they had been breathed onto Lorelei Yassky by God.

Leah counts to twenty for each of the four pins, two for the hands and two for the feet. Rana Fegrina does not struggle.

"Look at him," says Lorelei. "He died for your sins. You know what's weird about frogs?"

"Are you going to cut?" says Leah. Her voice is a handkerchief fluttering on a twig. She clears her throat. She wonders if there is such a thing as pushing Lorelei too far.

"What's weird about frogs," says Lorelei, "is they only recognize food when it moves. You set a dead fly in front of a frog, he'll fucking starve."

Leah imagines Rana Fegrina crouched before his dinner — a fly sizzling on a tiny white plate, size of a fingernail. Rana Fegrina secretes an ancient green wisdom through his pores. Rana Fegrina knows that time is a circle. Rana Fegrina knows that all things will pass. Rana Fegrina knows that sometimes a girl has to wait in the hall because her father is going to the bathroom in his bed. Rana Fegrina knows where the love goes when the body dies. The frog's thoughts coil along his hidden tongue, deadly as a bullwhip.

Leah decides to attempt a string of sentences.

"My mother's like that," she says. "She only recognizes food when it has no calories. If you put a steak in front of my mother she'd starve too."

Lorelei picks up the scissors in her right hand and, with the tweezers in her left, nips up the skin above Rana Fegrina's groin. She doesn't read the directions; she's done this before.

"My mother's a heifer," says Lorelei. She wrinkles her nose, jabs a scissor-blade into the pickled skin, and snips, unzipping the body cavity. "You put a steak in front of my mother she'll ask for thirds."

The heart of Rana Fegrina is a five-chambered thing. Three chambers have walls like the webbing between Rana's toes: the sinus venosus, the right auricle, and the left auricle. But two chambers are muscled like a father's bicep: the ventricle and the truncus arteriosus.

The heart of Rana Fegrina contains doors that open in one direction only.

The heart of Rana Fegrina cannot be broken. It can only be stopped.

What Leah suddenly notices, as she unsettles the liver with her probe and exposes the tiny purse of a gallbladder, is how Lorelei leans in so close that crabs could even now be leaping from her hair to Leah's. She imagines the crabs as a matrix of tiny translucent spiders so that if she were to actually look, Lorelei Yassky's pubes and scalp might appear to be a moving, shimmering mass.

She holds her breath.

"God, how do they get all these organs in one friggin' frog," says Lorelei.

Leah wonders if disgust is not that different from awe. She prods the gallbladder, marks it on her lab sheet. She says, "I think it's kind of beautiful."

"You need a doctor," says Lorelei.

"I just mean —" The probe starts trembling. She tucks the gallbladder back into its bed between the lobes. "I just mean the frog has everything it needs to be a frog," says Leah.

"You need an ambulance," says Lorelei.

"No, listen," says Leah, desperate to make sense. What is it her mother says? A perfect room has everything it needs and nothing else; it has a fireplace and a sofa and good lighting — but this is nothing Lorelei would want to hear.

Lorelei smirks. It is a sound she makes in her nose. "Have it your way," she says.

Leah looks at the wreckage that is Rana Fegrina, the flaps of belly-skin spread and pinned, the tumble of innards unspooled. She thinks of her jewelry box, dumped out on her bed.

"Ugly-beautiful," says Leah.

"Huh," says Lorelei.

Leah nudges a small nugget with the probe, holds it there in case Lorelei wants to see. But Lorelei is looking into the cup of her palm. "Kidney?" says Leah.

"Look, don't wait for me," says Lorelei. The edge of her knife is in her voice. Leah understands suddenly that the knife is a thing deep inside Lorelei; it is not a thing you would find in her sock.

Leah withdraws the probe. She slides her lab sheet into a central position on the table, so Lorelei can see. On the sheet is a mimeographed drawing of Rana, splayed and radiating lines from the organs. At the end of each line is another line for the organ's name. Leah has filled in most of hers.

Pancreas, she writes.

When Lorelei copies she could be filling in a grocery list. She drops the *r* from pancreas. The red smear in her palm stays hidden as she writes, a stain in the chamber of a shell.

"I could help you," Leah says.

"You missed stuff," says Lorelei, pushing the lab sheet toward Leah with the eraser end of her pencil.

Ureter. Cloaca.

"I could," says Leah. "For the final." Because now she sees something inside herself as clearly as she sees the knife in Lorelei: one single ability, the classification of living things, that could maybe save a person's life. Lorelei calls to her from under the waves, and she, Leah, walks into the water. Lorelei sits alone and wide-legged on a low wall after lunch, and Leah is the one who stops, extends a pack of Winstons. Other kids stare at them but they are safe in a fold of shadow, and Leah believes it is the shadow of Keith. Lorelei saying, *You'll get a reputation if you hang with me.* Lorelei saying: *I never had a friend like you.*

"Give it up," says Lorelei, her writing hand still in a nautilus around the pencil. "I got a D on the midterm."

Lorelei whispering: *The whole hot dog thing, Ivy started that, it was all a big lie.*

"I could tutor you," says Leah. "For nothing. I could get you a B."

She watches Lorelei yank the pins from Rana Fegrina and walk across the room with the tray. She watches Rana Fegrina slide into the trash as if he had never lived. She wonders what the body releases when it dies; she wonders if there is something she has forgotten to say.

"Wake up," says Lorelei. "It's next fucking Wednesday."

It takes Leah a minute to realize they are still talking about the final. She tries to look Lorelei in the eye. She almost gets there, but the machinery stops when she is looking at Lorelei's mouth.

Lorelei saying, *Trust me.* Her breath sweet.

"I could do it," Leah says. "After school. I just have to go home first."

This is not exactly true. The apartment is empty. Her mother will wait in a green vinyl hospital chair with a book on French furniture until they take away her husband's tray. Leah goes home every day and cleans her room because it is a thing she has to do. She works from a list of rotating jobs — burnish desk with lemon oil, dust behind books, line books up like teeth along edge of shelf, clean inside bureau drawers, recouple socks. By Saturday morning her room quivers like a heart in its new skin so that she is afraid to touch anything.

Lorelei looks at the ceiling as if seeking patience in the perforated tile. The movement slides the blunt gold edge of her hair down to the bone-wings on her back. Then she starts writing a number on a corner of Leah's lab sheet. Leah yanks it away. A green film glides down over Lorelei's expression like the secret eyelid of a cat.

"He'll make me do it over," Leah says.

They are not allowed to have notebooks at the lab tables. Leah pushes up her sleeve. Lorelei Yassky is halfway through the ballpoint tattoo of her home address when Leah detects it — the small, sharp twang of seaweed and salt.

Low tide.

She filters it through her memory.

It is the smell of seaweed thirsting on the sand; it is the smell of the horseshoe crab's shell after the crab has been returned to the physical universe.

It is the smell of Rana Fegrina, disemboweled for her sins.

It is the smell of Phisohex after the patient has been bathed — sponged and rolled and patted dry behind the curtain by a nurse in sympathetic shoes, a nurse who talks as if tending a frightened child.

It is gray ammonia sloshed from an orderly's yellow bucket, it is the Sea Breeze her mother strokes onto her father's slackening neck.

It is the smell of the body releasing. It is a tinge of lemony sweat.

It is the smell of B.O., though Leah cannot be certain whether it is Lorelei's or her own, and Whitman is wrong: The atmosphere is a perfume. It tastes of the distillation. She is in love with it, it is the beating of her heart.

ANDREA LEE

■

Golden Chariot

FROM *Zoetrope*

A musical comedy, or traveling minstrel show, starring a middle-class American Negro family and their brand-new 1962 metallicized Rambler Classic. All of them headed on an epic summer vacation trip across America, from Philadelphia to the Seattle World's Fair.

TIME:

August 3–24, 1962

CHARACTERS:

EARL B. HARMON, Ed.D., a high school principal
GRACE HARMON, his wife, elementary school teacher
WALKER HARMON, their son, a college freshman
RICHIE HARMON, their second son, age fourteen
MAUD HARMON, their daughter, age ten
THE GOLD RAMBLER CLASSIC

MUSIC:

No gospel, Dixieland, bebop, do-wop, ragtime, Delta blues, rhythm and blues, Memphis sound, Philly Soul, or Motown. Just 1962 summer AM middle-of-the-dial radio. Especially three songs: "Portrait of My Love," by Steve Lawrence; "Things (We Used to Do)," by Bobby Darin; and "Sealed with a Kiss," by Brian Hyland. These songs play over and over again, fading in and out of the pebbly roar of static that joins cities and towns, ranchland and mountains. The static is the real music.

Scene I

Sunrise. Somewhere heading away from Philadelphia on the Pennsylvania Turnpike. DR. EARL HARMON is driving the Rambler while the rest of the family sleeps around him. The roadsides in the burgeoning light are dense with Virginia creeper, and the speeding car shines like molten gold. The peaceful hills are dotted with black-and-white Mennonite cows.

DR. HARMON: Oh, it's the AAA that gives us the bedrock of security, the courage to take this leap. American Automobile Association. The name inspires confidence. All those A's, like the NAACP. The opposite of the KKK. The AAA guidebook tells us that it includes only hotels, motels, inns, Travelodges, campsites, and guesthouses where, and I quote, "no discrimination is made according to race, color, or creed." And there you are, there's the whole country open to us, like one big guesthouse. They can't slam the door in your face if they're in the guide.

Avoiding humiliation, that's been the thing. I'm roughly the color of Gandhi, but I would never go around in sandals and a diaper or flop down and let some Mississippi cracker spit on me. Oh, I went down to Birmingham because it was the right thing to do, but I kept well in the middle of the ranks as we marched along down streets lined with what looked like zoo animals to me. It was really just Southern white folks, offering their famous hospitality. They were howling for nigger blood, but it wasn't going to be mine. I made sure I was protected by a solid wall of sharecroppers, and then later I headed up a first-aid station where we treated the minor wounds of confrontation, my smooth brown hands on my simpler brothers' work-roughened skin. *Ebony* published a photo of me wearing a Red Cross armband, my brilliantined hair rippling back like Desi Arnaz's, an old black Alabama church deacon staring at me like I was the savior of the world.

Not everyone has to confront. I swallowed enough humiliation for a lifetime in Philadelphia when Mordecai Jackson and I were the first colored students at Central High, and they used to take fresh shit, I suppose it was their own, and put it in our lockers, in our desks, in our lunch bags, in our gym suits. Months of shit. There were some white boys with prolific intestines in that school, or maybe they bought it by the pound.

Now I live in a suburb where I don't have to smell shit unless they're spreading it on a lawn, in a five-bedroom fieldstone Colonial that the slick Irish realtor who was busy changing the neighborhood gave away to me for eighteen thousand the way he gave houses away to Hobell Butler and Melvin Duran and all the other Negro dentists and judges and preachers and doctors who left the old Philadelphia row-house neighborhoods to the poor niggers from the South. We're in a greener ghetto, and we like the walls. My oldest boy is in a good Protestant college, and the other two are on scholarship in private school, and my wife doesn't have to work if she doesn't want to. Education and integration are the keys to the future, as I tell the seniors at my school; and my kids have the future unlocked, with ushers handing them in.

It's time to give them the biggest present: the country. Not the South, where the air stinks of barbecued black flesh, but the West, the direction the covered wagons rolled. And in a gold car that's not one of those niggerish Cadillacs or Lincolns, but a Rambler, begotten by American Motors. Discreet luxury, one of the new metallic paint jobs, and a padded dash. Praise the Lord, as my mother would say, we are rolling toward the Pacific in a sort of temple, elect, protected under the signs of American Motors and AAA. Safe, as usual. Safe.

Scene II

Route 2, along the southern edge of Lake Michigan, between Sault Sainte Marie and Ironwood, Michigan. About three in the afternoon of the third day. Beyond fields and woods come occasional glimpses of the lake in dry brilliant sunshine. MAUD HARMON, in the back seat, opens her mouth in the air rushing in from the front, and lets the wind dry her tongue.

MAUD: A good thing about this trip is the bottle caps. Coca-Cola is having a contest in honor of the World's Fair and what they do is print a picture of a different city of the world in each bottle cap — you just peel the cork, and there it is: Bangkok, Paris, Amsterdam. Whenever we stop at a gas station, I dash over to the Coke machine and worm my hand down into the hole where the caps drop down after people open their Cokes. I'm lucky I have skinny hands. I have dozens of bottle caps now, my pockets rattle. I have all the countries now except Brazil and Denmark, they didn't print any of Russia because they're Communists. It's for a contest, but I don't think about that, I just like having all those cities. I like things that make you think about anything far away, whether it's other countries or millions of years ago. Among the books I brought with me is one about Marco Polo and another about digging up fossil men in Africa. Another is *Ivanhoe*. Sometimes I dream that I'm flying over the heads of my mother and father and brothers, gone somewhere else. They're sad but I'm not.

There was a big storm last night, which was our second night away from home. We were in a town called Mackinaw, which is a name that makes me think of old fish and worn-out raincoats, in a white little house that was part of a sort of motel near Lake Huron where the floor, if the three of us kids stood in one place, caved in about five inches, and where we had to wash the plates in the kitchen part *before* we ate dinner. Mom fixed minute steaks and corn on the cob and sliced tomatoes and the wind howled like a ghost story and the house shook like a giant was slapping it back and forth and I was disappointed that the roof didn't blow off.

In the morning I went outside before anybody else and met a white boy on the shore of the lake where the waves were slamming down like ocean waves. This boy came out of the bushes and he had a long green man's jacket that came down over his spindly legs like toothpicks, and hair cut so short it looked like a smudge on his head. He said his name was Spencer and that his dad owned land beside the lake and then asked like a retard was I a Negro. I said no I was a Polish Chink from Bessarabia, which was a joke I got from my oldest brother, Walker, and then I told him we were going to the World's Fair, and that's our car I said, that new gold one. It was funny to be talking to a white boy in the summer. I'm used to them at school, but we don't see each other after school or in vacations. This Spencer was quiet for a minute and said he'd show me something, and then he showed me that almost all the rocks on the shore had fossils in them, shells and sponges and trilobites. I picked up about fifteen fossils until my mother called me to come in and get my hair braided, and then it was time to eat breakfast and drive off in our golden chariot and leave old Spencer there waving like a little white doll in the middle of all of his million-year-old shells. See you later, alligator, I said. I felt sorry for him, stuck there while we set off to see the world.

Scene III

Bemidji, Minnesota. RICHIE HARMON stands at the foot of the giant statue of Paul Bunyan and his blue ox, Babe. Sixth day, about eleven in the morning. In the distance, paddleboats on Lake Bemidji.

RICHIE: Well, eighth grade history was good for something. I know the Mississippi starts here. At least I think it does. This would be a great home movie, but this cheap family doesn't even own a movie camera. Our friends do, but not us. Our mother says it's more educational to look than to take pictures so we're traveling with the oldest Kodak in the U.S.A., and we get to take a few crummy slides. On the *Wonderful World of Color,* people in the commercials are always filming each other in front of Pikes Peak or the Golden Gate Bridge. And what are we doing? We're not even modern. In exactly eight years, when I'm finished with high school and college, I'm going to be a famous photographer and I'll have the best equipment there is.

Nowadays, I buy photo magazines to check up on the new cameras, and because they're good for nudes. Every issue you get has two or three good ones. All the girls in the photo pix are white, the way all the girls in *Playboy* are, the way everybody is, everywhere in the movies, on TV, in everything we watch or read. I know five or six really cute Negro girls from our neighborhood or those pathetic Jack and Jill parties, girls so fine I'm half scared to ask them to dance or to say anything to them, but somehow they don't seem as real as the white girls in the pictures that make you touch yourself. It's like they exist less. It's like our family exists less than *Father Knows Best* or *Leave It to Beaver*. We're going across the continental United States of America in this fabulous car, but it's like no one can see us. It's too bad that we didn't bring a movie camera. We could make a television show of ourselves.

Scene IV

Eighth day. Devils Lake, North Dakota. Sunset in a motel parking lot with arid hills beyond. GRACE HARMON stands in front of stacked wooden boxes of empty soda bottles.

GRACE: These wide spaces scare me. The light is too strong. I feel unwelcome, caught like a cockroach out in the open. I like small places inside, places like my shiny kitchen when I have pots on all the burners and everything under control, the smell of greens cooking with ham bones, of chicken roasting, of yeast rolls and tapioca pudding. Or church, when the service has just finished, and we ladies are all standing in our gloves and hats à la Jackie Kennedy, and greeting each other and chatting so close that you can smell everyone's Arpège perfume and Alberto VO5 hair cream. There is a sense of salvation, and relief, because the Holy Word is still floating around us in the air, and yet we're all going home to eat soon.

Once when I was still a student at Philadelphia Normal School, I sat next to Eleanor Roosevelt at a tea to benefit the work camps, and she said to me that I must try to see as much as I could of this great country of ours. She was kind, but like an elephant in pearls, and it made me angry that she didn't stop to think that most of our great country didn't want to see me.

And I had traveled. The year before that I went with my cousin Minerva down to Palm Beach to work the winter season as a butter-water girl at the Fontainebleau Hotel. That was an experience: the dining room long as a football field, with all those dried-out white faces bent over their food, with Minerva and I and all the other pretty colored girls in our ruffled caps, skimming round tables where never in our lives could we have sat down. The manager's son, who was our age, used to walk around in jodhpurs and riding boots, not saying anything, just looking us over with hard blue eyes. We felt naked. That's the way I feel now, standing here under this big sky.

Scene V

Glacier National Park, looking over the Canadian border toward Waterton Lakes National Park and Calgary. A curving highway through a swarm of snowcapped peaks, resonance of early afternoon light over heights and distant forests. WALKER HARMON is behind the wheel, smoking a cigarette.

WALKER: One Winston and they're on my ass. They haven't been uncool enough to say anything yet, but Mom is muttering to herself and staring out at the Rockies as if she'd like to bite them off, and Pop looks like I just punched him in the stomach. Well, it had to be done, it's ridiculous that I'm eighteen and in college and doing half the driving and can't act like the hell I want. I was a fool to come on this trip. The whole thing is a mistake. It shows what's wrong with this pitiful family. The fight for civil rights is in the South, so we go west on a sightseeing expedition. My roommates at Oberlin, Joel Kagan and Marty Hubbard, are both down in Greenville, Mississippi, registering voters. Joel's sister from Bryn Mawr is with them, she wears dancers' leotards and skirts from Mexico, and twists her hair up in a style called the Marienbad. White students are lining up to risk their lives, and what did I do?

I came home from college in June like a good son, worked a summer job in the mailroom at the *Philadelphia Bulletin,* and dated Ramona Jenkins, who has tits like dirigibles and allows a lot of heavy action with bra and panties firmly in place and is already talking about how she wants to marry a doctor. Instead of acting like a man and volunteering for SNCC, I came on this trip, with Pop sweating over his AAA guide, and practically shitting in his pants every night when he has to go to ask for a room in one of these little cow-town motels. Terrified that he's going to hear that word "nigger" that would sweep us right off the map of the U.S.A. Sweep his precious family right off to Oz, like a black tornado.

Scene VI

Seattle World's Fair. High noon. The whole HARMON FAMILY stands together in the crowd.

THE FAMILY: We are standing at the foot of the Space Needle, which was our goal. It's as tall as the Eiffel Tower, and there's a rotating restaurant up at the top. We won't go up because there's a long line, and it costs four dollars a person, and because we're not the kind of family that does things all the way to the end. This is enough for us. The Space Needle points to the *Sputniks,* to the stars. It's like part of a cartoon about the future, something we think we have wanted for a long time. A prize the president might have promised us as an inalienable right. A giant ultramodern suburban kitchen appliance out of a dream.

Scene VII

Heading back home. The FAMILY MEMBERS speak in turns.

MAUD: On the Oregon Coast the Pacific was tall gray waves that turned my feet numb when I waded. There were dead trees like goblin trees scattered on sand that came from volcanoes. My father and brothers peed against one of the trees, and my mother said: "Don't look." It was the end of the country, and I wanted to stay there forever. I kept some sand in a bottle. I'd never seen black sand before.

DR. HARMON: White fellow who ran the lodge where we stayed in the Bighorn Mountains, a Pacific Theater vet, kept going on and on about the Indians when I went to pay the bill, about how they were shiftless and drank and so on. I think the son of a bitch thought I was going to laugh and chime in. Out here, Indians are niggers. Once my brother Ray, the minister who's the straightest-haired one in the family, was traveling across Oklahoma with some kind of fool Baptist tour group, and in a little two-bit café, they refused to serve him. But then the owner kind of slid up to him and asked if it was true that he was an American Indian. "No," says Ray, figuring he's not going to eat anyway. "I'm an American Negro." Damn if the cracker didn't shut up, smile, and bring him his apple pie.

RICHIE: At Yellowstone, the best thing wasn't Old Faithful, which you could hardly see because there were so many people around, or the bubbling pink sulfur mud that would probably parboil your foot if you wanted to make the experiment, it was two girls that Walker and I met at the campground canteen. They were a pair of not very pretty white girls with hair the color of grass when the green is burnt out of it at the end of the summer, one of them with pimples and one with a bow clipped on over her bangs. They started talking to Walker, who was very cool and said he was a sophomore at Oberlin and that impressed them into wild giggles and "Oh," they said to me, "You look older than fourteen, you look at least twenty." They went crazy over the Golden Chariot, and I showed them how the front seats flipped all the way back. We would have taken them for a ride except Mom was waiting for the hot dogs. "They were ready, little brother," said Walker, who the whole time had had this sort of constipated look on his face, that he gets when he tries to act suave. "It's a new age, the great and glorious West, gateway to the future. Be cool and the white chicks will flock like pigeons, they think we've got the Space Needle between our legs."

GRACE: When we got to Cody, Wyoming, we stopped in a big

general store that had traps and skins hanging from the ceiling and dusty old pickup trucks in the parking lot and we went in and all three of the kids bought blue jeans. No one we know wears blue jeans, except for white teenagers on television. The kids walk differently now: they amble like cowboys; they look, even little Maud, as if they all of a sudden know about distances, as if they're about to gallop away from me into a Technicolor sunset.

THE FAMILY: In the Black Hills of South Dakota, we, the Harmon family and our new car, were present at a historic event: the first intercontinental television broadcast using the *Telstar* satellite. At the base of Mount Rushmore we stood in a crowd looking on as the huge indifferent sand-colored faces of the Founding Fathers traveled magically across outer space to Paris. The Harmons — latest issue of the combination of a few Mid-Atlantic coastal Indians with certain unwilling West Africans shipped abroad for profit by their own warlords, and lightly mixed with the largely undistinguished blood of English debtors and Irish bond servants — stood and cheered with the rest of the crowd watching itself on an outdoor screen. Though we still can't vote or eat or pee with white men in many states, we love our country. Didn't we learn patriotism at school? We feel enlarged by a sense of history and destiny, even though inside each of us, in the dark space at the very center, is a secret question mark.

MAUD: The U.S.A. is like a big board game, Monopoly or Clue. We've been following signs for days along the highway: Burma-Shave; Little Stinker; and ads for the Corn Palace, in Mitchell, South Dakota. There it is, smack in the middle of the country, a royal palace really built out of corn. Cars all around it from every state. And if you look up in the sky, clouds of crows just gobbling it up.

RICHIE: I've grown three inches since I turned fourteen, and I have the biggest appetite in the family. I've been eating my way across America, and I say that the best root beer floats on the road are at A&W and the best barbecue is the Piggly Wiggly chain. I won a bet with my sister by drinking four bottles of Coke in less than five minutes in the back seat, when we were driving through the Badlands. And, out of intellectual curiosity, I ordered shrimp in Iowa, thousands of miles from either ocean. In Chicago, we went out to a restaurant run by Jewish people, and it was the best place I ever ate in my life. Papa Stein's. When they brought the meat, it looked like a rib out of an elephant, and they even served pickles that were made from whole tomatoes. The real Papa Stein himself, a cool old white-haired guy with a Mad Professor accent, came over to our table to say hello. Like we were celebrities or something.

WALKER: In Chicago, I didn't go out to dinner with everybody else. I stayed in the hotel, which for once was a deluxe one, a Holiday Inn — three A's of course. I needed to get away from them all, to breathe. I wanted to think about how I could start living my own life. After a while, I opened the curtains, and you could see the streets just lighting up in purple dusk, and I turned on the radio, and a wild tune stole out of that radio that was like the breath of the city. Jazz like I've never heard before. Spilling out of some mysterious black heart hidden out there under the lights. I sat and smoked a Winston, and for a few minutes, everything fell into place. The family trip didn't bother me anymore: I knew it was the last time for me. And that I was where I needed to be.

THE FAMILY: And so we returned, dashing across the last few states to Philadelphia, overcome by a sudden desperate urge to sleep in our own beds. Back East, nothing much was changed. It was still August 1962, the cicadas still at their summer wars in the treetops. Our new car, unmarred by the dust of prairies and alkali flats, was still a sumptuous gold. Were we the same? That was a question not one of us, for a long time, would think to ask. Not until years had passed, and other, far more sophisticated vacations had been taken — jaunts to Europe and Africa and Asia, paid for by credit cards and boosting us to a palmy level of worldliness we'd never dreamed of. Not until we Harmon children had gone our separate ways, and looked back suddenly to realize that this was the trip by which we would always judge all others. A journey that defined the ambiguous shape of our citizenship, when we moved across our country feeling as apprehensive as foreigners and at the same time knowing that every grain of dust was ours. And a private moment of glory, the kind every family has just once. When the highway belonged to us, and our car was the best on the road. "Swing low, sweet chariot," sang Dr. Harmon for a joke, as we turned the corner of our suburban street. And the Rambler Classic carried us home.

J. T.   L E R O Y

■

Stuff

FROM 7 × 7

I AM HIGH on a combination of cleaning solvents. All five of us are. We pooled our money to get a hotel room. It is a rare aligning of the supersensible regions when enough of us have the money and are willing to pass up buying a bag of heroin and chip in for a hotel room instead. Usually the concord has been brought about by a freezing wet spell that just won't let up, coinciding with a dearth of suitable street drugs.

Crayon is the only one who looks eighteen, is in possession of a believable driver's license, and has the prized credit card that a trick let him keep. It has a hundred-dollar spending limit, just enough to get us into this hotel room. It ain't fancy — they wouldn't think of trusting the folks who usually stay here with an honor bar, much less a bunch of scraggly street urchins like us. But it does have a thirteen-inch TV with HBO. After the cleaning staff hauls off, Serenity uses Crayon's maxed-out credit card to jimmy into the supply closet. There, sitting in plastic buckets on the pressed-wood shelves like croutons at Sizzler, are the cleaning solvents.

We sit on the floor, small brown paper bags sealed to our facial orifices as if we are in an airplane that did indeed run into a severe altitude problem.

We mean to mine this room for all the opulence it has to offer. All the bleach-scented, threadbare towels, the stained, inflexible sheets, even the cellophane-entombed plastic cups will come with us after we check out. We each, in turn, will push in the little silver lock in the doorknob of the bathroom door and take incredibly long hot showers, which we aren't able to take at the youth shelters. "Watch out world, I am an adolescent and there is a lock on this shower door!" is a phrase that is not bandied about in shelters. But, for now, we switch on the bolted-down TV, using the fastened-down remote, and go right away to HBO, for this, too, is a paid-for luxury, and we will use all of it — even if what we really crave most is to collapse on a bed that is ours for the night, without any grownup rules or regulations, no fear of cops or social workers. For we all know that swindle. Sleep is the same as shooting drugs: as soon as you inject it, you nod, and next thing you know, it's over and you are out in the cold, wet world again. Though a deep slumber is what we really require, it's too painful to have this glorious opportunity wasted by being unconscious. We sit congregated around our TV. George Carlin is doing his "A Place for My Stuff" routine. It's all about folks' stuff, how we all need to store our stuff, our lives are about accumulating stuff, then you have to get a bigger house to put all your stuff in.

I've heard it before; my mother had a trucker boyfriend who played Carlin tapes in his eighteen-wheeler as he drove. As Carlin spoke his outrage at our need to keep and store our stuff, the trucker announced with pride, "I own all my dang stuff in this here truck!" My mother did not like being categorized as his "owned stuff," and at the very next truck stop, she took our bag of stuff, and we became minus items on his stuff list.

My sinuses feel Brillo-padded by the inhaled oven cleaner. I look through a pixilated haze at our backpacks spread out behind us. No one is very far from his stuff — by habit we've arranged it so if we pass out, we'll land on our stuff, we'll wake if anyone tries to steal any of our stuff. I watch Gotti rise for her turn to use the bathroom and realize none of us is insulted that she takes all her stuff with her. We all do the same. Carlin is saying, "That's all you need in life, a little place for your stuff. That's all your house is: A place to keep your stuff. If you didn't have so much stuff, you wouldn't need a house. You could just walk around all the time."

And man, I think, not having a house, living on the street, you kinda *become* stuff. You're the stuff folks have to walk over, you're the stuff they have to deal with, have to move past without being guilted into digging out some change. And our stuff is the homeless-problem stuff. Some shelters let you keep some stuff there, but they go through it. They throw some of your stuff out if they want. Cops always want to take your stuff. Believe me, privacy is not for the homeless.

But I have a secret.

There are lockers at the Transbay terminals. There are rows of wooden benches, church pews, usually filled with homeless people sleeping off something. But at night, a lot of them never make it to a bench and travelers play body hopscotch to get to their Amtrak trains. I have a key, with a plastic orange square on it, the color of a prison jumpsuit. I keep the key tied to my waist, so if anyone took my other stuff, they wouldn't get my key. In the beginning I moved my stuff to a new locker every day. They had limits on storing stuff, and folks watched. Homeless folks watched, the occasional guard, and if it was too obvious you were storing your stuff, someone would bust in and empty it for you.

One bitter cold day when there had been no convergence of money, I woke up in a shelter and could not swallow. I got up and I fell down. And then I woke up at General Hospital. And I tried to explain that I had to get my stuff. I ripped at the tubes that ran into my arms until they had to tie my hands down. I screamed at them, I had to get my stuff!

"Your stuff will wait," a doctor told me and inserted some stuff into my IV that made me not care about my stuff anymore.

When I was released with a parting bag of stuff I was to keep swallowing, I headed to the Transbay. I knew my stuff wasn't going to be there. I knew I shouldn't even bother going.

George Carlin is saying, "And when you leave your house, you gotta lock it up. Wouldn't want somebody to come by and take some of your stuff."

I step over the bodies, layered in their blacks and grays like a topography map on my way to my locker. It's still closed. My heart pounds. I unfurl the string holding my key from around my waist like a train engineer. I'm on one of those game shows, I'm seeing if my key fits. What stuff have I won? I slide it in, and I flick my wrist. It does not move. I've seen them, they come in their uniforms, they come and, with a quick tug with shiny tools, they pull out the whole cylinder, change the lock, haul out the stuff inside. A new orange key inserted, waiting for a proper owner. This one's new key is gone, so I know someone else's stuff is in there. Probably someone with a house who only stores peripheral stuff in the Transbay lockers. Someone who lives by Carlin's words, "That's what your house is, a place to keep your stuff while you go out and get . . . more stuff!" I knock my head against the locker until I feel a hand on my shoulder. I spin around and the short woman in front of me holds out her heavy canvas-gloved hands.

"Whoa," she says, and makes a grip of her shielded fingers as if she were pulling back on reins. "Whoa there."

I know she's the one who confiscates stuff. I've seen her, gingerly emptying the lockers into garbage bags.

"Fuck off!" I shout into her face. I want to spit, but I also don't want to go to juvie, and I notice out of the corner of my eye that security is heading over at a rather nonleisurely pace. So I duck out of her reach and begin to sprint for the exit. "Wait!" she yells out to me. I turn and give her the finger. I won't turn and show her my face, she saw it once, I won't give her the satisfaction of seeing it again. I wipe fast at my eyes.

"I have your stuff!" she calls out. I keep moving till the words sink in. I spin around. The guard is now behind her. Without looking at him she gives him a fast, low wave, as if she were shaking bangles. He steps back reluctantly. "I have your stuff." She repeats quietly. Some of the bums have hoisted themselves into a better position to observe the action. The commuters walk by with their hurried clip.

I clear my throat. It still hurts when I swallow and I think that without the force of rage, it might not be able to produce words. I feel like the raccoons we watch them trap in the park in the dawn. "Come on baby . . . got some tasty stuff for you . . . come and get it."

"Where . . . where is it?" My voice cracks. I tighten my grip on my plastic hospital bag that reads "Personal Belongings" in bright blue.

She starts to walk toward me, I step back. She turns toward the guard behind her and says some words I can't hear. He nods and we both watch him walk away. She waves me over. I estimate the guard's distance versus mine. I judge it a mathematical equation that works out in my favor, so I stiffen my body and cautiously move toward the wall of lockers. She is holding something in her hand and at first I think she is going to play a game of "Guess which hand" with me, but as I approach, she turns over her palm to display a key. This one has a red plastic square, the color of blood in a specimen tube.

"Where's my stuff?" I whisper to her, my eyes on the key resting in the middle of the blackened suede-like cloth of her glove.

"It's in the lower locker, at the end." She points with her chin. "Why you gotta make a scene? Take this."

She holds the key out further and I peck it out fast, the way I've seen some of the park raccoons that have been around for a while do — they nab the food from the side, without getting into the trap. "What, you think I'm playing with you? I could get fired for this!" She frowns at me then follows it with a fast wink, which makes me confused as to how to answer. She reads my face and takes a quick breath. "That's your key. Don't lose it. It won't need no money." She turns and, just like that, walks away.

I watch her head through a huge, thick door marked "Personnel Only." I examine the key and look around. The guard is busy nudging a seemingly lifeless body with his foot. I head straight to the bottom locker the security guard pointed to and squat right in front of it. I don't know what I expect. I look around and no one is watching anymore. All the homeless are prone again. The commuters are still rushing past me in a blur. I try to detach myself as I fit the key in, the way I do when the men hand me my money and start to undo my pants. The lock clicks, making little gulping noises, and with a faint metallic gasp, it opens for me. I sit in front of the locker and stare at the contents. There are all my notebooks, stacked neatly and tied with twine like how schoolboys carried their books in the olden days.

"I like your stuff," the Transbay maintenance woman says from behind me. I don't respond. I just close the door of my locker and tie the key back around my waist.

She doesn't stop; the soft scuffle of her shoes travels past me. I lean back to watch her till she recedes into one of the cavernous rooms of the terminal. I slide my notebooks halfway out of the locker to shove into my Personal Belongings bag. I sit and stare at them, frozen, as if I just IDed a body in a morgue. I trace my fingertips along the careful bows she made on top of them. I turn and can see her vague form stuffing newspaper from the benches into the trash. I reach into my plastic bag and pull out two pages of stuff I wrote in the hospital and place it on top of the pile. I push it back in the locker, wrap the key around my ankle, and slam the door. "Don't touch my fuckin' stuff . . ." I whisper toward her, grab my bag, and leave.

And now, after I've gotten clean and I have a bed to sleep in every night, and some of the stuff in the locker's actually been published, I keep meaning to go back. To tell her. To give her the letter I've typed. And somehow it's years before I do make it back there. I feel as obscured as I always did among all those headed off hurrying with purpose, stuff to do. I enter the overly lit building.

But the lockers are gone. I knock on the Personnel Only door. I am told the lockers were torn out a year ago. The homeless are chased out now too. The terminal is not open all night anymore. I describe her, but the personnel guys only shrug — everyone I ask, he shrugs. I go to where the lockers once were, now just a wider corridor. And, like laying flowers at a plowed-over grave, I let fall my note to her. Telling her how my stuff is going to be published. Saying all I was unable to. I watch as the feet rumble by, trampling my note. Turning it black with footprints. As I walk out a Transbay employee is herding out a homeless woman. She reaches for her stuff from the worker, but he smiles brutally and tells her, "This stuff is confiscated." I imagine grabbing the bag from him and running with her into the street, into the dark, but I keep walking. I keep walking and wish I had that key to give her.

DOUGLAS LIGHT

■

Three Days. A Month. More.

FROM *Alaska Quarterly Review*

"WHEN YOU TURN TWELVE," Maria says, studying her younger sister Lena's breasts, "I'll give you my bra." Three days, a month. Their mother's left. They've been alone some time, Lena and Maria.

The room, hot from the late-spring sun cutting through the bare windows, smells of burnt onions and bad milk. "You itchy?" Lena asks her sister. She itches, has been itchy ever since Raho spent the night between her and Maria on their dingy, gray-sheeted bed, Raho and Maria squirming about every few hours.

"Why do they always think it's funny to put pants on a monkey?" Maria asks, more to the TV commercial than to Lena. The TV is always on, the sounds of voices, a distant family, issuing from the front room all hours of the day. Maria's father is not Lena's. They've never met either. "They think a monkey with pants," Maria says, "is funny."

Often Lena dreams they are comfortable, that their mother's returned and they are living in a clean apartment with peach-colored carpet, an apartment someplace south of 143rd Street, someplace other than west Harlem.

The TV shows grazing caribou, ice floes, then a woman in a red suit firmly saying, "Drilling in Alaska is our only viable option. The oil there is what we need."

"Shit, Alaska," Maria says. "How come you never meet no one

from Alaska?" she asks. "Puerto Rico, yeah, always, everywhere. Manhattan is Puerto Rico on vacation. But Alaska? You never meet people from Alaska."

"You itchy?" Lena asks again, and Maria looks at her surprised, startled, like Lena told her their mother returned.

"Let's," Maria says, standing, "get some ice cream."

Lena remembers her mother leaving, remembers the sound waking her at night. It was a sound of franticness, hurry and fright, of something moving through the walls, a sound similar to the sound of the crazy lady next door trying to cook the way she always cooks, by banging everything around. Then the TV was turned off.

A door shut and someone softly coughed in the hallway. "These sheets," Lena whispered to her sister, feeling the bedding they shared. It was eleven o'clock or midnight or three A.M. "They're suppose to be white."

"She's not coming back," Maria said, lying next to her.

"Where'd she go?" Lena asked.

"Just gone."

Three days, a month passed. "Don't pay no rent," Raho tells them, eyeing Maria as she moves around the kitchen. At age fifteen, he's a man. "The money you got, keep," he says.

The sink's filled with dishes from meals Lena can't remember eating. "You got six months," he says, studying Maria as she leans on the table, "before something happens. A good six months," he slowly says.

The bodega at the corner sells chocolate, vanilla, and coconut ice cream. Maria takes two beers from the standing cooler. "You ain't old enough," the bodega man says, eyeing Maria then Lena as they place the items on the counter.

"But my mama is," Maria tells him, then asks for a pack of Newport cigarettes and pays in quarters and dimes.

"Tell your mama," the bodega man says, "I ain't seen her in a while." He winks at Lena, offers her a broken orange Popsicle, the wrapper torn. "For free," he says. Maria's cautioned Lena about him, the bodega man, said he was not to be trusted. "He acts like he knows something," she said, "something he'll hold against us."

"Tell her," the bodega man says to Maria, half smiling, "I want to talk with her."

"Tell her," Maria says, grabbing the items, "yourself."

Eating ice cream from the small square box, Lena asks, "What's chocolate look like?" Artificial flavors, sugar, color no. 5, the ice cream box reads. They sit in front of the TV, the news accounting downward economies, a forest fire, and a kitten rescued from a storm drain.

"Like this," Maria says, and sticks her ice-cream-covered tongue out.

"I mean, on the tree, or wherever it grows."

Maria pours some beer. "What I don't get," she says, "is why some Puerto Ricans need to wave a Puerto Rican flag all the time."

"Mama's Puerto Rican," Lena says. "We're Puerto Rican." Often she dreams they are comfortable.

"Not that kind of Puerto Rican," she says. "Not the kind that waves a flag." On TV, a white woman says to the black man sitting next to her, "If you're honest with yourself, you'll see that we're all oppressed."

"Tell me something," Maria says. "What's the Alaskan flag look like?"

"I've never seen one," Lena tells her.

"You know why you've never seen one?" Maria asks, pointing her spoon. "Because Alaskans don't go crazy waving them around."

Raho comes by with friends and Chinese food, some beer. "Don't pay the rent," he tells them again.

"Don't you ever wash your sheets?" one of the boys asks Lena, looking at their bed, the dank sheets twisted and rumpled. Lena thinks of her mother, thinks of this boy in her room and the bra she'll get when she turns twelve. "Don't look like they've ever been white," the boy says, lightly kicking the mattress.

Leaving the room, Lena calmly slides her hand under her shirt, into her pants, and scratches. "Shit," the boy says, seeing her. "You too?"

There is no money but somehow Maria has money. Lena takes an old razor of her mother's and shaves her pubic area, the few random strands, but still she itches. Standing in front of the streaked bathroom mirror, she calls to Maria, "When do I get a bra?"

"Let's clean the place," Maria says from the kitchen, staring at the sink filled with dishes. They throw everything out, the dishes, the sheets, old underwear.

"I still need to talk with your mama," the bodega man says the next time they go for ice cream and beer. Outside, the fire hydrant is open, arcing a spray over the hot summer street, the sweating children, the passing cars. "Ain't seen her in a long while," he says, not smiling. "Tell her I got something she needs."

"You got sheets?" Maria asks him.

"Sheets?" he asks, confused. "What do you mean? Like, for a bed?"

"Listen," Maria says to Lena. "Mama's gone. What do you want?"

They sleep on the bare mattress, scratching through the night. In the front room, the TV blares: "I wish the world would stop." Three days, a month, more. Often Lena dreams they are comfortable.

The landlord comes by. "I'm not all that bad," he says to them. The door barely open, Maria eyes him through the crack. "When is your mother home?" he asks.

"Late," Maria tells him. "She's always working. Two jobs, double shift."

"Then she can afford to pay the rent."

"I'm thirteen years old," she tells him, "my sister's eleven." He seems to understand. They aren't the ones to talk to. They aren't the ones to pay rent.

"Don't pay him shit," Raho says. He is over more and more often, always calm and studying Maria. He buys them a set of sheets, new and dark blue. "They get dirty but it's hard to tell," he says.

"Mama's gone," Maria says to Lena. "What do you want?"

"I want to be a doctor," she tells her, "or a seamstress or someone who whispers on the phone like Mama use to."

"But what do you want," she says, "now that Mama's gone."

The TV speaks of aspirin, Odor-Eaters, pizza, and pantyhose. "I want one of those purple gowns and square hats like we see people wearing at City College every spring," Lena tells her. She chews at her nails, biting at the tips of her fingers. "I want to be older," she says. "I want a bra."

It is Sunday or Thursday or Monday. Raho moves in. Still, Lena itches. "Listen," he often says, and they stop to listen.

Maria moves Lena into their mother's old room so she and Raho can have the newly sheeted bed to themselves. Mama's room, with its empty air, stripped bed, and scarred bureau, feels like no one has ever lived there. The window and window ledge are marred with pigeon shit. Lena checks the drawers and finds a pair of socks, a T-shirt, a brown blouse, and red shorts, all smelling of a closed space. She can't remember her mother ever wearing these things, can't even picture what she'd look like in them. Can't picture her.

"How much money would you need?" Maria asks her.

The TV comments: "Seventy percent of our oil comes from the Middle East. We've got oil here, our own natural reserves. Not tapping them now is like going out to eat with a refrigerator full of food just waiting to rot."

The landlord starts coming by, knocking on the door every few days, asking for the rent. "I hate to do this," he says. The TV transmits false, empty voices, sounds of a world far away. The noise is the music of the apartment, the music of their lives. "I hate to do this, but we need to talk," the landlord says through the locked door. "I need the rent." Motionless inside, Maria, Raho, and Lena say nothing, remain quiet, like they are elsewhere.

"What do I need money for?" Lena asks Maria. "I have you."

"I'm saying, if you needed money," she asks, "if you were on your own, how much would you need?"

She is not on her own, she tells her. "I don't need money," she says. "I need Mama. I need you."

Three days. A month. Rarely do they leave the apartment. Raho moves about the place, opening closets then slamming them closed. "Why is this always on?" Raho asks of the TV, turning it off. "Tell me, why is it always on?"

"Leave it on," Maria calmly tells him. "Mama always had it on. It's home, it's sound," she says. "It's what makes me comfortable when I'm not." He looks to Lena for understanding, and finding none, turns the TV back on.

The issuing voices move from room to room, filling the hollow spaces.

The afternoons pass in a hot stupor, the weak, late-summer breeze failing to cool. "How much would you need?" Maria asks Lena, drinking beer. Barley, hops, yeast, the label reads. "How much?" she asks, her voice tight, strange. She sounds nervous, like the bodega man who has something he'll hold against them.

"Twenty or a hundred or five thousand dollars," Lena tells her. "What does ice cream cost?"

"The cost of ice cream," Maria says, thinking it through. "That's right, ice cream."

Raho buys them new clothing, Rocawear, Sean John, items like everyone else is wearing. "They're real," he says, showing them the labels.

"School started last week," Maria tells Lena.

"When did it end?" she asks, and they both laugh.

Hot baths and alcohol rubs soothe the itching.

"When's your birthday, Lena?" Raho finally asks, standing in the doorway and studying her closely for some time.

She doesn't mind him watching her the way he watches Maria. "What is today?" she asks, lifting her hand to feel her face. Sometimes she forgets the feel of her face. "What day is today?" she asks, lying calmly in the tub, the water warm and her pubic area shaved clean. "What month are we in?"

"Okay," Raho says, stepping away, his hands held up as a sign of surrender. "Okay."

Three days, a month, more. They throw the mail out, the envelopes bright yellow, the words *final notice* printed in red on the front. Evening comes earlier, the sun setting sooner. It is afternoon, one o'clock or two or five P.M. Sitting on the soiled tile floor, Maria takes her shirt off. "That shit with that Chinese guy lighting himself on fire," she says. "The government say all kinds of stuff and people believe."

"What?" Raho asks. "What the fuck are you talking about?"

There is a knock on the front door, then the rattle of the doorknob. Lena moves softly from the kitchen, stands before the door, one foot socked and her pants unbuttoned. Again, the doorknob rattles. A charge of anxiousness, of fright, cuts over her as she quietly leans to the doorframe, places her cheek to the cool, grimy wood and listens for a sound that is familiar, the sound of breathing or a cough that is her mother's.

From the outside hallway, a voice, distant and angry: "Rent by Friday. Tell your mother rent by Friday."

Lena thinks of Raho watching her bathe, thinks of his mouth and what it might taste like on hers.

"Listen," he tells her one afternoon. The day is cool; the leaves are turning the colors they turn when they die for the year. The TV is on, the volume loud. Maria is elsewhere, out buying ice cream or beer, or in the bedroom asleep. They sit next to each other on the couch, Raho and Lena. "Listen," Raho says, his eyes touching her.

Slowly, she lifts her skirt.

The air around them moves then stops moving and his hand is on her thigh, damp and forceful.

Often Lena dreams she is comfortable.

*

It hurt at first. But then, after some time, it no longer hurt.

"What do you want," Maria asks, moving about the room, "now that Mama's gone?" Her voice is a wall, solid and real. There is something different now. Somehow Maria knows of Raho, knows of Lena. That morning there was shouting, a door slammed, Maria crying. "Raho's not coming back," Maria told her, her eyes red and swollen.

"Where'd he go?" Lena asked.

"Just gone."

No longer are they sisters, Maria and Lena, no longer two girls from the same mother. Now they are two girls of different fathers.

"What do you want?" she asks again.

"I want to be a diplomat," Lena quietly tells her, picking at her toes, "or a model or someone who says 'Hi' to people when they walk into a store." She feels no different, feels no older. Still, she itches. "I want to be older," she says.

"But what do you want?" Maria asks, irritated.

The TV interviewer says, "One can't speak without fear of being castigated for common thoughts, truths that are true even if America doesn't believe them. How was Malcolm X killed? Tell me, who killed him?"

"Ice cream," Lena says.

"Ice cream," Maria answers, then hands her a twenty-dollar bill off a pile of bills. "That's right, ice cream."

The bodega man eyes Lena wearily as she sets the ice cream, a beer, and the twenty-dollar bill Maria gave her on the counter. Baby wipes, bandages, Kool-Aid, and Goya beans. Dust covers the items on the shelf. A Puerto Rican flag hangs over the cash register. Three days. A month. More. "Is your mama avoiding me?" the bodega man asks, embarrassed. "If she's avoiding me," he says, bagging the items, "tell her to forget about it." He hands her the change. "Tell her it's forgotten."

"You got Alaskan flags?" Lena asks.

"Alaskan flags?" he asks, confused. "What do you mean? Like, for the state?"

Returning home, an awkward stillness clouds the apartment. The TV is off, silence filling the space. Worried, she calls out her sister's name. "Maria," she calls, moving from room to room. The frail autumn sun casts a failing light through the dingy window. West Harlem is on the island of Manhattan. The bed is stripped of the dark blue sheets.

"Maria?" she says. "Maria?" she calls, frightened that she's alone.

There is a loud pounding on the front door, hollow and re-sounding. Silently, she moves along the hall, her breath still.

The knock sounds again, then the doorknob rattles.

"Maria?" she whispers, slowly leaning her cheek against the cool, grimy door frame. Today, she turns twelve. Still, she itches. "Maria?" she whispers, listening for a sound of something famil-iar. "Mama?" she says, listening for a sound that will make her comfortable when she's not.

NASDIJJ

■

Touching Him

FROM *Columbia Review*

NAVAJO BOYS grow up knowing this: There are monsters in the world. You learn early on, they're out there. Your grandmother will speak of them. She scares you, too. A little bit. Sometimes a lot. She has a lot of power. It scares you when Grandmother holds the sheep, the sheep struggles, and she cuts the animal's neck with her knife. She holds the sheep firmly as it dies. It knows it is dying. It tries to get away. But at some point it gives itself to her as she holds it like a baby. Kicking. You stand there, watching her. You are too scared to even run away. She does not ask you to help her hold the sheep. But she will. Someday. The day looms like bats. You hope it never comes flying from the cave. But it will find you, and you know it. Grandmother will have you touch and hold the sheep. Touching the animal as the life slips away. You know something of the power of touching things. Grandmother touches you, too, and sometimes firmly. She scares you, protects you, grounds you, and someday she will ask you to help her hold the sheep.

You learn early on the enormity of touching things.

Even writing, we are touching things. Pounding away like a sculptor chips away at the marble of what was. Writing the stories of what happened is a stone. The stone is not unlike a sheep. It has a life that belongs inherently to no one. You take it. Or not. You create the sculpture or not. You write the thing or not. All of it is monsters.

I am afraid to write about touching him. The monster of it lives outside with the bats. Touching the story of what touching him was like is, too, a chipping away at rock with hammers and a chisel. The thing emerges like the story in the stone. It has eyes. A nose. Fingers. Lips.

It has funny toes.

Awee had a penis, too. It came with being boy. All boy. Every inch of him. We do not discuss it. The penis is forbidden. Like death.

It bled, too.

He was always touching it. The foreskin did not retract all the way. He could peel it back so he could pee. Then, he would gently peel it back a little bit, and it would bleed. It did not need to be cut off (like most white people would be done with it), but just slowly over time, discovery, like death, is giving birth to what you are inside the layers of the thing.

In the morning, he would wake up with an erection, and there would be a little blood on his underpants, or his pajamas, or on the sheets (it depended on what he slept in, Awee preferred nudity as it was quite natural to him). He would grow alarmed, but more curious than alarmed. He wondered what it meant. He always wondered what things meant.

It meant he was a male. That is all it meant.

It did not mean that he was bad. Or that he was a bad person. Or that he was a criminal. Or that he was not covered in the skin of his morality. It was not a shameful thing, and we did not treat it like it was.

We simply acknowledged that Awee was male. AIDS had not robbed him of everything. Enough. But not quite everything. He had his gender, and he even liked it.

Most women want their sons to put it away. Get it out of sight. That is probably natural, too. Little boys do not walk around with erections.

And if you believe that, I have some land in the Everglades that I would like to sell you at a bargain.

Little boys walk around with erections. Men know when they care to remember beyond and past the moral injunctions erected by motherhood. The erections of the son, and the knife of the grandmother are not bats that touch, but stand in the darkness of the cave, wings folded tight, stiffly at attention.

I was not his mother. There are vast differences in the way men raise boys versus the way in which women raise boys. Most women would opt for circumcision. Let him squirm and suffer like the sheep. I opted for time, and knew that every hard-on he got would peel it back a little bit, and his penis (like his life) would emerge from the wetness of the skin that had protected it.

Awee was his penis.

My job was to protect him. Loving him was easy. It wasn't really work. Protecting him was work.

We had this Big Thing between us.

It was an agreement. Engorged with blood. The agreement was important. We had agreed that we would interrupt time itself (or events) to pose the question: What do you want.

Just ask it. No one, no one, no one would ever, ever, ever be punished for asking it. It deserved an answer.

What do you want.

I want to live.

Was an answer.

I want to be alive.

Was an answer.

I want to be in life.

How to do those things was never easy. They were hard to implement. Harder than a penis on a twelve-year-old could ever hope to be.

I want to play baseball with the other boys.

There was a lot to ponder. There was a lot to consider. There was a lot to protect.

There was a lot to touch in life. Touching him was magic.

Writing about touching him scares me. Because I live IN the world (and I understand how vindictive it can be) even when I try not to. How can you even hope to paint a picture of who he was without telling the story of touching him? You had to touch him to know him. You had to hug him to protect him.

This does not necessarily imply the touching of his penis (we are so focused on the poor thing). There wasn't much to touch. Awee had yet to go through the full-throttle of what is puberty, and at twelve, it loomed and squirmed like a sheep as Grandmother held it and deftly made the blood drain in spurts into her pan. I do not understand how the penis of a boy — even erect — can be perceived in a sexual context. The thing is just too vulnerable and exposed. It would be like calling a peanut a melon and expecting the taste to be the same. It won't be. The peanut is a taste. A marble is what boys play with. It is not a tomato. It will not cut nor will it spill red with seed.

His penis was only a possibility, and a thing he studied curiously like he might study the rules of a board game purchased in the toy department at Wal-Mart. It was private, too.

It was something that perplexed him, and he looked to me for guidance and for comfort. I only write this squirmy stuff here because if I do not, I will be dismissed as twisted and inappropriate, which I will be anyway.

Your penis is a contradiction. Any boy's penis is a contradiction. Thusly, you are prepared to deal with the other contradictions you will find in life. Millions of them. Your penis is the center of your body and your life. No matter what your mother tells you. You know that from day one. You know, too, that it can be put away so you might have a life.

What do you want.

Baby boys will tell you by their touching that they want their penis.

I want to live.

What do you want.

I want to be alive.

What do you want.

I want you to touch me.

He did not mean his penis.

He meant his life. Hold all of it. Held fast. Like Grandmother as she holds her sheep.

Touching him was my life. I don't know how you could deal with AIDS without touching him. I don't know of any way to approximate giving him what he wants without touching him. Wrapping him in hugs.

Touching him was magic. He was more than simply there.

It made me nervous. Touching him.

He was twelve. I was his dad. His new dad. His adoptive dad. He was all over me. With his hands, his kisses, and his hugs.

He had AIDS.

Let's be real. It was why I adopted him. Do-gooders doing good. The do-gooder shit runs deep. As deep and as liquid black as the loneliness in his lucid eyes. We were like lovers, too. I don't care what you think. It wasn't sex. I was not about to have sex with a twelve-year-old boy struggling with AIDS. I have crashed and burned before (many times) but not like this. It wasn't sex. It was, however, him in bed.

At night. When he was afraid.

Dreams. He was on Sustiva. It was just one of the HIV medications he was on. Sustiva makes you dream, and not just any dream. The research materials that describe the side effects of Sustiva use the term LSD-like. These were LSD-like dreams, and they would scare any twelve-year-old boy shitless.

They were electric. They were alive. They were visceral. They spoke to him in screams.

Him standing there at the side of the bed late at night. Weeping. He had either wet or shit the bed. AIDS is not a nice disease. I was exhausted. I would have to clean him up, clean his bedding, put it in the wash, and I let him sleep with me, I did. Him clinging to my leg like a remora. What was it going to hurt except the armchair psychologists and moral authorities who would dissect it later. Post-vivisection. You're not supposed to do that. It's against the rules. It's a big No No in our impenetrable culture. Him touching me. Hugging me. Wrapped around my numbness.

I gave him that. I gave him things I was not supposed to. Things that I hoped would prevent him from slipping away. Hold tight, boy. I was his rock.

It wasn't sex. I have to keep repeating it. It wasn't sex. It was survival. I do not know how I can separate him out from issues such as sex and AIDS when, in fact, he came from both. I believe his mother passed the virus to him. At birth. That is what I believe. I write this as though it were an indictment. It is perhaps unfair. He had been abused, too. What was fair about any of it? How he got AIDS was irrelevant, and a convenient way to get out of having to deal with the reality of him now. Denial is a snake of many colors. I do not know how I can separate him from the carnage that he came to bed with. I bought him blue pajamas. It was not enough. He could go through two or three pairs of pajamas in a night. Cleaning him was not sex. Nevertheless, it was soft and often intimate.

At first, my biggest fear was over shit. The smell of it. The feel of it. The disgust. It was not like having a baby. Or changing diapers. It was a lot of shit. The boy was twelve. He was far more disgusted (with himself) than I could ever be. There were times when he was in control of his body and his bowels. But there were other times, the not-good-times, when he wasn't in control of much. Finally, we evolved this struggle into a ritual, which helped. It helps to put these horrible things into rituals. I would pick him up and put him in the tub. I would wash him, touching him, and we did not talk much.

Sometimes he would cry. He had worked so hard at being independent. Now, our secret was that he was a baby once again, again and again, always slipping back, and I agreed not to tell anyone because he begged me not to. We had so many secrets.

In time, I did not think about his shit, or the smell of it. I do not remember it. I remember him.

What I remember is how nice he smelled in his blue pajamas.

I would wake up in the morning, and he would have soaked the bed in sweat, clinging to me again, with his twelve-year-old erection pressed against my leg. I ignored this. Who from invisibility has come to life in impotence. Not him. Not I. Some judge, some see, some hear, some speak in tongues and babble, some reaffirm the contradictions of their lives. Some disintegrate. Some find themselves in faith. I found mine in touching him. We were alive.

In the good times, there was a lot of touching him. Other boys did it quite a bit. Boys his age. It was normal. They did not know that he was sick: 1) because we did not tell them, and 2) he was quite good at covering it up.

During one of the good times (when the pain from his neuropathy could still be controlled by morphine, then later by a combination of methadone and Lamictal), I let him join a baseball team.

It was the world to him.

He was supposed to have a physical. I forged a doctor's signature. It was like being back in high school, and you needed a bathroom pass. Sue me.

He was quite clear about his desire to do this. "Look," he said. "I'm dying. We know that. But before I do, I just want to play some baseball."

What do you want.

I swallow all my fears like they are rocks inside my throat and say okay.

What do I do if he bleeds?

I sit in the stands with the other parents. In terror.

I am so nervous, my hands tremble uncontrollably, and I have to clench my Coke. He steps fearlessly right up into the balls. Swings. That crack. Home runs win him a lot of friends.

Now, they are touching him.

Arms around his neck. They're all over him with their shirts off. Late at night and summer hot and drinking Coke and the lights from the baseball field have illuminated not quite everything in truth.

I sit in the bleachers with the other parents who have arrived in their SUVs, and worry, worry, worry not about home runs but about stupid things like him getting bruised and blood, what if . . .

What If is the kingdom of the Board of Regents whose battlefields are littered with the corpses of the boys who have fallen there to protect the pleasure of the king.

What if.

Fuck.

What if he gets invited to his friend's house — other boys his age sleep overnight, and camp in backyards in their tents — what if all his secrets are found out? Can I? Can I? He wants everything.

I do say no.

Just no. Sometimes I am the bad guy, too.

"No, you can't sleep over at John's house."

"But, I want to."

That and fifty cents . . .

John's house. Where John and his brothers sleep with their friends in the basement in their sleeping bags, and stay up late, and eat chips, and cookies John's mom has made, and shine their flashlights on their dicks like look at mine.

Like I am not supposed to know. Give me a break.

I know John. I know his brothers. I know the basement. I know the friends. I know the cookies. I know the flashlights as if they were a lighthouse, and it would be my son who is the small ship lost out here in the bigger waves at sea. I know the laughing squeals of boys like I know antiquity. All of it is normal. All of it is fine. All of it is stuff that you have to let go of as you let them live their lives. As lives unfold. I know this: John will die at twenty in a frat house alcohol initiation. It will break his parents' hearts (they didn't know boys drink). Sam will live to be sixty-two, and he will always miss John. Frankie will live to be eighty-eight, and he will have four children, all of whom will grow up to be arrogant and rich. They will all have pools. Steven will finally become a doctor. Grant, contrary to everyone's expectations, will spend thirty years delivering mail. There is nothing wrong with it. Dennis will own a hardware store. Dan will move to New York where he will blow his brains out after twenty years as a junkie. Craig will visit Dan once, and never go back to a major American urban center again in his life. Mark will become a schizophrenic at nineteen, and will live on and off in a variety of institutions and group homes. He will hate his medication. Tom will sell new cars to people who play golf, and sometimes he will wonder what happened to everyone.

Every now and then, infrequently, but from time to time, they will all remember flashlights, and they will grow a little hot and blush.

"But I want to go to John's. Everyone will be there."

Not everyone.

I am essentially a selfish man.

It wasn't John I objected to. Or his mother with her cookies. It wasn't the basement with the boys. It wasn't sex or flashlights.

It was chaos. Anywhere.

AIDS is chaos imposed on time.

Awee would go (if I let him, and I would not), and lose himself in those quickly running moments in the wind where he was just a boy again, and essentially like them.

And he wasn't like them.

No matter the illusion of the medications he was on.

What they bought was time.

John had a few more years. Frankie had almost eighty. Mark was already showing signs of schizophrenia. They just weren't too visible yet, or obvious. His brothers would look back, and think: Oh yeah, there.

"But I want to go," Awee begged. A basement with sleeping bags. A mom. Cookies.

Now, who was going to give him his medication? Would he re-member it? Not likely. Mom? With her cookies. Dispenses out the antiretrovirals. Nada chance.

This is where he crawls up onto my lap again. To cry. I am his rock. His wetness is touching me. I am touching him.

It was not John or Mark or Tom or Steve he was going to miss. It was his childhood.

They were having theirs. John was already drinking, but no one knew it. Secrets are everywhere.

My purpose is to protect my son. Sometimes from himself.

He sulks to punish me. I am not amused.

What if he stops loving me.

These are the dragons of my discontent. What if he dies, and I'm not there to hold him.

He was something of a thief, and liked stealing bases. Slides into third. Skins everything. His thigh, his knee, sand and dirt ground into his skin.

Him screaming in the bathroom as I spray him in antiseptic.

"You DON'T have to hurt me!"

But I do.

All that hurt should steal such gentle shapes as this.

I was the one who held his hand when they put a catheter in his penis at the hospital.

"It will be okay," I lied.

It wasn't. He pulled it out. Now, blood again. They tied him down, and I was the one who wept.

"I HATE it! I HATE them," he screamed.

"I know," I said. Hopefully, I could touch him with my lies. But he was too smart, and usually he found them out.

Finally, I made them take the catheter out, and I would pick him up, and set him on the toilet so he could pee, and I would hold him.

I tried not to look at his penis. It was just a silhouette. Boys his age have usually discovered masturbation, and not as some comparative vernacular, but as the artillery of flesh. "I won't have children," he told me. Discovery comes at strange and inconvenient times. "I always thought I might."

"No, but you'll have other things."

"Like what?"

"Like sunsets. Don't we always try to see the sunset — even from the window — if we can?"

I could make him smile.

I could make him smile like no one else on earth. Only I could do it. Often, when I made him smile, he would reach out with his fingers and he would gently touch my eyes, and sometimes my lips, just to see if we were real. We were so real, we burned.

I bought him his own private flashlight to consult his penis with. I am a walking, talking advertisement for Wal-Mart.

It is the sun that falls.

What had once been torture for us — this touching — now was something else. He liked it when I washed his hair, and we spoke quietly in whispers. Soapy head. He would dunk himself down into the water of the bath and emerge more beautiful than god.

As people began to find out that he was sick with AIDS, that he was dying, there was less and less of them touching him. No more baseball boys with their arms draped in brotherhood around his shoulders. John, Mark, Steve, Tom, Dennis became his memories. He, too, would be one of theirs. Eighty-eight is a long time to carry them. Schizophrenia just loses them like luggage at the airport. Even my own friends and colleagues moved further and further away. "I can't deal with this," my literary agent said, which surprised me because she had never met my son. "I hope you understand."

I said I did.

But I didn't. I surely didn't.

Like she was even there.

People I worked with in publishing grew thin as smoke.

Even in the hospitals, no one came around. The nurses avoided him.

We held hands a lot.

It wasn't sex. We did not care what anyone thought about us holding hands. It wasn't about them or what they thought. It was about us. It always had been.

When I think of touching him, I remember how he held me. Hard around the waist. On the big bike when we could hold it up. Like the Acropolis clings to the burden of the cliff. The ancient citadel of Athens.

If it's true that good boys need no blush upon their cheeks, it's true, too, that men do not need epilogues. Come sit behind me, son, and touch me here and here. To wake the soul by tender, roaring strokes of bikes, and touching me through fear.

THE ONION

■

I'll Try Anything with a Detached Air of Superiority

FROM *The Onion*

I'M A PRETTY SOPHISTICATED, well-educated person. I went to Wesleyan, where I got my B.A. in comparative literature. I listen to *This American Life* on NPR. I've traveled abroad fairly extensively and even spent a year living in London. Given all this, you'd think I might be a little staid and stodgy, that I'd shun certain activities because I'm too good for that sort of thing. That is completely untrue. The reality is, I'll try anything with a detached air of superiority.

A few weeks ago, my friend Curtis organized a bowling party for his birthday. Can you imagine anything more tacky and all-American? But contrary to what you might think, I was more than game for it. I even bought a personalized bowling shirt so I could fit in with the common folk. I only bowled a 76, but I loved it. The people there were so into it, some of them actually did little dances when they got a strike. There was this one guy I called "One-Fist," because after every frame, he'd pump his fist in the air like some blue-collar Billy Idol. Never in my life have I had such a great time participating in townie culture while simultaneously sneering at it from a distance.

I guess that's just who I am. I'm open to anything, no matter how pedestrian or mainstream it may be. Last year, I decided to dive headfirst into the realm of the unwashed masses by attending a professional football game. What better way to experience the hive mind than by communing with seventy thousand drunken, frostbitten Americans who are only too happy to blow their meager wages cheering on their date-raping, steroid-enhanced gridiron heroes? I don't even remember which teams were playing. All I remember is yelling my head off while surrounded by a sea of jersey-wearing telephone repairmen and electricians, all the while thinking, This is so authentic!

I must admit, some of the mind-numbingly lame stuff I've exposed myself to has actually grown on me. I used to go to rummage sales for the sociological thrill of seeing commoners eagerly scrounge through their fellow commoners' crude, mass-produced possessions. You'd see all sorts of amusing parts and parcels from people's tiny lives. After a while, though, I started to enjoy finding good bargains. I even began collecting completed Paint-By-Numbers pictures. My favorite so far is a rabbit where the "artist" confused two of the colors, resulting in what I strongly suspect is the world's only purple-eyed hare. A true snob would never waste his time with something like that, but I am able to see the charm of my inferiors' sad little diversions.

When you think about it, it's really the mundane things that make life interesting. Attending pro-wrestling matches, shopping at the mall, riding a Greyhound bus, eating at McDonald's, seeing conventionally crowd-pleasing movies like *My Big Fat Greek Wedding* — such things may seem like lowbrow wastes of time, but they really help one maintain a sense of oneself. If you can do such things and still maintain your sense of haughty superiority, you've done more than merely lived. You've tasted the sickly sweet nectar that life has to offer and said, "I am above this. I am better than this. This is beneath me, but I will still do it because I'm open-minded enough to try anything and look down my nose at it at least once."

GEORGE PACKER

■

How Susie Bayer's T-Shirt Ended Up on Yusuf Mama's Back

FROM *New York Times Magazine*

IF YOU'VE EVER left a bag of clothes outside the Salvation Army or given to a local church drive, chances are that you've dressed an African. All over Africa, people are wearing what Americans once wore and no longer want. Visit the continent and you'll find faded remnants of secondhand clothing in the strangest of places. The LET'S HELP MAKE PHILADELPHIA THE FASHION CAPITAL OF THE WORLD T-shirt on a Malawian laborer. The white bathrobe on a Liberian rebel boy with his wig and automatic rifle. And the muddy orange sweatshirt on the skeleton of a small child, lying on its side in a Rwandan classroom that has become a genocide memorial.

A long chain of charity and commerce binds the world's richest and poorest people in accidental intimacy. It's a curious feature of the global age that hardly anyone on either end knows it.

A few years ago, Susie Bayer bought a T-shirt for her workouts with the personal trainer who comes regularly to her apartment on East 65th Street in Manhattan. It was a pale gray cotton shirt, size large, made in the U.S.A. by JanSport, with the red and black logo of the University of Pennsylvania on its front. Over time, it got a few stains on it, and Bayer, who is seventy-two, needed more drawer space, so last fall she decided to get rid of the shirt. She sent it, along with a few other T-shirts and a couple of silk nightgowns, to the thrift shop that she has been donating her clothes to for the past forty years.

Americans buy clothes in disposable quantities — $165 billion worth last year. Then, like Susie Bayer, we run out of storage space, or we put on weight, or we get tired of the way we look in them, and so we pack the clothes in garbage bags and lug them off to thrift shops.

When I told Susie Bayer that I was hoping to follow her T-shirt to Africa, she cried, "I know exactly what you're doing!" As a girl, her favorite movie at the Loews on West 83rd was *Tales of Manhattan* — the story of a coat that passes from Charles Boyer through a line of other people, including Charles Laughton and Edward G. Robinson, bringing tragedy or luck, before finally falling out of the sky with thousands of dollars in the pockets and landing on the dirt plot of a sharecropper played by Paul Robeson.

Bayer writes off about a thousand dollars a year in donations, and the idea that some of it ends up on the backs of Africans delights her. "Maybe our clothes change the lives of these people," she said. "This is Susie Bayer's statement. No one would agree with me, but maybe some of the vibrations are left over in the clothing. Maybe some of the good things about us can carry through." She went on: "I'd like us to be less selfish. Because we have been very greedy. Very greedy. Americans think they can buy happiness. They can't. The happiness comes in the giving, and that's why I love the thrift shop."

Twenty-four blocks north, up First Avenue, the Call Again Thrift Shop is run by two blunt-spoken women named Virginia Edelman and Marilyn Balk. They sit in their depressing back office, surrounded by malfunctioning TVs and used blenders and a rising sea of black garbage bags.

From a heap of clothing in front of her, Edelman extracts a baseball shirt that says YORKVILLE across its front. "Look at this. Who would want to buy something like this? It's just junk. Junky junky junk. This stuff bagged in a garbage bag, it's so wrinkled we don't even look at it. This is a Peter Pan costume or something — I don't know what the hell it is."

Edelman and Balk have been toiling at Call Again for two de-

cades. Their dank little basement, crammed with last year's mil-
dewing clothes, has no more space. The storage shed out back
looks ready to explode. The women inspect every item that comes
in, searching for any reason to get rid of it. Their shop space is limited, and their customers are relentlessly picky. This being the Upper East Side, the store displays a size-four Kenneth Cole leather
woman's suit, worn once or not at all, that retails for six hundred
dollars but is selling here for two hundred.

Edelman and Balk sit neck-deep in the runoff of American pros-
perity, struggling to direct the flow and keep it from backing up
and drowning them. "It's endless," Balk says. "Yesterday we got, I
don't know, five donations. It's like seven maids and seven grooms
trying to sweep the seas. Or Sisyphus, was it? Trying to roll the
rock?"

One day a few years ago, relief came to them in the form of a
young man named Eric Stubin, who runs Trans-Americas Trading
Company, a textile recycling factory in Brooklyn. He said that he
was willing to send a truck every Tuesday to haul away what the
women didn't want and that he would pay them three cents a
pound for it. "You never heard two people happier to hear from
someone in your life," Edelman says. Now every month 1,200 or
1,300 pounds of rejected donations are trucked to Brooklyn, and
every three months Call Again gets a check for a hundred dollars
or so, money that goes to charity.

Edelman estimates that more than a third of the donations that
Call Again receives ends up in Trans-Americas' recycling factory.
Goodwill Industries, which handles more than a billion pounds a
year in North America, puts its figure at 50 percent. Some sources
estimate that of the 2.5 billion pounds of clothes that Americans
donate each year, as much as 80 percent gets trucked off to places
like Trans-Americas.

Though the proceeds go to charity programs, these numbers
are not readily publicized. Susie Bayer isn't the typical donor. "Everybody who gives us things thinks that it's the best thing in the
world," Edelman says. "They feel as if they're doing a wonderful
thing for charity. And they do it for themselves — for the tax write-

off. Unfortunately, I don't think people know what charity is anymore. They would be horrified if they thought that they bought a suit at Barneys or Bergdorf's for eleven hundred dollars and we chucked it for three cents a pound because of a torn lining."

Susie Bayer's T-shirt goes straight into the reject pile. "We have a thousand of them," Virginia Edelman says. "Get it out of here."

This is where the trail grows tricky, for what had been charitable suddenly crosses a line that tax law and moral convention think inviolable — it turns commercial, and no one likes to talk very much about what happens next. A whiff of secrecy and even shame still clings to the used-clothing trade, left over from the days of shtetl Jews and Lower East Side rag dealers. The used-clothing firms are mostly family owned, and the general feeling seems to be that the less the public knows, the better.

The owners of Trans-Americas, Edward and Eric Stubin, father and son, are more open than most in the industry, though they wouldn't share their annual sales figures with me. In 2001, used clothing was one of America's major exports to Africa, with $61.7 million in sales. Latin America and Asia have formidable trade barriers. Some African countries — Nigeria, Eritrea, South Africa — ban used clothing in order to protect their own domestic textile industries, which creates a thriving and quite open black market. For years, Africa has been Trans-Americas' leading overseas market for used clothing, absorbing two thirds of its exports.

"There'll always be demand for secondhand clothing," says Eric Stubin, who reads widely about Africa, "because unfortunately the world is becoming a poorer and poorer place. Used clothing is the only affordable means for these people to put quality clothing on their body."

Edward Stubin agrees. "I have a quote: 'We can deliver a garment to Africa for less than the cost of a stamp.'"

Trans-Americas' five-story brick building stands a block from the East River wharves in Greenpoint, Brooklyn. Inside, sixty thousand pounds of clothes a day pour down the slides from the top floor, hurry along conveyor belts where Hispanic women stand and fling pieces into this bin or down that chute, fall through openings from floor to floor and land in barrels and cages, where they are then pressure-packed into clear plastic four-foot-high bales and tied with metal strapping — but never washed. Whatever charming idiosyncrasy a pair of trousers might have once possessed is annihilated in the mass and crush. Not only does the clothing cease to be personal, it ceases to be clothing. Watching the process of sorting and grading feels a little like a visit to the slaughterhouse.

"We get the good, the bad, and the ugly," Eric Stubin tells me as we tour the factory. "Ripped sweaters, the occasional sweater with something disgusting on it, the pair of underwear you don't want to talk about. We're getting what the thrifts can't sell." There are more than three hundred export categories at the factory, but the four essential classifications are "Premium," "Africa A," "Africa B," and "Wiper Rag." "Premium" goes to Asia and Latin America. "Africa A" — a garment that has lost its brightness — goes to the better-off African countries like Kenya. "Africa B" — a stain or small hole — goes to the continent's disaster areas, its Congos and Angolas. By the time a shirt reaches Kisangani or Huambo, it has been discarded by its owner, rejected at the thrift shop and graded two steps down by the recycler.

Standing in Trans-Americas' office, with wooden airplane propellers hanging next to photographs from Africa, Eric Stubin casts a professional eye on Susie Bayer's T-shirt. In a week, a 54,000-pound container of used clothes will set sail on the steamship Claudia, destination Mombasa, Kenya. Stubin spots a pink stain on the belly of the T-shirt below the university logo and tosses the shirt aside. "Africa," he says.

But there are many Africas, and used clothing carries a different meaning in each of them. Christianity tenderized most of the continent for the foreign knife, but the societies of Muslim West Africa and Somalia are bits of gristle that have proved more resistant to Western clothes. In warlord-ridden, destitute Somalia, used clothing is called, rather contemptuously, *huudhaydh* — as in, "Who died?" A woman in Kenya who once sold used dresses told me that not long ago Kenyans assumed the clothing was removed from dead people and washed it carefully to avoid skin diseases. In Togo, it is called "dead white man's clothing." In Sierra Leone, it's called "junks" and highly prized. In Rwanda, used clothing is known by the word for "choose," and in Uganda, it used to be called "Rwanda," which is where it came from illegally until Uganda opened its doors to what is now called *mivumba*.

At the vast Owino market in downtown Kampala, Uganda's capital, you can find every imaginable garment, all of it secondhand. Boys sit on hills of shoes, shining them to near-newness, hawkers shout prices, shoppers break a sweat bargaining, porters barge through with fresh bales on their heads. When the wire is cut and the bale bursts open like a piñata, a mob of retailers descends in a ferocious rugby scrum to fight over first pick. Between the humanity and the clothes there is hardly room to move. The used-clothing market is the densest, most electric section of Owino — the only place where ordinary Africans can join the frenetic international ranks of consumers.

I knew what this thrice rejected clothing had gone through to get here, but somehow "Africa" looks much better in Africa — the colors brighter, the shapes shapelier. A dress that moved along a Brooklyn conveyor belt like a gutted chicken becomes a dress again when it has been charcoal-ironed and hangs sunlit in a Kampala vendor's stall, and a customer holds it to her chest with all the frowning interest of a Call Again donor shopping at Bergdorf-Goodman. Some of the stock looks so good that it gets passed off as new in the fashionable shops on Kampala Road. Government ministers, bodyguards in tow, are known to buy their suits at Owino. Once in Africa, the clothes undergo a transformation like inanimate objects coming to life in a fairy tale. Human effort and human desire work the necessary magic.

My guide through Owino is a radio talk show host named Anne Kizza, a sophisticated woman who knows what she wants in dance-wear from reading South African fashion magazines. She always goes to the same vendors, whose merchandise and prices are to her liking; while I am with her, she buys a slim lime green dress for the equivalent of sixty cents and a black skirt for thirty cents. Price tags are still stapled to some items — THRIFT STORE, $3.99, ALL SALES FINAL — but just as Americans don't know what happens beyond the thrift shop, Africans don't know the origin of the stuff. Most Ugandans assume that the clothes were sold by the American owner. When I explain to a retailer named Fred Tumushabe, who specializes in men's cotton shirts, that the process starts with a piece of clothing that has been given away, he finds the whole business a monstrous injustice. "Then why are they selling to us?" he asks.

The big importers have their shops on Nakivubo Road, which is a hairy ten-minute walk through traffic from Owino. Trans-Americas' buyer in Kampala is a Pakistani named Hussein Ali Merchant. He is forty, with a beard and a paunch and a sad, gentle manner. A diabetic cigarette smoker, he seems to expect to die any day and extends the same good-natured fatalism to his business. "It's a big chain," he says, and all the links beyond Merchant are forged on credit. "Sometimes the people disappear, sometimes they die. Each year I'm getting the loss of at least thirty thousand dollars. Last year a customer died of yellow fever. His whole body was yellow. He died in Jinja. The money is gone. Forget about it, heh-heh-heh."

We drink tea in his dark shop among unsold bales stacked twenty feet high. Five or six years ago, when there were only a few clothing shops on Nakivubo Road, his annual profit was about $75,000. Today, with more than fifty stores, his profits are much lower. Merchant is one of Africa's rootless Asian capitalists. Before coming to Uganda in 1995, he twice lost all his money to looting soldiers in Zaire. Between disasters he went to Australia and pumped gas for three months, but he fled back to Africa before his visa expired. "I've been sitting like this for twenty years here. In America you have to work hard, no money, things are very expensive. Here, it's easy. I want to do hard work in America? For what?" Merchant has a frightening vision of himself squeezing price tags onto convenience store stock at midnight in Kentucky. As for Karachi, it terrifies him, and he goes back only once a year to see his family, his doctor, and his tailor. "I'm a prince here," he says. "I'm a king here in Africa."

Merchant's warehouse — "my go down," he calls it in local slang — is in an industrial quarter of Kampala. On a Saturday afternoon in December, the truck carrying the Trans-Americas shipping container with Susie Bayer's T-shirt pulls in after its long drive from the port of Mombasa on the Kenyan coast. Seven customers — wholesalers from all over Uganda — anxiously wait along with Merchant. Among them is a heavy woman in her forties with a flapper's bob and a look of profound disgust on her fleshy face. Her name is Proscovia Batwaula, but everyone calls her Mama Prossy. As the bales start leaving the container on the heads of young porters, Mama Prossy literally throws her weight around to claim the ones she wants. Merchant, standing back from the flurry, murmurs that a week before, she bloodied another woman's nose in a scuffle over a bale of Canadian cotton skirts.

Eric Stubin has stenciled my initials on the bale containing Susie Bayer's T-shirt. But I never imagined 540 bales coming off the truck at a frantic clip, turned at all angles on young men's heads, amid the chaos of bellowing wholesalers in the glare of the afternoon sun. Finding the T-shirt suddenly seems impossible. When I try to explain my purpose to Mama Prossy, she answers without taking her eyes off the precious merchandise leaving the truck: "What gain will I have? Why should I accommodate you?" She scoffs at the idea of publicity benefits in New York, and as bales disappear into wholesalers' trucks, I start getting a bit desperate.

Then Mama Prossy learns that I teach in American universities. She badly wants her son to attend one; for the first time she takes an interest in me. Moments later, more good luck. Merchant spots my bale coming off the truck, the initials "GP" all of three inches high.

Mama Prossy insists on the right to tear it open and have a look. The used-clothing trade in Africa is fraught with suspicion and rumor and fear of bad bales. Wholesalers bribe the importers' laborers to give them first crack at the most promising stock, based on the look of things through clear plastic. But what Mama Prossy extracts from the top of my bale makes her lip curl in ever-deepening disgust. It is a pink woman's T-shirt. Women's clothes are not supposed to be mixed in with men's. "I will lose money," she announces, and pulls out another piece. "Is this for a fat child? Where are they in Africa? We don't have fat children here in Uganda."

She is angling for a price cut from Merchant, who reminds her that she still owes him fifty thousand Ugandan shillings (thirty dollars) from last week. She starts calling him "boss." After all, he is higher on the chain, and she needs him more than he needs her. They settle on the equivalent of sixty dollars for the bale, a price that amounts to nineteen cents a shirt. Merchant has paid Trans-Americas around thirteen cents each, excluding freight charges; he will have little or no profit on the bale, which was graded "mixed," Africa A and B.

Mama Prossy turns to me. "You say this bale is best quality, better than the others?" It wasn't what I'd said, but I keep my mouth shut. "I doubt," says Mama Prossy, looking me over with quite naked contempt. "We shall see."

A Kampala journalist named Michael Wakabi told me that Kampala has become "a used culture." The cars are used — they arrive from Japan with broken power windows and air conditioners, so Ugandan drivers bake in the sun. Used furniture from Europe lines the streets in Kampala. The Ugandan Army occupies part of neighboring Congo with used tanks and aircraft from Ukraine. And the traditional Ugandan dress made from local cotton, called gomesi, is as rare as the mountain gorilla. To dress African, Ugandans have to have money.

Twenty years ago, when I was a Peace Corps volunteer in Togo, all the village women wore printed cloth, and many of the men wore embroidered shirts of the same material. The village had at least half a dozen tailors. The mother of eight who lived next door dreamed of making clothes in her own market stall and asked me to help her buy a hand-cranked sewing machine. Used clothes were sold in limited and fairly expensive supply; a villager wore the same piece every day as it disintegrated on his body.

Then the floodgates opened. With the liberalization in Africa of the rules governing used-clothing imports in the past ten years,

Africans, who keep getting poorer, can now afford to wear better than rags. Many told me that without used clothes they would go naked, which, as one pointed out, is not in their traditional culture. And yet they know that something precious has been lost.

"These secondhand clothes are a problem," a young driver named Robert Ssebunya told me. "Ugandan culture will be dead in ten years, because we are all looking to these Western things. Ugandan culture is dying even now. It is dead. Dead and buried." The ocean of used clothes that now covers the continent plays its part in telling Africans that their own things are worthless, that Africans can do nothing for themselves.

But the intensity of the used-clothing section in every market I entered suggests that if something called "Ugandan culture" is dying, something else is taking its place. The used clothes create a new culture here, one of furious commercial enterprise and local interpretation of foreign styles, cut-rate and imitative and vibrant.

For all this, Uganda is quite capable of mass-producing its own clothes. On the banks of the White Nile, at its source in Jinja on Lake Victoria, a textile company called Southern Range Nyanza uses local cotton, considered the second best in the world after Egyptian, to manufacture 13 million yards of fabric a year. With the Africa Growth and Opportunity Act of 2000 opening the American market, Southern Range has begun exporting men's cotton shirts to New York — so shirts that begin in Uganda might make a double crossing of the ocean and end there as well.

Viren Thakkar, Southern Range's Indian managing director, insists that he can sell the same shirts in Uganda for three dollars — less than twice the cost of a used shirt — but the dumping of foreign clothes makes it impossible for him to break into the market. "The country has to decide what they want to do," he says, "whether they want to use secondhand clothes continually, or whether they want to bring industry and grow the economy." Globalization has helped to destroy Uganda's textile industry, but Ugandans simply don't believe that their own factory could make clothes as durable and stylish as the stuff that comes in bales from overseas.

In Jinja's market, Mama Prossy sits like a queen on her wooden storage bin and watches the morning trade. At her feet, half a dozen retailers poke through the innards of the Trans-Americas bale. "You see how you are picking very, very old material," she scolds me. "And you are mixing ladies'. My friend, why are you mixing ladies'? And too much is white."

"I told you," I say, "I don't work for them."

"But you put your initials on it."

She will lose money on my bale, Mama Prossy insists; she will never buy Trans-Americas again. But the entries she makes in her ledger book show a profit of ninety-eight dollars — more than 150 percent.

Her retailers sort the T-shirts by their own three-tier grading system. Susie Bayer's is rated second-class and goes for sixty cents to a slender, grave young man in slightly tattered maroon trousers who seems intimidated by the queen on her throne. His name is Philip Nandala, and he is the next-to-last link in the chain. Philip is an itinerant peddler of used clothes, the closest thing in Uganda to the nineteenth-century rag dealer with his horse-drawn cart — except that Philip transports his fifty-pound bag from market to market by minibus or on his own head, five days a week on the road. "If I stay at home," he says, "I can die of poverty."

His weekly odyssey begins in Kamu, a trading center on a plateau high above the plains that stretch north all the way to Sudan. I follow Philip and his bag of clothes through the market, watching him dive into one scrum after another as bales burst open. Out comes children's rummage, and Philip fights off several women for a handful of little T-shirts that go into his bag: MS. Y'S GOOFY GOOF TROOP, 2 BUSY + 2 SMART FOR TOBACCO = 4H and FUTURE HARVARD FRESHMAN.

The sun beats down, and Scovia Kuloba, the woman who introduced Philip to the trade, sits under an umbrella among mounds of clothes. Her barker scolds at the market crowd: "People leave the clothes to buy fish! They let their children go naked! This white man brought the clothes with him — don't you want to buy?"

When I explain to Scovia Kuloba that her goods come from

American charities, she stares in disbelief. "Sure? I thought maybe we Africans are the only ones who suffer. The people from there — I thought they were well off. I think they don't even work."

Her teenage daughter, Susan, whose braids and clothes look straight out of Brooklyn, adds: "I don't want to be poor, you just cry all the time. I hate the sun. I hate Africans." She'll only marry a *mzungu,* she says, because she knows from movies like *Titanic* and *Why Do Fools Fall in Love* that white men are always faithful, unlike Africans.

Slowly, I become aware of the sound of amplified American voices nearby, along with gunshots and screeching tires. Next to the used-clothing market, an action flick plays on video, with speakers hooked up outside to attract customers. In a dark little room, two dozen adults and children, who have paid six cents apiece, sit riveted to *Storm Catcher,* starring Dolph Lundgren.

The end of the road is a small hilltop town, green and wind-swept, called Kapchorwa, about 110 miles northeast of Mama Prossy's stall in downtown Jinja. Clouds hide 14,000-foot Mt. Elgon and, beyond it, Kenya. Philip spreads his wares on a plastic sheet at the foot of a brick wall and works hard all day, a tape measure around his neck. Poor rural Ugandans, the chain's last links, crowd close, arguing and pleading, but Philip is now the one with power, and he barely stirs from his asking price. One young man comes back half a dozen times to try on the same gray hooded coat. It fits perfectly, and it has arrived just in time for the chilly season that is blowing in. But Philip wants $4.70, and the customer only has $1.75.

"This coat is as thick as fish soup," Philip says. "The material lasts twenty years."

"You are killing me," the customer says. "The money is killing me."

"I am not killing you. I bought it at a high price, I ask a high price."

The customer finally walks away, and Philip returns the coat to his pile. The thrift shop's price tag is still stapled to the back: "$1.00." At the sight of it, I suddenly feel sad. I think of Virginia

Edelman and Marilyn Balk back on the Upper East Side, tossing out truckloads of the stuff, desperate to get rid of it. I remember the torrent pouring down the chutes at Trans-Americas' factory in Brooklyn. On balance, in spite of its problems, I have become a convert to used clothing. Africans want it. It gives them dignity and choice. But now that I have seen them prize so highly, and with such profound effects, what we throw away without a thought, the trail of Susie Bayer's T-shirt only seems to tell one story, a very old one, about the unfairness of the world as it is.

The T-shirt is buried deep in Philip's pile. My flight back to New York is leaving in four days, and I am concerned about missing it. So I reach into the pile, wanting to position the T-shirt more advantageously. As soon as I touch it, the shirt flies out of my hand. An old man in an embroidered Muslim cap and djellaba, who is missing his lower front teeth, holds it up for inspection. Tracing with his finger, he puzzles out the words printed in red and black around an academic insignia: "University Pennsylvania," he says. He dances away, brandishing the shirt in his fist. Ninety cents is his first offer, but Philip won't budge from $1.20. Eventually, the old man pays. Yusuf Mama, seventy-one, husband of four, father of thirty-two, has found what he wants.

I ask him why, of all the shirts in the pile, he has chosen this one. "It can help me," he says vaguely. "I have only one shirt."

Later, when I tell the story to people back in Kampala, they shake their heads. Yusuf Mama wanted Susie Bayer's T-shirt, they say, because a *mzungu* had touched it.

ZZ PACKER

■

The Ant of the Self

FROM *The New Yorker*

"OPPORTUNITIES," my father says after I bail him out of jail. "You've got to invest your money if you want opportunities." We're driving around Louisville in my mother's car. Who knows why he came down here, forty miles south of where he lives, but I don't ask too many questions. I just try to get my father, Ray Bivens, Jr., back across the river to his place in Indiana.

My father just got a DUI — again — though that didn't stop him from asking for the keys. When I didn't give them up, he sighed and shook his head as though I withheld keys from him daily. "C'mon, Spurge," he'd said. "The pigs aren't even looking."

It's 1995. He's the only person I know who still calls cops pigs, a holdover from what he refers to as his Black Panther days, when everyone raked their globes of hair with black-fisted Afro picks, then left them stuck there like javelins. When, as he tells it, he and Huey P. Newton met in basements and wore leather jackets and stuck it to whitey. Having given me investment advice, he now watches the world outside the Honda a little too jubilantly. I take the curve around the city on the Watterson Expressway, past the backsides of chain restaurants and malls, office parks, and the shitty Louisville zoo.

"That's your future," he says. "Sound investments."

"Maybe you should ask the pigs for your bail money back," I say. "We could invest that."

He doesn't respond. By now he's too busy checking out my mom's new car. Ray Bivens, Jr., doesn't own a car. The one he just got his DUI in belonged to a friend.

He takes the Honda's cigarette lighter out of its round home, stares into the unlit burner, then puts it back as if he'd thought about pocketing it but had decided against it. He drums a little syncopation on the dash, then, bored, starts adjusting his seat as though he's on the Concorde. He wants to say something about the car — how much it cost and how the hell Mama could afford it — but he doesn't. Instead, out of the blue, voice almost pure, he says, "Is that my old dress jacket? I loved that thing."

"It's not yours. Mama bought it. I needed a blazer for debate." The words come out chilly, but I don't say anything else to warm them up. And I feel a twinge of childishness mentioning my mother, like she's beside me, worrying the jacket hem, smoothing down the sleeves. I make myself feel better by recalling that when I went to post bail the woman behind the bulletproof glass asked if I was a reporter.

"You keep getting money from debate, we could invest."

When most people talk about investing, they mean stocks or bonds or mutual funds. What my father means is his friend Splo's cockfighting arena, or some dude who goes door to door selling exercise equipment that does all the exercise for you. "Didn't you just win some cash?" he asks. "From debate?"

"Bail," I say. "I used it to pay your bail."

He's quiet for a while. I wait for him to stumble out a thanks, or promise to pay me back with money he knows he'll never have. Finally, he sighs and says, "Most investors buy low and sell high. Know why they do that?"

Before I can respond, I hear his voice, loud and naked. "I *axed* you, Do you know why they do that?" He's shaking my arm. "You answer me when I ask you something."

I twist my arm away from his grasp to show I'm not afraid. We swerve out of our lane. Cars behind us swerve as well, then zoom around us and pull ahead.

"Do you know who this is?" he says. "Do you know who you're talking to?"

I haven't been talking to anyone, but I keep this to myself.

"I'll tell you who you're talking to — Ray Bivens, Jr.!"

He used to be this way with Mama. Never hitting, but always grabbing, groping, his halitosis forever in her face. After the divorce, he insisted on partial custody. At first, all I had to do was take the bus across town. Then, when he couldn't afford an apartment in the city, I had to take the Greyhound into backwoods Indiana. I'd spend Saturday and Sunday so bored I'd assign myself extra homework, work ahead in textbooks, whatever there was to do, while waiting for Ray Bivens, Jr., to fart himself awake and take me back to the bus station.

That was how debate started. Every year there was a different topic, and when they made the announcement last year it was like an Army recruitment campaign, warning students that they'd be expected to dedicate even their weekends to the cause. I rejoiced, thinking that I would never have to visit my father again. And I was good at debate. My brain frowned at illogic. But I don't think that my teachers liked me because of my logical mind; they liked me because I was quiet and small, and not rowdy like they expected black guys to be. Once, my history teacher, Mrs. Ampersand, said, "You stay away from those drugs, Spurgeon, and you'll go far." I could always think of things to say about U.S.-China diplomatic relations, or deliver a rebuttal on prison overcrowding, but with someone like Mrs. Ampersand all debate logic fell away, and in my head I'd call her a bitch, tell her that the strongest stuff in my mother's house was a bottle of NyQuil.

We've crossed the bridge into Indiana, but my father is still going. *"That's right! You're talking to Ray Bivens, Jr.! And don't you forget it!"*

Autumn is over, and yet it's not quite winter. Indiana farmland speeds past in black and white. Beautiful until you realize the world is supposed to be in color.

Later, calm again, he says, "Imagine a stock. Let's say the stock is the one I was telling you about, Scudder Mid Cap. The stock is at fifty bucks. If it's a winner, it doesn't stay at fifty bucks for long. It goes to a hundred, let's say, or two hundred. But first it's gotta get to fifty-one, fifty-two, and so on. So a stock increasing in price is a good sign. That's when you buy."

I thank him for telling me.

"Doesn't matter what you invest in, either," Ray Bivens, Jr., says. "That's the beauty. Don't gotta even think about it. That's something you won't hear from an accountant."

"You mean stockbroker. A stockbroker advises about stocks. Not an accountant."

His face turns bitter, as though he's about to slap me, but then he thinks better of it and says, "So you know who to go to when you get some extra cash."

"Look. I just told you, I don't have any money."

"You will, Spurgeon," he says. He puts an arm around me, and I can smell his odor from the jail. I don't have to see his face to know exactly how it looks right now. Urgently earnest, a little too sincere. Like a man explaining to his wife why he's late coming home. "I'll pay back every penny. I mean that."

"I believe you," I say, prying his arm from where it rests on my neck.

"You believe me," he says, "but do you believe *in* me?" He puts his arm back where it was, and now he's some suburban dad, a Little League coach congratulating his charge.

"I believe in you."

His arm falls away as he settles deeper into his seat with this knowledge, the leather sighing and complaining under him. I take the exit that promises a Citgo, park at a gas pump. The fluorescent lights stutter off and on as I begin pumping gas. I can hear what my mother would say — that my father is a cross I have to bear, that the Good Book says, "A child shall lead them," and all that crap, which basically boils down to "He's *your* father. Your blood, not mine."

Ray Bivens, Jr., leans against the car and stretches. Then he cleans the windshield with a squeegee. When I'm finished filling the tank, he says, "Hey, Spurgeon. How about breaking off a few bills? You know, they frisked me clean in lockdown."

I give him a twenty and wait in the car. He's in the Citgo so long

I get out and wipe off the squeegee streaks he left on the windshield. Finally, he comes back with a six-pack of Schlitz and a family-sized bag of Funyuns. "Listen," he says, handing me a beer. "We have to make a quick stop in Jasper."

Jasper, Indiana, is where his ex-girlfriend Lupita lives.

"I knew it," I say, and hand back the unopened beer before starting the car. "You're in trouble."

One of the fluorescent lights overhead blinks out. "What the hell are you talking about?"

"Why do we have to go to Jasper, all of a sudden?"

"If you shut your mouth and go to Jasper you'll find out."

"This is Mama's car," I remind him. "She wants it back."

"Why you gotta act like everything I ask you to do is gonna kill you? You my son. I tell you to do something, you obey."

I try to imagine what he's running from — men who'll tie him up at gunpoint and demand the twenty dollars he owes them, police officers waiting at his door — but those thoughts give way to the only thing we'll find in Jasper: Lupita, watching TV, painting her toenails. I've been to Lupita's place twice. It's full of birds. Huge blue and gold macaws. Yellow-naped Amazons. Rainbow lorikeets that squirt their putrid fructivorous shit on you. Tons of birds, and not in cages, either. I don't think my father liked them perching on his shoulders any more than I did, but the birds could land anywhere on Lupita and she'd wear them like jewelry.

Then it occurs to me that this is the only reason he cleaned the windshield.

"You're going to make me drive you and Lupita around so the two of you can get drunk. I knew it."

"If you don't shut up —"

I don't speak to him, and he doesn't speak to me. We pass a billboard that reads, WHEN LIFE GIVES YOU LEMONS, MAKE LEMONADE. I try to think of what my mother will say. She let me borrow the car to get him out of jail. But she wasn't about to pay bail, and she definitely won't want me coming home at midnight, her car smelling of cigarettes and Mad Dog.

My father sees me fuming and says, "I told you I was going

to get your money back, right? Well, there's going to be a march tomorrow. A million people in Washington, D.C. One. Million. People."

"No," I say. "Dear God, no."

"Exactly," he says.

At one point, I'd wanted to go to the march. I imagined it would be as historic as Dr. King's March on Washington, as historic as the dismantling of the Wall. The men's choir of my mother's church was going, but I didn't want to be trapped on a bus with a bunch of men singing hymns, feeling sorry for me because I'd been born with Ray Bivens, Jr., for a father. And, what's more, I had a debate tournament. I imagine Sarah Vogedes, my partner, prepping for our debate on U.S. foreign policy toward China, checking her watch. She'd have to use our second-stringers, or perhaps even Derron Ellersby, a basketball player so certain he'd make the NBA that he'd joined the debate team "to sound smooth for all those postgame interviews." This was the same Derron Ellersby who ended his rebuttals by pointing at me, saying, "Little Man over here's going to break it down for ya," or who'd single me out in the cafeteria, telling his friends, "Little Man's got skills, yo! Break off some a your skills!" as if he expected me to carry on a debate with my tuna casserole.

I picture Sarah Vogedes's composed face growing rumpled as Derron agrees with our opponent. I imagine Derron, index cards scattered in front of him, looking as if he'd been faked out before a lay-up, saying, "Yo! Sarah V! Where's Little Man? Where he at?"

For once I'm glad Ray Bivens, Jr., is scheming so hard he doesn't see me smiling. If he sensed in *any* way that I might be willing, he'd call the whole thing off.

"That's in Washington, D.C.," I remind my father. "Nearly seven hundred miles away."

"I know. But first we're going to Jasper," he says. "To get the birds."

Technically, the birds are my father's, not Lupita's. He bought them when he was convinced that the animals were an investment. He tried selling them door to door. When that didn't work and he couldn't afford to keep them, Lupita volunteered to take care of them. Lupita knew about birds, she'd said, because she owned a rooster when she was five, back in Guatemala.

It is completely dark. I ask, once more, what he plans to do with these birds, and he tells me that he's going to sell them.

"But you couldn't sell them the first time," I say.

"I didn't have a million potential buyers the first time."

I tell him that I can take him to Jasper, or I can take him home, but that I absolutely cannot, under any circumstances, cut school and miss my debate tournament to drive him to D.C.

"Don't you want your money back?" he says. "One macaw alone will pay back that bail money three times over."

"What are a million black men going to do with a bunch of birds? Even if you could sell them, how're you going to get them there?"

"Would you just drive?" he says, then sucks his teeth, making a noise that could almost be a curse. He stretches out in his seat, then starts up, explaining things to me as if I'd had a particularly stupefying bout of amnesia: "You're gonna have Afrocentric folks there. Afrocentrics and Africans, tons of Africans. And what do Africans miss most? That's right. The motherland. And what does the Mother Africa have tons of? Monkeys, lions, and guess what else? Birds. Not no street pigeons but real birds, like the kind I'm selling. Macaws and African grays. Lorikeets and yellow napes and shit." He might as well have added, "Take that."

I say nothing, thinking quickly but driving slowly. Off the interstate, the road turns narrow and insignificant. We pass through Paoli Peaks and Hoosier National Forest before finally arriving in Jasper.

We pull into Lupita's driveway. In the dark, her lawn ornaments resemble gravestones. Motion-detector floodlights buzz on as my father walks up to the house. Lupita stands on her porch, wielding a shotgun. She's wearing satiny pajamas that show her nipples. Pink curlers droop from her hair like blossoms.

"What do *joo* want?" Her eyes narrow in on him.

I stay in the car. She and my father disappear into the house while I watch the pinwheel lawn daisies spin in the dark. The yelling from inside the house is mostly Lupita: "I am tired of your blag ass! Enough eez enough!" Then it stops. They've argued their way to the bedroom, where the door slams shut and all is quiet.

But the calm doesn't hold. Lupita breaks out with some beautiful, deadly Spanish threats, and the screen door bangs open. My father comes out clutching cages, each crammed two apiece with birds. I can hear birdseed and little gravelly rocks from the cages spill all over the car's interior when he puts them on the back seat. He doesn't say a word.

He makes another trip into the house, and returns with another cageful of birds. Lupita follows him, but she stops halfway from the car. She stands there in her ensemble of sexy pajamas and pink sponge curlers and shotgun.

"Don't get out," Ray Bivens, Jr., says to me. "We're going to drive off. Slowly."

Lupita yells after us, "Joo are never thinking about maybe what Lupita feels!" For a moment I think she's going to come after us, but all she does is plop down on her porch step, holding her head in her hands.

Once the birds get used to the rhythm of the road, they swap crude, disjointed conversations with one another. A Mexican redhead sings "Love Me Do," but gets the inflections all wrong. A lorikeet says, "Where the dickens is my pocket watch?" then does what passes for a man's lewd laugh. If there's a lull, one will say "*Arriba, riba, riba!*" and get them all going again.

"Bird crap doesn't have an odor," my father says. "That's the paradox of birds."

"She loved those birds," I say. "And you just took them away."

"They learn best when stressed out," he says. "Why do you think they say '*Arriba!*' all the time? They get it from the Mexicans who're all in a rush to get them exported."

I stick to the point. "Don't try to make excuses. You hurt her. And what about the birds? You didn't think to get food, did you?"

"You are a complete pussy, you know that? You need to go to this march. When you go, check in at the pussy booth and tell 'em you want to exchange yours for a johnson."

I check the rearview mirror, then cross all lanes of I-65 north until I'm on the shoulder.

"You better have a good reason for stopping," he says.

"Get out," I say. The birds have ceased their chatter, and when I turn around they're looking from me to him as though they'd placed bets on who will go down in flames.

Ray Bivens, Jr., clamps his hand to his forehead in mock dumb-foundedness. "You ain't heard that before? Don't tell me nobody never called you no pussy?"

"Get out, sir," I say.

"Yeah. I'll get out all right." He opens the passenger-side door just as a semi whooshes by. He slams the door and traps the cold air with me.

It's late — past midnight. I stop at the next exit to call my mother. She says if I don't get my tail back in her house tonight she'll skin me alive. I tell her I love her, too. She likes to pretend that I'm the man of the house, but it's at times like this that it's clear that the only man of the house is Jesus.

I buy a Ho Ho at a gas station, and, as I separate the cake part from the creamy insides with my teeth, I think about how Derron would have shrugged Ray Bivens, Jr.'s schemes away with a goodhearted hunch of the shoulders. "Pops is crazy," he'd say to the mike in an NBA postgame interview, then put his gently clenched fist over his heart like someone accepting an award. "But I love the guy."

I get back into the car. I return to the last exit before heading north again, going slowly in the right-hand lane. When I see my father, I pull over to the shoulder, pop open the electronic locks. He acts like he knew I would come back for him all along. We don't talk for nearly an hour, but everything is completely clear: If I am not a pussy, I will cut school, forget about the debate, and go to D.C.

Just outside Clarksburg, West Virginia, I pull over. I can't make it to the exit. Twice I almost nodded off. When I slump onto the steering wheel, my father gets out and rouses me enough for us to exchange places, even though he's not supposed to be driving.

I don't know how long I've been asleep, but I wake to an umbrella cockatoo chanting, "Sexy, sexy!" My eyes adjust to the dim light, first making out the electric glow of the dash panels, and then the scenery beyond the cool of the windows. We are on a small hilly road. It is so dark and so full of conifers that I feel like we're traveling through velvet.

Ray Bivens, Jr., I can tell, has been waiting for me to wake up. At first I think he wants me to take over the wheel, but then I realize he wants company. He raps on the car window and says, "In ancient Mesopotamia it was hot. There was no glass. What they did have was the wheel —"

The yellow-naped Amazon breaks into the Oscar Mayer wiener jingle before I can ask my father what the hell he's talking about.

"Shut up!" he yells, and I sit up, startled, thinking that he's yelling at me. The bird says *"Rawrk!"* and starts the jingle over, from the beginning.

"Here's why windows are called windows," he says with strained calmness when the bird has finished, but a lorikeet interrupts. "Advil works," the bird says, "better than Tylenol."

My father blindly gropes the back seat for a cage, seizes one, and slams it against another cage. All the birds revolt, screeching and shuffling feathers. But Ray Bivens, Jr., raises his voice above the din. "The Mesopotamians cut out circles, or 'O's, in their homes to mimic the shape of the wheel, but also to let in the wind!" he yells. "And there you have it. Your modern-day window. Get it? 'Wind-o.'"

I look to see if he's taking himself seriously. He used to say shit like this when I was little. I could never tell whether he was kidding me or himself. "You're trying to tell me that the Mesopotamians spoke English? And that they created little 'O's in their homes to let in the wind?"

"All right. Don't believe me, then."

We make it into Arlington at eight in the morning, park the car at a garage, and take the Metro into D.C. with the morning commuters. White men with their briefcases and mushroom-colored trench coats. White women with fleet haircuts, their chic lipstick darker than blood. The occasional Asian, Hispanic — wearing the same costume, but somehow looking nervous. Mostly, though, we see black men — groups of black men wearing T-shirts with the names of churches and youth groups emblazoned on them. Men in big, loose kente-cloth robes; men in suits with the traditional Nation of Islam bow tie.

My father hands me two cages, and he hefts two. While the morning commuters eye us, he discusses the bird prices loudly. Once we get closer to the Mall, we can hear African drums, gospel music blaring from the loudspeakers, and someone playing rap with bass so heavy it hurts your heart. Everything has an early-morning smell to it, cold and wet with dew, but already thousands have marked their territory with portable chairs and signs. Venders balance basketfuls of T-shirts on their heads; D.C. kids nudge us, trying to sell us water for a dollar a cup. The Washington Monument stands in front of us like a big granite pencil, miles away, it seems; and everywhere men shake hands, laugh like they haven't seen each other in years. They make pitches, exchange business cards, and congratulate each other for just getting here. But, most of all, they speak in passwords: "Keep Strong," "Stay Black," "Love Your Black Nation."

As we work our way through the masses, Ray Bivens, Jr., keeps looking off into the distance in search of the perfect customer.

"Brother," one man says, shaking his head at me. "I don't know if them birds males or not, but they sho ain't black!"

I nod in my father's direction and say, "Looks like you've got a customer."

He shoots me an annoyed look. "Let's split up," he says. "We'll cover more area if we're spread out."

"Okay, chief," I say. But I stay where I am.

After a few speeches from Christian ministers, a stiff-looking bow-tied man introduces Farrakhan and the Nation of Islam. I'm so far back that I have to look at the large-screen TVs, and as Farrakhan takes to the stage the Fruit of Islam phalanx behind him applauds violently.

I make my way toward the edge of the crowd to get some air. Though I'm already as far away from the main stage as one can be, it still takes me half an hour to push through the crowd of men, most of whom pat me on the back like uncles at a family reunion. Some black women cheer as they stand on the other side of Independence Avenue, but others wave placards that read LET US IN! or REMEMBER THOSE YOU LEFT HOME. It occurs to me that I can stay here on the sidelines for the entire march. A hush falls over the crowd, then it erupts into whistles and cheers and catcalls, and people begin chanting, "Jesse! Jesse!"

On the screen, Jesse Jackson is clasping hands with Farrakhan, but he doesn't do much more than that. It seems that the day will be a long one, with major speakers bookended by lesser-known ones.

Now a preacher from some small town is on the podium. "Brothers, we have to work it out with each other! How are we going to go back to our wives, our babies' mothers, and tell them that we love *them* if we can't tell our own brothers that we love them?"

At first, he sounds like every other speaker, breaking a cardinal rule of speech: reiteration, not regurgitation. He reads from a letter written in 1712 by William Lynch, a white slave owner from Virginia. Farrakhan read from this same letter, I realize, but the content got lost in his nearly three-hour speech. The letter explains how to control slaves by pitting dark ones against light ones, big-plantation slaves against small-plantation slaves, female slaves against male ones. The preacher ends by telling everyone that freedom is attained when the ant of the self — that small, blind, crumb-seeking part of ourselves — casts off slavery and its legacy, becoming a huge brave ox.

"Well, well, well!" An elbow nudges me. "Wasn't that powerful, brother?" A man wearing a fez extends his hand for me to shake.

I shake his hand, but he doesn't let go.

"Powerful!" the fezzed man shouts above the applause.

"Yes," I say, and turn away.

I must not be convincing enough, because the guy taps me on the shoulder and says, "Feel this! The power here! This is powerful!"

"Don't get me wrong," I say, "but I'm just here because my father made me come."

The man in the fez screws up his face in the sunlight, features bunched in confusion. He puts his hand to his ear.

"My father!" I yell. "My father made me come!"

"Made you come? Made you? This, my brother, is a day of atonement! You got to cut your father a little slack for caring for your sorry self!"

Other men's eyes are on me now, but I'll be damned if this man who doesn't even know me sides with Ray Bivens, Jr. "I thought the whole point of all this was to take responsibility," I say. "Put an end to asking for slack. If you knew my father you'd know that his whole damn life is as slack as a pants suit from J.C. Penney!"

"Hold up, hold up, hold up," a voice says. The voice comes from a man with a bullet-smooth head. The pistils and stamens of the monstrous Hawaiian-flower-print shirt he's wearing seem to stare at me, and suddenly his face is so close I can smell the mint of his breath.

"You need to learn that responsibility is a two-way street!" The Hawaiian-shirt guy points to my chest. "You have to take responsibility and reach out to him."

Many more people have turned to look at us, thanks in no small part to the constant squawking of the birds in their cages. The Phalanx of Islam is on its way, moving in the form of crisp, gray-suited men wearing stern looks and prison muscles.

"Let me ask you a question, my brother," he says. "Why are you here? You don't seem to want to atone — not with your pops, not with anybody."

Those around me have formed a sideshow of which I seem to be the villain, and they look at me expectantly. The Hawaiian-shirted man folds his arms across his chest and jerks his chin up, daring me to answer him.

"Atoning for one's wrongs is different from apologizing," I begin. "One involves actions, the other words." I don't want to say anything now that the crowd around me is silent, listening; now that the sun in my eyes is so strong I feel like crying. I can feel the debate judge mouthing "Time's up," can see the disbelief and disappointment in the men's faces. An oxford-shirted security guard grabs me by the arm.

"What," he says, "seems to be the problem, son?"

"Look," I finally say to him and anyone else who'll listen. "I'm not here to atone. I'm here to sell birds."

I spot my father by the cages balanced on his shoulders when the marchless march is pretty much finished. The sky is moving toward dusk, and though speakers are still coming up to the podium, you'd stick around to listen only if they were your relatives. My father and I get pushed along with other people who are trying to leave.

I don't bother telling him how security guards clamped me on the shoulder and sat me down on the curb like a five-year-old and gave me a talking-to, reminding me of the point of the march. I don't tell him how they fed me warm flatbread and hard honey in a hot plastic tent and gave me bean pies, some pamphlets, and a Koran. But he can tell how pissed off I am.

He can see I haven't sold any birds, and I see he hasn't, either. Ray Bivens, Jr., grabs a man by the arm. The man's T-shirt reads, VOLUNTEER: WASHINGTON, D.C.

"Where's a good bar?" my father asks. "That's cheap?"

The man raises his eyebrows and says, "Brotherman, we're trying to keep away from all that poison. At least for one day." His voice is smooth and kind, a guy from the streets who's become a counselor, determined to give back to the community. He smiles. "You think you can make it for one day without the sauce, my brother?"

The bar we end up in is called the Haven. The bartender looks at the birds and shakes his head as if his patrons never ceased to amuse him.

Even though Ray Bivens, Jr., is sitting in the place he loves most, he still seems mad at me. So do the birds. None of them are speaking, just making noises in their throats as though they were plotting something. I ask the bartender if the birds will be safe outside; whether someone will steal them.

"Not if it's something that needs feeding," he says.

"Speaking of feeding," my father says, "I'm going to get some

Funyuns. Want any?" He says this more to the bartender than to me, but I shake my head. The bartender spray-guns a 7-UP in a glass for me without my even asking, then resumes a conversation with a trio of men at the end of the counter. One man has a goiter. One has processed waves that look like cake frosting. While those two seem to be smiling and arguing at the same time, the third man says nothing, smoking his cigarette as though it were part of a search for enlightenment.

The Smoker ashes his cigarette with a pert tap. "You been at the march, youngblood?"

"Yeah. How'd you know?"

They all laugh, but no one tells me why.

The bartender dries some beer glasses. "Anybody here go?" When nobody replies, he says to me, with a knowing wink, "These some shiftless niggers up in here!"

There's general grumbling. I tell him I was glad I went. "I was more relieved than anything else," I say.

"Relieved?" the Smoker asks, his voice wise and deep, even though he's just asking a question. "What you need relief from? You ain't old enough to be in preschool."

I try to think. "I don't know. I just get tired of feeling like I'm a fucking mascot or something," I say, surprised that I said the f-word out loud, yet shaking my head as though I said words like that every day. "I get tired of it. You skip it for a day and it feels like a vacation."

The Smoker stares at me.

"It's like I'm in this class, surrounded by white folks. Like they just pick one, even after the good grades and staying after school and everything — even after all that, they still make you feel like *they* picked you. Token until proven adequate. Adequate until proven competent. Competent until proven worthy." I meant it to sound like I was pissed off, not only because I was, but because I thought they'd be pissed off along with me.

"Man," the guy with the goiter says, "I'm happy to hear that. You got the luxury of feeling tired. Back in the day, before you were born, couldn't that type of miscegenation shit happen."

"You mean integration," I say.

"We the ones fought for you to be in school with the white folks," he says, his goiter looking as if he'd swallowed a light bulb. "Now you talking 'bout a vacation!"

They all laugh like it's some sort of secret code that got broken.

"You'll be all right, youngblood," the Smoker says. "You'll be all right."

Just as I begin to realize they're humoring me, Ray Bivens, Jr., comes blustering through the door. He flashes a wad of money. "Luck," he says, smiling, "is sometimes lucky."

The trio at the bar high-five each other in anticipation of free drinks.

"Who," I say, "did you take that from?"

"Take?" He chucks his thumb toward me as if to say get a load of this guy. "Sold the birds. Rich white dude. Convenient store. I said, 'I got birds.' He said, 'I got money.' Six hundred bones."

I'm upset, though I don't know why. Six hundred bucks. Who in this neighborhood even had six hundred bucks? I lean toward him and whisper, "I bailed you out of jail, remember."

"Don't worry," he says. "I'll buy you a drink."

Three hours pass, and my father has beaten all the regulars trying to win money from him at pinochle when a woman appears. Her skin is the color of good Scotch. She sits between me and my father, twirls around on her barstool once, and points a red enameled finger toward the goiter-man changing songs on the jukebox. "Play 'Love the One You're With.' Isley Brothers."

"I was going to," says the Goiter. "Just for you."

She spins around on the barstool again, so that she's facing the bottles lined up on display. "Farrah," she says, and extends a tiny limp hand in my direction. "Farrah Falana."

"That's not your real name," I say.

"Yes, it is," she says dreamily. "Farrah Falana. I was named after that show."

Now I see that she's going on fifty. She smiles at me with her mouth closed, and, for a moment, looks like a beautiful frog.

My father makes a long, admiring appraisal of her seated behind. "Farrah and Ray," he says. "I like how that sounds."

"I like how it sounds, too," Farrah says, sliding her barstool toward him.

My father and Farrah get drunk while I play an electronic trivia game with the Goiter. He knows more than I gave him credit for, but he's losing to me because he bets all his bonus points whenever he gets a chance. The Goiter and I are on our tenth game when Ray Bivens, Jr., taps me on the shoulder. I look over to see him standing very straight and tall, trying not to look drunk.

"You don't love me," he says sloppily. "You don't *understand* me."

"*You* don't understand you," I say.

Farrah is still at the bar. I plunk three quarters in the game machine. "Your go," I say to the Goiter.

"Does anybody understand themselves?" Ray Bivens, Jr., says to me softly, and for a second he looks perfectly lucid. Then he says it louder, for the benefit of the whole bar, with a gravity only the drunk can muster. "Does *anybody*, I say, under*stand* themselves?"

The men at the bar look at him and decide it's one of their many jokes, and laugh, though my father is staring straight through me, as though I were nothing but a clear glass of whiskey into which he could see both the past and the future.

"Let me tell you something," Ray Bivens, Jr., says, almost spitting in my face. "Lupita *understands* me. That woman," he says, "*understands*. She's It."

Farrah smacks him on the shoulder and says, "What about me? What the fuck about me?"

An hour later he says, all cool, "Gimme the keys. Farrah and I are going for a ride."

I've had many 7-UPs, and I've twice asked my father if we could go, told him that we either had to find a motel outside the city or plan on driving back soon. Now it's nearly three A.M. and he's asking for the keys. The car is all the way over in Arlington, and even the Metro has stopped running.

"Sir," I say, "we need to drive back."

"I said, Spurgeon, dear son, that Farrah and I are going for a ride. Now give me the keys, dear son."

A ride means they're going to her place, wherever that is. His going to her place means I have to find my own place to stay. Giving him the keys means not only that he'll be driving illegally, which I no longer care about, but that the car will end up on the other side of the country, stripped for parts.

"No," I say. "It's Mama's car."

"Mama's car," he mimics.

"Sir."

"Maaaamaaa's caaaaar!"

I leave the bar. I'm walking for a good minute before I hear him coming after me. I don't even know how I'm going to get back to the car, but I pick a direction and walk purposefully. I hear the click click click of what are surely Farrah's heels, hear her scream something that doesn't make sense. The streetlights glow amber, and my breath makes smokelike puffs in the October air. Then I'm spun around as if for inspection, and that's when I see his face — handsome, hard-edged, not the least bit sloppy from liquor.

Sure. He's hit me before, but this is hard. Not the back of the hand, not with a belt, but punching. It's a punch meant for my face, but it lands on my shoulder. Then there's another hit, this one all knuckles, and my jaw pops open, automatically, like the trunk of a car. I try to call time-out, but he's ramming into me not with his fists but with his head. He leans into me, his head tucked into my stomach, both of us wobbling together like lovers. Finally, I push him away, and wipe what feels like yogurt running from my nose into the raw cut of my lip. I start to lick my lips, thinking that it's all over, when he rushes straight at me again, and I break my fall against a newspaper stand. Sheaves of weekly newspapers fan the ground like cards spilled from a deck. I kick him anywhere my foot will land, shouting at him, so mad that I'm happy, until I kick at air, hard, and trip myself up. I don't know how long I'm down, but he's now picking me up like a rag doll. "What the hell are you talking about?" he says, as if to shake the answer out of me. "What the hell are you talking about?"

I only now realize what I've been screaming the whole time. "Wind-o!" I yell at him. "You and your goddamn wind-o! There was never any wind-o! And you don't know shit about birds! *Arriba! Arriba!"*

Then I remember something I know will kill my father. He dodged the draft. They weren't going to get this nigger was his view of Vietnam. It was the one thing I'd respected him for, and yet somehow I said it: "You didn't know fucking Huey P. Newton. You never even went to Vietnam!"

"Vietnam?" he says, once, as if making sure I'd said the word.

I'm quiet. He says the word again, "Vietnam," and his eyes somehow look sightless.

I go to put my hand on his shoulder, but a torrent of people, fresh from the march, has been loosed from a nearby restaurant. They slap one another's backs, smelling of Brut and Old Spice, musk-scented African oils and sweat. Already, my father has gone.

Ray Bivens, Jr., left with the car, and Farrah left with someone else. The birds are gone. My blazer is gone. After I have a Scotch the bartender says, "Look, I can float you the drinks, but who's going to pay for that, youngblood?" He points to one of the bar's smashed windowpanes.

I pay, and then have no money left for a cab or a bus. The bridge over the Potomac isn't meant for pedestrians, and it takes me half an hour to walk across it. For a long time I'm on New Hampshire Avenue, then I'm on Georgia. I ask for directions to the train station.

Perhaps he's right about Lupita. When she sat on the porch and held her head, it seemed she felt sorrier for him than she did for herself — it wasn't pity but sympathy.

I walk by an old-fashioned movie theater whose marquee looks like one giant erection lit in parti-color lights. People pass by, wondering how to go about mugging me. A well-dressed man asks if I'm a pitcher or a catcher, and I have no idea what he means. It's good that Ray Bivens, Jr., and I fought, I tell myself. People think that you need something worth fighting for. But it must be the fighting that decides what matters, even if you're left on the sidewalk to discover that what you thought mattered means nothing after all.

*

"Where do you want to go?" the Amtrak ticket agent asks.

"East," I say. "Any train that goes east this time of night."

"You're in D.C., sir. Any further east and you'll be in the Atlantic."

Of course, I'm not going east. I've been going east for the last day and a half. I can finally go west now. Go home.

But it would be me who gets the snottiest ticket agent of the whole damn railway system. I look into his gray eyes. "West, motherfucker."

The ticket agent stares at me, and I stare right back. He looks down at his computer, and then at me again. "Where, pray tell, do you want to go? 'West,' I'm afraid, is a direction, not a destination."

"Louisville, Kentucky," I finally say. "Home."

He enters something into his computer. Tilts his head. He smiles when he tells me there is no train that goes to Louisville. The closest one is Cincinnati.

I walk away and sit down. How am I going to pay to get to Cincinnati, then from Cincinnati to Louisville. The only white person in the station besides the ticket agent is an old woman in a rainbow knit cap, who is having an intelligent conversation with herself.

I'll have to call home, ask my mother to give her credit card number to this prick. A man approaches the ticket counter with his son, half asleep, riding on his back. He probably just came from the march. Probably listened to all the poems and speeches about ants and oxen and African drumming, but still he'd had this kid out in the hot sun for hours, then in the cold night for longer. It's almost five o'clock in the morning, and all this little boy wants, I can tell, is some goddamn sleep.

"Hey," I say to the man. When he doesn't respond, I tap him on the nonkid shoulder. "It's pretty late to have a kid out. Don't you think?"

He puts his hand up like a traffic cop. "Dude, I don't know who you are, but you'd best not touch me."

I sit down on a wooden bench. The old white woman next to me carefully pours imaginary liquid into an imaginary cup. The man with the kid goes up to the ticket agent, who stops staring into space long enough to say, "May I help you, sir?"

"Do y'all still say 'All aboard'?"

"Excuse me?" the ticket agent says.

"My son wants to know if y'all say 'All aboard.' Like in the movies."

The boy jiggles up and down on his father's back, suddenly animated. The ticket agent sighs, hands grazing the sides of his face as if checking for stubble. Finally, he throws his arms up in a sure-what-the-hell kind of way, and disappears into the Amtrak offices. The father sets the boy down on the floor. An intercom crackles, and a voice says:

"All aboard!"

The voice is hearty and successful. The boy jumps up and down with delight. He is the happiest I've seen anyone, ever. And though the urge to weep comes over me, I wait, holding my head in my hands, and it passes.

JAMES PINKERTON

■

How to Write Suspense

FROM *Modern Humorist*

LIKE MOST PEOPLE between the ages of eighteen and thirty-six, you're probably writing a suspense novel. Perhaps you've written your first book, and realize that it doesn't have any suspense in it at all. Maybe you've written a suspense novel, but it's the wrong sort of suspense. The details are irrelevant — what matters is that you are awful at writing truly great suspense, and it infuriates you. With my program, you'll learn how to inject those blood-curdling hooks into every nook and crevice of your writing. You'll discover how to construct suspense-packed sentences, and how to "end" those sentences with edge-of-your-seat punctuation.

On to the first lesson!

Lesson 1: General Suspense Tips

The opening sentence is essential to a great suspense novel, as it lets the reader know what the story's going to be about. I've included a sample opening sentence below, to show you how it's done right:

John crossed over to the living room and lit a cigarette.

Note how I have successfully introduced a character, a location, and an action. Now let's crank up the suspense:

John crossed over to the living room and lit a cigarette. Or did he?

Doubt sets in. Our reader begins to question everything he or she has come to believe. Who is this John character? Can we really trust him? How can we really trust anybody? Chilling questions. Luckily, you don't have to answer them. Remember: Great suspense lies in what you don't tell your readers.

Having placed the seed of doubt in our readers, we quickly move on to something else, distracting the hell out of them.

John then went to work and nothing happened.

This is a perfectly acceptable follow-up sentence, right? Wrong. This sentence isn't suspenseful at all. Let's try that follow-up sentence again:

~~*John then went to work and nothing happened.*~~ *John went to work. His day was a roller-coaster ride of intrigue and mystery.*

Did you see what made the "right" sentence suspenseful and what made the "wrong" sentence utterly worthless? If not, you might be making the same mistakes and not even realizing it.

TIP:
Try practicing writing in a mirror. Watch yourself as you write. What are you doing wrong?

Lesson 2: Writing the First Chapter

Read the following opening paragraph and try to locate where the suspense is coming from:

The gunman adjusted his gay hat as he powled the misty ooftops, knowing his pey would show soon. Sweat stuck to his shit as he contemplated what he must do. The one-eyed man who had killed his fathe would finally pay the pipe.

An excellent opening to a great suspense novel. Where are all the r's? Is it a typographical error? Does the writer simply not like r's? Or are there mysterious deeds at play, and are the r's somehow involved? All of these questions spiral through the readers' minds as they find themselves in the taut grip of suspense.

In the next paragraph, we release this grip:

> *The one-eyed man had stolen all the r's.*

Goosebumps, yes? If you felt a cathartic release while reading that sentence, you're not alone. Why? Because that was great suspense.

A simple lesson can be gleaned from this: A suspense novel should start with a very suspenseful opening paragraph, then release the suspense in the second. After this you just write the rest of your book. The reader knows what kind of powerhouse suspense writing to expect, and your work is done.

TIP:

Lightning is so suspenseful it's not even funny, so always use it for everything. Lightning makes the reader notice whatever happened before the lightning, so also remember to put in a lot of suspense before the lightning crashes. Just pack it in there, no one will mind.

Lesson 3: Writing Suspenseful Dialogue

Read the following dialogue and watch for the "end parts" of the sentences. These are the parts of the sentences where you're probably going to be able to fit most of the old suspense in.

> *"I never thought you'd be capable of murder," said Janet, crossing to the living room to light a cigarette. Or did she? "I've known you since the first grade. You've never harmed a fly."*

> *"Maybe that's true," said John. "Maybe it's not true. Maybe I've harmed lots of flies." He looked over at Janet, who may or may not have been lighting a cigarette. "You don't know me, Janet."*

> *"Or do I? I know you're not capable of murder, John. Sure, maybe flies. I'll give you that. But people? That's stupid."*

Janet put the lighter she may or may not have been using to light a cigarette on the table. Then Janet saw an enormous bloody knife on the table.

"Is this knife yours, John?" she asked.

"No," John replied. "I'm pretty sure it's not mine."

"Are you lying to me, John?"

"No, probably not."

Lightning crashed!

Egad! Is John a *murderer?* Possibly! That's the thing — who knows? Good suspense dialogue should crackle off the page for your reader, as the preceding dialogue just did for you. Always keep the reader on their toes by being ambiguous about everything. Leave out important details, locations, names, even events integral to the plot. Remember, the more the reader has to guess at, the more powerful your novel becomes.

Lesson 4: Ending Your Suspense Novel

A good suspense novel must have a surprise twist ending to leave the reader completely dumbfounded. If you've done your job well up to this point, then readers should have no clue what's happening, who your characters are, or what it is they're so worried about. Time for the final turn of the screw to make them jump out of their seats! Observe:

John and Janet had finally solved the murder. It had been some other guy all along. They were just sitting down to a delicious lasagna that Janet had baked when suddenly —

How would YOU end the tale? Write out your ending now. Then read my ending to see why yours is wrong.

GOOD:

— Janet's head exploded! Janet had been injected with a toxin that explodes heads. John stopped eating his lasagna.

Or did he?
The End

BETTER:

— *a big bomb dropped on the house, killing both of them, but mostly Janet. The bomb had been launched in Iraq because of a war there, but the guidance system had shorted out, so it went over to Janet's place instead and flew right into her head. John had a mouthful of lasagna at the time and was flabbergasted.*

Everyone else was flabbergasted, too. "We never saw that coming," they said.

It turned out that John's last name was Saunders. Nobody had ever known that.

The End

SUSPENSETASTIC:

— *a murderer walked in the house!*

"Oh no, a murderer!" John said as he stopped eating his lasagna. The murderer chased John all through the house and murdered him while Janet escaped. She ran outside and flagged down a policeman who was driving by.

"There's a murderer in my house!" Janet said.

"He's not in your house," said the policeman. "He's ME!" Holy shit! The policeman was the murderer! He murdered Janet.

The End

Parting Thoughts

Alfred Hitchcock once wrote: "It's either great suspense, or it's a large pile of my stool." These words are as true today as they were two hundred years ago, when he first made suspenseful films. No, dear readers — great suspense writing is not easy. But with a lot of practice and determination, you will, I assure you, never be as good as I am. You will, however, still be among the great suspense writers of the twentieth century. Dear readers, I leave you to it. Also: *Lightning crashed suddenly!*

Sorry to scare you like that.

DAVID SEDARIS

■

Rooster at the Hitchin' Post

FROM *Esquire*

THE NIGHT THE Rooster was born, my father slipped into my bedroom to personally deliver the news. I was eleven years old and barely awake, yet still I recognized this as a supreme masculine moment: the patriarch informing his firstborn son that another player was joining the team. Looking around my room, at the vase of cattails arranged just so beside the potpourri bowl, he should have realized it was not his team I was playing for. Not even a girl would have decoupaged her own electrical sockets, but, finding it too painful to consider, my father played on, going so far as to offer me a plastic-wrapped cigar, the band reading, IT'S A BOY. He'd gotten one for each of us. Mine was made of chewing gum, and his was the real thing.

"I hope you're not going to smoke that in here," I said. "Normally I wouldn't mind, but I just Scotchgarded the drapes."

For the first six months, my brother, Paul, was just a blob, then a doll my sisters and I could diaper and groom as we saw fit. Dress him appropriately and it was easy to forget the tiny penis lying like a canned mushroom between his legs. Given some imagination and a few well chosen accessories, he was Paulette, the pouty French girl; Paola, the dark-wigged bambina fresh from her native Tuscany; Pauline, the swinging hippie chick. As a helpless infant, he went along with it, but by the age of eighteen months he'd effectively dispelled the theory that a person can be made gay. Despite our best efforts, the cigar band had been right. Our brother *was* a boy. He inherited my sports equipment, still in its original wrapping, and took to the streets with actual friends, playing whatever was in season. If he won, great, and if he lost, big deal.

"But aren't you going to weep?" we'd ask. "Not even a little?"

We tried explaining the benefits of a nice long cry — the release it offered, the pity it generated — and he laughed in our faces. The rest of us blubbered like leaky showerheads, but for him water production was limited to sweat and urine. His sheets might be wet, but the pillow would remain forever dry.

Regardless of the situation, for Paul it was always all about the joke. A warm embrace, a heartfelt declaration of concern: In moments of weakness, we'd fall for these setups, vowing later never to trust him again. The last time I allowed my brother to hug me, I flew from Raleigh to New York, oblivious to the sign he'd slapped on the back of my sport coat, a nametag sticker reading, HELLO, I'M GAY. This following the hilarity of our mother's funeral.

When my sisters and I eventually left home, it seemed like a natural progression — young adults shifting from one environment to another. While our departures had been relatively painless, Paul's was like releasing a domestic animal into the wild. He knew how to plan a meal but displayed a remarkable lack of patience when it came time for the actual cooking. Frozen dinners were often eaten exactly as sold, the Salisbury steak amounting to a stickless meat Popsicle. I phoned one night just as he was leaning a family pack of frozen chicken wings against the back door. He'd forgotten to defrost them and was now attempting to stomp the solid mass into three six-inch portions, which he'd force into his toaster oven. I heard the singular sound of boot against crystallized meat and listened as my brother panted for breath. "Goddamned . . . fucking . . . chicken . . . *wings*."

I called again the following evening and was told that after all that work, the chicken had been spoiled. It tasted like fish, so he threw it away and called it a night. A few hours later, having decided that spoiled chicken was better than no chicken at all, he got out of bed, stepped outside in his underpants, and proceeded to eat the leftovers directly from the garbage can.

I was mortified. "In your *underpants?*"

"Damned straight," he said. "Rooster ain't getting dressed up to eat no fish-assed-tasting chicken."

I worried about my brother standing in his briefs and eating spoiled poultry by moonlight. I worried when told he'd passed out in a parking lot and awoken to find a stranger's initials written in lipstick on his ass, but I never worried he'd be able to make a living. He's been working for himself since high school and at the age of twenty-six founded Sedaris Hardwood Floors, a successful floor-sanding company. The work is demanding, but more tiring still are the nitpicky touchups, the billing and hiring, and the endless discussions with indecisive clients. When asked how he manages to keep all those people happy, he credited the importance of compromise, explaining, "Sometimes you got to put that dick in your mouth and roll it around a little. Ain't no need to swallow nothin', you just got to play on it for a while. You know what I'm sayin'?"

"Well . . . *yeah.*"

At an age when the rest of us were barely managing to pay our own rent, he had bought a house. Four bedrooms and the place was his, as were the trucks and sport utility vehicles that spilled from the driveway and onto the lawn he paid to have mowed. All this from a business philosophy based on the art of a blow job.

Paul referred to his house as "the home of a confused clown," but to the naked eye, the clown seemed absolutely sure of himself. There was the farting mound of battery-operated feces positioned on the mantel, the namesake rooster inlaid into the living room floor, the bright green walls and musical butcher knives. "No confusion here," you'd say, tripping over a concrete alligator. It was an awfully big place for just one clown, so we were relieved when a girlfriend moved in, accompanied by an elderly pug named Venus.

My brother was overjoyed. "You want to talk at her? Hold on while I put her on the phone."

I prepared myself for the voice of a North Carolina girlfriend, something like Paul's but lower, and heard instead what sounded like a handsaw methodically working its way through a tree trunk. It was Venus. Months later, he put me on the phone with their new dog, a six-week-old Great Dane named Diesel. I spoke to the outdoor cats, the indoor cats, and the adopted piglet that seemed like a good idea until it began digesting food. They'd been living together for more than a year when I finally met the girlfriend, a licensed hairdresser named Kathy. Erase the tattoos and the nicotine patch and she resembled one of those tranquil Flemish Madonnas, the ubiquitous Christ child replaced by a hacking pug. Her grace, her humor, her fur-matted sweaters — we loved her immediately. Best of all, she was from the North, meaning that should she and Paul ever bear a child, it stood a fifty-fifty chance of speaking understandable English.

They announced their engagement and planned a mid-May wedding tailor-made to disappoint the Greeks. It would not take place at the Holy Trinity Church but at a hotel on the coast of North Carolina. The service would be performed by a psychic they'd found in the phone book, and the music provided by a DJ named J.D. who worked weekdays at the local state penitentiary.

I flew in from Paris two days before the wedding and was sitting in my father's kitchen when Paul came to the door dressed in a suit and tie. A former high school classmate had committed suicide, and he'd dropped by the house on his way home from the funeral. Since I'd last seen him, my once slim brother had gained a good sixty pounds. Everything seemed proportionally larger, but the bulk seemed to have settled about his face and torso, leaving him with what he referred to as Dick Do Disease. "My stomach sticks out further than my dick do."

The added weight had softened certain features and swallowed others altogether. His neck, for instance. Obscured now by a second chin, his head appeared to balance directly upon his shoulders, and he walked delicately, as if to keep it from rolling off. I told myself that if I looked at my brother differently, it was because of the suit, not the weight. He was a grown man now. He was going to get married, and therefore he was a changed person.

He took a sip of my father's weak coffee and spit it back into the mug. "This shit's like making love in a canoe."

"Excuse me?"

"It's fucking near water."

Then again, I thought. Maybe it *was* just the weight.

I drove to the coast early the next morning with my sister Lisa and her husband, Bob. Mention Paul, Kathy, or even Atlantic Beach and Lisa's eyes would well with tears of joy. "I just never thought I would see this day," she would sigh. "Never, never, never." From Morehead City on, she pretty much cried nonstop, provoked by the landmarks of our youth. "Oh, the bridge! The pier! The midget golf course!"

Atlantic Beach was where we had vacationed when our mother was alive, and it had changed a lot over the last ten years. Paul was to be married in what used to be the John Yancy Hotel but was currently called the Royal Pavillion. The remodeling had been extensive, and what had once been a modest oceanfront hotel now boasted reception rooms and a wedding gazebo. Waitresses wore bow ties and pushed the scampi, explaining that it was Italian. Had you spent the eighties in a coma, you might have been impressed with the fake columns and pastel color schemes, but as it was there was something sad and mallish about it.

While the ceremony would take place at the Royal Pavillion, guests would be staying next door at the Atlantis Lodge, a three-story motel essentially unchanged since the early space age. It's where we'd spent weekends as young adults, when trips to the beach became trips *at* the beach. Mushrooms, cocaine, acid, peyote: I'd never checked in without being, at the very least, profoundly stoned, and on arrival I was surprised to find the furniture actually standing still.

"Didn't these beds used to vibrate?" I asked my sister Tiffany.

"Don't they still?" she said.

My brother had chosen the Atlantis not for its sentimental value but because it allowed the various family dogs. Paul's friends, a group the rest of us referred to as simply "the dudes," had also brought their pets, which howled and whined and clawed at the sliding glass doors. This was what happened to people who didn't have children, who didn't even know people who had children. The flower girl was in heat. The rehearsal dinner included both canned and dry food, and when my brother proposed a toast to his "beautiful bitch," everyone assumed he was talking about the pug.

An hour before the wedding, the men in my family were scheduled to meet in Paul's room, no women or dudes allowed. I went expecting a once-in-a-lifetime masculine moment, and, looking back, that's probably what I got. While my room was immaculate, Paul's was dark and littered with bones, like the cave of an animal. He'd arrived only the previous afternoon, but already it looked as though he'd been living there for years, surviving on beer and the bodies of missing beachcombers. I spread out a newspaper and sat on the bed as my father, the best man, attached my brother's cummerbund. It was five o'clock on one of the most important days of their lives, and both of them were watching TV. It was a cable news channel, a special report concerning a flood in one of those faraway towns senselessly built on the banks of an untrustworthy river. Citizens stacked sandbags on a retaining wall. A wheelbarrow floated down the suburban street. "And still," the announcer said, "still the rain continues to fall."

I'd heard once, probably falsely, that when filming the movie *Gandhi,* the director had hired extras to play the roles of sandbags, that it had actually been cheaper than finding the real thing. It seemed like a worthy conversational icebreaker, but before I could finish the first sentence, my father told me to put a lid on it. "We're trying to watch some TV here," he said. "Jesus! Do you mind?"

Over in the bridal suite, they were systematically applying makeup and crying it back off. Noteworthy things were being said, and I couldn't help but feel I was in the wrong room. My father turned my brother to face him and, with one eye on the television, began knotting his bow tie.

"Water like that will fuck the shit out of some hardwood

floors," Paul said. "Those motherfuckers are looking at total re-
placements, I'll tell you what."

"Well, you're right about that." My father helped the groom into
his jacket and turned to give the flood victims one last look. "All
right," he said. "Let's get married."

It was a busy day at the Royal Pavillion. The five o'clock wedding had gotten a late start, and we watched from the sidelines as a
Marine Corps chaplain finished marrying an attractive young couple in their early twenties. My sisters Lisa and Amy gave the relationship three years at the most. My other sister Gretchen and I
put it closer to eighteen months, and Tiffany suggested that if
we wanted the real answer, we should ask the psychic, who stood
beside a scrub pine entertaining Paul's godmother. She was a
tall, conservatively dressed woman with flesh-colored hair and
matching fingernails. Sunglasses hung from a chain around her
neck, and she wiped their lenses while reciting her credentials. It
seemed that, aside from her regular Friday night tarot-card read-
ings, she also cured cancer, diabetes, and heart disease by touching the sufferers in secret, hard-to-reach places. "I've had the gift
since I was seven," she said, "and, believe me, I am very good at
what I do."

When it came to weddings, she psychically read the prospective
bride and groom, divining their innermost selves and using her
findings in order to tailor unique, personally significant vows.

"Well, I, for one, think that that is really beautiful," Lisa said.

"I know you do," the psychic said. "I know you do."

The marines filed out of the gazebo, and we moved in to take
their seats. "Who does that woman think she is?" Lisa whispered.
"I mean, come on, I was only trying to be polite."

"I know you were," I said. "I know you were."

J.D. the DJ was stuck in bridge traffic, so the ceremony com-
menced without the prerecorded wedding march. Lisa predictably
started howling the moment the bride rounded the Coke machine
and came into view on the arm of her father. The dogs followed
suit, and, determined not to join them, I looked beyond the psy-

chic's shoulder to a small patch of ocean visible through the trees. It was the place where, almost twenty-five years ago, my brother had come close to drowning. We'd been horsing around at high tide and looked up to find ourselves on the other side of the waves, drifting farther and farther from the hotel. It wasn't natural to be out that far, and so I swam for shore, thinking he was right behind me.

"Greetings, friends and family," the psychic said. *"We stand on . . ."* She looked at the bride, towering over my pint-sized brother. *"We stand on tiptoes this afternoon to celebrate the love of . . . Paul and Kathy."*

He wasn't supposed to be out at that time of day, especially with me. "You wind him up," my mother said. "For God's sake, just give it a rest." When accused of winding up my sisters, I'd always felt a hint of shame, but I liked the fact that I could adequately enthuse a twelve-year-old boy. As an older brother, I liked to think that it was my job and that I was good at it. I swam for what felt like the length of a pool, then stopped and turned around. But Paul wasn't there.

"This love cannot be bought . . . in a store," the psychic said. *"It cannot be found . . . under a tree, beneath a . . . shell, or even in a . . ."* You could see her groping for a possible hiding place. *"Even in a . . . treasure chest buried centuries ago on the . . . historic islands that surround us."*

A swell moved in, and my brother went under, leaving only his right arm, which waved the international sign for "I am going to die now and it's all your fault." I headed back in his direction, trying to recall the water-safety class I'd taken at the country club. *Think,* I told myself. *Think like a man.* I tried to focus, but all that came to me was the instructor, an athletic seventeen-year-old named Chip Pancake. I remembered the spray of freckles on his broad, bronzed shoulders and my small rush of hope as he searched the assembled students for a resuscitation victim. *Oh, choose me,* I'd whispered. *Me. Over here.* I recalled the smell of hamburgers drifting from the clubhouse, the sting of the life jacket against my sunburned back, and the crushing disappointment I felt when Chip selected Kimberly Matthews, who would later describe the experience as "life changing." These are not the sorts of memories that save lives, so I abandoned the past and relied instead upon instinct.

"We ask that this marriage be blessed with as many graces as there are ... grains of sand in the ... ocean."

In the end, I just sort of grabbed Paul by the hair and yelled at him to lie flat. He vomited a mouthful of seawater, and together we kicked our way back to the beach, washing ashore a good half-mile from the hotel. We were lying side by side, catching our breath in the shallow surf, and it seemed a moment in which something should be said, some declaration of brotherly love.

"Listen," I started. "I just want you to know —"

"Fuck you," Paul had said to me.

"I do," Paul now said to Kathy.

"I just never thought I'd see this day," Lisa whimpered.

My brother kissed his bride, and the psychic looked out at her audience, nodding her head as if to say, "I knew that would happen."

Cameras clicked, and a wind kicked up, blowing Kathy's veil and train straight into the air. Her look of surprise, his frantic embrace — in resulting photographs, it would appear as if she'd dropped from the sky, caught at the last moment by someone who would now introduce himself as the luckiest man in the world.

At the reception, my brother danced the worm, throwing himself on his belly as the dudes chanted, "Party, fat man, party!" My father delivered a brief, awkward speech while waving a rubber chicken — not a rooster, but a chicken — and again the cameras flashed.

"I cannot believe you," I said. "A rubber *chicken?*"

He claimed he'd been unable to find a rubber rooster, and I explained that that wasn't really the point. "Not everyone has the ability to improvise," I said. "Where were your notes? Why didn't you come to me for help?"

If I was hard on him, it was because I'd wanted to deliver the big speech. I'd been planning on it since Paul was a boy, but nobody had asked me. Now I'd have to wait until his funeral.

At 1:00 A.M., the room rental ended and plans were made to move the reception onto the beach. Kathy changed out of her gown while Paul and I took the dogs for a quick walk across the front lawn of the Atlantis. For the first time since the wedding, we were alone, and I wanted to force a moment out of it. The operative word here, the source of the problem, is *force*. Because it never works that way. In trying to be memorable, you wind up sounding unspeakably queer, which may be remembered, but never the way you'd hoped. My brother had spent his life saving me from such moments, and now he would do it again.

A light rain began to fall, and just as I cleared my throat, Venus squatted in the grass, producing a mound of peanut-sized turds.

"Aren't you going to clean that up?" I asked.

Paul pointed to the ground and whistled for the Great Dane, who thundered across the lawn and ate the feces in one bite.

"Tell me that was an accident," I said.

"Accident, hell. I got this motherfucker trained," he said. "Sometimes he'll stick his nose to her ass and just eat that shit on tap."

I thought of my brother standing in his backyard training a dog to eat shit and realized I'll probably continue thinking about it until the day I die. Forget the tears and brotherly speeches, this was the stuff that memories are made of.

The Great Dane licked his lips and searched the grass for more.

"What was it you were going to say?" Paul asked.

"Oh, nothing."

From their perch atop an endangered dune, the dudes emitted a war cry. Kathy called out from the door of her room, and, together with his dogs, my brother set forth, spreading a love that could not be found under a tree, beneath a shell, or even in a treasure chest buried centuries ago on the historic islands that surrounded us.

JASON STELLA

■

Astroturf

How Manufactured "Grassroots"
Movements Are Subverting Democracy

FROM *Shout*

SHE HAD ONLY one name, Nayirah, when she came before the Congressional Human Rights Caucus on October 10, 1990. It was just after the Iraqi invasion of Kuwait, and Nayirah testified to having witnessed Iraqi soldiers tearing Kuwaiti infants from hospital incubators, leaving them to die on the floor. As she spoke, tears streamed down her face.

The videotape of her testimony circulated through every nook of American media, and then-president George Bush cited the incident frequently in building a case for military action. A country that polls had shown to be evenly split on intervention as late as December 1990 slowly became primed for war. When the Senate finally voted on its war resolution on January 12, it passed by five votes. And the number who said they voted because of the baby incubator incident? Six.

Nayirah had appeared under the auspices of an American grassroots organizing committee, Citizens for a Free Kuwait. She was part of a larger mobilization, in which CFK provided American news organizations with color photographs of Kuwaitis of all ages who reportedly had been killed or tortured by Iraqis. CFK also distributed videotapes that showed Iraqi soldiers apparently firing on unarmed demonstrators, as witnesses related tales of horror.

Their campaign turned the Gulf War into a moral battle, a fight of good against evil that stands today as the reason to oppose Saddam Hussein. It's the genesis of the "Evil" in the Axis.

After the war, *Harper's* publisher John R. MacArthur visited CFK while researching his book *Second Front: Censorship and Propaganda in the Gulf War.* That's when he discovered a conspiracy, at the center of which stood the Kuwaiti government and its PR firm, Hill & Knowlton, which had created CFK from scratch.

Among the piles of war photos shown to MacArthur were depictions of tortured Kuwaiti citizens who had apparently suffered gruesome deaths.

"But when I looked closely at the photographs," recalled MacArthur, "I saw that they were mannequins dressed up to look like torture victims."

MacArthur dug further and found that the entire campaign itself had been manufactured by Hill & Knowlton on behalf of the Kuwaiti government, which had a lot invested in appearing the victim. Of the $11.8 million raised by CFK, only $17,861 came from actual citizens. The rest was supplied by the Kuwaiti government.

Moreover, the supposedly anonymous young girl who had so tearfully testified was actually the daughter of the Kuwaiti ambassador to the United States — not a hospital volunteer, as she had testified. She lived in the United States and the events she recounted had not occurred. The Gulf War, it turns out, was waged not on a lie, but rather on a mountain of them.

Enter Astroturf

In 1967, Monsanto Industries patented "monofilament ribbon file product," and they saw that it was good. Said They, "A primary object of this invention is to provide a synthetic product which simulates the physical characteristics and general appearance of natural turf." Then, baseball was played upon it, by the Astros in Houston, and They saw that it was good. And They named it, AstroTurf.

In 1995, *Campaigns & Elections* magazine defined a new brand of Astroturf as "a grassroots program that involves the instant manufacturing of public support for a point of view in which either uninformed activists are recruited or means of deception are used to recruit them."

One of PR's most active recruiters has been Edward L. Bernays, nephew of Sigmund Freud, and the most influential pioneer of modern public relations tactics.

To sell cigarettes as a symbol of women's liberation, he convinced a group of women's rights marchers to hoist Lucky Strike cigarettes as symbolic "torches of freedom." Within months, sales of Lucky Strike were soaring as a new niche of nicotine addicts became "liberated."

Bernays would later find out that the practical application of his own theories proved greatly effective for Joseph Goebbels, minister of propaganda for Hitler's Third Reich. As Bernays writes in his autobiography, "[Goebbels] was using my book, *Crystallizing Public Opinion*, as a basis for his destructive campaign against the Jews of Germany. This shocked me."

Today, such tactics are commonplace. The creation of illusory grassroots groups is a time-tested process, one which is not exclusive to wartime propaganda. Corporations rely on Astroturf groups to rally support for or opposition to legislative measures that threaten to siphon cash from the corporate till.

To those seniors concerned about rising prescription drug costs, Citizens for Better Medicine (CBM) might seem a worthy advocate for their cause. Billing itself as "a grassroots organization that is working to strengthen and improve Medicare," CBM is actually a front for the Pharmaceutical Research and Manufacturers of America (PhRMA), a trade group made up of the world's largest pharmaceutical firms.

Through CBM, PhRMA spent $65 million in the 1999–2000 election cycle on ads and direct mailings which featured the skeptical senior "Flo," who stressed the importance of "keeping big government out of our medicine cabinets." Flo, a fictional character, was played by Diana Sowle, who is best known for playing Charlie Bucket's mother in the 1971 hit *Willy Wonka and the Chocolate Factory*.

CBM's ads talked about protecting seniors and their prescription drug coverage. They were really about protecting industry's profits from commonsense reform. Through CBM's ads, seniors were invited to call Congress and oppose the very measures that would help them control the skyrocketing cost of life-saving prescription drugs.

Whether they manufacture consent for war or prey on the vulnerability of senior citizens, public relations firms are using Astroturf and other veiled tactics to dupe the public into thinking that they are supporting a grassroots, nonprofit, or independent organization, when in fact they are unwittingly supporting the very causes, corporations, or policies they might otherwise wish to denounce. In so doing, they create for the public the illusion of active participation in the democratic process.

The overall PR strategy for manipulating and maintaining this illusion is one of triangulation between three camps of traditionally liberal opposition: radicals, idealists, and realists. Speaking before the National Cattlemen's Beef Association, Ron Duchin, senior vice-president of the PR firm Mongoven, Biscoe, and Duchin, outlined his firm's basic divide-and-conquer strategy for defeating activist groups.

The first step is to isolate and marginalize the radicals. Radical activists "want to change the system," and have "underlying socio/political motives — I would categorize their principal aims right now as social justice and political empowerment," Duchin said to his sympathetic audience. To isolate them, PR firms will try to create a perception in the public mind that people advocating fundamental solutions are extremists, fear mongers, or social malcontents with anarchist aims.

After marginalizing the radicals, the next step, Duchin said, is to identify and "educate" the "hard-to-deal-with" idealists — concerned and sympathetic members of the public — by convincing them that the changes advocated by the radicals would hurt people. Idealists, Duchin said, "have a vulnerable point. If they can be shown that their position in opposition to an industry or its products causes harm to others and cannot be ethically justified, they are forced to change their position — thus, while a realist must be negotiated with, an idealist must be educated."

With the proper "educating," Duchin explained, idealists and realists can be counted on to cut a deal with industry that can be touted as a "win-win" solution, but that actually serves what Duchin calls "the final policy solution."

"Realists are able to live with tradeoffs; willing to work within the system; not interested in radical change."

If successful, this strategy should force the public to fear the radicals, view the uneducated idealists as unrealistic, and view the realists as trusted leaders whose endorsement of the corporation or its product validates the corporation's claims.

In Bernays's 1928 book, *Propaganda,* he explains the full dimensions of propaganda, PR, and Astroturf in tones that echo the covert darkness of the postwar era. "The conscious and intelligent manipulation of the organized habits and opinions of the masses is an important element in democratic society," he wrote. "Those who manipulate this unseen mechanism of society constitute an invisible government which is the true ruling power of our country."

And it was this ruling power that engineered consent for the Gulf War. In the minds of Americans, the available facts did not seem to warrant military intervention. But when Nayirah's teary testimony paired with photos of dismembered mannequins entered the debate, fiction blurred fact, setting in motion a conflict that still exists today.

This kind of manipulation is nefarious because it turns good intentions against their very ends. The danger of Astroturf comes not from its subversion of democracy, but in the way that it tricks us into subverting it ourselves.

Rugburn: Astroturf's Top Ten

Activistcash.com
Activistcash.com attempts to discredit activists by suggesting that there is something disreputable about the money they have re-

ceived from foundations. The site refers to activists as "nannies," "anti-choice zealots" and "hypocrites." Ironically, Activistcash.com makes no mention of its own funders, mainly the tobacco and alcohol industries.

National Smokers Alliance
As internal tobacco industry documents make clear, the NSA was invented by Big Tobacco in 1993 with the help of public relations giant Burson-Marsteller to counter antitobacco legislation.

The American Tort Reform Association
The ATRA claims to be comprised of the "average citizen," but is in fact a corporate front for the chemical, tobacco, pharmaceutical, and auto industries.

The Global Climate Coalition
Run by New York PR firm Ruder Finn, the GCC represents the big oil, gas, coal, and auto corporations. In 1997, the GCC distributed a video to hundreds of journalists claiming that increased levels of carbon dioxide would increase crop production and help end world hunger.

Contributions Watch
Posing as a "public interest" campaign reform organization, CW's hidden agenda is to dig up dirt at the state level for the corporate clients of its creator, the State Affairs Company (SAC), and the funder, Philip Morris. SAC and CW work to attack the political enemies of their clients, and to smear the "hidden, undisclosed consumerist agendas" of real public interest groups like Consumers Union, the Center for Science in the Public Interest, Ralph Nader's Public Interest Research Group, and Trial Lawyers for Public Justice.

Arctic Power
Working to promote oil drilling in the Arctic National Wildlife Refuge, AP bills itself as a "grassroots, non-profit citizens' organization with 10,000 members." Its board members include repre-

sentatives from the Alaska Oil & Gas Association, Resource Development Council, Alaska Miner's Association, and Alaska Forest Association.

Environmental Conservation Organization
ECO is an anti-environmental umbrella outfit counting more than three hundred Wise Use groups as members. With a phone and fax network and a monthly newsletter, *eco-logic,* fronting as an eco-friendly publication, ECO promotes Wise Use efforts to stop the global warming treaty and to push founder Henry Lamb's conspiracy theories of a United Nations New World Order.

New York Institute for Law and Society
Donald Trump funneled at least $118,000 to an anti-Mohawk ad campaign run by the Institute to block the St. Regis Tribal Council's plans for a Catskills Native American–run casino. Trump and his lobbyist Roger Stone were hit with a record $250,000 in fines for violating state lobby laws.

Keep America Beautiful
A front for the packaging and waste-hauling industries, KAB lobbies against mandatory recycling laws, especially the passage of a national bottle bill in the United States.

Consumer Alert
This Astroturf group calls global warming science "scare stories," and funds the Web site Globalwarming.org. Consumer Alert's networking project, the National Consumer Coalition, formed the so-called Cooler Heads Coalition (CCC), "to dispel the myths of global warming." Consumer Alert is funded by the Chemical Manufacturers Association, Chevron, Monsanto, Philip Morris, and other large corporations.

JOHN VERBOS

■

Lost Boys

FROM *Pindeldyboz*

Pittman

The new kid arrived today, halfway into the semester. His name: Pittman. We hung our heads and shook them slowly as soon as we saw him. His next few months will be hellish. Mr. Clean, the hairless headmaster, gave him a tour around the campus. Even Mr. Clean shook his head.

We Few, We Happy Few, We Band of Brothers

We wear jackets. We wear ties. We have to; there's a dress code. And there we are, reading *Henry V* out loud to each other in English class. Because we have to. Some of us don't mind this as much as we mind the ties and jackets. Pittman reads Hal. He does a surprisingly good job, we think, and then we look around to make sure that everyone else is in agreement. Everyone else seems not to care one way or the other.

The Ladykiller Murders The Indian

To be honest, The Texan has us worried. He was always a little screwy, but in the last few days he's gone over the edge. It all started when The Ladykiller murdered The Indian in chemistry lab. The Ladykiller didn't know what he was doing; he just sat down on his stool next to The Texan, like he did every other day, except that this time The Indian was already sitting there. The Indian was invisible, so how was The Ladykiller to know? He crushed The Indian, we suppose, but we don't know for sure and The Texan won't talk about it. The Texan just mopes around the halls, staggering into lockers, muttering to himself. His boots are dull, scuffed, and cracked.

Wendy

We call him The Ladykiller because of three things: the way he wears his pants slung low across his hips, the way he walks with this slow cat's gait — actually, those two kind of go together. The third thing is Wendy. Second thing. Whatever.

Peanut's Hex

Mr. Shields gave Peanut detention for casting a hex on a teacher. Presumably Mr. Shields is the teacher in question, but none of us was there to verify that fact. We have only the carbon copy of the detention slip to go by. Peanut retaliated by killing a squirrel with a rock and putting the carcass in Mr. Shields's Ford Tempo. At least that's what we think happened. Again, we don't have any proof. Mr. Shields may have killed the squirrel himself. We know that Mr. Shields and Peanut are not on the best of terms, but we are uncertain as to how deep their mutual disaffection runs. And neither of them is forthcoming about it. Mr. Shields only speaks to students in Latin and Peanut doesn't talk to anybody without a very good reason. He certainly doesn't talk to us. Regardless, we doubt that he'd answer our questions about whether or not he killed the squirrel and how, if he did, he got it inside Mr. Shields's Tempo.

Study Hall

— Psst. Hey you.
— What?

— You're the new guy, right?
— Yeah.
— Are you gay?
— What?
— Are you gay?
— No.
— Do you have a girlfriend?
— No.
— I see.
— That doesn't mean I'm gay.
— Right. Right.
(scribble scribble flip flip scribble)
— Hey Sweetie.
—
— Hey Sweetie, hey new guy.
— I have a name.
— Right. Sweetie. That's your name.
—
— Hey, Sweetie, you got a pen?
— Just the one I'm using.
— Can I borrow it?
— What?
— Can I borrow your pen, Sweetie?
— No. I'm using it.
— I just need it for a second. I'll give it back.
—
— Come on, Sweetie.
— Fine. But I need it back.

Threats from Beyond the Grave

The Ladykiller (or Indiankiller or just Killer) has been getting
death threats from The Indian. The dead Indian. Threats from beyond the grave, some whisper. These threats come on half-sheets
of college-ruled paper and are scrawled in a childish hand. We fish
them out of the trash after The Ladykiller has discarded them.

We have a record. INDIAN COME BACK TO KILL YOU, the first one said, underneath a drawing of a stick figure wearing a head-dress decapitating another stick figure labeled YOU. They've gotten worse. And more complex. Terrible deaths for the Ladykiller are outlined. Horrible things. Skinning him alive, for example, and then setting him in front of a big industrial fan. The Lady-killer, however, is not fazed. He reads each new day's threat, smiles and snorts, then crumples it up and defiantly chucks the ball into the trash. His bravado is baffling.

Rounds

The Sheriff clicks his way down the hall. He's checking for irregu-larities: ties knotted incorrectly, shirttails in the breeze. The Sher-iff will take any and every opportunity to slam somebody up against a locker and sneer at him through his drooping black mus-tache. That there ain't regulation, he'll say. Then The Sheriff will drop the boy like a sack of taters and continue on his clicking in-spection of the halls and dorms. We scatter like rats when we hear that clicking. We've trained ourselves to hear it from across the campus. The Sheriff clicks even when he's walking through the mud. Nobody's gotten close enough to get proof as to whether The Sheriff is actually wearing spurs or just making the clicking sound with his tongue. Those who have suffered at the hands of The Sheriff never think to look at his heels. All they report is that his eyes are like blasting caps and that his teeth look like ice cubes when he shows that cold cold sneer.

The Debatable Origins of Wendy

Wendy is from another school. Certain persons (scribbling love letters on off-white stationery) would argue, at this point, that she is from another world, that Earth has never produced such a crea-ture. Regardless of her origins, she attends an all-girls day school that was founded by a woman who wrote a famous book on an-cient Greek mythology. Again, certain persons (mooning out the open window and sighing) would interrupt here to announce that Wendy is much like some of the goddesses in that book. These persons have been warned about making such comments out loud, even though we've all thought them. Wendy sneaks onto the campus at certain designated times and meets The Ladykiller at certain designated places. We have their schedules memorized. We watch them through high-powered binoculars and sometimes creep up closer on our bellies. We know that this is not correct. We're also pretty sure that The Ladykiller knows we're watching. One of us, probably Allergic Jones, sneezed one time and The Ladykiller looked in our direction, right at us, and then went about his business. Allergic Jones swears that The Ladykiller winked at him. Whether he knows we're watching or not, things between The Ladykiller and Wendy have gotten more animated. They've gone further, been more brazen when flinging their clothing. They've been louder. We scattered like rabbits when a pair of red panties landed inches from our hiding spot. We'd like to think that we've had a positive effect on the situation, but if The Ladykiller is in on the game, then Wendy might be too. Just a thought, one of us says, and then shrugs.

Polls

The election is coming up. The Ladykiller has put up signs and given speeches that imply that providing pussy and beer for all will be his first priority if elected. This strategy seems to be working well for him. If The Sheriff gets wind of this, however, it's curtains, but so far there's been no sign of that happening. The Texan has entered the fray as well. He has promised nothing, implicitly or otherwise. He is trailing The Ladykiller by quite a margin in our polls. When asked why he's running, The Texan says nothing but gives us a look that says, You know why. A candidate that nobody's ever heard of before has registered on the charts by appearing in priest's robes and forgiving everyone for everything. It appears that The Ladykiller will win in a landslide. The Texan gives us a look that says, Just wait.

What Allergic Jones Has Been Up To in the Lab

Allergic Jones has been concocting a paste that makes a loud BANG! when you apply pressure to it with a metal object. He holds a gray gob of it in his fat hand and explains how it works. We are impressed. We nod sagely and scratch our barren chins.

The Last We Saw of Peanut

Peanut has disappeared. He was last seen heading into The Sheriff's office. The Sheriff said, Shut the door, and Peanut did. That was days ago. We have no illusions about what happens in that office.

A Necessary Explanation of the Dynamics of This Place

It is a fact that Pittman minces. He can't do anything about it, any more than Allergic Jones can help being allergic. Most of us overlook it, the same way we overlook The Ladykiller calling Pittman a fag and making his life generally miserable. The Ladykiller is not an exceptionally good person. If The Ladykiller didn't razz Pittman, then someone else would. And of the available razzers, The Ladykiller is the only one who does not cross the line into physical violence. Pittman, however, does not understand this, does not understand that he is comparatively lucky. We tell him that it's a good thing that The Texan seems to have gone off his rocker and that Peanut has disappeared. Otherwise . . . We don't continue. We let it sink in. Pittman looks nonplussed, and so we explain that this sort of thing is bound to happen and it's best to find a way of dealing with it. If it weren't his wrists and his lips and the way he walks, up on the balls of his feet, then The Ladykiller or somebody worse would've found something else to pick on. The list of infractions is long: being poor, not driving the right car, not wearing the right pants, being smart, being dumb, having dark skin, being pale, having curly hair, talking too fast, not speaking enough, being too short, being too tall and awkward, being too fat, having bad skin, having no discernible sex drive, wearing thick glasses, having misshapen lips, being unable to grow facial hair, being an albino, having a limp, having a lisp, having a withered arm, having a hump, a stutter, a wandering eye, a peg leg, a hook instead of a hand . . . et cetera, ad infinitum, ad nauseam. Pittman looks at us. He has not taken Latin.

The Room When We're Not There

There are thirty chairs in each room. At the moment none is occupied. The moonlight is the only light, and it comes through the two windows on the east side of the room, the side that faces the street. Blue everything. There's a lectern on the desk at the front of the room and behind it looms the chalkboard, cleared of all the notes and scribbles, streaked from being washed with a wet sponge. The floor is hardwood, misaligned and warping at the ends. Booksbooksbooksbooksbooks. Posters of cities on the wall. Paris, Rome, Moscow, Venice, Calcutta, Athens, London, Budapest. The posters are dimmed in the moonlight and look like two-dimensional monsters chained to the wall. They have snarling teeth and sharp bloody claws, but they no longer possess the will to attempt freedom.

Operation

Allergic Jones applies the paste with his finger and then gently pokes it into the keyhole with a Popsicle stick. Two of us train flashlights on the work site. Another watches the halls. We have people posted at the exits and in the stairwells. It is such a large-scale operation because nobody wanted to be left out. Otherwise it would've been a two-man gig. Pittman refused our invitation. When Allergic Jones has filled every keyhole one of us gives the signal and we all disappear.

Snarl

All hell breaks loose on the day before the election. BANG! BANG! All over the building. The Sheriff is snarling and squatting down to inspect a door. No damage, except to the nerves of the teachers. Snarl. We're alternately trying to look very busy and check the heels of The Sheriff's boots for spurs. However, we get caught on, are mesmerized by, the note sticking out of his back pocket. It looks like another one of the suicide notes that keep showing up, signed by Pittman but not written in Pittman's hand (simple handwriting analysis will bear this out, we're certain). It might be The Indian reaching out from beyond the grave, trying to get The Ladykiller in trouble. This is a highly dubious theory, as it seems much too troublesome and far too complicated, even when taking into account the craftiness of The Indian. As further research into this matter is needed, some of us cause a ruckus to draw The Sheriff's attention, while others steal the note from The Sheriff's back pocket. Then we scatter, like antelopes this time. Snarl.

The Suicide Note

This is a superior suicide note, better than ours, we're afraid. Ours are all half mocking, half serious. But we are poor note writers. We have a collection of these notes, hidden away in a filing cabinet on the top floor. We compare our notes to those we've collected. Everyone, it seems, has written a few. Even The Texan, although his have only started appearing recently. Our favorite, its source unknown, is "Got bored, went out window." We also have a collection of love letters to Wendy. Everyone writes these too, but they are harder to come by because their authors guard them carefully. We suspect that The Sheriff wrote one of the letters to Wendy that we have managed to acquire. It is penned on stiff paper, with icy blue ink.

Assembly

The Sheriff has gone on the warpath, so to speak. He is clicking up and down every hall, looking for the guilty. We've never noticed his monocle before. When he leaves a hall, the clicking sound remains. Click click click. You get the idea. It's like we're inside a very large clock. Or a very large crocodile. We are all assembled, the entire body of jacket- and tie-wearing adolescents. The Sheriff glowers at us from behind the podium. He sneers. The temperature in the room drops ten degrees, even with the increase in body heat among all present, hot and nervous and sweating, shoved, as we are, into the bleachers in the always stifling gymnasium. We are all guilty, in one way or another. Some more than others. It is a matter of what the offense in question is. Boys are pulled at random from their seats and inspected by The Sheriff. He is desperate, he is accusatory. He holds up a Ziploc bag with a small gob of gray paste in it. He presents us with a bouquet of suicide notes. He pulls from his inside jacket pocket an impossibly long and multicolored rope of panties, tied one to the next, like handkerchiefs. Do you know anything about this? The Sheriff hollers, shoving the panties in Pittman's face. We are secretly jealous. Pittman sputters and waves his arms. The Sheriff asks, What's the matter, boy? You gay? Roars of laughter. Silence. The Sheriff looks around the room through his monocle, scanning the room for remnant gigglers, boys biting their faces, red-cheeked and teary eyed. You will all suffer, The Sheriff says, unless someone comes forward. Allergic Jones is aching to unburden his conscience, but we have the ether at hand. More silence. An arched eyebrow from The Sheriff. He takes off his black hat, runs his hand through his gray hair, fills the hat with the evidence, and puts it back on. He clicks away, through the door. The Texan stumbles out from his seat and shouts. His eyes are unfocused and bloodshot. Hey, he shouts again. The Sheriff stops in his tracks and wheels on The Texan.

The Texan Speaks

Fine, The Texan says, I did it. All of it. Everything. The suicide notes, the underwear, whatever that weird gray crap in the baggie is. There you go. Fuck it. I'll take the rap for whatever you want to pin on me. Let's go. What's the punishment? No sense these fellas here takin' the blame for something they didn't do. Am I right? Come on, what's the punishment? Let's do it right here, friend.

I'm ready. I'm not afraid of you or your sneer or your clicking, which, I'm convinced, has nothing to do with spurs.

What We're Thinking in This Moment of Crisis

A) What's his game here? Is he trying to win votes? Is this a ploy?
B) Is he drunk?
C) Crazy bastard. The Sheriff will eat him alive. Kill him, even.
D) I wonder where Wendy is right now. I wonder if she's wearing that sweater that she wears, the one with seven buttons of which she always only buttons four or five.
E) Well, The Texan might have gone around the bend, but he's got my vote. Besides, look at The Ladykiller, smug and silent over there. Letting another man take the fall for him. Damn unpresidential of him, damn unpresidential.

The Sheriff Responds

Pistols, he says. Dawn.

A Sleepless Night

The crickets, oh the crickets. We blame them for our insomnia, but the truth is that we're anxious. Tomorrow things will change. We must have every confidence in The Texan. If our faith is well placed, if we're right, not only will The Sheriff fall, but The Texan is sure to win the election that afternoon, after such an act of stupid courage. And we're certain that if The Texan is elected, his first act will be to send The Ladykiller to the stockade for killing The Indian, which puts a new twist on the Wendy situation. And we extrapolate further, to love letters and marriage, but there is a fog beyond which no predictions can be made. We take a turn around the campus and listen to the crickets and watch for signs of life. We perch on the wall that encloses the campus. Pittman, we see, through our binoculars, is shadowboxing furiously, sweating fiercely, and generally looking like a bad motherfucker in his dank and piteous room. Poor Pittman. Allergic Jones falls off the fence with a mighty sneeze.

Love Letters to Wendy

We write these late at night, when we can't sleep. Some letters are long ramblers, encyclopedias of the irrelevant. Some authors aim for a particular number of pages or words. In all of them, love and/or Wendy are the themes, at least on the surface. A few of the more artistic of us compose letters entirely out of pictures. The French students among us use that language whenever possible, while the Latin students stick entirely with English. Popular openings: Wendy, Dear Wendy, Love, To Wendy Who Makes the Moon Pale and the Sun Burn with Jealousy, Beloved Wendy, My True Love. Popular things described: Wendy. Specifically: Wendy's eyes, Wendy's hair, the way Wendy smells, Wendy's lips, Wendy's smile, Wendy's bosom. Popular things lamented: not being with Wendy, not being able to describe the beauty of Wendy, not being The Ladykiller, the existence of The Ladykiller, not having the guts to tell Wendy how one feels. Popular things longed for: a night of blissful passion, Wendy to smile in one's direction, a chance. Popular poets quoted: Shakespeare, Byron. Popular threats made: suicide, various publicly embarrassing displays of one's love for Wendy. Popular incidents recounted: the first time one saw Wendy. Popular closings: Love, All My Love, Passionately, Longingly, Hopefully, Sincerely, I Love You, Burningly, Achingly, Collapsing Under the Weight of My Love. Sometimes there are tears, or maybe they're just drops of saline. The most pathetic letters claim a life-threatening illness. The saddest are those whose tone is that of a soldier at war who never expects to return.

Dawn

We find the crowd gathered in the library. Who knows why this site has been selected. We curl ourselves atop the bookcases and look down and smile. It is a sight. Tension. Hats. Tables and card catalogs have been moved out of the way, some have been toppled onto their sides. A weeping librarian pores over the tiny slips of paper, shouting at the spectators, calling them heathens and so forth. She is subdued with ether. The Texan is already there, dressed all in a neutral gray. We nod approvingly at his choice of color and of outfit. Gray boots, freshly shined, gray jeans, a gray belt, a gray button-down shirt with shiny silver buttons and two buttoned breast pockets, a large gray cowboy hat. His six-shooter hangs off his right hip. He is our hero and we wave our hankies at him and swoon. The Sheriff arrives a moment later, kicking open the library door. He clicks inside and sneers. He has waxed his mustache to a curl. He is dressed in solemn black, from his boots all the way up to his hat. Someone mentions that the two men are wearing identical shirts in different colors. That individual is subdued with ether and tossed onto the heap with the rest. We notice that there seems to be quite a heap. But no time for that now: The Sheriff and The Texan are standing back to back and counting off ten paces.

Bang! Bang!

The Texan is gunned down rather unceremoniously. It's a shame, really. The crowd is stunned, silent. The Sheriff holsters his gun, wipes his face with a handkerchief, and walks out. The Texan's body is hoisted by a clutch of boys and carried out to the pile of constantly burning leaves, where he is cremated. We remain atop the bookshelves. We shake our heads and begin planning ballads and epic tales about the bravery of The Texan and his terrible end at the hands of a vicious and cheating tyrant.

The Outcome of the Election

The election has been postponed, due to one of the candidates having been shot in the library at dawn. There is no indication as to whether the election will be rescheduled or simply canceled. The Sheriff made the announcement, visiting each classroom in turn, but he has made no further announcements since. We thought we saw a tear in his eye. We do not feel bad for him. He has locked himself in his office and has not emerged. Even this has not moved us.

Monastery

Pittman has cloistered himself. He no longer speaks, not even when he is called on in class to read the parts of Hal or Romeo or Richard or Hamlet or Lear. He refuses with a vigorous shake of his head. When he is not in class we spy him studying in his third-floor room. We watch him reverently following lines of text with a long index finger.

The Epic Tale of The Texan

We begin thus:
Once there was a — there was THE — Texan. Now, THERE was a man, and there never was quite another man quite like that man. He stood six no seven no ten no twenty no forty no seventy-five no one hundred feet tall. And he was taller in his hat. Which was a very tall and very impressive hat, so much so that when he wore it he was significantly taller than he was when he didn't.

It stalls out there. Describing the size of The Texan's hat. We are poor writers of suicide notes, love letters, and epic tales.

A Defiant Gesture

The Ladykiller has left, and he's taken Wendy with him. We watched him sprint toward the old brick wall, pulling Wendy by the wrist. We watched him climb up to the top of the fence, and then help her up. We watched a silhouette of Wendy disappear over the other side. We watched The Ladykiller look back at the school, raise his middle finger in our general direction, and then turn and jump down. Gone.

We Accidentally Blow Up the School

Allergic Jones made a slight miscalculation.

Kidnapped!

We decide that Wendy has been kidnapped. We are going after her, and we will rescue her from the clutches of The Ladykiller. It will be a daring rescue, we say, a real swashbuckling affair with silk and swords and wild, feathered caps. We reassure each other of this as we stand on the top of the wall. We take a last look. Everything has been decimated. A burning, smoldering mess. One thin boy, his hair sticking out all over, stands on top of a collapsed dormitory. We shake our heads. We imagine the future. On the outside of the fence, we will paint two words in white, four-foot-tall letters. LOST BOYS. Then we will run, following a trail that we can only hope exists. Beyond that, we see nothing but a fog.

Resurrection

We climb down off the fence and walk back toward the buildings, which resurrect themselves as we pass, the campus growing like chemical stalagmites planted in the bottom of a water-filled pickle jar. We cast strange shadows. We reach out our hands for the thin boy with hair like a thick feather crown.

Stick-Figure Indian

Pittman shadowboxes with his eyes closed and feet bare, in the damp grass, backlit by the moonlight.

DANIEL VOLL

■

Riot Baby
(Life in South Central Los Angeles)

FROM *Esquire*

TEN YEARS AGO, in the wake of the Rodney King verdicts, American society ruptured in South Central Los Angeles, resulting in the worst riots in our nation's modern history. Ten years later, the people are still poor, there's not enough work, and the gang violence is bad and getting worse. One other thing hasn't changed in South Central: Little boys still grow up there. This is the story of South Central since the riots.

This is the life story of Jelani Stewart, who came into this world as his city burned.

The black circus is dark and smoky and magic. And it is loud and it is black. The ringleader, Casual Cal, is black, and he's got a black midget sidekick, and the trapeze artist is black and the guy on stilts is black and the guy who vaults thirty feet high and flips and lands on a tiny chair perched in the air is black and the magician is black and the showgirl he makes vanish and who reappears in the tiger cage is black. The audience is black, too, and at the moment, to a person, all two thousand are going completely nuts, especially Jelani Stewart, who is not quite ten years old.

Look at this boy, Jelani. He's about to have a heart attack, y'all! He screams, No! No! No! as the girl contortionist from Africa bends over backward, curving her spine back, back, back until her perfect brown face is between her thighs and she is smiling up into the audience and rolling her eyes. Jelani grabs his cousin Kiana's hand. Oh, my gosh!

Casual Cal pumps the crowd. "I say, Big Top, you say . . ."

"Circus!" Jelani shouts, leaning his head back, staring into the heavens of the circus tent. It's like it's not real! A family is up there on the high wire riding bicycles without nets. The deejay is spinning, and it is loud! I'm a sucker for cornrows and manicured toes. . . . Mommy . . . what's poppin' tonight?

Jelani's been waiting all year for the UniverSoul Circus to come back to Los Angeles. For one thing, he gets to eat cotton candy and nobody says a thing about cavities. For another thing, all of the people who matter the most are here. There's LaTonya, his mom, who loves him beyond words; Nana and Paw-Paw, who let him play on their computer at home; his seventy-five-year-old great-grandmother, Elouise, who raised seven kids in Watts and South Central; his auntie LaTrice and his uncle Tommy, who works at the airport; and his other cousins Tarik, Karlie, Karol, and Tommy Jr. The big-top tent is up across from a cemetery in the parking lot of the Hollywood Park racetrack. Paw-Paw sprang for ringside seats at $18.50 a pop.

Paw-Paw has a round, bearded face, short dreadlocks springing off his head, wire-rim glasses, and an earring. His name is Cornelius Reffegee, and he's LaTonya's stepdad. He is forty-nine years old and has been married to Pat, LaTonya's mom, for fifteen years.

"Soul Train time!" Casual Cal announces. "I need volunteers over thirty!" Before Jelani can sing, "We're gonna get funky, funky, funky!" Nana — who is old, y'all, she's fifty-one! — is center ring, shaking her booty in a Soul Train line. The whole family is up, stomping their feet, chanting, "Go, Pat, go! Go, Pat, go!"

Jelani's never seen Nana onstage before, but this is the circus, and all things are possible. He looks over and sees his mom howling with laughter, tears rolling down her cheeks. Three elephants gallop into the ring, and one stops short. Jelani pokes Kiana in the ribs. Look, he's taking a poop. The elephant wraps its

trunk around the waist of a pretty girl in glittering tights and picks
her up. Look, he's got her legs and stomach inside his mouth.

What if he bites her?

He don't got no teeth!

A light-skinned acrobat scampers onto the high wire. "Brother
looks like a half glass of milk," purrs Casual Cal, who is really on
now. "I want all the large-sized women to stand up and let us see
you," he hollers. "We're proud of you sexy ladies. And young men,
pull your pants up! Nobody wants to see your underpants!"

Outside it's bright California sunlight, but inside the big top
there's a chalky smell in the air from the smoke machines, and the
colored lights are spinning, and everything just glows. Jelani was
born just up the street from here, and he and his mom live a few
miles east, in the heart of South Central Los Angeles, just past the
intersection of Florence and Normandie. And that's what this
story is all about, Jelani being born. Because the boy's about to
turn ten, and y'all, what a ten years it's been! Because people sometimes tell him that something weird was happening when he was
in his mom's stomach, waiting to come out, and when he was little, his nana used to call him Riot Baby. Because he was born in
fire. But he doesn't really know much about that. What does he
know? "I never ever want the circus to ever ever end!" he says. Casual Cal is worked up, too. "A man has to want to change!" he
shouts in benediction. He is drenched in sweat and gleams in the
purple air. "Never conceive in your mind to do anything evil to another human being."

April 29, 1992, evening, and LaTonya Potts, aged twenty-five, is
in labor in Centinela Hospital in Inglewood, squinting up at the
TV between contractions. An angry crowd is shouting and beating
people on the TV and somebody says that you can smell smoke in
the hospital and LaTonya wants her mother, who is there trying to
help, to just back off. The nurse has been saying Any time now for
five hours. And now, smoke and fire.

The pain is worse than anything LaTonya's ever felt. Can somebody just turn the damn TV off? She tells herself she'll make good
choices from this point on. She just wants the baby to be born,

soon, and naturally. No getting cut open. She knows it's a boy from the ultrasound but has kept this a secret, even from her mother.

Her family has begun to drive in from all over South Central. She hasn't seen the baby's father, Daryl, in six months. She hadn't trusted that man and hadn't meant to get pregnant, and she's only going to stay with people she trusts from now on, period.

Not far away, a man LaTonya has not yet met, Bo Noble, thirty-one and still on parole from a drug conviction, is racing his gray Cadillac toward Florence and Normandie. He's been watching the verdicts on television, and then the images, live from a news chopper, of a mob looting Tom's Liquor at the corner there. Bo picks up his gun, chambers a bullet, clicks the safety on, and tells his homegirls: "I'm gonna get me some."

As he approaches the intersection, a Latino couple with an infant is attacked in their car. Helicopters fly overhead, broadcasting live. Anyone who is not black, and even some light-skinned blacks who are unlucky enough to enter the intersection, are pulled from their cars by the mob and beaten to a pulp on live television.

LaTonya recognizes the intersection on the TV. Florence and Normandie is only a couple blocks from where she grew up. The contractions pound. This baby is big. A white man is being dragged out of a truck and beaten. Reginald Denny, hauling twenty-seven tons of sand in his rig to an Inglewood cement-mixing plant, had rolled into the intersection of Florence and Normandie at 6:46 P.M. He was listening to an all-music country station and didn't hear news of the Rodney King verdict, but something is going on up ahead of him. Rocks and bottles fly past. As Denny slows, rocks and chunks of concrete smash his windshield, his doors are yanked open, and he is pulled from the cab. He is knocked to the ground and beaten in the head with a hammer; when he tries to move, another man crushes his skull with something that looks like a fire extinguisher. Mommy, please turn off that damn TV! Oh my baby, oh my baby.

Bo parks his car off Normandie and pushes through the crowd. The corner is Eight Trey Gangster territory. It feels like a party. Bottles of Olde English 800, looted from the liquor store, are being passed around. A gauntlet has formed, and guys with baseball bats are smashing all the car windows. Bo knows some of these guys from his days living in the neighborhood. There's Football Williams! He and Bo are both Crips, though from different sets, and they smoked a little weed together when Bo was living a few blocks from here with an old girlfriend. Football was always a big guy, and there used to be talk that the pros might be interested. Now Football grabs something that looks to Bo like a cinder block and smashes a white guy in the head. There is no sign of the police.

An hour ago, the police field commander for the 77th Street Division ordered his thirty officers in the area to retreat. "I want everybody out of here!" he shouted into his radio. "Florence and Normandie. Everybody get out! Now!" When two officers in a lone squad car return to rescue a Korean woman who has been beaten unconscious in her car, the officers are pelted with rocks and bricks and almost can't escape. The crowd chants, "It's Uzi time!"

At 6:30 P.M., as the worst riots of the century are developing in his city, Daryl Gates, the Los Angeles police chief, leaves headquarters to attend a fundraiser in Brentwood. The city has known since early afternoon that the verdicts would be delivered, but Gates did not put his department on tactical alert, and a dozen of his captains are out of town at a training seminar. Gates and Los Angeles mayor Tom Bradley haven't spoken in more than a year. After the field commander for the 77th Street Division orders his officers to withdraw from Florence and Normandie, they retreat to a command center thirty blocks from where Reginald Denny lies. During the next few hours, the police lose the city. Pawnshops that stock weapons are looted, putting thousands more guns on the street.

LaTonya's family is being told that no one should leave the hospital. Mayor Bradley imposes a citywide dusk-to-dawn curfew. Cornelius, Pat, and the rest of the family will sleep in the waiting room.

Once the sun sets, looting and burning and killing begin in earnest. Bo kicks in store windows, grabbing what he can. Sunday

Mays, who is thirty and has been in the gang life since she was twelve, rides shotgun in the Cadillac. Sunday grew up slashing and shooting, but she also loves Barbra Streisand, and she's singing "I Want Everything" from *A Star Is Born* as they ride. She and Bo feel the lawlessness like a drug, and it's euphoric. Children ride stolen bicycles; women lug bags of shoes and toilet paper. Whole families. Retribution, baby, Bo says. Payback time. Liquor stores, corner groceries, and fast food restaurants are torched. A new fire is reported every four minutes. Firefighters are shot at and can't put the fires out.

Bo holds his fist out the window of his Cadillac. Ash falls like snow. Fire on every corner. A laundromat is lit, now a fish market, crowds moving from building to building with torches. The K-mart and the Sav-on are looted and the Newberry's burned down. Korean shop owners, armed with shotguns, are on rooftops. Bo jacks a woman at a gas station, steals her wallet. Some Mexicans put a chain around a cash machine and pull it down the street, sparks trailing behind.

It pisses Bo off that Latinos have joined in the looting. "Rodney King wasn't no Mexican," Bo says as he puts a pistol to a guy's head and steals his wallet.

Bo and Sunday bring in their first haul. When Sunday's landlord asks her where she got all the TVs and boxes of shoes and electronic equipment that she's carrying up her stairs, she answers: "I'm a black business owner. I'm just trying to protect my stuff." Bo fills his bathtub with meat, stacks his bedroom with TVs and VCRs and liquor. Open season. Once in a lifetime, Bo says. He's dreamed of something like this since he was a boy back in Ohio.

LaTonya's baby doesn't come all night, as if he knows.

In the morning, the second day of the riots, the doctor breaks LaTonya's water, but it doesn't help. Nobody told her it would hurt this much. The doctor drips Pitocin into her vein, and the contractions come with more force now, but the baby is not moving. Then he takes what looks like a pair of spoons, and he reaches inside with them and tries to pull the baby out, but nothing works.

Bo can't believe there are no police in the streets, and it's late afternoon by the time the National Guard shows up (having had what the governor calls an "ammunition problem": their bullets had failed to arrive). The looters — black, white, Latino — are swarming the stores with a crazy sense of exhilaration. Gang members and mothers with children. At 4:00 P.M., the first national guardsmen take up position at Martin Luther King and Vermont and other hot spots, armed with M16s, but it's easy for Bo to avoid them. The looting spreads toward Westwood, up Hollywood Boulevard. An eighteen-year-old Korean is killed trying to protect a pizza parlor.

"Let's go to Beverly Hills," Bo tells Sunday. "Shit, yeah, we fixing to bust into Tiffany's, get us the good stuff."

But Beverly Hills is one of the only neighborhoods protected by police in riot gear. Bo wants to pull out his pistol, but Sunday says it isn't going to help against that heat, and they turn around.

The riot spreads throughout Los Angeles County and up into the Valley. The TV shows a department store with no police around, and looters show up five minutes later. The city is burning. There are no cops. People come up in taxicabs, keep the meter running, grab VCRs. Police cars are turned over and set afire in the street. Flights can't leave LAX because of the smoke.

As evening falls again on the city, LaTonya, after thirty-two hours of labor, asks for a C-section. Get this baby outta me, please. At 5:49 P.M., while the city burns outside and the sirens wail and gunshot victims, the dead and the dying, are being treated in the emergency room downstairs, LaTonya is cut open and the boy is taken out. He weighs eight pounds, ten ounces. He is footprinted and cleaned and brought back to his mother's arms.

As LaTonya takes the baby to her breast, in a speech announcing that thirty-five hundred federal troops have been dispatched to Los Angeles, President Bush vows to use "whatever force is necessary to restore order." She names the baby Jelani, from a book of African names. It means mighty and strong. She talks to him all that night. "Now I understand why you didn't want to come out," she says. "When you get older, you're going to hear people talk about this day."

Making his way through the roadblocks and the fires, Jelani's father, Daryl Stewart, arrives the next day. Cornelius meets Daryl at the door. "Don't you go in there unless you plan to stay with her." Daryl shoulders his way past him. He says it is the happiest day of his life and he wants to make things work. He's gotten himself a job, and can't they try again? LaTonya wants her son to have a father, but for now she wants to stay with her family. On Monday, the curfew is lifted, and the city returns to work and school. As she's returning home from the hospital, most everything she sees out her window has been burned down. Plywood is being nailed up. Folks are sweeping. Fifty-four people are dead, making this the most violent urban uprising in modern American history. Twenty-three hundred wounded. Twelve thousand arrested. One thousand fires. Eight hundred businesses burned down.

LaTonya and Jelani stay with Cornelius and Pat for six months, and then they move into a one-bedroom apartment. LaTonya decides to give Daryl Stewart another chance. Daryl got himself a job, pest control for Orkin. Every morning he goes off to work, kisses her goodbye, a man in a uniform. But when she calls his job one day, she learns that Daryl was fired, weeks ago, actually. "But he dresses and goes to work every day," she says to his boss. Then her phone rings and it's a drug dealer, telling her that Daryl has traded her car for crack cocaine, and would she like to buy it back? She files a police report, and apart from a brief visit in Las Vegas years later, Jelani has never again seen his father, nor has LaTonya ever received child support. "If I saw my dad on the street," Jelani says, "I wouldn't know what he looks like."

Jelani wakes up slowly. He goes into the bathroom. He's got to get through his mom's room to get there. His mom's boyfriend, Bo, is snoring in her bed; he'll be snoring for hours. Jelani doesn't think it's right that Bo sleeps all day and watches TV. Not that Jelani doesn't like watching TV, he sure does, but a man gets up and goes to work or school or something. There is a list taped to the wall next to the bathroom sink: "Jelani's daily bathroom chores. Good morning! 1) Wash face 2) Brush teeth 3) Put deodorant on 4) Pick up clothes off floor 5) Hang wash towel up 6) Make sure water is turned off and lights are out. Thank you son. I love you." Jelani's mom believes if you write things down, especially dreams, they come true. She learned that from the Bible, and her list is thumbtacked to the kitchen wall: "1) To own my own daycare business 2) For my business to be successful 3) To own a black shiny new Pontiac Grand Am, with a license plate that reads: CALIFORNIA PRYR WKS! 4) To own my own home 5) To be the best mom and provider I can be."

Jelani's mom is in the kitchen making oatmeal. She is dressed in nice pants and loafers with tassels. Jelani is walking around the house in his long underwear. A couple TVs are on in different rooms, as always, and he is not getting dressed. "Put on your clothes. Now!"

The walls of Jelani's house are decorated with squares and circles cut from colored construction paper. They are labeled CIRCLE, SQUARE, TRIANGLE. On the stove, a handwritten sign says STOVE, and underneath in red letters is the word HOT! Jelani's mom is getting ready to run her daycare business out of the house, and he has helped her make the signs. She told him, I'm an entrepreneur. He liked that word, and it felt like a project they were doing together. When she had to learn pediatric CPR, they practiced on each other, and now her certificate is framed on the wall.

As Jelani and his mother head outside, he's shoving his homework into his backpack. Divine, a pit bull that lives in the backyard next door, throws himself against the chain-link fence that separates the yards. Jelani's mom wants to be saying, Don't be teasing that dog, but what's the use, she's said it a thousand times. She's worried that the pit bull will scare the families that she hopes will come to have her babysit their kids.

Oh, shit, she needs Bo to pay the electric, and she'd better remind him because he'll never remember otherwise. Jelani waits by the gate as LaTonya sticks her head back in the door. Of all the places they've lived, this little South Central rental with the palm trees outside is his absolute favorite.

After Jelani's father disappeared, LaTonya found another apartment, for less rent, and for the next year and a half, she raised

Jelani alone. She loved feeding him and washing his clothes. She didn't have much furniture, just a bed for the both of them, but she kept the place spotless. It felt good to be on her own, but sometimes she got lonely. She got a job with the school district at a daycare in Venice. Sometimes she took Jelani with her, and other days she walked him to a babysitter who lived around the corner.

Bo was dealing crack out of an apartment on Highland when he saw LaTonya walk by holding her son's hand. She was slim and pretty, wearing a pants suit. She seemed from another world, a better world. Bo was living the gangster life, and mostly he met girls who wanted drugs for sex — strawberries, he called them. But this girl was different. She didn't seem to want or need anything. "There goes an angel," he whistled. "That's my future."

And so the next morning, Bo raced outside when he saw her at the mailbox. He was still in his pajamas. He introduced himself and told her she smelled nice. He asked if he could call her. She just laughed. "Don't you got a girlfriend?" He was out there again the next morning, and every morning for the next week. Sometimes he'd walk beside her a ways. He made her laugh. Finally she gave him her number. Sure, he was probably wild, she knew that from the start, but he was handsome, and, well, he was paying attention to her.

The scar is not the first thing you notice about Bo, but once you get past the bulk of him — he's six feet and 225 pounds — then you might notice it. It's a dark, jagged line across his forehead. He got it back in Lorain, Ohio, when he was hit by a car at age three. His head was busted open, his arms and legs broken. He was in a coma, hooked up to life support, and his mother sat at his bedside even when everybody gave up hope. Sometimes he still hears her voice — Why you playing in the streets? You gonna be okay, I'm with you. Junior, I'm gonna whup you when we get home.

Jelani stayed with his grandparents when Bo and LaTonya had their first date. Bo blended her a drink with gin and ice cream and pink lemonade; he put whipped cream on top — pink panties, he called it.

LaTonya never knew what crack looked like until she met Bo.

She'd never known a gang member. Before Jelani was born, she'd been a nanny for seven years, starting with an affluent white family in suburban Chino, an hour outside Los Angeles. She'd gotten the job through church. Bo called her square. Her daddy had smoked weed in front of them as children, funny-smelling cigarettes that he would roll in the car as he drove them to school. She didn't like it then and she didn't like it now, but nobody had ever paid her this much attention before, and it felt good to have somebody think she was pretty. Soon he was staying overnight.

"Bo was extroverted, and I was Bo's girl, and nobody could touch Bo's girl, and I was made up to be some kind of queen," she says. Daryl had been introverted and sneaky, stealing off for his drugs. Bo was more out with it, and she liked that. He was upfront: This is who I am.

For the first time in his life, Bo felt that, in LaTonya, he really had something special. And for the first time, he felt like he had a lot to lose. But a man's got to make money. He worked the alley behind their apartment, selling crack. "He had twenty cars in that alley all lined up," she says. "White folks, every color." She was always telling him, "You got to put up that money, invest it." He thought it was going to last forever. He always told her, "I know what I'm doing."

LaTonya never smoked crack. Bo told her if she ever did it, he'd beat her up. He wanted her pure and clean. Crackheads brought furniture and stereos and jewelry as payment, and these things furnished the apartment. LaTonya had rules: She didn't allow Bo to deal in the house while Jelani was home. Crack addicts didn't scare LaTonya; some were middle-aged men who just a few months earlier had families themselves and had held down jobs. Her own father had been a family man until he'd tried crack.

Jelani spent most weekends with his grandparents, and often during the week he'd be with LaTonya's grandmother, a retired nurse. "I knew it wasn't good for him to be with me, the way things were going," LaTonya says. Paw-Paw bought a refurbished computer from Nana's younger brother, Joseph, who opened a successful computer-training business after the riots with the goal of helping black youth enter the technology age. With Jelani on his lap, Paw-Paw ordered CDs and books online. Paw-Paw introduced him to jazz recordings, the more obscure the better, and for laughs, they'd tune in Dr. Demento. Jelani was the son Cornelius never had and the grandson he'd always hoped for. Most Sundays, Jelani went to church with Nana, who sang in the choir, and LaTonya sometimes came along.

When Jelani wasn't around, she'd be out in the alley with Bo, but when her son was home, she stayed inside. Bo's idea of how to play with a child was to crush things between his hands and shout, "This is Bo!" At three, Jelani started preschool at a local daycare. A teacher there said that Jelani was hyperactive and that he should be checked by an expert. So LaTonya took Jelani to UCLA, where he was diagnosed with attention deficit disorder. The doctor prescribed Ritalin, but when LaTonya researched the drug, she didn't like what she learned, especially that some kids seem to turn into zombies. She refused to give it to her son. And he seemed to settle down fine.

LaTonya wanted to believe Bo would outgrow selling crack, especially when his gang friends started going to jail. Dre, who brought Bo into the life, got twenty-five in Pelican Bay after he was picked up twice for robbery and selling crack. But Bo figured he was smarter than the police. "Don't be trippin', baby," he told her. "Everything's going to be okay." At night, he'd count out hundreds of dollars, sometimes thousands. She told him, "You should buy a house with that." "We got this place, baby, what I need a house for?"

Sometimes the police came around and jacked Bo up against the wall, and sometimes they took him downtown for questioning. LaTonya was with Bo in the alley the first time she saw the police handcuff him. They wanted to talk to him about a murder. "Don't worry," he said. "I ain't trippin' on this." Bo promised he'd be home that night, and he was. The police rattled Bo's cage every now and then, but it wasn't until 1997 that he was arrested again, and this time it was LaTonya who filed the complaint.

Almost a hundred thousand blacks have left Los Angeles in the past twenty years. A good many have gone to the cemetery, a good many have gone to jail, a good many more have made it to the sub-urbs, some have made the migration back home to the South. But South Central is LaTonya's home. This is where she's staying.

To get to the house where Jelani lives, you exit the Santa Monica Freeway at Vermont Avenue and drive south, passing first the red-brick buildings of the University of Southern California and then the new Science Center, built since the riots, and the L.A. Coli-seum, before crossing Martin Luther King Boulevard, where na-tional guardsmen were stationed with M16s. A block farther south is where the first person was killed. As you drive, consider that many of the businesses on Vermont for miles south of here were reduced to ashes — a mix of storefront groceries, mom-and-pop shops, and the occasional Korean-owned liquor store. Notice that Payless Shoes and Taco Bell, as promised, have rebuilt, as have a couple banks.

Jelani's street intersects with Vermont just before the railroad tracks at Slauson Avenue. A pink storefront church is on the cor-ner, and there is a laundry just up the alley, and also a barber col-lege. During the riots, while many businesses were gutted, not a single house was burned. The low-slung wooden bungalows, built in the 1920s, remain the pride of South Central. Should one come on the market, it will fetch upwards of $150,000.

There are palm trees on both sides of Jelani's street. They are very tall and skinny palm trees. The sky is pale blue overhead, the air very still. Most front lawns are well kept. Most windows have burglar bars. There are no high-rises here, nothing more than a couple stories. Even in the neighborhood known as the Jungle, off Crenshaw Boulevard, four miles west of Jelani's street, they've got lawns.

Jelani and his mother live in a small brown house in the back-yard of a larger bungalow owned by Miss Allbirdie Jones. They have been here for two and a half years now — the longest they've been in one place since Jelani was born. LaTonya feels lucky to have found the house, and she pays four hundred dollars a month for rent. Jelani likes living behind Miss Jones's house, set back away from the street. He feels safe back here, and if trouble comes through the door, he knows to hide in the closet.

Jelani is looking out the screen door. A few kids have gathered in the driveway next door. "What are they doing, Mom?" he asks.

"Is that your business?"

He shakes his head.

"That's right," she says. "It's not your business."

LaTonya doesn't let him play with neighborhood kids, except his cousins when they come to visit his great-grandma, who lives across the street. If LaTonya could keep Jelani inside forever, she would. She only recently began to let him walk the five blocks home from school alone. She used to wait at the school door, until he said, "I want to walk all the way home by myself." That five blocks is Jelani's favorite part of the day. He'll walk home with Brittani and Jahnae, who tease him and tell corny jokes and sometimes hold both his hands. They're all in the fourth grade. Jelani has a bounce to his walk and big, brown, long-lashed eyes. "Jelani, all you has to do is change that little smartie attitude into a positive attitude," Brittani tells him. "Like today we were doing history and you made us laugh — that was not a good opportunity." She's got braids and long legs in bright pants and a great attitude, and Jelani's in love with her. She's not going to marry him because he's not serious enough.

Fart is Jelani's favorite word. As in, "Bo likes to fart" or "All Bo does is sleep, eat, and fart." Jelani has a slight Louisiana accent from his grandma's side of the family, and he elongates the vowel: faaahrt. When he giggles, his shoulders shake. Jelani likes words, and has since he was a little boy, when his mom first read him *Curious George*. Some nights, for homework, he must learn a dozen new vocabulary words and use them in a sentence. "I slew my enemies," he says, balancing on the curb. "I will not indulge in bad behavior."

Now here's LaTonya waiting on the corner of their block. She has heard that a ten-year-old kid in the neighborhood is already gang-banging, and she says that drugs are being sold from two houses on the block. The 77th Street Division is the deadliest in

California, with eighty-two homicides last year, about fifty-five of those gang killings. But there is no safe place anywhere, LaTonya says. "I like my neighborhood. I don't want my son to think he has to move out. To where? Everywhere there are bad apples."

When Jelani saw the Columbine shootings, he wanted to know if it was real or just TV. Then he wanted to know how the students got guns. LaTonya told him about gun shops and background checks. If he ever saw a gun, he promised, he'd come right home and tell her. She wanted to know how it made him feel to see those kids shooting. "Maybe they needed their moms and dads," he said. He thought, Yeah, it's dangerous here, but look at that. He felt sorry for those white kids.

Bo is sleeping as LaTonya and Jelani leave for church. Sometimes LaTonya thinks that Bo is just using their place as a safe house, a retreat from his thug life, and all he seems to do is sleep. He says he's not living the life anymore, but last night he was washing blood off his hands and face in the shower. And last week, she found a deep bruise on his sternum where somebody had tried to stab him in the heart. She'd long ago stopped asking him to join her in church, or in anything; but it's Bo she is thinking about as she listens to the soloist. Storms they keep a-raging in my life, goes the song. The congregation is on its feet; the snare drum and the organ are keeping tempo. LaTonya is up, rocking back and forth, and she hears herself shouting out loud with the others, Amen!

The family church is in Watts, a fifteen-minute drive. Jelani's great-grandmother kept coming here even after she moved to South Central; she is up in the choir today, in African garb and headdress, looking regal. The usher at the door wears white gloves. Outside is Nickerson Gardens, one of the most notorious housing projects in America. It was near here in 1965 that the Watts riots, which killed thirty-four, began. To this day, cops are not easily trusted. Last week officers came to serve a warrant and were confronted by a hundred angry residents, some throwing rocks and bottles; extra units were called in to protect the officers from what was described by police as a "near riot."

Every Sunday, the women in LaTonya's family drive here for church. LaTonya's mother also sings in the choir, and once a month, Jelani sings up front with the children's choir. Today, along with thirty other kids, Jelani is in junior church.

Good morning, junior church!

Jelani wears corduroy pants and a checked shirt. He slouches and twists, all shrugs, like a boxer ducking punches. He is in the front, sitting with his cousin Kiana. The stained-glass window is etched with white orchids. Men in suits move among the children, keeping order. Brother Saunders, a volunteer Sunday school teacher with a bushy mustache and suspenders, is up front, asking questions.

"How many of you pray?"

Jelani raises a hand.

"How many of you pray every day?"

Jelani doesn't raise his hand. He pulls at his cousin's shirt.

"How many of you do things that are wrong?"

Jelani looks around, then puts up his hand.

"God says, 'If you do things wrong and you come to me, I'll forgive you.'"

Brother Saunders walks over like he might hit Jelani, rears back his open hand.

"If I hit Jelani, what is he supposed to do?"

"Forgive you!" the children shout.

"That means Jelani is not supposed to hit me back, right?"

"Why not?" a kid asks, totally perplexed.

Yeah, why not? thinks Jelani. In karate class, the teacher says, Jelani, your body is your house, your arms are your gates, don't let anybody in your house. Protect your house! Nothing about forgiveness there. And there was that time last year when the bully was all over him. What was he supposed to do, forgive the kid, who was twice his size? Uh-uh. He got somebody twice the bully's size. Bo went and had a serious talk with him, and poof, no more bully. Isn't that the way the world works? And that's when it's good to have Bo around, too. That's when it seemed to Jelani that they were almost a real family. He wasn't much good for doing stuff or playing ball — Tomorrow, he would always promise Jelani — but having Bo in the house made Jelani feel secure sometimes. Except a couple times, when he was so mad that it seemed like he was going to do violence against LaTonya, and maybe Jelani, too.

"Now, I'm not saying that Jelani should not defend himself!" thunders Brother Saunders. "Jelani, you say, 'Brother, I will defend myself, and then at an appropriate time, I will forgive you. And I will do both of these things vigorously.'"

The real trouble with Bo started in 1997, when Jelani was five. Up until then, Bo had been the man of the house, Jelani's real father figure, except of course for Paw-Paw Cornelius, who was such a good man and who hovered over LaTonya and Jelani as much as he could without interfering. Cornelius said that of all his grandkids, it was Jelani he worried over most, because of that man Bo.

Bo had always been volatile. When his mother died a few years before, he went back to Ohio alone for the funeral. He broke down at the funeral home and pulled out his gun and waved it around until everybody cleared out, including the preacher. That's what Bo said happened; LaTonya was never sure. But now he became moody and violent at home. He started lighting his crack pipe in front of LaTonya, and he would dip his cigarettes in a mixture of embalming fluid and PCP that he called sherm. It got to where she felt safer around the crackheads than Bo, and one of Bo's regular customers even told her, "You need to leave him — he's going to bring you down." Things got so bad that LaTonya went to court and had a judge issue a restraining order to keep Bo away.

"Defendant has been physically violent toward me throughout our three-year relationship," the complaint stated. "He has punched me in the nose, blackened my eyes, slapped and hit me on numerous occasions, and has thrown a chair at me. He also repeatedly makes threats to harm me, my son, and family members."

The legal voice then gives way to Bo's voice: "I'll kill you and your family."

When LaTonya's mother read the restraining order for the first time, she was devastated. "Why didn't you tell me?" she said.

When LaTonya was growing up, Pat had been beaten up by her first husband and later by a boyfriend. LaTonya recalls looking "into my mom's room, and her boyfriend is sitting on top of her, just punching her, and the next day, he's this nice man in the house who did things for us and bought things for us."

On the nights when her father was violent, LaTonya would gather her sisters in the other end of the house and read them stories as loud as she could. He had a job at the hospital, and nobody was a more careful dresser or responsible provider. Before her daddy turned to drugs, he was Mr. Clean. A piece of lint outraged him. One night when he was threatening, Pat and the kids fled, and LaTonya still remembers standing in the rain and the dark, waiting for the bus.

After LaTonya got the restraining order, Bo's luck began to run out. He was arrested five days later for possession of cocaine with the intent to sell. He called her collect from the county jail. "I got stuck and I'll let you know what happens," he said. He was sentenced to 270 days in jail. Within weeks of getting out, he was arrested again, this time in Venice with a 69th East Coast Crip named Lil Too Cool, for possession of crack. A few months later, he was busted again for drug possession, and in September 1998 he was sent to prison.

Jelani was six. He didn't know anything about crack cocaine or jail. All he knew was that Bo was gone and there was no money left to pay the rent.

At around age ten is when it will start for Jelani. What gang you from? is the most dangerous question he can be asked in this neighborhood. The question is coming, and there is no right answer. I don't bang is the answer mothers tell their sons to say. "Jelani, you say, 'I don't bang,'" LaTonya says. And hope for the best. I don't bang got two kids killed just before Christmas. For all his swagger in the world of gangs, Bo cannot protect Jelani; in fact, Bo is a liability. Gang violence is spiking again, and Jelani's street is Hoover territory, and the Hoover Crips are a large and serious gang known for their ruthlessness. Bo's a Crip, too, but his set and the Hoovers are sometimes enemies. One neighborhood gang-banger puts it this way: "When little niggers from Hoover see Bo, if they smoke him, they get more stripes because they got a OG. So Bo in more danger than a little homie."

The mothers in this neighborhood attribute all this business to the Devil. Devilment is a big word here. The police officers beating Rodney King was the Devil's work, and the riots were the Devil, too. Damian "Football" Williams hitting Reginald Denny in the head with the cinder block was the Devil. When Williams was arrested thirteen days later, he sobbed and said, "I never seen my daddy. I bet if I had a father, I wouldn't be in this predicament that I'm in right now." He told his mother that he was guilty, and she said, "Dame, you know you were wrong, but that was the Devil."

Gangs are the Devil. Selling crack is the Devil, and smoking it is the Devil, too. It was devilment when Bo hit LaTonya, and it was devilment that one time when he hit Jelani square in the face, and it is devilment to just sit there and not do anything about it.

LaTonya decided to do something about it. Jelani's house is in the flight path to LAX, and from his yard he has always loved watching planes come in low over the palm trees. Until September 11 he wanted to be a pilot and would get Paw-Paw and Nana to take him in the airport to watch takeoffs and landings. But after the skies go quiet, Jelani doesn't want to be a pilot anymore. He wants to be a judge with a gavel, like the black lady judge on TV who sends people to prison. The planes crashing got Jelani thinking about his own life, and this is what he realized: 1) that he, Jelani Stewart, is the man of the house, and 2) the world is made up of good guys and bad guys and very little in between. Jelani wants to judge people and pronounce them bad if they're bad. After September 11, when LaTonya meets him on the corner after school, Jelani will ask her, "Is he here?" And if Bo is at home, LaTonya will nod her head yes, and Jelani's face will just fall.

Jelani's started talking back to Bo. "When you gonna stop making my mama cry?" he says to him. "When you gonna leave us alone?"

"Jelani talks so intelligent," a fourth-grade mom tells LaTonya at school.

"You think so?" LaTonya laughs.

"He's always polite and well mannered," the mom says. "How'd you do it? Mine talks back to me. He's ten years old and he's already sagging his pants, cussing, and looking like a thug."

"Mine grew up with a thug," LaTonya says. "So he's already seen the life and decided he didn't like it."

Bo got out of prison two and a half years ago. He had been calling collect and writing, I'm gonna change. I just want my family back. He said he'd go to counseling with LaTonya. He had gotten strong in jail, and Jelani was impressed when he saw him. "Here's the thing about jail," he told Jelani. "If you sleep and drink a gang of water, you won't age much. I'm in the best shape of my life."

Bo settled back into LaTonya's little three-room house, and the romance rekindled for a while, and she even had fleeting thoughts that maybe they'd get married. When he was in jail, LaTonya had had fantasies of taking Bo away from his homeboys and the three of them just living a simple life, but where? She even searched the Internet to find an apartment in Lorain, Ohio, where they all could live. But she knew better. And Bo began to stay away at night, and soon he was back in the thug life. The restraining order from years before had done some good, though; if Bo was still a thug, at least he was a mellower thug.

LaTonya will never quite understand what happened next. It may have had something to do with the night two years ago when she was mugged.

It was a Friday night, and LaTonya was wearing her uniform when she got off the bus and began her walk home. She'd been training for a $7.25-an-hour housekeeping job at the Marriott in Manhattan Beach and had cleaned twenty rooms that day. It was her birthday. Her house was just ahead when she heard footsteps behind her; a kid walked past, a sweatshirt hood over his face. His hands were in his pockets, and when he got in front of her, he turned and pulled out a gun. He pointed it at her face, stepped toward her. It all happened so fast. Then he reached out and grabbed her purse. A car pulled up and the kid was gone.

Jelani and Bo were home waiting to celebrate her birthday when LaTonya pounded on the door. "Bo opened it and my mama was crying and she hugged him," Jelani says. "Bo said, 'What happened, what happened?' She could barely breathe. I thought she got shot. I was crying, too. I was crying so hard."

Bo ran out to the street to see if he could catch the robber or find the purse. LaTonya called the police. "If the police are coming," Bo said, "I can't be here. I can't have nothing to do with the police."

Bo left, the police came, and Jelani's stomach got sick that night. "I thought that man was about to come to our house."

And LaTonya lay awake, holding Jelani, feeling abandoned, thinking, How many times has Bo done that to people — scared them, pulled a gun, maybe killed? And from that night on, LaTonya has said a prayer. She might backslide, and the Devil will try to make her fail, but please, God, deliver me and my son, Jelani, of this man Bo. He's not meant to be here. I cannot do this alone. I am a sinner, Lord, and I have only myself to blame, but I ask your mercy. Thy will be done.

Finally, this is what happens:

One recent weekend, LaTonya drives into the desert in a rental car with her mother, on their way to Palm Springs to attend a women's prayer conference. A few thousand African-American women are there, filling an auditorium, hands in the air, some warbling prayers in tongues LaTonya can't decipher. She is hoping that God will give her a sign.

When Jelani feels fear, he always feels it in his stomach. The day before his mom leaves for the desert, he goes with her to the laundromat on Vermont. He is riding his scooter in the parking lot when he sees the man with the gun. LaTonya is inside, folding laundry. The man is in the alley next to the laundry with his back to Jelani. The man pulls the gun out of his pants and aims; he does this again and again. Jelani gets a good look at the gun and at the man's hand and the way his hand fits around the gun. Jelani doesn't want the man to catch him looking, so he takes his scooter inside the laundry and stands next to his mom. He doesn't want to tell her about the gun, doesn't want to scare her. All night he has a stomachache.

LaTonya left Bo the key to the house.

"Don't be bringing none of your friends here while I'm gone," LaTonya said.

"Don't you worry, nigger."

"I'm not worried. I'm telling you."

"Okay."

"I got spies."

Jelani is staying at Paw-Paw's while LaTonya is gone. It's fun at Paw-Paw's, like a vacation; Jelani gets to play on the computer, and Paw-Paw always cooks. Paw-Paw is just about the opposite of Bo. He and Nana take Jelani on trips, and Paw-Paw always has a project for Jelani. Today's project: build a shed.

Bo walks into the American Barber College on Vermont to get a shave before heading to see his parole officer. He pays his two bucks and sits in an old-fashioned barber chair. The apprentice barber is nineteen years old and just out of jail; his pants are belted low on his hips, and four inches of striped boxers show. FREAK is hand-jagged on his left forearm in wide Old English lettering. "You in a gang?" he asks as Bo sits down. Bo nods. "First Street. East Coast." The barber is a Crip, too, like Bo, but from another set, the Watergate gang on Crenshaw and Imperial. Bo is wearing a crisp blue shirt with a motocross design and wide blue pants and blue Converse All Stars. When the barber sees Bo wearing Crip colors, with his hair pulled back in a tight ponytail, he sees an OG, an original gangster, a term that signifies a leader, a survivor. The barber tells himself: This nigger's been doing this shit twenty years longer than me. You've got to respect him. Even though he's not from my hood, he's still a G.

Out at the desert hotel, LaTonya prays, and others pray for her, a chorus of voices: "Let him go. . . . You're strong. . . . There's no good for you there. . . ." She catches herself feeling sorry for him but then remembers how she sent him to pay the electric bill last week and he kept half the money.

Paw-Paw and Jelani set to work clearing the back for the new shed. But soon after he starts raking and piling leaves, Jelani begins to wheeze — a deep, gasping, desperate wheeze, like a drowning boy. First, Cornelius just thinks it's dust, and he sits Jelani in his car with cool air running. "I need my inhaler," Jelani says. "It's at my house." Jelani's house is locked up, and when Cornelius knocks on the door, Bo isn't there.

Bo is at the parole office, sitting through a mandatory job-training seminar. The jobs lady up front has a list of places that might employ ex-convicts. "When you go for a job, don't announce right away that you're a convict," she tells them. "Somewhere down the line you're going to have to tell them. By then maybe they'll be on your side."

In Palm Springs, songs of praise are bouncing off the rafters, and the lady evangelist is up front exhorting her sisters to "Rejoice and surrender!" LaTonya is in the middle of the crowd, but she feels alone. So many choices she wishes she'd made different. "I want you all to get up now, sisters," the evangelist says. "I want you to jog around this hall. Feel God's energy, His love for you." LaTonya starts to move.

Taking the bus back from the parole office, Bo stops at the Home Depot. For a moment, he feels inspired. Maybe he'll get a job. When he first came to Los Angeles, before he started slagging crack, he worked as a security guard, first for Bank of America and then for an art gallery. He worked construction for a while, helped build a Howard Johnson. I'm not afraid to work, he tells himself, but as he walks into the massive Home Depot, with its endless neat aisles of lumber and nails, he feels something like fear. He goes toward the counter, where the manager is standing by a stack of applications, and blurts out, Do you hire convicts?

The manager shakes his head no, resigned, and even as Bo watches the manager, heart racing, he is not sure whether he just said those words or imagined it.

That night when Cornelius checks on Jelani, something's definitely not right. The boy's breathing is still labored, and he's sleeping with his eyes open, which he's never done before. By dawn, he seems a little improved, but later, as Paw-Paw barbecues outside, Jelani starts wheezing loud enough for a neighbor to suggest that Cornelius take him to the hospital.

LaTonya is up on her feet, like the other women in the auditorium, and yes, she's jogging, wringing her arms, trying to shake off the old, the depression, the sense of failure. Surrender and rejoice! She can feel the energy in the air. Moving down the aisles, threading past the stage. Suddenly, out of the whole crowd, the lady evangelist reaches out her hand and touches LaTonya's shoulder, anointing her. She looks into LaTonya's eyes. "You are going to make a change in your life. Let the walls come down. Trust God." Out of thousands, it is LaTonya who is anointed. It has happened, the sign she has been waiting for. And she weeps, each new breath filling her with hope.

When LaTonya gets back to her hotel room, an urgent message: It's about your son. On the phone, LaTonya can hear Jelani's lungs fighting for breath. Asthma is serious in the neighborhood. Jelani's friend Jahnae would die from an attack. "We've done this before," she tells her son. "Everything's going to be okay. Just breathe."

"Can you come home?"

"Let me speak to Paw-Paw," she says, and she instructs Cornelius to a nearby hospital where they've got Jelani's records. "Call me as soon as you get back," she says.

Bo is heading to the corner of Washington and Rimpau, the corner where he became a gangster. He slagged crack here for five years out of the laundry, which everybody called the wash house. It's a clear day, and he can see the Hollywood sign to the north. He used to stash his rock cocaine in a broken washing machine, and the man working the cash register was on his payroll. All the money went straight into the cash drawer, so when the police came, which they did every other day or so, frisking Bo up against the window, he never had drugs or cash in his pockets. Bo was a natural businessman. Back in Ohio, he had worked as a hospital orderly, and sometimes when old folks in that hospital were getting ready to die, they asked for Bo to sit with them. He had a gift with people that way, the same gift that made him a good drug dealer.

Cornelius and Jelani tear through the streets to the emergency room at Midway Hospital. Jelani is hooked up to machines, blows into a tube to test his lung capacity.

People respect Bo in this neighborhood. This is his turf. Wherever he's lived, he's always come back here. It's his corner. He's got nothing to sell tonight, and nobody's got any money, but this is where life happens. Bo climbs into a van. Hey, it's me, Bo! Damn,

Bo. Bo smokes a little Thai stick with the guy in the van, Tupac's on the radio, they pour something into a cup, drink it. These days he doesn't hang out here so much. There are other destinations at night, cryptic journeys and transactions, minor hustles. This is the street, this is the life, he tells himself, and I'm a Crip till I die. LaTonya knows it; her mother knows it. I'll be representing till the casket drops. He takes another hit. I'm a thug, a killer. I'm a gangster. I'll blast you. I'll shoot you. I'll rob you. I'll kill you. They all know it comes along with the gangster life. They don't want that in their family! He stomps like an angry bull, and then comes a low wail, like a wound.

LaTonya has a choice to make, whether to leave now and return to Jelani. But she prays and prays on it and decides she must stay in the desert. When God is getting ready to bless you, the evangelist says, the Devil always attacks the person closest to you, trying to take you off your path. Don't give in.

She can feel the rising voice, all that is ahead, and it scares her. She does not want the confrontation, she does not want to say Go! Jelani sucks the inhaler, a deep breath, a gasp, forcing his lungs open. Paw-Paw holds his hand. Bo lights his crack pipe, sucking the smoke into his lungs. I'm a thug. I'm an OG. And Jesus got angry at those that would desecrate his house! LaTonya knows what's ahead, and it is terrible. When she returns from the desert, she makes a small sign with a colored marker and tapes it to the front door: CAUTION! GOD IS AT WORK IN THIS HOUSE.

And he says, You're worthless. He calls her a bitch; that's the least of it. It's all f-this and f-that. But Jesus got angry. She calls him a bitch back, just to let him know that she's not going to back down from the Devil. Then he says, I'm going to smoke you. The wind is howling, her own voice yelling back. He says, I'm going to bust all the windows! She knows he is in despair, angry at himself. He wants her to fight back. She feels the rising heat convulsing her body; letting go is like childbirth itself. I can't forgive you anymore, I'm not your mama. I have a son.

"You sad, Mama, when I was born?"

"No, I was happy. I was tired and in pain, but I was happy."

"I thought you didn't feel anything."

"I did feel, but not when they was taking you out, 'cause I was asleep."

"I never know a baby can be in your stomach. I never know that."

"Yes. Remember on TV when we watched ER, and they were cutting the lady's stomach to get the baby out?"

"They cut you open with scissors?"

"Knife. They had to cut through six layers to get you out."

"They cut you open all the way around?"

"Yes, like a smile."

Jelani doesn't know what else happened when he was born; she hasn't told him yet, and nobody seems to talk much about the riots anymore anyway. All he knows is, "I came out of her all wet." But he does have some questions. "I heard at school that babies come out of your butthole. Is that true?"

The other morning, Jelani made snacks for the four new babies in LaTonya's care, and then he read them a book. He's about to start baseball. Paw-Paw will take him to practice. He's taking Brother Saunders's etiquette class, which teaches young men how not to behave like thugs. LaTonya now believes that you can't protect your child from devilment in all its forms, but when you invite the Devil in, you can invite him to leave.

And she packed Bo's bag and he's back on his corner. He's been gone a month now. She hadn't wanted to tell this story. She'd hidden Bo at first, embarrassed by those years when Jelani was little and she was too comfortable with crack and thugs. But LaTonya decided that telling was testifying, and testifying is a Christian act, and that maybe this is all a part of God answering her prayers. So here it is, the story of the life of her little boy, good and bad. Jelani Stewart is ten years old. On April 30, there will be a big party at a park near LaTonya's house, with a black clown and a piñata. Everybody he loves will be there. He made the guest list himself.

Sherman Alexie is a Spokane/Coeur d'Alene Indian and was named one of the "Twenty Writers for the Twenty-first Century" by *The New Yorker*. He went on to direct the film based on his first book of poetry, *The Business of Fancy Dancing*, which premiered at the Sundance Film Festival in 2002. Alexie's first collection of short stories, *The Lone Ranger and Tonto Fistfight in Heaven*, was later made into *Smoke Signals*, the first feature film produced, written, and directed by American Indians. Alexie is the author of the novels *Reservation Blues* and *Indian Killer*, the poetry collections *Old Shirts & New Skins*, *The Summer of Black Widows*, and *One Stick Song*, and the short story collections *The Toughest Indian in the World* and, most recently, *Ten Little Indians*. He lives in Seattle with his wife and two sons.

Lynda Barry is a writer and cartoonist whose work has appeared all over tarnation. She was born in the Midwest, grew up in Seattle, and moved back to the Midwest as fast as she could. She lives with her husband on a farm, where they work on native plant propagation and prairie restoration.

Ryan Boudinot received his M.F.A. at Bennington College and a B.A. in creative writing from Evergreen State College. He has written a novel about selling ice cream. He lives in Seattle.

Mark Bowden is the author of six books, including *Black Hawk Down* and *Killing Pablo*. He is a national correspondent for the *Atlantic Monthly* and a columnist for the *Philadelphia Inquirer*, and he teaches journalism and creative writing at Loyola College of Maryland. His other books are *Doctor Dealer, Bringing the Heat, Our Finest Day*, and *Finders Keepers*. He has also written for *The New Yorker, Sports Illustrated*, and the *New York Times*, among other publications. He was born in St. Louis, Missouri, in 1951, and grew up in Glen Ellyn, Illinois, Port Washington, New York, and Timonium, Maryland. He graduated from Loyola College of Maryland in 1973 with a B.A. in English literature. From that year until 1979 he wrote for the now defunct *Baltimore News-American*. Bowden lives in southeastern Pennsylvania. He is married and has five children.

Michael Buckley is from Long Beach, California, and is a graduate of California State University at Dominguez Hills. "Meticulous Grove" was written among the eucalyptus groves of that university and is the first story he has had published in a national literary journal. He is currently at work on a novel of great length and brilliance. He spends his days working with middle school children.

Judy Budnitz grew up in Atlanta and attended Harvard University. She was a fellow of the Provincetown Fine Arts Work Center and received her M.F.A. in creative writing from New York University. Her fiction has appeared in *Story*, the *Paris Review, Glimmer Train*, and *Harper's Magazine*, and her first collection of stories, *Flying Leap*, was published in 1999. Her novel, *If I Told You Once*, was short-listed for England's prestigious Orange Prize.

David Drury is a writer and editor in Seattle. He earned a master's degree in interdisciplinary Christian studies from Regent College in Vancouver, British Columbia, where he wrote a children's novel (unpublished) as his thesis project. "Things We Knew When the House Caught Fire" is one of a dozen short stories and travel narratives inspired by a twelve-day road trip between California and

Texas. He intends to see the collection, tentatively titled *12 Strangers,* published in 2004. His e-mail address is DavDrury@hotmail.com.

Jonathan Safran Foer was born in 1977 in Washington, D.C. He is the editor of the anthology *A Convergence of Birds,* and his stories have been published in the *Paris Review* and *Conjunctions.* He is the author of the international bestseller *Everything Is Illuminated,* parts of which appeared in *The New Yorker.* He lives in Brooklyn, New York, and is at work on his second novel, which takes place in a museum.

Lisa Gabriele's work has appeared in *Vice,* the *New York Times Magazine,* Salon.com, *Nerve,* and the *Washington Post.* She has directed and shot award-winning documentaries for the Life Network and the History Channel. Before that she worked at the CBC, in TV and radio, for many happy years. Her first novel, *Tempting Faith DiNapoli,* was published internationally and was a bestseller in Canada — for two weeks! She hopes to smash that record with her second novel, to be published by Simon and Schuster, if she can finish it. She currently lives in Toronto's Little Italy, after years in Washington, D.C., New York City, Buenos Aires, Dawson City, and Whistler, British Columbia, where she drove rich people around in a taxicab, often wishing she were one of them. For some reason it hasn't worked out that way.

Amanda Holzer wants to apologize for her unhealthy relationship with lists, although in this case it seems to have worked in her favor. She has received many a mix tape from eager young boys hoping to impress (read: undress) her, and has always felt there was a far more telling message behind the songs chosen. Amanda understands that your personal list might possibly include Aerosmith's terribly revealing "Dude Looks Like a Lady" or, even more likely, Devo's "Whip It," and still she encourages you to create your own mix-tape tale. The author does not, however, encourage you to give it as a break-up gift.

Chuck Klosterman is the author of *Fargo Rock City: A Heavy Metal Odyssey in Rural North Dakota* and *Sex, Drugs, and Cocoa Puffs: A Low Culture Manifesto.* He is a senior writer for *Spin* and has also contributed to *GQ,* the *New York Times Magazine,* and the *Washington Post.*

K. Kvashay-Boyle is a student at the Iowa Writers' Workshop. "Saint Chola" is her first published story, and it was written for the triumphant and admirable Summra Shariff.

Dylan Landis is working on a novel and a collection of stories, all interlocking. Her fiction has appeared in *Tin House,* the *Santa Monica Review,* and *New York Stories* and is anthologized in *Bestial Noise: The Tin House Fiction Reader.* She has won numerous fiction awards, including the Ray Bradbury fellowship, and in a past life wrote six books on interior design.

Andrea Lee is the author of *Russian Journal,* which was nominated for a National Book Award, and the novel *Sarah Phillips.* Several of her stories have been included in the O. Henry Prize Stories and Best American short story anthologies. She lives with her husband and two children in Turin, Italy.

J. T. Leroy is the author of the international bestsellers *Sarah* (being made into a film by Steven Shainberg) and *The Heart Is Deceitful Above All Things* (being made into a film by Asia Argento). His third book will be published in 2004. His Web site is found at www.jtleroy.com, and he is part of the rock band Thistle (www.thistlehq.com), currently recording their debut.

Douglas Light's work has appeared in the *Alaska Quarterly Review* and the *O. Henry Awards: Prize Stories 2003.* He has recently completed a collection of short stories and is at work on a novel. He lives in New York City.

Nasdijj grew up a migrant worker and learned to write on his own in migrant camps by writing journals. His avocation is adopting children with special needs, and these are currently the human subjects he writes about. He is the author of *The Blood Runs Like a River Through My Dreams* and *The Boy and the Dog Are Sleeping*. His next memoir of growing up in migrant camps is called *Geronimo's Bones* and will be published early in 2004.

The Onion is a satirical newspaper and Web site published in New York City, Chicago, Madison and Milwaukee, Wisconsin, and Denver, Colorado. It can be found on the Web at www.theonion .com.

George Packer is the author of four books: *The Village of Waiting*, about his experience as a Peace Corps volunteer in Togo, West Africa; *Blood of the Liberals*, a history of his family and American liberalism in the twentieth century, which won the 2001 Robert F. Kennedy Book Award; and two novels, *The Half Man* and *Central Square*. He is also the editor of *The Fight Is for Democracy: Winning the War of Ideas in America and the World*, an anthology of original essays that appeared in September 2003. He has reported from many foreign countries and written about politics and literature for the *New York Times Magazine, Mother Jones, Dissent, Harper's Magazine*, and other publications. A 2001–2002 Guggenheim fellow, Packer is a staff writer at *The New Yorker* and lives in Brooklyn.

ZZ Packer was raised in Atlanta, Georgia, and Louisville, Kentucky. Her stories have appeared in *The New Yorker, Harper's Magazine, Story, Ploughshares, Zoetrope All-Story*, and *The Best American Short Stories 2000* and *2003*. Her collection of short stories, *Drinking Coffee Elsewhere*, was published in March 2003.

James Pinkerton pays the bills with a boring desk job in Canada but dreams of someday making enough money to quit his job, buy a solid gold desk, and sit behind this at home instead. His work has appeared in countless online humor publications, and he recently took on the duties of a very overworked editor/Webmaster on www.thetrailertrash.com. He hopes to leave Canada one day, and in the event that he is asked if he is from there, to lie shamelessly. His event-filled life was the subject of the 1992 film *Ski School 2.*

David Sedaris is a humorist and social critic whose commentaries are heard on National Public Radio. He is the author of the best-sellers *Barrel Fever, Naked,* and *Me Talk Pretty One Day,* and he contributes essays to such magazines as *Esquire, Allure, The New Yorker,* and *Travel and Leisure.* Under the name the Talent Family, he and his sister Amy Sedaris collaborate on plays, one of which — *One Woman Shoe* — received an Obie Award. He lives in Paris.

Jason Stella cannot figure out what to do with himself. He is a free-lance journalist, stage performer, playwright, and videographer. His one-man show, *Guide to Health and Strength,* was critically acclaimed but far too ahead of its time to reach a wide audience. He was director of photography for the 2002 short film *I Was a Quality of Life Violation,* written by Reverend Jen Miller and directed by Nick Zedd. Jason is currently in a hypomanic cycle and is blazing through a novel titled *Causal Attributions.* The book is a comedic, tragic, and far too honest autobiographical whirl in which he addresses the unjust stigmatization of goats; why most pornography is not a depiction of a sexual situation; his best friend from second grade; and how he manages his manic-depression. He lives in Manhattan with Ted Koppel and a goat.

John Verbos writes: "After 'Lost Boys' was published, a woman I'd never met before (and whose face I cannot recall today) looked at the story's title and then, with arched eyebrows, asked me, 'Is this about vampires?' I'd like to lie and say that I coolly answered, 'No, it's about cowboys,' and then took a sip of my dry martini, but it's probably closer to the truth to say that I gave her a long and *very serious* summary of the story's plot while gesticulating wildly and spilling Pabst on myself . . . But that's not the point. *This* is: It took me a year to realize that she was absolutely right. Vampires."

Daniel Voll is a contributing editor at *Esquire.* His short stories, investigative journalism, and essays have appeared in *The New*

Yorker, Vanity Fair, the *New York Times,* and *Story.* His documentary film, *Army of God,* premiered last year on HBO. He recently moved with his family from New York to Los Angeles, where he spent nine months reporting "Riot Baby." He says, "Jelani and his family were fearless as I reported the story, and I tried to write it in that spirit."

NOTABLE
NONREQUIRED READING
OF 2002

DOROTHY ALLISON
  Compassion, *Tin House*.
JANE AVRICH
  Trash Traders, *Ploughshares*.

AMY BLOOM
  Your Borders, Your Rivers, Your Tiny Villages, *Ploughshares*.
ARTHUR BRADFORD
  Radsh.

MATTHEW CALLAN
  The Lemon Pledge, Freezerbox.com.
RON CARLSON
  Some of Our Work with Monsters, *Ploughshares*.
BROCK CLARKE
  For Those of Us Who Need Such Things, *Georgia Review*.
  The Lolita School, *Story Quarterly*.
MICHAEL COLTON
  Admission Impossible: The Perfect College Essay, *Modern Humorist*.
PHILIP CONNORS
  Driving and Drinking in a Poet's Footsteps, *Croonenbergh's Fly*.

KATHERINE DARNELL
  Fiji, *Drunken Boat*.

ELIZABETH DENTON
Taco Bell, *Virginia Quarterly Review.*
MATTHEW DERBY
The Sound Gun, *Conjunctions* on-line.
CALLA DEVLIN
Borderlines, *Watchword.*

ELIZABETH ELLEN
How the Homeless Funambulist and Lonely Somnambulist Met and
Shared a Melon, *Pindeldyboz.*
JULIA ELLIOTT
Father's Kitchen, *Fence.*

PAUL FEIG
Bound and Gagged: A School Dance Story, Nerve.com.
STEVE FELLNER
Greek Mafia Connections, *Northwest Review.*
MICHAEL FINKEL
To Wait or Flee, *New York Times Magazine.*
IAN FRAZIER
That's Militiatainment!, *Mother Jones.*

TODD GITLIN
Blaming America First, *Mother Jones.*
GERSHOM GORENBERG
The Thin Green Line, *Mother Jones.*

JOE HIRSCH
Instant Ghetto, *3AM Magazine.*
GABE HUDSON
The American Green Machine, *Conjunctions* online.

HILLARY JACKSON
The Hanging, *Story Quarterly.*
MAT JOHNSON
Will Cory Booker Be the First Black President of the United States?, *Shout
Magazine.*
CAMDEN JOY
Dum Dum Boys, *Little Engines.*
TIM JUDAH
The Sullen Majority, *New York Times Magazine.*

SYBIL KOLLAR
   Freud's Throat, Poetserv.org.

ALEX PERRY
   How I Bought Two Slaves, to Free Them, *Time*.
PAUL POISSEL
   The Facts of Winter, *Fence*.
KEMP POWERS
   The Shooting, *Esquire*.

JOANNA SMITH RAKOFF
   My Salinger Year, *Book Magazine*.
DAVID REES
   Get Your War On, Mnftiu.cc.
CYNTHIA RIEDE
   The Girls Upstairs, *Story Quarterly*.

KEVIN SAMPSELL
   New Suburban Lit: 2 Stories, *Pindeldyboz*.
GEORGE SAUNDERS
   My Flamboyant Grandson, *The New Yorker*.
DEBORAH SHAPIRO
   Happens All the Time, *Open City*.
MONA SIMPSON
   Coins, *Harper's Magazine*.
CHERYL STRAYED
   The Love of My Life, *The Sun*.

JORDAN J. VEZINA
   A Vanishing Breed, *Thought Magazine*.

JOE WENDEROTH
   Agony, *Fence*.
KERI R. WOODWARD
   Tom's Last Funeral, Yankthechain.com.
TARA WRAY
   Flatbed, Seabed, *Pindeldyboz*.

THE B·E·S·T AMERICAN SERIES ™

THE BEST AMERICAN SHORT STORIES® 2003
Walter Mosley, guest editor • Katrina Kenison, series editor

"Story for story, readers can't beat the *Best American Short Stories* series" (*Chicago Tribune*). This year's most beloved short fiction anthology is edited by the award-winning author Walter Mosley and includes stories by Dorothy Allison, Mona Simpson, Anthony Doerr, Dan Chaon, and Louise Erdrich, among others.

0-618-19733-8 PA $13.00 / 0-618-19732-X CL $27.50
0-618-19748-6 CASS $26.00 / 0-618-19752-4 CD $35.00

THE BEST AMERICAN ESSAYS® 2003
Anne Fadiman, guest editor • Robert Atwan, series editor

Since 1986, the *Best American Essays* series has gathered the best non-fiction writing of the year and established itself as the best anthology of its kind. Edited by Anne Fadiman, author of *Ex Libris* and editor of the *American Scholar*, this year's volume features writing by Edward Hoagland, Adam Gopnik, Michael Pollan, Susan Sontag, John Edgar Wideman, and others.

0-618-34161-7 PA $13.00 / 0-618-34160-9 CL $27.50

THE BEST AMERICAN MYSTERY STORIES™ 2003
Michael Connelly, guest editor • Otto Penzler, series editor

Our perennially popular anthology is a favorite of mystery buffs and general readers alike. This year's volume is edited by the best-selling author Michael Connelly and offers pieces by Elmore Leonard, Joyce Carol Oates, Brendan DuBois, Walter Mosley, and others.

0-618-32965-X PA $13.00 / 0-618-32966-8 CL $27.50
0-618-39072-3 CD $35.00

THE BEST AMERICAN SPORTS WRITING™ 2003
Buzz Bissinger, guest editor • Glenn Stout, series editor

This series has garnered wide acclaim for its stellar sports writing and top-notch editors. Now Buzz Bissinger, the Pulitzer Prize–winning journalist and author of the classic *Friday Night Lights,* continues that tradition with pieces by Mark Kram Jr., Elizabeth Gilbert, Bill Plaschke, S. L. Price, and others.

0-618-25132-4 PA $13.00 / 0-618-25130-8 CL $27.50

THE B·E·S·T AMERICAN SERIES

THE BEST AMERICAN TRAVEL WRITING 2003
Ian Frazier, guest editor • Jason Wilson, series editor

The Best American Travel Writing 2003 is edited by Ian Frazier, the author of *Great Plains* and *On the Rez*. Giving new life to armchair travel this year are William T. Vollmann, Geoff Dyer, Christopher Hitchens, and many others.

0-618-11881-0 PA $13.00 / 0-618-11881-0 CL $27.50
0-618-39074-X CD $35.00

THE BEST AMERICAN SCIENCE AND NATURE WRITING 2003
Richard Dawkins, guest editor • Tim Folger, series editor

This year's edition promises to be another "eclectic, provocative collection" (*Entertainment Weekly*). Edited by Richard Dawkins, the eminent scientist and distinguished author, it features work by Bill McKibben, Steve Olson, Natalie Angier, Steven Pinker, Oliver Sacks, and others.

0-618-17892-9 PA $13.00 / 0-618-17891-0 CL $27.50

THE BEST AMERICAN RECIPES 2003–2004
Edited by Fran McCullough and Molly Stevens

"The cream of the crop . . . McCullough's selections form an eclectic, unfussy mix" (*People*). Offering the very best of what America is cooking, as well as the latest trends, time-saving tips, and techniques, this year's edition includes a foreword by Alan Richman, award-winning columnist for *GQ*.

0-618-27384-0 CL $26.00

THE BEST AMERICAN NONREQUIRED READING 2003
Edited by Dave Eggers • Introduction by Zadie Smith

Edited by Dave Eggers, the author of *A Heartbreaking Work of Staggering Genius* and *You Shall Know Our Velocity*, this genre-busting volume draws the finest, most interesting, and least expected fiction, nonfiction, humor, alternative comics, and more from publications large, small, and on-line. *The Best American Nonrequired Reading 2003* features writing by David Sedaris, ZZ Packer, Jonathan Safran Foer, Andrea Lee, and others.

0-618-24696-7 $13.00 PA / 0-618-24696-7 $27.50 CL
0-618-39073-1 $35.00 CD

HOUGHTON MIFFLIN COMPANY   www.houghtonmifflinbooks.com